CONSCIOUSNESS AND PERCEPTION

*A Part-Fictionalised Reflection
On Humanity's Struggle
To Know Reality*

By

Tony McKay

Copyright © Tony McKay 2019
This book is sold subject to the condition that it shall not, by way of trade or otherwise, be lent, resold, hired out, or otherwise circulated without the publisher's prior consent in any form of binding or cover other than that in which it is published and without a similar condition including this condition being imposed on the subsequent publisher.
The moral right of Tony McKay has been asserted.
ISBN: 9781916132306

This is a work of fiction. Names, characters, businesses, organizations, places, events and incidents either are the product of the author's imagination or are used fictitiously. Any resemblance to actual persons, living or dead, events, or locales is entirely coincidental.

DEDICATION

To Lesley Haddow

CONTENTS

ACKNOWLEDGMENTS i

CONSCIOUSNESS AND PERCEPTION iii

PROLOGUE 1

PART I 4

BOOK ONE: SNAPSHOT OF A PLAYGROUND 4

    1 4
        Scene 1: Coal 4
        Scene 2: Time trials 10
        Scene 3: See-saw 12
    2 19
        Scene 1: Only swings, no roundabouts 19
        Scene 2: Dot-to-dot 21
        Scene 3: Walking in sleep 23
        Scene 4: The show must go on 25
    3 27
        Scene 1: Carefree 27
        Scene 2: The eye of the beholder 30

PART II 37

BOOK TWO: KEEPING IT REAL 37

    4 37
        Scene 1: Happy New Year! 37
    5 42
        Scene 1: Tender 42
        Scene 2: As you do 46
    6 50
        Scene 1: As you see 50

PART III 56

BOOK THREE: KENYA 56

    7 56
        Scene 1: Coming to terms 56

8	60
Scene 1: The story so far...	*60*
9	76
Scene 1: As long as it takes	*76*
10	81
Scene 1: The Initiates	*81*

PART IV 85

BOOK FOUR: ACCEPTED 85

11	85
Scene 1: Picking up	*85*
Scene 2: Wolf whistles	*88*
Scene 3: Party on!	*90*
12	94
Scene 1: Fear	*94*
13	96
Scene 1: In keeping with appearances	*96*
14	100
Scene 1: Level crossing	*100*

PART V 107

BOOK FIVE: THE OLD NEW DAWN 107

15	107
Scene 1: Resolutions	*107*
Scene 2: 'See'	*115*
16	119
Scene 1: Never again	*119*

BOOK SIX: TIME 121

17	121
Scene 1: Decorations	*121*
Scene 2: A few hours	*133*

BOOK SEVEN: RIPPLES 134

18	134
Scene 1: In the wake	*134*
Scene 2: Held	*138*
Scene 3: Darkness	*140*

BOOK EIGHT: SEARING 145

    19 145

        Scene 1: Pain *145*

BOOK NINE: PRETENCE 151

    20 151

        Scene 1: Prep *151*

        Scene 2: Clocked *162*

        Scene 3: Business *163*

BOOK TEN: PARTING WAYS 171

    21 171

        Scene 1: Passing *171*

PART VI 174

BOOK ELEVEN: HANGING ON 174

    22 174

        Scene 1: Out in the open *174*

        Scene 2: Keeping it civil *177*

        Scene 3: Cycles *179*

BOOK TWELVE: ONGOING 185

    23 185

        Scene 1: Day to day *185*

        Scene 2: Shell *187*

PART VII 188

BOOK THIRTEEN: EVERYTHING 188

    24 188

        Scene 1: Something of an Apologia *188*

        Scene 2: Reflections *217*

PART VIII 229

BOOK FOURTEEN: FORGETTING AND REMEMBERING 229

    25 229

        Scene 1: Prognosis *229*

        Scene 2: Lost and broken *231*

26	233
Scene 1: Journey - Looking back, looking forward	233
Scene 2: Regrouping	234
Scene 3: Time out	235

BOOK FIFTEEN: HOME	236
27	236
Scene 1: As you go As you are	236

BOOK SIXTEEN: MOVEMENTS	275
28	275
Scene 1: Stuck	275
Scene 2: Out	277
Scene 3: Chance	278
Scene 4: Gone	280

BOOK SEVENTEEN: CLOSURE	282
29	282
Scene 1: Joy and Sorrow	282
Scene 2: Chase	284

BOOK EIGHTEEN: SIGNS AND SIGNALS	285
30	285
Scene 1: Yes or no	285
Scene 2: Siren	287
Scene 3: Asunder	289
Scene 4: Anew	295

EPILOGUE	297
A SPECIAL THANKS FROM THE AUTHOR	300
SELECTED BIBLIOGRAPHY	301

ACKNOWLEDGMENTS

This book was inspired by the writings of John Jacob Raub and further encouraged by the works of Evelyn Underhill, Aldous Huxley, Thomas Merton, and Fyodor Dostoevsky among others (see Selected Bibliography).

It would never have been possible, however, without the unconditional love and selfless support given to me throughout my life by my parents, Thomas and Isabella (née Roy) McKay, my brothers and sisters: Tommy, Archie, Catherine, Alex and Mary, and my partner, Jane Wangechi Wambugu. No words can express what you mean to me, or the love I feel for you. Thank you!

At risk of leaving a single person out, there are of course countless other remarkable people who have touched and continue to support me in my life, and I am forever indebted to them. They know who they are. Please know that you too have also contributed to this book, and that without you, it would have been incomplete.

Thank you!

Love always,

Tony

CONSCIOUSNESS AND PERCEPTION

A PART FICTIONALISED REFLECTION ON HUMANITY'S STRUGGLE TO KNOW REALITY

***A note from the author for a potential reader:**

In our consumerist society and the faster pace of life often associated with the Western world many people now consume books today barely drawing breath.

This is a person's prerogative of course and if you are a person who likes their books this way then that, of course, is perfectly fine. However, if this is the case I must let you know at this point that perhaps this book is not for you, and you may probably find yourself putting it down after a few pages, never to return to it, or, worse still, lobbing it into the nearest bin – not unless of course it's still on your eBook reader at the time!

In addition, it should also be noted that this book is intentionally not as constrained or rigidly tied to the conventions of a 'typical' novel. Indeed, for some readers, it is quite possible that their experience of the book may turn out to be somewhat similar to the saying there are some so blind that they cannot see, and some so deaf that they cannot hear; and as such, just don't 'get it', thus part of the reasoning behind this note.

Indeed, for if a reader is to take away anything from this book they must know from the outset that its main purpose is to raise awareness of the grave need for humanity to move out from its current yet predominant state of egoic consciousness (i.e., if it is to have any hope of coming to know True Reality).

And so, in consideration of this, it is perhaps advisable for the reader to keep this main theme in mind while reading through the material; particularly, when confronted with the changes in narrative that occur later within the book, and which are specifically designed to encourage a deeper consideration and critical questioning of the topic.

With a proposition presented to the reader to consider the 'surface level' events in the characters' lives, and by way of looking at this later in the book through a reflective and contemplative discussion between protagonists, the all-important and often out of sight *why* of our human struggle is hopefully made clear as we approach the denouement i.e. in the suggestion of what is truly real within ourselves, within our environment, and within our shared world.

Direct knowledge of the [Divine] Ground cannot be had except by union, and union can be achieved only by the annihilation of the [false] self-regarding ego, which is the barrier separating 'thou' from 'that'.

Aldous Huxley (Writer, Novelist and Philosopher)

The Perennial Philosophy, Chato & Windus, London, second impression, 1947.

PROLOGUE

Anno Domini 28

At the height of the storm, reaching the shore with the boat still intact and everyone accounted for seemed impossible.

Daylight had not yet arrived. They had lost all direction and the wind and the waves would soon condemn them to the abyss.

In coming to this conclusion, the decision was made: no longer could the master be left just to rest. They would wake him and plead with him to do something, for the alternative was death.

When he opened his eyes, four relayed their terrifying reality to him, while the other eight looked on with expressions echoing what was spoken.

He, in turn, rose and made his way graciously through them, at once providing consolation, before coming to a standstill in the foremost part of the vessel.

As they watched him from their huddled and crouched positions, as he faced and tamed the elements, their fears were soon removed and belief strengthened.

Meekly, without words, they began to emerge slowly from their confines and looked around in awe.

The stillness they were experiencing within seemed in communion with what were now the conditions everywhere.

Their master had smiled on them as one who was their father and reinforced the message by rhetorically questioning their faith.

Yet, despite this earlier lesson, it was to be the quick succession of events, from disembarking in the Gerasenes, to the people there begging them to leave, that would become the talking points going back across the lake – back to the homeland they had left just the evening before.

When he was sure the master was at the stern, Simon Peter approached the others, and crouching down, spoke loudly enough to talk over both the sound of the oars cutting through the water and the voices of those already involved in discussion: 'He came from the tombs towards us as we approached the shore. Didn't you see him?'

'Imagine! The people had said that he had lived there. *There,* among the dead!' Andrew recalled.

'I noticed the man when the master leapt from the boat and made his way towards him, then I heard the shouting and saw the man prostrate himself at the master's feet,' James offered.

'And what about the man's face? Did you see how contorted it was before, and the hacks and the scars, and those eyes, what about the man's eyes?' John said, his own eyes frantically searching the others for something – anything – that could be used as confirmation.

'Yes,' Simon Peter acknowledged, 'inhuman surely, even unlike anything in nature.'

'But how, how is it possible, and how can they have so much influence over a man? I mean that they can take ownership of him,' said Philip, thinking out loud, but not expecting an answer.

And no answer came.

Here, they were stuck. Their lack of knowledge made them feel vulnerable. If it could happen to the man, it could also happen to one of them.

Simon Peter wiped his forehead in a response of sorts, and part exasperation. 'Before, I mean, could it be that the master was silently communicating with them from here, on the boat, just before we reached the shore?'

'Mmm, perhaps,' James said, wringing his hands as he stared into the bottom of the boat, gazing at nothing in particular.

'Or,' John began, 'maybe he was calling what was his.'

'What are you saying? Called what was his? Tell me you are not saying this, this,' Simon Peter wanted to say 'blasphemy'.

'The man is what I'm saying! Our master was calling the man; this man who was his!' John insisted. 'When he called us, our situations were all different. Each calling was different. Surely, this man was called by him also.'

'Yes, of course, John. Very good. And then the master somehow made them talk. Yes, it makes some sense of it all,' Simon Peter said, greatly relieved.

'And what about them? No matter how many, they knew who the master was, didn't they, calling him Son of the Most High?' Andrew reminded them.

'Truly they knew. They even begged the master to send them into the pigs,' James marvelled. 'No wonder so many people came out to see what had happened. I mean, with what the swine herders must've told them.'

'Yes, that their pigs had charged down the cliff and drowned in the lake. Yes, the people would have to see the bloated carcasses for themselves,' Simon Peter added.

John, contemplating the lead-up to the drowning, expressed what was puzzling him. 'Do you think they would've asked to go into the pigs, if they'd known what was to happen?'

'Huh?' Simon Peter grunted. 'Who could know such a thing? Maybe the master would know.'

'And calling themselves Legion!' exclaimed Philip. 'Can you imagine? Demons grouped in a Legion, possessing a man?'

All fell silent for a moment, each trying to make sense of what they had encountered.

Andrew grunted, shaking his head in what would have been disbelief had he not witnessed what they had all seen. Gazing out across the shimmering lake, he recalled the words that had been spoken; words that were now etched forever in their minds: 'My name is Legion, for there are many of us.'

PART I

BOOK ONE:

SNAPSHOT OF A PLAYGROUND

(RULES, ROLES AND SPECIAL GUEST STARS)

1

Scene 1: Coal

Friday 4 January, 1974, Forgewood, Motherwell, Scotland.
The Railway Depot, 8:00 p.m.

When he crosses the next track and gets in among the trees, John knows he'll be free from the clutches of the security lights. The first part will be over.

'Hey there, mister!'

John's instinct is to run, but he realises he's kidding himself on in these conditions. It was bad enough trying to walk across the snow and ice-covered rocks. *No, too late, I'm caught*, he tells himself. *I'll lay it on thick, but then again, it's the truth.*

He turns to face who called him and is relieved to see a watchman, and better still, he's on his own.

Taking the man in, John sifts through the possible eventualities in his mind, but deep down, there is only one. The breadth of the man makes him appear shorter than he actually is, and his movement is definitely restricted, particularly that of his upper body.

John discarded the thought of treachery as quickly as it came.

He was proud of the fact that he'd never taken liberties nor fought with anyone who couldn't defend themselves properly. Even if he was getting on in years and feeling that bit older, he wasn't going to change his ways now. The security lights at the watchman's back were a concern though. He'd have to position himself so that he wouldn't be blinded, should they get down to business.

'You can't leave here with that, mister,' the watchman said, drawing the shortened pick shaft from the inside of his donkey jacket.

John released his grip on the sack of coal he was carrying on his back, letting it fall to the ground.

At this, the watchman came to a halt approximately ten yards away.

On closer inspection, John saw that the watchman's face was lean and that he was probably in his early thirties. His clothing made him look a lot broader. It was the same for most people who had to venture outside in this weather; well, the ones who had the clothes for it, he thought.

As he watched, the younger man put his right hand through the loop attached to the crude home-made club, clenching his fist around its base. John smiled and shook his head in resignation. He would never understand why some men had to become monsters every time they were given a wee bit of authority. In his younger years it had made him angry. Now though he was just saddened by it.

'Look, son, I wouldn't be here if I didn't need to be. I've a wife and four weans at home freezing and hungry.'

The watchman had heard all the stories before, but not from this man.

'Mister, if I let you take that coal, I could get sacked. You people from the scheme are up here every night. Yees'll end up emptying this place.'

'Huh! If you'll let me. What kinda man are you? Would you let your family freeze in a hoose with no fire on a night like this?'

'No, I wouldn't. I'd buy the coal if I needed it.'

'Aw, aye, I get it now, so you're better than me because today, you've got a couple a' bob. You're working class like me, son. Remember that.'

'I didn't mean it like that. You could've got a loan off somebody. What good are you to your family, if you were to get lifted for stealing?' the watchman said, trying to soften his tone.

Despite the way it was delivered, the comment from the younger man stung John.

Before he had given in to the last resort of stealing the coal, John had already felt embarrassed at having to ask his friends for the money he had lent them; money they were supposed to have paid back ten days ago. But then, they too were struggling; they too had nothing, he reminded himself. He could either be arrested in the railway depot or in the housing scheme on the way back, he was told. Inwardly he cringed as he recalled how making his way through the scheme was said to be the riskier of the two.

'So, you're going to get the polis?' John stated half-heartedly. He sensed the watchman might be looking at things a bit differently, but he needed to know for certain.

'Mister, look, just leave the coal where it is, and I won't get the polis.'

'Come oan son, give me a break here. Look! Look at the wagons. They're overflowing with it. A sack here or there won't go amiss for God's sake. If you like, I can return it next week, on Friday. How's that? Once I get my wages.'

In response, the watchman dropped the club, letting it hang from the loop around his wrist before simultaneously shrugging his shoulders and turning his open hands outwards in the gesture, 'What can I do?' which also meant, 'It's not going to happen'.

'Well, my friend,' John started, 'it's as simple as this. Me and you are gaun'ae have to come to blows over it, because I cannae leave here tonight, with nothing.'

The watchman was riled and considered this prospect. He was no easy touch when it came to going ahead, and despite being a good ten to twelve years younger than his opponent, he knew to take nothing for granted, but he'd never used the club on someone before, and only carried it in the hope that it would prevent confrontation. Every other time he'd come across people from the scheme, they'd always run off towards the trees when they'd seen him. People often hid there until the watchmen had passed by, only to come out again to get some coal 'once the coast was clear'. All the watchmen knew that. It was par for the course, he remembered. The depot was even too big for the watchmen to secure effectively – the managers had said as much. There was really no sense in what this man was doing; no need for any kind of confrontation. It didn't need to be this way – it was total madness and could really only mean one of two things: this man had never tried to steal coal from here before; or worse still, he was a headcase. Yet, in the earlier exchanges, the man had seemed quite humble. Even so, he had a strong presence. His open collar, and bulging neck muscles told their own story.

John and the watchman had shown each other respect, and the watchman had learned over the years that a man who respected others should not be considered weak. It was more likely to be the opposite in his experience; definitely game, and probably handy with it too. However, the watchman came back to the respect, appreciating it first. He wasn't afraid of the older man and now understood that this – dare he say it – *thief* was in genuine need. It was more than just the coal: the man was fighting to provide for his family.

If he wanted to, the watchman could walk the short distance to the office and contact the police; the man would surely know that. At the watchman's word, they would be waiting to arrest the man when he re-entered the scheme. The man would surely know that too.

Weighing it all up, this threat of violence was really this man's final attempt, a last desperate cry for help, the watchman reasoned.

Removing the loop from his wrist, the watchman slipped the club under his left arm, clamping it against his side. 'I'm Davie, Davie McKellar,' he said, offering his open right hand to John.

As they made their way towards each other, John chose to arc his route across the hazardous surface.

Seeing this, the watchman came to a standstill and with his arm still extended, turned his body to accommodate John's move.

Only in doing so, however, when he was forced to close his right eye because of the brightness of the lights, did the watchman realise that he was seriously out of his depth. In panic, the thought of grabbing for the club flashed into his mind, but it was too late. In that moment his hand was gripped firmly.

'John McLeod,' the man said, lowering the tone of his surname, as if somehow trying to lessen the impact.

At these words the watchman froze.

His senses were in a heightened state of awareness, but he was trapped in a body experiencing momentary paralysis. He was suddenly struck by the silence of the night and how alone he felt. The depot's reek of diesel fuel engulfed him, turning his stomach in a nauseous twist that threatened to erupt in boak. If the stories about this man were true, he could have been lying unconscious by now. These were the first of the new thoughts to register. The watchman battled for composure.

'Nice to meet you, Mr McLeod, I've heard so...' *What am I doing? Shut the fuck up!* he told himself.

John believed that people didn't really know him; only his family and close friends had any idea of the type of man he was. He spoke up, attempting to alleviate any anxiety in the younger man. 'A pleasure to meet you, Davie. You seem like a good man,' he replied, releasing his grip.

'Thanks, Mr McLeod.'

'Well, what I was meaning, Davie, was I could get the coal back to you next week, and you could throw it on another wagon for the steelworks just the same.'

John was also a thoughtful and generous man, and known within the town to do you a good turn before he'd do you a bad turn, Davie recalled with relief. He was grateful that this was the John McLeod he was now experiencing.

'No bother, Mr McLeod, but you don't need to bring it back. It's alright. If anybody seen us, they'd wonder what we were up tae. The other day there, a guy on the dayshift got suspended. They say he was taking money off people and then letting them take the coal.'

'Aye, is that right? I see what you mean, Davie. Okay, son, listen. I really appreciate what you're doing for my family tonight. I'm not always in this kind of position, you know. If ever I can help you with something, give me a shout. I'll do what I can.' With that, John offered his hand, and he and Davie shook hands a second time.

'I will do, Mr McLeod, but I'm just thinking maybe somebody is watching us the now. They'll see us talking and you walking away with the coal. It'll put me in bother. What if I carry it back over and leave it on the nearest wagon. You walk back into the treeline, and let me walk down behind the shed, then you could come back for it when I'm out of sight. There's nobody else working down this side of the depot, but it would keep me right, just in case.'

'Aye, I see what you're saying, Davie. No problem. You're a good man. If you can leave it on the nearest that would be great,' John said, looking at the first line of wagons approximately thirty yards away.

'Will do, Mr McLeod, and mind and watch yourself going through the streets with this,' the watchman replied, making his way over to the sack of coal.

'Aye, I will, Davie, and don't be worried about me mentioning anything about *us* if I get a pull.'

'Thanks, Mr McLeod.'

'Thanks, Davie, I really appreciate it, son. All the best to you and your family,' John said, as he headed towards the trees.

'Aye, and a good New Year to you and yours, Mr McLeod.'

Scene 2: Time trials

'Look, Mammy, I'm smoking!' Ninian said to his mum, as he puffed away on the imaginary cigarette he was holding in two fingers, blowing out as if trying to make smoke rings.

Both watched the effects of his warm breath on the sub-zero air.

His mum, Agnes McLeod, strained a smile, as she readjusted his balaclava and buttoned his coat at the collar for the second time of the evening. At least his callipers were still fastened, she thought. The other three kids all had their coats on, and were sitting close together on the couch. They seemed warm enough for now. She would let them stay up for a little while yet.

Agnes stood up from the chair, so her vision was no longer impaired by the thicker ice that had steadily congregated near the bottom of the living-room window throughout the day. Still no sign of John. What was keeping him? she wondered.

At the window, her silhouette was surrounded by the mild yellow glow from the streetlights. The light filtering in created the illusion of warmth, but that was all it was. On the fireside wall, her shadow joined the speckled patterns that the iced glass had helped to provide.

'Mammy, look! Lourdes is on the wall. There's the Virgin Mary!' Ninian exclaimed, blessing himself, as he focused on one such pattern on the woodchip wallpaper.

'Aye and there's Donald Duck beside it!' said Andrew, the eldest of the children, aged sixteen; Paul, who was eleven, laughed at the joke, before eight-year-old Margaret joined in.

'That's enough now,' Agnes said, turning to face the three on the couch and trying to hold back a smile.

'It is, Mam!' Andrew continued, with his right arm raised and pointing. 'Look, there's its beak and there's the feathers sticking oot its bum.'

Everyone was laughing except seven-year-old Ninian. 'Mammy, tell them, tell them!' he pleaded, not far from tears.

'Right, that's enough now,' Agnes said smiling. 'I know what we can do. Who wants to play a treasure-hunt game?'

'Aye, Mammy,' Margaret said excitedly, struggling to get up from the depressed seat on the couch, on to the floor.

'Okay, listen carefully now. I want you to help each other and look in all the cupboards all the wardrobes, and under the beds, and bring me all the shoes that you can find. Andrew will be the timekeeper and we'll see how fast you can be. Okay? Are yees ready?'

'Aye, Mammy!' yelled Margaret and Ninian, holding their arms high and jumping up and down in unison, while Paul wondered what the treasure was.

'Okay, are you ready, timekeeper?'

'Aye, Mam,' Andrew grinned; it wasn't so long ago that he'd been the one trying to "beat the clock" during time-trialled tasks.

'On the count of three then… One. Two. Three. Go!' said Agnes, as the children scampered out of the living room on the hunt.

'Can you look for some paper, Andrew, and I'll prepare the fire?'

'Aye, Mam,' replied Andrew, before thinking out loud. 'Mammy, what are you going to do?'

'We can look through the shoes when the weans bring them. I'm sure there'll be some that are auld and done. We can get a wee fire going with them; they might burn long enough to boil some water for the tea.'

Scene 3: See-saw

John was both pleased and relieved at how things had turned out in the depot. Thoughts of Agnes and the kids carried him quickly along the trail through the clearing. He had told himself this would be the last. Never again would he put or leave his family in such a predicament.

The fact that the job was half-done was also of little consolation and the absurd thought that he was well on the way to redeeming himself, by getting the coal, made him laugh aloud and curse in self-ridicule.

Almost immediately afterwards, he began to muse on how he would've swallowed a thought like this in his younger years. *Aye, getting older had its benefits. A shame though that all his life experience couldn't prevent his latest fuck-up!* John drew a sharp breath and blew out a volley of swear words, shaking his head in an attempt to throw the criticism from his mind.

He believed and understood that there was no redemption in providing the coal in this way, and yet, here he was, *still* trying to blank out distracting thoughts. *What was I meant to do? The job had to be done, plain and simple. I knew it. Agnes knew it. That was the way of it,* he told himself again. *And, anyway, home's the place to look at what you've done the day. Not here. Later. Stay focused.*

After dragging the sack of coal down the slippery embankment at the boundary of Braidhurst High School's playing fields, John, looking over the five-foot railings, scanned the upper stretch, of the first street, at the edge of the scheme, Dalriada Crescent.

Beyond the orange glow from the solitary streetlight, the weary row of six in a block, three storey flats, looked back at him.

Strands of smoke dispersed quietly across the rooftops, as, underneath, tired, disjointed eyes, flickered and waned, through net curtain lids.

John felt exposed here. True, it was also a bad night in terms of the weather, but things in this part of the street were a bit too quiet, he thought. The route from the school's grounds definitely meant less time in the open street, but it still seemed far, maybe too far.

John was now walking back and forth along the inside of the school's boundary fence, whispering in a mantric fashion. 'Lord Jesus Christ, Son of the living God, have mercy on me, a sinner.'

John so wanted to be home. *What the fuck am I doing here?* he thought.

Chilblains were beginning to make his feet feel as though they were about to burst from his boots. *No more. This is it. I need tae move.*

Watching for police cars and officers "on the beat", John lifted the sack of coal over the five-foot railings and dropped it on to the pavement, and into the street. He then wrestled his way to the top of the icy fence and jumped off.

As he landed on his feet, beside the coal, two police officers walked out from the close opposite. A sickening feeling rose in John's stomach as he cursed in silence. His thoughts came again to Agnes, the kids, his parents, his in-laws. Unknowingly, he put his hands over his face, his fingers moving up and down, pressing into his forehead. This time there would be no escape. One of the officers had recognised John instantly, and they now made their way across the road towards him.

'*Soooo,* you're the infamous John McLeod, eh? I've just been in there sorting one of your pals oot,' the taller of the two sneered, thumbing in the direction of the block of flats they had just come from.

John put his thoughts aside. 'Hello, officer,' he said, addressing the policeman who knew of him, but ignoring the taller one who had spoken.

'Hello, John. I'm Police Constable George Miller and this is Police Constable Douglas Robertson. Constable Robertson used to work in Glasgow, but started working with us this week,' the younger policeman said, as both officers stepped on to the pavement.

'Aye, and I was hearing that you think you're a bit a' a ticket. Is that right?' PC Robertson taunted.

'No' me, son. That's no' my game.'

'Well, I heard it is, and I'm here to sort your kind oot.'

'Aye, is that right? Good for you. George,' John said, turning to the younger officer, 'whit's goin on here, son?'

'Let's just leave George oot a' this,' the taller officer continued. 'How about it, hard man? Me and you right now?'

'Come on, Dougie, there's no need for this,' the younger officer cut in timidly. '*What?*' replied PC Robertson, all the while looking directly at John. 'I'll no' be two seconds wi' this fuckin' mug.'

John knew Robertson was on a mission, but felt he had to try. 'Look, lads, you've got the coal and you've got me. That'll do us for the night.' he said, raising his arms in a gesture of surrender, before returning them to his sides.

'Huh, is that right now?' PC Robertson said, smirking. 'That's all well and good, *but* as me and my colleague here were trying to get you to come along quietly, you were resisting, so I had to use force. Isn't that right, Georgie boy?'

PC George Miller smiled uneasily, not knowing what to do, or say.

John turned to the younger man. 'So this is the way you operate as well, George, eh? I didn't think you were into these games, son.'

At these words from John, the young PC looked at the ground.

Seeing this reaction from his colleague, PC Robertson howled with laughter, raising his head to the sky. 'Please tell me yer fuckin' jokin'?' He now looked with a quizzical expression at the younger man. 'Don't let this cunt play with yer heid, George. You're a better man than he'll ever be,' he said, as he drew his truncheon and pointed it casually in John's direction. 'Look at him. *Scum*! Just another wide boy that needs a good doin' to square him up. It's the only way they ever learn, and this cunt'll learn plenty the night, I can assure ye.'

'So that's it, eh? You're here to tame the town?' John said, inwardly readying himself for the inevitable.

'Aye, that's right! And it's your turn to be tamed,' PC Robertson replied, eyes wide, looking somewhat crazed.

'Ah, suppose a big tough guy like you will need a truncheon then, eh?' John questioned, stepping on to the road, so he and PC Robertson were no longer separated by the coal at their feet.

John didn't want to even attempt to take his denim jacket off. He didn't know what this man was capable of, but he knew it wouldn't be Queensberry Rules.

'Here, George, hold these the now, and for fuck's sake turn yer radio off!' PC Robertson said, all the while looking at John, as he started handing over his truncheon, radio and hat to the young officer.

John watched and waited. He was relieved to see that PC Robertson had taken the bait and was passing the truncheon, but it also came to him then just how hopeless his own situation had become. 'Yees know there's nae need for any of this, don't yees?'

However, he was not allowed to finish his sentence.

To get all of his strength into the punch, PC Robertson drew his left arm wide as he darted on to the road. In doing so, however, he had unknowingly handed John the initiative almost immediately. As PC Robertson began propelling his punch forward, John had already moved in and was transferring his body weight from his right side to his left, by means of an upward, curving, short right hook.

As he connected with the left side of PC Robertson's chin, John felt the impact of the precision-strike travel up through the muscles of his fore and upper arm. The force of the punch carried the length of the policeman's body, making him slip on the black ice on the road, lifting his feet off the ground. Falling heavily, he never felt his coccyx shatter, as a result of the crippling contact with the frozen tarmac, and with arms limp by his side, he was unable to prevent the whiplash as he fell backwards, smashing the base of his skull, against the kerb with a sickening crack.

John and PC Miller looked speechlessly at each other.

Suddenly, their eyes were drawn towards the steam rising from the warm urine emanating from PC Robertson's loins, as the liquid flowed to meet the blood that was now trickling from his right ear on to the ground.

'Dear God, help us,' John murmured, as he started unbuttoning his jacket with the intention of placing it under PC Robertson's head.

As he knelt down beside the injured man, however, he had no idea how to proceed. There was even more blood.

At a loss, John eventually placed his jacket over PC Robertson's chest and taking the officer's left hand in his hands, he began rubbing it gently.

Praying in silence, John overheard PC Miller behind him, calling for an ambulance and back-up on the police radio.

The latter was not lost on John. Immediately, he rose from his kneeling position, only to meet the full force of the truncheon strike.

The blow opened up the skin under his right eye, depressed his cheekbone and knocked him sideways, causing him to stumble and lose his footing. Going to ground, he instinctively threw out his left arm to take the impact.

Instantly, John knew he didn't have long. He needed to see Agnes and the kids and knew that if he didn't get out of this situation, he might not see his family again as a free man for a very long time.

These thoughts drove him as he tried to push himself up to run, but his limbs would not cooperate. PC Miller's downward swing had cut across his temple, causing a delayed reaction.

John fully understood that if he attempted any sudden movements, he could collapse at any moment.

Getting himself to his knees, he sat back on his heels. He looked at the officer expectantly, but PC Miller stood back from him some yards away, still wary.

This indecision from the young constable allowed John valuable seconds. He gently patted the gaping wound on his cheek with his right hand, but in truth steadied his breathing, before pushing himself upright.

'George, George, George,' he said, in endearing tones, as he staggered backwards slightly. John knew his only chance was to draw the young officer into a conversation and to let him do most of the talking. This would hopefully give him more time to clear his head, because there was no doubt, if PC Miller decided to rush him now, he'd probably have more of a struggle on his hands than would normally be the case if he was fully compos mentis.

'I'm sorry, John!' George blurted out. 'But what am I meant to do? He's lying there oot the game and the man who done it...Well, how does it look? I mean, when the back-up comes, and they see I haven't done anything, I mean. He's supposed to be my partner for fuck's sake!'

'I wisnae looking for bother, George. I told you that I was coming wi' yees freely! No resisting! And noo look what's fuckin' happened!'

Shouts from the flats could now be heard.

'That's out of order what you're doing with that man!' a woman's voice called out.

'Aye and Ah seen the fuckin' lot by the way!' a man shouted from a veranda.

'Aye. A fuckin' disgrace!' another raged.

'Get yourself up the road, John,' one man in his forties, accompanied by another, said, approaching the scene. 'We seen what these jokers were up tae.'

'Be careful, sir!' young PC Miller cautioned, trying to keep control of the situation. 'Walk on. This is none of your business. Walk on or you'll be arrested for being an accessory.'

'Aye, is that right, officer? I'd say it's you who should be careful,' the man warned, looking around at the people now gathering.

'Aye, officer,' his drunken friend continued, 'or who knows what might happen. For all we know, you could end up lying on the road beside yer pal there, wi' the pish runnin' oot ye.'

At these words, PC Miller became silent.

More and more residents were coming out into the street. One of them, an older man, approached John. 'On you go, John. Go home to see Agnes for a wee while before they come. There's nothing you can do here now. And here… hold that against your face, son,' he said, offering John a scarf.

'Aye, thanks a lot,' John replied, as he looked around at those who had congregated.

Making his way through the small crowd, John stopped at the feet of PC Robertson, who was still lying on the ground with the denim jacket covering his chest. The officer had his eyes closed and was mumbling.

John knew then that both their lives, and the lives of their families, would never be the same again. Breaking into his thoughts, the sound of the police siren brought its own realisation – he had to move, *now*! Turning from the scene, he ran towards his house on the Bellshill Road.

Crouching down beside his colleague, PC Miller again raised the radio to his mouth.

2

Scene 1: Only swings, no roundabouts

In a row, along the front of the hearth, Paul and Margaret knelt, while Ninian stood. The three children had continued to watch the remnants of the old shoes smoulder in the fireplace. They had burned quickly, giving out little in the way of heat, but watching the flames had somehow brought them comfort.

Keeping vigil at the window, Agnes, finally saw him running out from Dalriada Crescent. The nee-naw blare of the police siren, now louder, instantly confirmed her worst fears. She rushed to the front door; her eldest son, Andrew, following at her back.

When she opened the door, John was standing on the pavement on the other side of the road. He was looking directly at her and continued to stand there. Hearing the sound of the engine, Agnes understood. Turning to her right, she saw the police vehicle already reducing its speed.

Passing her neighbours' block, the Black Maria swayed as it mounted the kerb and coasted along the empty pavement, coming to a standstill immediately outside Agnes's front gate, eclipsing her view of John.

Charging from the house, Agnes hurried along the icy path to face what awaited her. The officers had leapt out with their truncheons already drawn. Agnes had not expected this show of force from them. 'No' for coal. No' all this for coal,' she murmured.

As she stumbled closer, shouts from the ongoing commotion tore into her mind, threatening to overwhelm her. Through the open gate, she edged sideways to the left, palming her way along the side of the empty police van. The shouting had stopped, she realised.

Agnes slumped against the passenger door. Whimpering, she eventually rounded the vehicle.

On the road, one of the officers, on his hands and knees, gasped for breath. His hat lay next to him, some feet away. She then looked at John. The right side of his face was dark with blood. He stood, holding the downed officer's truncheon, as the other five policemen made moves to surround him.

Feeling the tug on the back of her three-quarter length coat, Agnes turned to find Margaret and Ninian. Paul and Andrew stood behind them.

'Daddy!' Margaret called out.

Ninian joined in. 'Daddy! Daddy!'

Catching sight of his family, John shouted to the officers. 'Right that's it. That's enough!' before turning his attention to his wife. 'Take the weans in the hoose, Agnes.'

Margaret and Ninian wanted to go to their father, but Agnes held them back.

'I'm sorry, Agnes. Take them in. *Please*,' John hurried.

Agnes gave no reply. She didn't know what to do for the best.

'Right, that's me. I'm throwing it down. Okay?' John called out, making a deliberate show of casting the truncheon aside a few seconds later.

No words were spoken by the officers. None were needed. Their eyes communicated their intentions.

John knew what was coming and prepared himself the best he could. The batons and punches rained in heavily from all sides.

Margaret let out a squeal, and, with hands clasped to her ears, buried her face in her mother's coat. Ninian stood, with arms outstretched, reaching out to his father; beckoning him to come and collect him. His callipers rattled together at the inside of his legs. Babbling through tears, he didn't recognise the initial warmth, only the coldness – the coldness that told him that he had wet himself.

With Paul rooted to the spot, Andrew made a forward move to help his father, but catching on, Agnes called out, instantly putting an end to the young man's thoughtless plans of vengeance.

Looking on again at her husband, Agnes pushed away the tear arriving on her left cheek with the palm of her right hand. 'It'll be over soon, John,' she whispered.

Scene 2: Dot-to-dot

In her upstairs bedroom, Agnes stood, resting her forehead against the frozen window. Each breath steamed up the glass, but just as quickly disappeared. With shoulders slouched and fingers part through the worn lining in her coat pockets, she let the tears roll down her face in silence.

Gazing down into the yellow glare from the street, she recalled what she had said to John earlier in the evening: 'Let the ones who owe us the money go and get the coal for us, John. It's only fair. They're the ones that let us down. It's no' right!'

He would hear none of it though. 'I couldnae let them do that, Agnes, whether they owed me the money or no'. I'll no' be long. Don't worry,' he had said, as he'd left the house.

'*I'll no' be long. Don't worry.*' Agnes grimaced at the irony.

She'd be able to find out what he'd be formally charged with 'in the morning', one of the officers had said.

Margaret, her daughter, let out a quiet yawn. Hearing this, Agnes stiffened. She was afraid to turn round and find that the child had woken up. Margaret had become hysterical on seeing her father being beaten and dragged semi-conscious into the police van. Right up until the time when she had finally fallen asleep, she had remained unconvinced that her daddy would be okay.

Standing motionless for a few seconds, Agnes carefully adjusted her position to check on her daughter. Relieved that the child was still sleeping, she returned to the window. Her thoughts now came to her eldest son, Andrew.

The boy had done well, she acknowledged. He had tried to remain strong, even though he too was deeply affected by what he had witnessed. Agnes knew he had been in a daze, plagued by thoughts of what he felt he should have done. But on entering the house the situation with the children had jolted him out of it, and no wonder – she had never seen the young ones in such a state. The maelstrom of raw emotions had made her fearful. She was sure that at least one of them would fall ill.

Thankfully though, Andrew had picked up on, and followed her lead. And together they had tried their best to calmly play down each child's concerns for their father's well-being, despite harbouring the same grave fears themselves.

In the end, however, it had played out the way she had hoped and partly expected.

Only when hunger and exhaustion had finally caught up with the children were they ready for bed. It had, for the most part, been a waiting game.

Moving from the window with her thoughts of the children's plight, Agnes crept over the warped floorboards and lowered herself gently on to the edge of the bed. She again broke down. Her body began to shake, as she fought to restrain the noise of her heartache.

Scene 3: Walking in sleep

In their double bed, Ninian lay flat on his back, dozing, while his brothers slept on either side.

His head, sticking out from under the heavy coat that lay across the blankets, rocked gently from side to side, on the edge of a pillow.

The people that made up the crowd were making a lot of noise shouting and laughing, and Ninian was soon laughing too. They were bumping into him and pushing him forward, through to what seemed to be the front of the crowd. The shouting and laughing was becoming louder and louder. Near the front, he caught glimpses of the faces of those who formed part of the crowd on the other side. Ninian began to feel uncomfortable. The people didn't seem to have happy faces after all: some were very, very angry. Others were even spitting, and another man threw a stone. Some were trying to break free from the crowd, but were being pushed back by men armed with spears: soldiers.

Yet, even so, further to the right, one man managed to break free and throw out a kick as another on Ninian's side rushed out with his left hand raised and clenched in a fist. Women, in tears, cried out against the men. As the men were grabbed and forced back in line by the soldiers, a gap suddenly appeared and Ninian was nudged forward, further out into the open.

Through the sandy-coloured dust cloud hanging just below his line of vision, Ninian could now see a man lying sprawled out with his face on the ground. His bare back was scored and bloody. A huge soldier, who had been holding the mob back, now turned his attention to the man on the ground. He shouted angrily as he walked over and, taking something from his belt, raised his arm high, before bringing it down, forcefully lashing the man on the ground. The crowd cheered more loudly.

Ninian started to cry and, rubbing his eyes, began to wail.

Andrew was the first to wake. 'Ninian, Ninian, it's okay. Look. It's bedtime. You're in yer bed with me and Paul. You're okay. Shh. Go to sleep,' he told him quietly.

Ninian wailed all the louder.

Paul now woke. 'Ninian. Aw, Ninian! I'm soakin'. He's peed the bed!' he moaned, as he slid out from under the weight of the assorted sheets and makeshift bedclothes.

With Ninian's crying not showing any signs of letting up, Agnes came into the unlit room.

'He's wet the bed, Mammy,' Paul told her.

'It's okay, son. I'll take him in with me. Change your clothes if they're wet,' she said quietly, 'and change the bottom sheet, boys. Yees can borrow the one off Margaret's bed for the night. I'll sort it all tomorrow. And remember, give the tarpaulin a wipe before you put the dry sheet on.'

Under his breath, Andrew groaned. Even with a dry sheet on top, the plastic-coated tarpaulin that stopped the mattress from getting wet always felt cold on entering the bed. It seemed to take ages for the combined heat from their bodies to dispel the dampness. Winter was the worst – and this had been the worst night.

It had been the same for all of them though and coming to his senses, he soon thought better of complaining. Besides, he was to be the man of the house in his father's absence. 'No bother, Mam,' he said, as he pushed out from under the bedding.

Ninian continued to cry, as his mother helped him from the bed. 'The devil was making me laugh at God, Mammy. I didn't mean it, Mammy,' he bawled.

'It's okay, son,' she said, before turning to her second born. 'I wonder if this altar-boy idea was a good one, Paul.'

Paul took some seconds before answering. 'Maybe after he does it tomorrow he'll start to get used to it, Mam, and then he'll be alright.'

'Aye, well, we'll see,' Agnes said, suddenly taken aback at the sound of her dispirited tone. 'Och, what am I saying? I know you'll watch him, son, and it'll all work oot fine. Goodnight, Paul. Goodnight, Andrew. See yees in the morning.'

'Goodnight, Mammy,' the boys replied, as Agnes turned, and left the room, carrying the sobbing Ninian in her arms.

Scene 4: The show must go on

With all the noise, Margaret was now awake, and was sitting up in bed crying, as Agnes and Ninian came into the room.

'It's okay, Margaret, I'm here ma darlin',' Agnes whispered, as she sat Ninian on the edge of the bed and began stripping him of his wet clothes. This time, after drying him, she quickly buttoned him up in one of his daddy's shirts.

For the first time in the night, Agnes became aware of the burning sensation in her nostrils when she breathed in. The room was bitterly cold, too cold for children. She took her coat off and laid it beside her older one, on top of the bed clothes, and wasted no more time in getting Ninian and herself under the covers with Margaret.

Being in bed with their mum had calmed the children. Margaret, close to sleep, cuddled up to Agnes's right side, resting her head on her mother's shoulder, while Ninian lay on his back, as he always did, holding on to his mum's left hand.

'It was a trick, Mammy. The devil tricked me into laughing at Jesus. That's what it was: he tricked me, Mammy!'

'I know, son. Don't worry about it. Jesus knows that too. Try and go to sleep now. Altar boys need to get a good rest before they serve, especially when it's going to be their first mass,' she whispered.

'Aye, Mammy. Paul told me that too. He's the best altar boy, Mammy. Even my teacher Mrs Donnelly said he was.'

'Aye, he's good, son, but you'll be good. Just listen and do what he tells you tomorrow and it'll all be fine. After a wee while, you'll be the top altar boys in Motherwell.'

'Do you think so, Mammy? I'll try my best, Mammy. Maybe me and Paul can serve at all the masses, together, Mammy.' Ninian's mind swirled with excitement before he said, 'Will my daddy be at the man's funeral too, Mammy? Will he be there to see us serving on the altar?'

'No, he won't make it this time, son, but he'll see you do it another day,' she answered, unable to come up with anything else.

Looking at the ceiling, made visible by the streetlight, Agnes's bottom lip trembled as she drew in short, panicked breaths through her nose.

In an attempt to conceal her grief, she freed herself of Ninian's hand, and gently slid her arm under and around his neck, drawing him closer. *You're of no use to the children like this. They can't see ye crying. They need to have hope.* 'Go to sleep now, son.'

'Goodnight, Mammy. I said my prayers in my own bed, Mammy.'

'That's good, son. You're a good boy. Night, night now.'

'Night, night, Mammy.'

Ninian, she thought, closing her eyes to push the tears out. *Had there ever been a time in his short life where she and John had said he'd be okay, and honestly believed it?*

'It was the way he was lying in the womb,' the doctors had told them. That was what they'd said had caused the problem with his legs. Time would tell whether persevering with the callipers would make any difference.

He was already a nervous wee soul, even before being fitted with them; never quite had the confidence of the other children at any time really. But the attention-seeking! Och, aw the weans were like that, it was part of childhood. But Ninian's methods… *Stop it*! Agnes gripped herself. She knew this train of thought well, and knew exactly where it led to: a night without sleep; hours of toing and froing from one scenario to the next, thinking whether he'd turn out like him, or whether he'd grow up a normal child.

Not tonight. I can't, she told herself. *Just accept it. Was there really any more wondering to be done? It wasn't a case of will he or won't he now, surely? Accept it, stop living in denial. It'd be better to just accept it. That was the answer. Accept the fact that he was becoming more and more like him – like Iain. It was obvious what was going to happen.*

No, please not tonight. Agnes tensed her whole being, forcing her head back deeper into the pillow. *No, please God. Don't let him go the same way as ma wee brother Iain. Please no' another tragedy,* she lamented inwardly.

Choking back tears, she held the children tighter.

3

Scene 1: Carefree

Light snow had started to fall as Paul and Ninian, hand in hand, made their way towards St Luke's Parish Church in Forgewood.

On the way, they decided to pass by the local shops on Kylemore Crescent, primarily to see if Paul's friends, Eddie (aka Eldo) and Gary, were around.

Paul smiled as he saw Rover, a black and brown mongrel with a stick in his mouth, bounding across the road towards the shops. The other two mongrels that Eldo had – one resembling a whippet, and the other a Labrador – chased after it, followed by another couple of dogs belonging to people from the scheme.

Eddie was standing outside the newsagent with Gary. They didn't have their bags, so Paul knew they would've handed them back, having finished their paper rounds for the day.

Catching sight of the brothers, Eddie and Gary ran across the snow-covered pavement, before going into a slide over the last few yards, barging into Paul and Ninian, who almost lost their footing.

'Paul, what happened?' Eddie said nervously. 'Did your da kill a polis? Everybody's oan aboot it?'

'Naw, nothing like that, He was in bother, but…' Paul struggled, feeling embarrassed.

'I'm telling ye! Tell him, Gary! Tell him what your uncle Rab said!'

'Aye, Paul. Ma Uncle Rab said yer auld boy leathered a polis in Dalriada last night, and that the polis got taken away in an ambulance. They think the polis is deid.'

'Naw. It cannae be. We seen ma da getting lifted outside oor bit, didn't we, Ninian?'

Ninian nodded in agreement, without looking up.

'Honest, Paul, that's what everybody's saying. The whole scheme's talking aboot it,' Gary confirmed.

'It cannae be true. It cannae be,' Paul said, as if trying to convince himself. 'Anyway we've got to go. We've to serve at Mr Cuthbert's funeral. We better hurry, or we'll be late.'

'Alright, Paul,' Eddie started, changing the subject. 'Are you coming oot to play in the afternoon? We're going over to North Motherwell for a game a' fitba'.'

'What, the day? Look at the place,' Paul replied, dragging his right foot across the snow.

'Aye, Ah know,' Eddie answered, 'but it's just a kick-aboot, maybe four a side or something. Once the snow's trampled down it'll be fine. You can come too, Ninian. It's no' far, just through the level crossing a wee bit. Gary's taking his new ball. And we're wearing our Scotland tops, Paul! Did Ah tell ye? Ma Uncle Frank says that he's taking me tae the World Cup!'

Standing slightly behind Eldo, out of view, Gary raised his eyebrows and tilted his head wryly towards him, before pulling a funny face and smiling at Paul.

Paul latched on immediately. 'Are ye? That's great Eldo! Was Frank bevvied when he told ye?'

Eddie spun round quickly to Gary and laughed as he tried to punch him in the stomach, but Gary was already out of distance, and turning to Paul, he found that he too had backed off.

Eddie laughed with his friends at his own useless attempts. He began calling Gary and Paul all sorts of vulgar names, and telling them what he would do to them when he got them, causing them to laugh all the louder.

'Stop yer daft carry-on. We need to go,' Paul said through his laughter, all the while keeping his eyes on Eddie some yards away. 'We'll come in the afternoon, won't we, Ninian?'

Ninian nodded shyly again.

'We'll come for you about half twelve then, Paul, alright?' Gary said.

'Aye, we'll be ready. See ye, Gary. See ye, Eldo,' Paul told them.

'See ye later, Paul. See ye, Ninian,' said Eddie, now returned to his senses. 'And, Paul... Hope your da's alright, mate.'

'Aye, I hope everything turns oot okay, Paul. See yees,' Gary added.

'Thanks, lads. We'll team up later and have a laugh.'

Scene 2: The eye of the beholder

Within the church, the deceased man's immediate family stood close together in the front pews, while extended family and friends were spread out randomly in the ones behind.

St Luke's was almost half-full and the mourners now awaited the Gospel reading from Father Thomas Reilly.

Already in position, on either side of the lectern, acting candle-bearers, Ninian and Paul stood motionless, facing each other.

Ninian, because of the height of the lectern, was having difficulty seeing Paul, and came to realise that if he could just move a wee bit to the left he'd be able to see his big brother much better.

Deciding to check on everything one more time before making his move, Ninian tightened his grip on the wooden shaft of the candleholder, and smoothly followed it from the floor up through and above his hands, raising his head still further until finally he saw the golden shimmer on the glass sleeve.

They had told him in the sacristy that it was a wee bit big for him, but that if he just held the processional candleholder straight, the way Paul had shown him, he'd be 'doing a very good job'. All he had to do was 'just let the wooden shaft rest on the floor and hold it firmly, keeping it straight'.

Father Reilly had added that if they carried out this task effectively, both their candles would remain at an equal height above the lectern, 'in accordance with protocol'. Ninian remembered he'd to ask Paul what this meant later.

Glancing at Father Reilly on his left, Ninian worked out that if he really was going to make his move, he'd have to do it fairly soon. It would be very bad to make his move when the priest was reading from the Gospel. No, he could never do that.

He'd do another final check. And only then, when everything was okay, would he make his move – *just a wee bit*.

Almost convinced that everything was as it should be, with fists one on top of the other, Ninian twisted his grip on the wooden shaft, holding it fast. Looking up to face Paul, he readied himself for the final time. *Go.*

In moving his left leg and taking a small step sideways, Ninian accidentally lifted the candleholder from its resting place on the floor. Now free, its top-heavy weight began tilting to the right, throwing out the bottom to the left – jarring his wrists.

Filled with terror, Ninian stabbed the candleholder downwards.

The sound of the shaft striking the varnished floorboards startled him, as did the stinging vibration that flew up through his grip, shaking the candle in its brass housing.

Fighting desperately to keep the candle, and holder together, Ninian almost cried out.

Yet miraculously, after a few exhausting seconds, somehow he managed to rebalance, and stabilise the movement. With his panic subsiding, and very pleased at having retrieved the situation, Ninian soon became annoyed that no one had come to help – a thought that succeeded in pushing out his bottom lip.

Continuing to dwell on what he had come through, he was suddenly struck by the dawning of a horrendous possibility.

Nervously, his eyes traced the length of the wooden shaft reaching up to the brass holder. *Please,* he pleaded, before looking up to the cylindrical glass sleeve that encased the candle and protected it. Finally, he saw its palpable warm glow – the flame had not gone out after all.

Smiling over to Paul, his opposite number, Ninian was reassured by seeing his big brother wink back at him discreetly.

Paul was the best. In his white vestments, he looked like one of the statues, Ninian thought. Paul knew what and where everything was in the sacristy and on the altar; in fact, he knew everything in the whole of St Luke's. He would be a great priest when he was older. And yes, Ninian would follow in his footsteps.

Wrenched from his daydream by an icy draught biting into his clammy fists, Ninian hoped that it wouldn't be long before James, the other senior altar boy, returned to take the candleholder from him. After all, he'd only been given the job because James had to help Father Reilly with the censer.

After the Gospel, Ninian remembered; that's when James would come back and take the candleholder away.

As Father Reilly held the chains and reverently waved the censer in the act of blessing the book of Gospels on the lectern, Ninian watched intently. It was great being an altar boy. It was the first step to becoming a priest. The clashing of the chains, the pouring smoke, and the wafting smell of the burning incense, in some way drew Ninian deeper and deeper into his otherworldly realm.

By the third and final wave of the censer, he was completely gone, totally lost in the mesmeric dance of the smoke's silky blue plumes curling and folding, rolling and tumbling, falling and rising.

Coming to the belief that the smoke had a life of its own and moved as it pleased, Ninian watched as the billowing greyish-blue mass seemed to contract then expand, breathing in and blowing out, each time increasing in size, yet thinning, becoming translucent, stretching out, to hang mysteriously in the air.

Just in front of the lectern, Ninian now noticed that there was something different within the cloud. A small bright light like a sparkler on bonfire night was emerging and growing rapidly almost violently.

Yes. It was an entity; an entity of light…

Convulsing in metamorphosis…

Writhing with an urgency…

Eagerly awaiting its release…

A being of unimaginable beauty…

Miraculous in her splendour…

Rippling the surface of the cloud as she now flowed graciously underneath gazing and smiling lovingly as she made her way majestically covering the length of the cloud.

Gliding back and forth…

Gaining momentum, back and forth…

Growing in strength, back and forth…

Impossible speeds, back and forth…

Becoming a blur, back and forth…

Becoming the *cloud*…

Now, somehow, the movement was no movement at all.

Now, somehow *all* was made still, until gradually, in the silence of her brilliant light, the ethereal being rose up magnificently high above them, effortlessly scouring the area above their heads, before gracefully swooping down to twist around them and become, once again, the bluish grey plumes that were now stretching stealthily in their *search* outwards, outwards from where they stood at the lectern *still outwards* beyond the communion rail, passing over the coffin, becoming wider, seeping between the bodies of the mourners, standing in the pews...

Drifting...

Probing...

Purging...

Yes, *them...*

Forcing them from their hosts, dark, hideous, vaporous forms, momentarily bound on contact with the cloud, but then released to recoil and flee in all directions back into non-existence.

And so the cloud continued to advance with ease further and further still, purging as it went, until suddenly, in an instant, its awareness was alerted anew. The presence of a more powerful evil had been detected. From all areas of the church, the tendrils began streaming rapidly towards a place of convergence, frantically snaking their way between the bodies of the mourners in an almost desperate race to confront their enemy, but incredibly they were dissolving as they approached touching distance, they were having no impact on the *boy* who stood at the centre, and soon the cloud was no more.

The sound of the priest's voice – 'The will of He who sent me is that I should lose nothing' – passed by on the horizon of Ninian's perception.

Ninian's eyes sharpened. The boy stood at the end of a pew across the aisle, roughly 30 feet away. He looked to be about three or four years older than Ninian and was slightly taller. His gleaming black hair was plastered to his head and his grey jumper was much too big for him. He was looking up to a red-haired woman and seemed to be talking to her. His mouth moved at an incredible speed, but she wasn't paying him any attention.

Paul's eyes stared at his brother's head, willing him to turn around. He had told Ninian in the sacristy not to look at the congregation when holding the candle. Out of reach, however, he could do nothing without causing a scene.

Ninian continued to watch the boy mouth to the woman, but still she took no notice.

Before Ninian had time to realise or understand how it had happened, the boy glared back at him. Ninian didn't see him turn his head, yet he'd been looking at him all the while.

Frightened, Ninian turned away to find his brother Paul giving him a look that screamed 'Ninian!'

Ninian was jolted back and returned to his senses, gripping the candleholder tightly, as if by instinct. He now clearly heard Father Reilly – 'This is the Gospel of the Lord' – which signalled the end of the reading.

Ninian lowered his head. He felt how bad he'd been.

There was one consolation, however. At least James would now come to take the candleholder from him and he'd be able to return to his chair. He would concentrate from now on though, and he'd begin by listening to Father Reilly's homily.

'*Ninnnniaaan,*' the whispering voice breathed.

Turning his head to his right, Ninian half-hoped to see James, but there was no one between himself and the congregation.

'*Ninnnniaaan.*' He heard the voice again; its sound seemed to swirl around him

Tightening his grip on the candleholder, Ninian looked down through the space between his arms, following the wooden shaft to the shiny wet floor. Ninian was standing in a big puddle. *It wasn't me, it wasn't me*, he told himself. *No, no, no, not here, please.*

Glancing to his right it was worse. The puddle was trickling along the varnished floorboards towards the communion rail. Returning to look at the base of the candleholder, however, Ninian noticed that there were tiny ripples on the water. The ripples had slight delays between them, but they seemed constant. Like the tiny waves of a tide they flowed in a steady stream from left to right and were broken as they washed up against the bottom of the candleholder's wooden shaft.

Turning his head slowly to his left, hoping to find the source, Ninian's eyes searched their way along the silvery stream. It seemed that the water was only flowing past Ninian's side of the lectern. Continuing to look upwards along its course, Ninian soon noticed that the distance between the ripples was becoming shorter. Instinctively, Ninian drew in his stomach. His bladder almost emptied. Further along the water, he could see the distorted reflection of the boy. The boy was now somehow standing there watching him.

Ninian turned his head quickly, bringing it back to look at the base of the candleholder.

Closing his eyes as tightly as he could, he then opened them slowly only to find that the boy had drawn closer, and was now standing beside him.

Ninian, with his head still lowered, could see that the woollen sleeves of the boy's jumper stretched down past his grey shorts. Heavy drops of water fell from them, splashing in the puddle at their feet. The boy's soaking, black leather shoes had no laces and had burst open at the insteps. His thick grey socks had some broken twigs sticking in them and were pulled up below his pale knees that were scarred with dark purple gashes.

'Ninian, I can take it now.'

Turning his head slightly to the right, to where the voice came from, Ninian saw James approaching.

At that precise moment, however, Ninian felt a cold wet hand come to rest on his left wrist. Wincing at the contact, Ninian squeezed his eyes closed and lowered his head. He could feel the slender fingers curl caressing him in a gentle hold.

Suddenly the hold tightened.

Instantly, Ninian felt them rushing deep within. Their whispers quickly became a roar; guttural sounds from a ravenous multitude. The invasion snapped his body to attention. His chest was thrust out, as his head whipped upwards, opening his eyes to a tremendous light, but then the light was gone. Ninian fell deeper and deeper into darkness. He tried to scream, yet nothing would come out.

In terror, he turned to the boy. The boy's eyes were closed and his head was lowered. Water cascading from him. Ninian fought to wrestle free.

Suddenly, the boy's eyes flicked open, but they weren't there, only total blackness – deep, black glistening pools.

Ninian let out a scream as he pulled himself free, but his callipered legs remained rigid, causing him to bend sharply in front of the lectern. In the movement, the candleholder veered to the right, its top-heavy weight dragging him to the floor.

Terrified and confused, Ninian put all his strength into hurling himself back upright, but it was more than was required. His momentum carried him too far past a comfortable standing position, past the point of recovery.

He fell backwards, with the candle older held firmly in his fists. Rushing to catch him, James, the senior altar server, never saw it coming. The dull clink of the candleholder's glass sleeve breaking as it gouged James's face was met with horrified gasps and cries.

PART II

BOOK TWO: KEEPING IT REAL

(19 YEARS LATER)

4

Scene 1: Happy New Year!

Friday 1 January, 1993. Kylemore Crescent, Forgewood, Motherwell, Scotland, 11:30 a.m.

Ninian had slept where he had fallen, and lay sprawled out, face-down, on the three-seater couch, in his living room.

'Ninian, get the door!' Karen, his girlfriend, shouted from the bedroom.

Again, the letterbox was rattled, this time, more forcefully.

'Ninian! Get the door!'

'Aye, Ah hear ye!'

'Well, get the door then! There's somebody at the door!'

Ninian pushed himself from the couch and, sitting up, he immediately felt the cold, wet, beer-soaked carpet on the soles of his bare feet.

Rubbing his eyes with his right thumb and index finger, he leaned back on the couch, and let out a muffled groan.

The letterbox rapped again.

'Ninian!' Karen pleaded once more.

Standing up and turning to his right, his first step knocked over an unwanted glass of vodka and his second scrunched on the loose tobacco and cigarette papers that someone had abandoned on the festive TV guide.

Lifting his left foot to wipe off the debris, Ninian cursed as he stumbled slightly.

Taking the TV guide in his hands, he folded it in half before sliding it, along with its contents, under the middle cushion on the couch.

Scanning for further evidence, he gathered cigarette papers and a small lump of cannabis from the mantelpiece, and stuffed them into the right-hand pocket of his black denims. Then turning to the two armchairs, he picked up two ashtrays from the floor, emptying their contents into a plastic bag bulging with empty beer cans.

Entering the kitchen, he dumped the carrier bag beside the others at the bin and looked around. He groaned and blew out, closing the door on his way out. *Later,* he thought.

In the hall, he clawed at his bare chest as he made his way towards the front door. 'Some clown must've left it open when they were leavin'.'

The letterbox was rapped again.

'Aye, I'm coming.'

Reaching the door and opening it further, Ninian found Claire, his Community Psychiatric Nurse.

'Morning, Ninian. I was to drop in and see you today. Remember?'

'Aye, aye. In ye come, Claire.'

'Rough night?' Claire asked, as she closed the front door and followed him down the hall.

'Naw, nothing major. Just a few friends round after the Bells,' he replied, entering the living room. 'Have a seat, Claire. Oh, I almost forgot… Happy New Year.'

'Happy New Year to you too, Ninian. All the best,' Claire said, shaking his hand, before taking her seat on the armchair, beside the partially opened window.

'Can I make you a tea or a coffee, Claire?'

'Thanks, Ninian, but my husband's waiting for me outside in the car. Maybe some other time. I won't be staying for long. I'm just here to see how you're managing over the holidays.'

'No bother, Claire. Thanks,' he said, picking up his T-shirt from where it lay in a crumpled heap on the floor and pulling it on over his wiry frame before taking a seat on the couch.

'So,' Claire began, 'what's been happening, Ninian? Has everything been okay?'

Ninian rubbed at his eyes. 'Aye, fine, Claire, thanks. How's it been for yersell? The family and everybody doing well?'

'Yes, they're all doing great, Ninian, thanks. We had a nice Christmas with family and friends. We're going to my in-laws when I leave here. The kids are already there, keeping them on their toes, I suspect. And what about you, Ninian? Tell me, how have things been? Any plans for the rest of the holidays?'

'Aye, much the same as yersell, Claire. I saw my family over Christmas, and went to a couple of parties wi' ma pals. I've to go over to my mam and dad's later for dinner. We usually gather there on New Year's Day. Paul's still in Kenya right enough. But he's getting to come home after Easter for a break. It's been years since we've seen him.'

'That's nice, Ninian. And you were saying you had some friends over last night too.'

'Aye, that's right, Claire: a couple of ma pals and their girlfriends. My own girlfriend Karen joined us later. She's in there having a long lie,' Ninian answered, smiling awkwardly.

'Good, Ninian, that's good. Sounds like you've had plenty company and a busy schedule too!'

'Aye, it's been fairly busy, Claire.'

'Good, that's good, Ninian, and how has that worked out for you, Ninian? You know you've been off medicine now for almost two months.'

'Aye, fine, Claire. No problems,' he replied, looking beyond Claire, out through the window, hoping to look as though he'd been distracted by the sound of a car in the street, three floors down.

'That's good, Ninian. So there's been no delusions, no voices?'

'Naw. Nothing, Claire.'

'Okay great. And there's been no… er, shall we say, you haven't seen any unwelcome guests, or have you?'

'Naw, nothing like that, Claire. That's aw behind me now.'

'Okay, Ninian. Well,' she said, getting up from the chair, 'you'll contact me, or your doctor, if you're not feeling too good, won't you?'

'Aye, I'll phone, Claire. I've got the numbers.'

'Okay, Ninian, I'll see you soon. Oh, I almost forgot. You've got a review coming up at the end of this month. You'll get a letter informing you of the time and date, probably by the end of next week. Right, I'd better get going. Look after yourself, Ninian, and remember, give us a call if you're feeling out of sorts.'

'Aye, I will, Claire. Thanks. Hope the rest of the holidays go well,' he said, walking her to the front door.

'Thanks, Ninian, I hope you have a nice time too. Cheerio,' Claire replied as she opened the door and let herself out.

'See ye, Claire, all the best.'

Closing the door behind her, Ninian ran the fingers of both hands through his hair, interlocking them at the back of his head. With his eyes now closed, he blew out heavily. *Nightmare,* he thought. *What a fuckin' nightmare! Of aw the days!*

Walking back into the living room, he picked up the solitary cigarette that lay on top of the hi-fi. Sitting back down on the couch, he lit and drew heavily on the cigarette, blowing out the smoke towards the window. *No way,* he thought. *Absolutely no fuckin' way! You've come too far, and anyway, what are ye meant to say? Not one person has ever believed ye. Aye, and you've learned that the hard way, from when ye were a laddie. Could she really honestly expect that, after everything, you'd keep telling her the truth? Where exactly has that ever got ye, eh? Dubbed up in a fuckin' hospital. Continually pumped full a' the next wonder drug, and then left sittin' aw day like a fuckin' space chimp. Naw. No fuckin' more. I'll take my chances.*

Taking another draw on his cigarette, Ninian smiled and sniggered. The involuntary movement forced the smoke out through his nose, making him cough repeatedly and causing his eyes to water.

Rubbing his eyes, he continued to laugh. *Aye,* he thought, *maybe ye should've just told her the truth; the truth that when ye opened the door the boy was there too, standing behind her; the truth that he had followed her in; the truth that he'd been sitting beside her all the while on the arm of the chair… the truth that the voices telling ye to do evil things were real.*

5

Scene 1: Tender

Friday 1 January, 1993, Bellshill Road, Forgewood, Motherwell, Scotland. 3:10 p.m.

John watched Ninian across the kitchen table. His son was hardly eating anything. The beads of sweat were steadily congregating on his forehead and his hands, despite resting them at either side of his plate while holding his knife and fork, couldn't hide the shakes.

'Are ye still with us, son, or are ye somewhere else?'

'Eh, naw, sorry. Just feelin' a bit rough,' Ninian replied, trying to show a renewed interest in his steak pie dinner.

Agnes scowled at John.

'Whit is it, missus?' John asked, as Agnes shook her head and continued with her meal.

'Too much a' the auld soup last night, eh, Ninian?' John continued.

'Och, John, give it a rest, would ye. He's still a laddie, int ye, son? He's not doing anything that any of the other young ones aren't doing. And anyway, it's the holidays, int it, son?' she said, resting her knife on the table, before reaching over to ruffle the locks of Ninian's mousy brown hair. She knew John was right though – their son was in danger of making an already hard life even harder.

John winked playfully at Ninian as Agnes returned to her plate, before John said, 'When I was a child I talked like a child I reasoned like a child. But when I became a man I put those childish ways behind me.'

Agnes looked up from her food and tutted. 'Would ye listen tae it, Ninian. We've got the Bishop sitting wi' us noo.'

John let out a mischievous laugh.

'Aye, no' bad, Da,' Ninian replied. *Where did he learn that one,* he thought, *in Barlinnie? When he was in doing 'es ten stretch for leavin' a polis like a cabbage.*

'Aye, if only I'd taken heed of those words of wisdom, *maybe,* just maybe,' John said, sticking a small roast potato into his mouth, 'I'd have saved us aw a lot of bother.'

'Dear God! I know it's New Year and we can manage yer gibbering, but don't start getting aw sentimental oan us! A' Ninian, we couldn't cope with that one the day, could we, son?'

'Och, whit are you oan aboot, wummin? Can a man no' hold his hands up and admit he got it wrong every now and again? It's healthy, is it no'?'

Ninian discreetly wiped his forehead and smiled over at his dad. The auld boy wisnae the worst, he thought. *He'd done his time inside, ten years, but he was still doing it here on the outside. He'd tried to make amends, but he still couldnae really get over what he had done. The auld dear had been good wi' him as well. Even after all these years, she still tried to reassure him.*

'So,' John started, turning once more to Ninian, 'what about this lassie Karen? Are ye no' thinking aboot poppin' the question? She seems nice.'

'Pfft, settle doon, Da.'

'Settle doon, Da! Would ye listen tae it, missus? Aw kiddin' aside, Ninian, it's a good wummin like yer mam here ye're needin', and it's aboot time ye were thinking aboot settlin' doon wi' a nice lassie.'

Agnes sat quietly. She couldn't pretend anymore. She knew, like John, that they wouldn't always be there for him.

'We'll see what happens, Da,' Ninian said, rolling some peas around his plate with his fork, *I'm oot a' here shortly,* he thought. *He's daein' ma fuckin' napper in.*

'Right, John, give it a rest, eh? Let's try and enjoy the day, will we?'

An uneasy silence followed.

'Who wants some rhubarb crumble and custard?' Agnes asked, getting up from her chair, and lifting her dinner plate from the table.

'Aye, ye can always get round us with yer culinary delights, ma dear. What aboot it Ninian? Are ye up for some of yer mam's speciality?'

'I'd like tae, Da, and thanks for making ma favourite, Mam, but

I'm no' feeling too great, to be honest. I was gonnae head over to the flat and get a lie doon, if it was alright wi' yees?'

'Aye, no bother, son. I'll put some in a bowl for ye and ye can put it in yer fridge and get it when you're ready for it.'

'Thanks, Mam. Sorry aboot that.'

'No bother, son.'

Ninian started to rise from his chair at the table, as his Mum prepared his dessert.

'Whit aboot Andrew and Margaret, Ninian?' John asked. 'Will ye no' be able to stay for a wee while until they come? They'll be here shortly wi' the weans. And Paul… we're still hoping he'll be able tae phone fae Kenya as well. Ye'll miss them aw if ye go.'

'I'm sorry, Da. Would you tell them I'm sorry and that I'll catch up with them later?'

'Ninian!' John started. 'Listen, Andrew and Margaret ye can see later, and that's bad enough since it's New Year's Day, and a day for the family, but it's now eight years since we seen yer brother Paul, and we've not spoke to him on the phone since August. What'll we say to him if he calls, and asks to talk to you, like he always does, and you're no' here, again?'

Ninian was silent for a moment, before answering. '*Da*, Paul knows I love him and he'll understand that if I'm no' here it's because I'm no' feeling well.'

John thought for a few seconds. He knew Ninian was right, but he knew also that Paul was a great influence on Ninian, and hoped that if he did call, he'd be able to talk to Ninian, talk some sense into him. 'Alright, I'll let him know,' John said, the sound of defeat in his voice.

'Thanks, Da. Right, I'll away over the road.'

'Here's yer pudding, son,' Agnes said, handing Ninian a bowl covered in tin foil.

'Thanks, Mammy, and thanks for dinner as well, Mam,' he replied, kissing her on the cheek and giving her a cuddle.

'See ye, Da,' he said, turning to John.

'Okay, son*,*' John replied, getting up from his chair and walking round the table to his last born. 'Listen, ye know I'm no' trying to be on yer case and giving ye a hard time all the time, don't ye? Me and yer mammy love ye and things have been hard enough for ye over the years. We just want what's best for ye, son. Life's hard enough.'

'Ah know, Da. Ah know. I love yees tae and I appreciate everything. Ah dae.'

'C'mere,' John said, almost crushing Ninian in his arms, and kissing him on the cheek before releasing him. 'And mind now, we're graftin' on Wednesday. Watch whit yer doing wi' that drink. I need ye fresh. We've got a lot of work oan and Ah cannae have ye up on the roofs if yer no' a hunner per cent.'

'Aye, Ah know, Da. I'll be ready. I'll probably see yees over the weekend. Mind and tell everybody I'm sorry I missed them.'

'Alright, son, take care, and watch yersell oot there,' John said, as he and Agnes followed Ninian into the hall.

'Aye, Ah will,' Ninian replied. 'See ye, Mam. See ye, Da,' he said, opening the front door.

'See ye, son. God bless,' John replied.

'See ye, Ninian. Watch yersell, son,' Agnes added.

The two of them waved to their youngest, as he made his way across the frosty path and out through the open gate.

John closed the front door only when Ninian had passed from their sight and had entered the scheme.

Scene 2: *As you do*

As Ninian entered the close to his flat, he found Gary, his friend, walking down the stairs towards him, carrying a plastic bag containing the customary 'New Year' requirements, which, on this occasion, consisted of cans of beer and bottles of wine.

'Where have you been? I was rattlin' yer door there for ages.'

'Just up at my mam and da's,' Ninian replied, holding up the bowl. 'I could've done withoot it right enough, but they would've came doon tae the flat if I never made it up for dinner.'

'So, how are they doing? Are they doing alright?' Gary asked, as they headed up the stairs.

'Aye, they're doing fine, Gary, thanks.'

'And what about Paul? Have yees heard anything?'

'Naw, nothing yet,' Ninian replied, almost instinctively. Yet, as soon as the words that had come from his mouth had sunk in, Ninian, at that moment, came to a deep and sudden realisation; a realisation of something that could only be described as heartfelt pain. Gary's innocent question had brought about a quivering response from the innermost part of Ninian's being. And so Ninian was now, once more, left with that familiar feeling; a feeling of sadness and regret he had faced throughout his life. The times when he'd felt, and come to know, that he'd somehow been unfaithful; the times when he, that same old Ninian, had somehow failed or somehow let down those that he loved.

Ninian came to a halt on the stairs. 'You know, Gary,' he began solemnly, 'it's good that Ah can talk tae ye. Ah don't think Ah really realised. Ah mean, Ah didnae really realise until this moment until your question about Paul, my ain brother. Honestly, Gary, you wouldnae believe it. Fuck knows whit I've been doing. Fuck knows whit's been goin' on in ma ain heid. I haven't even written or spoken to Paul, for absolutely fuckin' ages, and do you know whit? Do you know whit's actually the worst oot the lot? At some level, Ah don't even know if it's even fuckin' registered. Ah mean, I'm not even sure if it's even been there in ma heid tae dae it, tae contact him! How the fuck is that even possible Gary?

'Ah mean, put it this way: take you, me and Eldo, for example… We obviously always talk aboot Paul fae time tae time, just as I do with ma family, but where the fuck have Ah been? Have Ah really been there, tuned in, fully switched oan, paying attention, or even fuckin' listening?

'The auld boy was just saying before I left that it was August when they last heard fae Paul! Where the fuck have Ah been, Gary? Eh? Not even knowing that aboot ma ain big brother, ma ain blood. And it's the fuckin' presidential elections o'er there the noo tae!

'Ma maw and da, the whole family, they'll aw have been oot their fuckin' minds the whole time wi' worry. And me? Whit the fuck have Ah been doin'? Fuck all! Walking aboot, plugged in tae the fuckin' moon as usual! As if they've not got enough oan their plates withoot ma fuckin' stupidity!'

Ninian proceeded to sit down on the steps, still holding on to the bowl with both hands. 'And Paul…' he continued. 'Fuck. He always phones. Well, when the phones are working o'er there.' Tears began to well up in Ninian's eyes.

Gary sat down beside his younger friend. 'Look, Ninian,' he said, putting his right arm over and around Ninian's shoulders. 'Paul knows the score wi' ye. He loves ye and you love him. He's with ye always, Ninian. Fuck, he told ye that before he left, didn't he? Nothing can ever change that love, Ninian. It's alive and it's eternal. Forever. No matter whit! Just as you're always wanting the best for him, he's always wanting the very best for you, at all times. And I'm sure he'll phone when he gets a chance and let yees aw know that e's awright.'

'Aye, I hope so, Gary. It's just… it's just the way that things seem tae pass me by at times, or maybe it's the way I somehow let things get oot a' hand and then they aw somehow conspire tae create what then become these major fuck-ups. And the saddest thing is, of course, is that I genuinely don't even know. Ah genuinely don't even know that I've fucked up until later, when it's too late. Then Ah think aboot it aw; think aboot aw the things that Ah should've done, if you know what Ah mean. Who knows? Maybe it wouldn't be as bad if it was just the wee things that Ah fucked up, *but it's no'*. It's the things that really matter, Gary; the most important things; relationships! Aw ma relationships wi' family, friends, loved ones. Ah mean, for fuck's sake, how much longer does it have tae go oan like this? I'm fuckin' sick a' it, Gary.'

'Hey, hawd oan a minute, young yin. Ah know whit yer sayin', Ninian. Listen. Don't let yersell be kidded here, cause I can tell ye right now, we're aw in the same boat, bro'. Every single one a' us. We aw make a right cunt a' it fae time tae time.'

Ninian wiped his tears with his right hand and sniffled. 'Thanks, Gary. I'm sorry for unloadin' oan ye. It's just so fuckin' exhausting, so fuckin' sore.'

'Here, gie yersell a break, young yin. Don't be so hard on yourself, Ninian. Mind, you've come through a lot and yer aff aw they tablets that you've been oan as well. Aw that'll be having an effect oan ye tae, Ah mean, as ye adjust, and get used tae being aff them. Just take yer time and be patient wi' yersell.

'Look, they say every day's a school day. Yer still young, Ninian, and Ah don't mean that in a patronising way cause we're aw still learning, *always*, no matter whit age we are. Just try not tae worry so much, that's aw I'm tryin tae say. Things'll be awright. C'mon. It's New Year; a time for seeing oot the old and bringing in the new; another chance; a new start for us aw, Ninian, eh? Whit dae ye say, bro'?'

'Aye, Ah suppose. Thanks, Gary, ye're a good yin.'

Taking a deep breath, Ninian blew out heavily, hoping this would push out his anxiety and bring about a renewed sense of composure. 'Anyway,' he continued, 'enough aboot me. Whit aboot yersell? You, Michelle and the wean? Everything alright?'

'Aye, they're fine, Ninian, thanks. Michelle's taking the wean up to her maw's and getting her to watch her for the night cause a' the party we're havin' in oors a bit later. Yer still coming, int ye? Your Karen said she'd come!'

'I don't know, Gary. I'm no' feeling too clever, to be honest.'

'Come oan!' Gary said, standing up with a heightened sense of optimism. 'Don't even think aboot letting let me doon! It'll be a great night, just like last night. Huh, come tae think a' it, you were in some nick last night by the way.' He smiled down at Ninian. 'When I left ye, ye were lying right oot it.'

Ninian got up slowly from the step. 'Aye, Ah know,' he replied, feeling embarrassed. 'I don't know whit happened. I ended up getting drunk awfy quick last night.'

'Nae wunner! When I came in they were telling me ye had already started bevvying well before the Bells. You already had a good drink in ye when I seen ye.'

As they turned to continue heading up the stairs, Gary put his left arm around Ninian's shoulders, before changing his accent and talking in character. 'You need to learn to pace yourself, young Skywalker.'

Ninian smiled. 'Aye, nae bother, Uncle Obi.'

Gary sniggered and raised the carry-out bag in his left hand. 'But don't you worry, son! This'll no' be long in getting ye thegither.'

'Naw. I couldnae face it the day, Gary.'

'Come oan, it'll square ye up,' Gary told him, as he watched Ninian put the key in the Yale lock.

'Quick! I nearly forgot. Get the telly oan. *Oliver's* oan! I love that film,' Gary said excitedly, quickly changing dialect to assume the tone and manner of a proper English gentleman. 'Of course, it reminds me of my own childhood, my humble beginnings, those bygone days! The good old days! Those days when my white and frozen, pale yet blue baldy arse shone through the threadbare tapestry that I once knew to be my trousers! Oh the trials, the tribulations!' he exclaimed, gazing solemnly at the floor, the thumb and index finger of his right hand stroking at imaginary jowls.

Ninian turned from the door to find Gary sniffling and dabbing at fictional tears. 'And they say I'm the cunt that's no' right in the nut!' Ninian exclaimed.

The two friends laughed at each other as Ninian opened the door to the flat.

6

Scene 1: *As you see*

Friday 1st January, 1993, Kylemore Crescent, Forgewood, Motherwell, Scotland, 4:15 p.m. (GMT + 0.00)

Watching the black-and-white film, Gary, sat at one end of the couch, while Ninian sat at the other. With the festive TV guide resting on his lap, Gary was well into the process of preparing another spliff, and was burning a piece of cannabis on the end of his lock knife.

Throughout the film, he had taken to speaking in a posh English accent and burst into song as Ninian, once again, filled their glasses with Buckfast.

'Wine, glorioooous wwwwine! I'm going to get honnnnkinnnnng! Lah lah lah lah laaaah! Lah lah lah. Lah lah. Laaaah!'

'You've done yer nut,' Ninian said, laughing, as his friend continued to hum the tune of the song.

'Ninian! Are ye in?' someone shouted through the letterbox.

Ninian got up from the couch, and made his way out of the living room and down the hall.

Opening the door, he became anxious. Eldo was standing with Phil Murray. *Eldo knows fine well Gary's got no time for this guy. What's he up tae?* he thought.

'Alright, Ninian? Is Gary wi' ye?' Eldo asked, slurring his words slightly.

'Alright, lads. Aye, he's here. Come oan in.'

'Cheers, Ninian. How was the New Year? *Was it okay?*' Phil asked, as he entered.

'Aye, well, whit Ah can mind a' it,' Ninian laughed. 'All the best, Phil.'

'Aye, Ah know the feelin'. Aw the best, Ninian,' Phil said, as they shook hands and headed down the hall.

'And what aboot this fuckin' headcase?' Phil laughed, seeing Gary as he entered the living room. 'Whit's the score wi' the long black hair and the Goth gear? Are you no' watching the wrong film? Should it no' be Dracula or something you're watchin'?'

'Ah!' Gary replied, still in character. 'My, my, my what a delight! If it isn't our friendly neighbourhood stoat-the-ball!' he exclaimed, taking a draw on the joint and gently blowing out, before getting up from the couch. 'Look at yooooo!' he continued, 'all grown-up and walking around with the merriment of an imbecile! Pray tell,' he motioned, as he casually put his right arm over and around Phil's shoulders, 'are you still interfering with yourself at regular intervals? Mmm, I must say, I do admire your... erm... how shall we say? Yes, that certain *je ne sais quoi*. And tell me, did your parents not explain to you that in vigorously pursuing such interests that you may, indeed, end up with eyes like Grasshopper's Master? Oh, *such rudeness*. Please forgive me. Where are my manners? Please join us as we partake in a small libation that we may indulge ourselves further in your nonsensical ramblings.'

Phil could only laugh at Gary's reply before responding, 'Okay, you win, smartarse. Have ye got any draw you can sell me? Some of ma punters are looking for a dod.'

'Indeed! And what wares are you peddling yourself during this fine season of good will?' Gary replied, keeping on with his act, as both sat on the couch, while Ninian poured wine for his new visitors.

Phil sniggered at Gary's amateur dramatics. 'Well, if you must know, there's some Temazepam, as usual. And I've managed to get a hold of a regular supply of Peach Palfium.'

Gary tutted and shook his head. 'Dear, dear, dear! And what is one expected to do with those? Apart from soil their undergarments of course.'

'Look,' Phil said, becoming frustrated. 'Are you selling me a bit or no'?'

'Alas, my dear Phil, I only have a bit of personal to see me through the weekend,' Gary replied, taking another draw of the joint, and nonchalantly blowing the smoke out, upwards, into the air.

It was no secret that Gary supplied his friends with cannabis. And everyone in the room knew he was lying about not having any left, but he didn't care, such was the dislike he had towards Phil.

'Right, nae bother. I'm off. I'll see yees later,' Phil replied, having had enough of Gary's games. 'I'll come down later for some of that gear, Eldo, alright? You'll be in, won't ye?'

'Aye, I'll be in aboot sixish, Phil.'

'Right, nae bother. See yees later, lads,' Phil said, heading out of the living room, followed by Ninian, who escorted him down the hall.

'See ye later, Phil,' Ninian said, as he opened the door.

'See ye, Ninian, have a good one.'

Closing the door, and walking back down the hall to the living room, Ninian heard the raised voices of his two friends.

On entering, he found Gary standing in the middle of the living room, pointing with his right hand at Eldo, who was sitting on the chair, near the window.

'And that better be the last, Eldo, I'm telling ye! Ah better no' see him in ma company again. I'm sick a' telling ye. I'll end up plungin' that cunt one a' these days.'

'Hawd oan a minute, Gary,' Eldo slabbered. 'If it wisnae for Phil, I'd be sittin' doon in that flat wi' fuck all. Ma wife wouldnae have had anythin' for her Christmas and neither would ma wean.'

'How many times dae Ah need to tell ye, Eldo? Aw ye need tae dae is tell me if you're stuck an' I'll square ye up wi' a couple a' bob!'

'Gary, ye just don't get it, dae ye? Do ye think Ah like getting money aff ye aw the time, eh? Do ye think it makes me feel good running aboot wi' fuck all and hivvin' tae keep asking you for dough, eh? And then goin' into ma wife and tellin' her that I got mair money aff ye. Aw the while feelin' like a total fuckin' arsehole.'

'Okay,' Gary replied, relatively calmly, 'and so it's better tae keep a stash a' pills in yer hoose for that fuckin' bam? Is that what yer tellin' me? Whit if yer hoose gets turned o'er, eh? Do you ever think a' that? And do you think he'll be goin' intae the jail wi' ye? Eh? Nae fuckin' danger! He just wants to play the gangster, that fuckin' real yin. But here's the thing, Eldo: You'll be the mug that's doin' the time and missin' yer wife and wean! No' that cunt!'

'Ah know what yer saying, Gary, I'm no' fuckin' daft. I'm just daein' it for another few weeks tae get a joab. It's money every week. He just comes doon takes some a' the pills and then bails oot and brings mair when he gets them. There's nae drama!'

'There's nae fuckin' talking to you, Eldo. I love ye, ye're ma brother, but there's nae fuckin' talking tae ye. Ye never listen tae any cunt. Ye'r full a' the drink every day and ye're no' seein' the bigger picture here. That guy's bad fuckin' news! Nothing but fuckin' bother! And I'll tell ye, it'll aw end in tears, mark ma fuckin' words. It's a fuckin' certainty! And I'll tell ye something else. Do not tell that cunt anything aboot ma business, or who I supply. That fuckin' bam could get us aw the jail.'

Eldo didn't respond to Gary.

Ninian picked up what was left of the last bottle of wine and poured it into their glasses.

'Cheers, Ninian,' Gary said.

'Aye, thanks Ninian,' Eldo added.

The three friends sat quietly.

'I'm sorry, Eldo,' Gary said eventually, getting up from the couch with his glass in his hand, and walking over to where Eldo was seated. 'Cheers,' he continued, holding the glass out to Eldo.

Eldo stood up and pushed his glass against his friend's. 'Cheers. Don't worry aboot it.'

'Ah fuckin' worry aboot ye!' Gary said, putting his left hand around the back of Eldo's neck and gripping it.

'Ah know. It's cool. Don't sweat it.'

Gary embraced Eldo. 'Thanks, mate,' he told him, before turning to rest his glass on the hi-fi. Taking a backwards step, he moved to stand in the centre of the living room.

Pushing his chest out, Gary, using both hands, gripped the insides of his open neck shirt. Letting them hang there, he turned to Ninian, who was sitting on the couch, *smiling*, in anticipation, of Gary's next performance.

'And what of this young whippersnapper?' Gary started, looking down at Ninian.

Eldo smiled, laughed and quickly joined in, blinking his right eye, in his act of adjusting a monocle. 'Whippersnapper indeed, wot, wot!'

'I say we beat the impudence out of him. And what of you, Giles?' Gary said, trying to look serious as he turned to Eldo.

'*Hmm*. Quite so, Basil, quite so. A bounder and a fraud!' Eldo replied.

Ninian laughed at his two friends as they tried to keep up their act, drawing menacingly close to him on the couch. 'Careful, my erudite companions!' he told them, 'please remember that I find myself in an extremely fragile situation at present *and*, quite frankly, if the truth be told I am, indeed, frightfully unstable. And what a tragedy it would indeed be, *if, perhaps, unbeknownst to myself*, I were to reach over, and take the lock knife in my hand *and,* overcome by a wave of evil, proceed to *stab out* indeed, indiscriminately in all directions!'

'*Hmm*, a fearful insight indeed,' Gary said, pulling at his cheeks with his left hand. 'I never quite thought of that, Giles.'

'*Hmm*, me too, Basil, me too. Perhaps now would be a good time to vacate the premises, *I mean get tae fuck so to speak.*'

The three friends laughed at their stupidity.

'Right!' Gary said, clapping his hands and rubbing them together, before moving to sit back down on the couch and taking his can of beer from the floor. 'So, what about the party? Yees are still comin', int yees?'

'Aye I'll be doon about half seven,' Eldo said, returning to take his seat on the chair. Linda won't make it though. Her and the wean are goin' up to stay with Linda's auld dear for the night. The auld yin's no' keepin' too good.'

'Is she no'?' Gary asked, gulping a drink from his can. 'Is she right no' well?'

'Naw she'll be awright. She's just loaded wi' the flu. But she's no' managed oot the door for the last few days. Ah think Linda's just goin' up tae watch her, and make dinner an' that.'

'That's good, Eldo,' Gary said, turning to Ninian. 'And what aboot you, Ninian? You're coming wi' Karen, int ye?'

'Aye, Ah suppose,' Ninian said smiling.

'Ah, that's ma boy. Ah telt ye I wouldnae be long in gettin' ye thegither, didn't Ah?' Gary said, pleased with himself. 'Here, Eldo, roll wan up, wid ye. It's your turn, ma son,' he said smiling, as he passed the TV guide holding the paraphernalia.

'And whit aboot drink or that? Dae ye want us to bring anything?' Eldo asked, as he took the paper from Gary.

'Naw, just bring yersells. There's plenty drink and plenty draw and I'm sure there'll be plenty other gear tae. There's some acid there annaw if yees fancy it.'

'Maybe I'll bring some pills just in case,' Eldo told them. 'There's nothing worse than comin' aff acid and then havin' fuck all tae help ye get the nut doon.'

'Aye,' Gary laughed, 'bring some then, Eldo. Ye're right, they'll dae us a turn.'

Ninian was becoming agitated. 'Do me a favour, Gary, wid ye? Don't give me any of them. Even if I'm drunk and I'm doin yer nut in for them. Don't give me any. I'm finished wi' them. Honest. I've got enough goin' on in ma napper as it is, withoot drappin' acid.'

'Here, Ninian,' Gary said, genuinely concerned, 'that's easier said than done. Tell him, Eldo. Tell him whit he's like when he's got a drink in him and pesterin' us tae give him whatever's oan the go.'

Eldo smiled and nodded. 'Aye, ye're murder, Ninian. Honest. Ye don't take naw for an answer. Ye're like a dug wi' a bone.'

'I know I can be miles oot sometimes when I'm bevvied, *but* just throw me oot yer hoose if I'm startin' ma daftness,' Ninian said, almost pleading.

'Come oan, Ninian, for fuck's sake, turn it up. It's us yer talking tae. As if that's gonnae happen,' Gary said, leaning over and ruffling Ninian's hair.

Ninian lifted his glass and emptied it in one gulp, cursing inwardly. His friends were right. He was his own worst enemy.

PART III

BOOK THREE: KENYA

7

Scene 1: Coming to terms

Friday 1 January, 1993, Our Lady of Victoria Monastery, Kipkelion, Rift Valley Province, Kenya, 7:10 p.m. (GMT+3)

Missionary priest, Father Paul McLeod, sat at the desk in his room. For the first time in many weeks, a calm smile of acceptance broke out on his gaunt, bearded face.

Taking the first, of the two letters he had just written, he angled it nearer the small lit candle, and lowered his head accordingly.

Dear Mum and Dad,

I can't imagine what it must be like for you at this time, but I pray you experience the Lord's strength to overcome any bitterness or feelings of hatred.

I too have had to tell parents here that their sons and daughters have passed on to be with the Lord, and I fully understand the trouble the Brothers will have there in telling you the same about me.

I am very sorry for the pain and suffering my death has caused you all.

I love you so much, Mum and Dad. I know you know this, as it was you who made us the close loving family that we are, but I would like to take this moment, if I may, to express my sincere thanks for the love you have showered upon me, as a son and guest in your family.

You have always put your children first and sacrificed a great deal throughout your lives, in providing me – and indeed all of us – with a privileged upbringing. Even now that we're adults, you're always there to guide and support us.

For all of this and more, I am eternally grateful. I am truly blessed to have you as my parents.

As I write, I realise it would be easy for me to start feeling sorry for myself, but the reality of my whole life is one in which I have received so much. Indeed, so much more than I could ever possibly have given. Yet this is, and has been, the true nature of my life – and what a gift!

As with all of us, this is the wonder of life; a life made and born into Eternity.

In October, I had a week-long retreat at a Benedictine monastery in Nairobi. I thoroughly enjoyed my time there, and during my stay, I wrote a short reflection about 'us' and what I now know to be our inseparable union with our loving God. I hope you like it. Here it is:

> The wind is free
> so like me
> when through His grace
> I can see
>
> This gift to be embraced by all
> in acceptance of the inherent call.
> Placed therein by His breath
> so we may too, know no death.
>
> Unending Love, Unending Light,
> Creation praises You, day and night.
> All is Yours and is alive in You
> Eternal, here and now, is true!

Can we hold to this belief
in times of trouble, in times of grief?
A wind of change, we've stepped outside
Where to run where to hide?

Your separation from Me is never complete
I AM awaiting my child, with open arms to greet!
We are together, in part the same,
through your Brother, within Our Flame

What We have, is Ours to share,
do not cry, do not despair.
A life is not lost, or thrown away.
For All is Alive, in Me, to stay.

The wind is free
so like me
when through His grace
I can see

Mum and Dad, I remember you used to tell us when we were children that everyone makes their journey to the Lord. I have come to understand this as a great truth on so many levels.

Always hold on to the fact that our God is a God of love and a God of the living. We are together always!

Please pass on my love to Andrew, Margaret and Ninian, and please thank them on my behalf for their love and kindness throughout my time with them. I am truly blessed to have you all in my life – my family. Thank you!

Always remember, He who is in you is greater than he who is in the world.

May He continue to bless and guide you in everything!

Love always. Your loving son and brother in Christ,

Paul x

Paul folded the letter and slipped it into the readied envelope. Using some of the Sellotape that he had cut, and part-stuck to the edge of the desk, he sealed his message and placed it face-up in front of him.

With the tip of his right thumb, he made the sign of the cross over the words 'Mum and Dad' and whispered a blessing. He prayed a last farewell to his family, and, taking the envelope in his hands, pressed it against his lips, before returning it to the desk.

The other letter he had written now demanded his attention.

Dom Leonard Melrose, based at Sancta Maria Abbey in Scotland, was someone Paul greatly admired and loved.

When Paul had entered the monastery, shortly after he'd left school, the then Father Leonard had guided him in the ways of monastic life, becoming his formator and, in due course, his spiritual director.

With the passage of time, however, Paul's old teacher had moved up the hierarchy. Dom Leonard Melrose was now head of their Order.

Paul forced his shoulders against the backrest of the wooden chair, causing a creak that ruptured the silence, then gently rolled them forward to relax again in their natural position. Taking a deep breath in through his nose, he filled his lungs and blew out slowly through dry lips, quickly coming to focus on the questions that would be asked once they were gone.

Pensiveness now replaced his earlier contentment.

Everyone in the Order had played their part consistently. They'd done everything to encourage dialogue between the tribes. *Yes*, he nodded, oblivious to the gesture. *That was the fact of the matter.*

But it had made no difference.

Acknowledging the fear arising within, Paul now picked up the letter he had written to his superior.

8

Scene 1: The story so far...

Fr Paul McLeod
Order of the Divine Servant
Our Lady of Victoria Monastery
Kipkelion, Kenya
1 January, 1993

Dear Dom Leonard,

Greetings in Christ,

I pray this finds you in good health, my dear Brother.

I'm sorry it's been a long time since we last communicated, my dear friend. And I'm sorry also for the sad news that I now share.

Our Abbot, Dom Stephen, is very ill. He's been bedridden for two weeks, and this morning, at first light, Brother David drove him to the Nairobi Hospital.

As you know, he's been attending this hospital as an outpatient for the past eight months or so. Indeed, he is due to see the oncologist there next Tuesday. However, with his condition worsening daily, we realised that if he waited here at the monastery until then, he'd be too weak to travel.

If the truth be told, my dear Brother, it would've been better if he'd gone to the hospital five days ago when we first asked him, but he would hear nothing of it. I believe he felt that he was abandoning us by going, and this from a man who has given us everything!

I can't tell you how relieved we all were last night when he finally said that he'd make the journey today.

At first light, we carried him out to the vehicle, and then lay him on the pillows and blankets that we'd laid out on the back seats.

In Brother David we have our best driver. He's particularly good at negotiating a way down over the rocks that lie between the monastery and the road. No doubt he'll do everything in his power to ensure our dear Brother gets there as safely and as comfortably as possible.

I should mention also that we agreed with Dom Stephen, once he's admitted, that Brother David would stay at his bedside and help with his care. Brother David will also phone you from the hospital to give you an update, my dear friend, as soon as our sick Brother has settled in. I would've called you myself to inform you of all of this, but the telephone wires in the surrounding area have been down for months now, as a result of the violence.

Here at the monastery, we endeavoured to give our Brother the best care possible, and there has always been at least one of us with him round the clock. We've given him his painkillers as prescribed, but the look of anguish on his face of late suggests they're barely having an impact. We pray that the hospital staff manage to get his pain under control as soon as possible, and that his appetite may also come back to something like it once was.

Before he left for hospital, he asked that I write to you, Dom Leonard. He wanted me to explain his *situation* and *everything* that's been going on here.

I pray I've not left anything out regarding our dear Brother, and I apologise in advance if some of what follows is already known to you.

Around one month ago, we opened the doors of the church once again to a large number of people who had been chased from their homes. Over a period of a few days, they came from all areas of Kipkelion. At its height, the number totalled 248 (men, women and children). However, as the weeks have passed by many have left.

This could be seen as being good in itself, but, unfortunately, it doesn't tell the whole story.

For while it's true that we've managed to assist a number of families to flee to their homelands during lulls in the violence, it's the indigenous tribe that has allowed their safe passage, on the condition that they never again return to this area.

As I write, it is the old, who have nowhere to go, and the sick, who are too ill to travel, who remain with us. We continue to provide them with food, shelter and basic medicines, but it remains to be seen what the final outcome will be.

Despite this uncertainty, however, in caring for this group over this past month, we've come to know even more about their predicament, my dear friend. Indeed, from our discussions, it has dawned on the Brothers and I that these specific outbreaks of violence, which have caused them to seek shelter here, began in 1991.

This is of some significance, Dom Leonard, for 1991 is also said to be the year that President Moi, under increased pressure from the American Government, finally reintroduced multi-party politics to Kenya.

From what we can gather, it would certainly appear that from around this period onwards people being chased from their homes became something of a regular occurrence.

Yet as terrible as this is, today we seem to have reached a point where we are now seeing a marked change in the way these heinous acts are being carried out.

Indeed, those we have spoken with have told us that when they were forced out in times gone by, they were usually allowed to return to their 'empty houses' after a fortnight or so, when tensions had died down.

These days though it's very, very different. Now, when they're being chased away, their homes are wiped off the land, destroyed and removed, not with tools, but by the indigenous peoples' bare hands!

When you consider how long it would take to do this, and the energy required, I feel it illustrates the heightened intensity of the hatred. It seems that the 'outsiders', as they are now commonly referred to, are to be systematically cleared out, once and for all.

It's so sad, my dear brother. When I look at the indigenous population and see how they've changed in these months leading up to the election, it's hard to believe that they are the same people who were once, humble, dignified members of our church.

Indeed, it doesn't seem so long ago that the Brothers and I were playing football with the local men every Sunday afternoon.

Regardless of who was from what tribe, we had some great laughs together, trying to show off our skills on an unforgiving cow field. As you might imagine, the women and children had great fun too, watching us from the sidelines. How those days now seem like a lifetime away, my dear friend.

I've really never seen anything like what I have witnessed of late. There is almost an image of frenzied joy on some of the men's faces, or something like crazed glee. To see men turn on their neighbours, people from certain tribes, picking them out for expulsion, or worse, is difficult to comprehend.

In all our work, Dom Leonard, as always, we pray, contemplate and question ourselves before and after any kind of intervention with the community, but I cannot deny how harrowing it is to see what men are truly capable of.

Over the past week or so, we've recovered the bodies of fourteen young men. Some were brutally castrated and left to bleed to death, others had limbs hacked off and were burned alive, while others still were mercilessly beaten and stoned to within an inch of their lives.

The fortunate are killed outright. Those who are alive but unconscious are mutilated further. Indeed, of those who are knocked unconscious, as they lie on the ground some have their eyelids cut off and their eyeballs carefully plucked out. I say *carefully*, as it's the intention to remove the eyes in such a way whereby their attachment with the optic nerves remains intact. This then allows the nerves to hold the eyeballs 'in place' so to speak (i.e., 'fully exposed', resting on their unconscious victim's cheeks).

Disturbingly, this practice seems to be becoming ever more commonplace, Dom Leonard.

Indeed, just the other day, having rushed out to find and collect the dead, on hearing news that people had been killed in a small rural settlement not far from the monastery, we came across another such instance.

As we arrived at the scene, during what we have come to know to be this eerie stillness of the 'aftermath', our presence disturbed some of the more familiar scavenging birds of prey (kites), forcing them to take flight.

The men's bodies – four of them – were lying on the ground

outside each of their partially destroyed mud houses, the flames on the thatched roofs beginning to taper off.

Yet, in spite of all of this, and taking us completely by surprise, one of the men, the furthest from us as we drew near, regained some consciousness and somehow got to his feet. His bare back was gleaming, the sunlight reflecting off the blood pouring from his machete wounds.

Trying to stumble towards his house, he was calling out names, probably those of his wife and children.

We, too, were shouting out to him as we ran towards him. It was just an instant reaction. I think we were afraid he would fall. And, on hearing our cries, he shuffled round to face us

It was only then, however, that we were able to see the full extent of his injuries. The man's eyeballs were hanging from their sockets, barely attached to the ends of overstretched nerves. He mumbled sounds in confusion, perhaps struggling to process whatever it was he was still able to visualise

It was such a pathetic image that, for a moment, I glanced to the ground, hoping to find a large boulder. I wanted to kill him there and then, to end the suffering, but, later that evening, I wondered about this. Whose suffering was I really trying to end? Was it his, or was it my own suffering; in having to look on him; and tend to him in his agony? Still, I do not know. God forgive me.

Brother Thomas and I managed to get hold of him. We sat him on the ground and held him close, rocking him gently – waiting. I can still hear his mangled screams for his wife and children. We gave him the final sacrament and watched the life go out of him.

In the hours that followed, we buried the bodies in the grounds of the monastery. We managed to contact the relatives of one and have kept the details of the other dead for those relatives we couldn't trace – it's believed they'd already left Kipkelion.

On the other side of the coin, of course, are those who carry out these and similar atrocities. Some of the young men have, no doubt, been led against their will, and made to do terrible things. And others have done so against their better judgement.

We've heard it said that when these youths return from attacking the *outsiders'* homes, a cleansing ceremony takes place, where a goat is sacrificed in a ritual.

Whether this is an attempt at absolution or to prevent curses from falling on their people, only the tribe's elders will know. However, despite these interventions, there are reports that a few of the young men have taken their own lives, as a result of being unable to live with what they've done, and others are supposedly wandering in torment, alone, through the forest: 'Wandering in their own living hell, with their curse upon them,' as the local women say.

There are no winners here, Dom Leonard.

And yet, with the presidential election taking place last Tuesday, 29 December – and the results due out anytime soon – it seems that we might, at least, be approaching some sort of finale, my dear Brother – indeed, in more ways than one.

I say this, Dom Leonard, for we too have now received death threats.

A few days ago, sketched *drawings* were stuck to the church doors and others were scattered around the monastery. They showed 'us' – the Brothers – decapitated, our heads raised aloft on spears. This afternoon, however, the threat was made more direct.

In being summoned to a meeting of the local tribesmen, I was told plainly, by one of the tribe's elders, that, 'The work will be finished by midnight'.

Whether we, the Brothers, gave the *outsiders* up, or whether we died with them, was said to be 'irrelevant'. 'The monastery will no longer provide sanctuary, it will burn, if necessary, with everyone inside.'

I was then dismissed from the meeting. They are done with talking, Dom Leonard.

As a result of these developments, when I came back to the monastery, I told our young novices to gather their things and change into their civilian clothes. I've given them travel expenses to their homes and food for their journeys. As I write, with darkness drawing near, they are almost ready to depart. I informed them also to enjoy the New Year with their families, and that we'd be in touch with them soon, making no mention of the threats we'd received earlier in the day.

Dominic, our eldest novice, is from this area, and he will post this letter. You will notice that I've also included a note to my parents, Dom Leonard. I would be very grateful if you would pass it to them, should you learn news of my death.

I also pray that this letter reaches you safely, my dear Brother, as hopefully, it can help to explain some of what is going on here and perhaps provide a 'possible context'. Indeed, in an attempt at trying to gain an understanding of these events ourselves (to inform our response), the Brothers and I, at the instruction of Dom Stephen, have been delving into all that we could find on Kenya's history.

With the violence escalating, we stepped up our efforts in urging tolerance and peace during our meetings with the indigenous tribesmen. However, at a time when tribal identity is everything, many still cling to the old stereotyped views of other ethnic groups.

It really is heartbreaking to see the *Mwananchi* – ordinary people – being encouraged by their leaders to hold these hostile attitudes, Dom Leonard.

Horrifically, these poisonous views have become so ingrained that they are now held up as some great truth, or something that's to be understood as being what common sense tells them about a group of *different* people.

And what is it that they're being told? Well, perhaps ironically, it's really the regurgitated lies that the British introduced and spread as a means to divide and rule the tribes during the colonisation of their lands.

In saying this, of course, one cannot deny that historically the tribes wouldn't have had, let's say, old *rivalries* or *suspicions*, or even clashes with neighbouring peoples on their borders, before the colonialists arrived. But once the British found out what these suspicions were, there is no doubt that they added – and continued to add – their own divisive anecdotes to them. Indeed, in using this ploy, maintaining and managing a certain level of ethnic tension soon became the norm, which of course assisted in the exploitation of the people and their lands.

It really is quite shocking and yet, remarkably, the fact that these stereotyped views have been spread for so long, and so convincingly across the whole country, it seems to have reached the stage where they've now even been internalised by the very same peoples that they are said to be about!

For example, one of the tribes was told they were lazy and good for nothing; another was said to be hard-working and good in business (and, as a result, money mad); another was told that they were good at working the land; while another still was said to be good with cattle.

Yet, in coming to accept these views as *truths* about themselves, it's clear that some of the tribes' people feel that they now have to live up to these and other such gross generalisations, so much so that you often hear people say, 'It's who we are!'

Sadly, it appears there is some truth in the saying that if we are told something often enough, we'll come to believe it must be true.

Yet, with all of this no doubt contributing to the current unrest, what is seen as being the main reason for chasing the *outsiders* off Kalenjin territory is an issue that has become known as 'the land question'. And this issue too has its origins in colonialism.

When the British came here in the early part of the nineteenth century, there was no land or nation called Kenya. There was, however, a large number of proud peoples (tribes) with their own identities, traditions, languages, culture, heritage – and lands.

Yet, the British were to change all of this.

Invading these lands, they confined these communities to geographical boundaries which became known as the British Protectorate, and after 1920 became known as the Kenya colony.

It is a woeful tale. The colonisers really did carve the place up with impunity. Not content with physically moving and regrouping diverse peoples within localised artificial boundaries, they also created national boundaries where none existed. The fact that some Kenyan academics insist that Kenya itself isn't even a nation, but a collection of tribes forced to live in reset demarked territories, surely highlights the damage done by the then British Establishment's indifference.

Moreover, the story continues that on reaching the best areas for their purposes, the British then cleared them of indigenous populations, and with the forced labour of the previously conquered tribes in their possession, they shaped the land in a way that would maximise profits. All of this was, of course, maintained by continuing to keep the people in check: by brutalisation, disinformation, setting them against one another, and detaining them in concentration camps – where the use of rape, castration and murder was the order of the day.

Yet, I imagine that after gaining independence from Britain in 1963 and electing their first President in Jomo Kenyatta, one would've hoped that the exploitation of the Kenyan people might have ended. But, as is the case, sadly during these years of transition – that is, from British to Kenyan rule – deals were struck between the then supposedly *outgoing* British elite, and the newly forming Kenyan elite, ensuring once more that in many ways it would be 'business as usual' – all at the expense of the 'ordinary' Kenyan citizens.

President Kenyatta filled his Government with fellow Kikuyu tribesmen and allies, and soon Moi himself – the then leader of the opposition and a member of the Kalenjin tribe from here in the Rift Valley – would also get involved, becoming Minister for Home Affairs in 1964, and effectively making Kenya a single-party state.

And so, in taking advantage of these new roles, this select group not only held all the power, but also controlled the majority of the country's resources.

As the years moved on, Moi became the Vice President in 1967 and continued in this role until Kenyatta's death from ill health, in 1978, from where he went on to become President, despite the best efforts of his political enemies to prevent this from happening. Indeed, four years later, Moi's presidency overcame an attempted coup.

Yet, in defeating the coup, Moi was then able to reshuffle his cabinet and thereby give senior posts to those loyal to him. From this position of strength, it's believed that he and his associates soon gained even more power and control, and with it *possession* of almost all of the country's assets.

I'm sorry if, as the saying goes, I have brought you a long road for a shortcut, my dear friend, but, tragically, these events continue to impact on Kenya's current situation, particularly here in the Rift Valley, where 'the land question' is used to stir tension among the poor.

In going back to the time when the handover between Britain and

Kenya was taking place – that is, around the time when some of the colonialists were leaving, and Kenya became 'independent' – those peoples who had been previously 'conquered' and taken by force from their homelands during colonial rule, and made to work for their 'colonial masters' in 'different' tribal regions, soon found out that they had now been effectively *abandoned* in these areas.

In this predicament, these people had to try and make new lives where they found themselves. This was partly due to the fact that they were too poor to go back to their historical homelands, and partly because, over the years, they had raised families in those places under colonial rule.

With this being the case for many Kenyans, the State, however – having received funding support from the British Government – responded to the situation by introducing a loan scheme.

Through this loan scheme, Kenyan citizens could take out small loans on good terms, and buy small plots of land from the Kenyan Government, and also from the outgoing colonialists.

For the first time, this allowed Kenyans of different tribes to stay legitimately (with title deeds) where they were, and provide for their families on their own small plots of land; for example, by growing crops for sustenance, or keeping cattle.

It seems that this was not foreseen as a problem at the time, as, with independence, *all* land within its borders was now seen to be Kenyan.

However, with the newly formed alliances of the new Kenyan elite running the show, they too, of course, were to access this money, in huge amounts. And so, through forming small groups among themselves, and by making deals with the British elite, these individuals then went on to gain massive areas of some of the most desirable and profitable lands in the country (particularly here, in the Rift Valley).

Sadly, however, this information is not common knowledge.

Indeed, today, a different story is in place; a story which has been continually spouted by those in power as we approached the elections; a story that has not only continued to divide ordinary Kenyans, but one that has blamed 'the neighbour' and 'the self-same poor' as being the cause of every hardship experienced by the indigenous peoples. In other words, the story tells the indigenous people that it's the *others*, who have stolen settled and now prosper in the land — the land that didn't, doesn't, and never will belong to them.

And so, in this way, the ordinary people are continually being manipulated, all the while unaware that a small number of their very own indigenous elite has taken vast areas of their land, and has been using it to profit themselves.

So, as you can see, it's a real travesty. Kenya's political leaders and their elitist friends are continuing in the same way as their British counterparts.

In doing so, of course, this also means that several generations of ordinary people have been bombarded with the same old divisive generalisations, based on hearsay, that have now become accepted within society as truth, thus perpetuating a cycle where the poor continue to fight each other over the crumbs that fall from the table of the elite.

If only the ordinary people could see that they are being conned, my dear Brother; conned into believing that their troubles are tribal in nature, when in fact, they are politicised.

Yet, unfortunately, they can't. And so the sorry tale goes on, with the political leaders inciting tribal tensions and using them as a smokescreen, keeping the poor suspicious of each other and encouraging them to fight in the false belief that they will regain their land — their birthright!

And what happens to the poor who are chased away? Well, if they are able, some return to their homelands and go on to tell their fellow tribesmen of what they've had to endure. And so revenge attacks soon follow on the poor of the *unfavourable* tribes there, making victims of one place become the perpetrators in another.

One can only wonder at how long this will go on in Kenya, Dom Leonard.

Yet, could we really have expected any less, when we see the seeds that have been sown by the British elite in these lands: seeds that have been forever soaked in their unfathomable arrogance, their ridiculous notion of 'entitlement', the offspring of their psychopathic 'because we can' attitude, a perversion of nature that's to be endlessly watered by the tears of those they ride roughshod over and so continuously feeding their unquenchable desires with the blood of their injustices while, of course, trying to convince the rest of us to accept perhaps their biggest delusion – that the ends justify the means; showing us all the while that they undoubtedly have no notion, feeling or care for the truth; the truth that it is God's Providence alone that has brought mercy to their victims; God's Providence that has brought deliverance from their murderous ways.

And what of the many ordinary British people that they have conned into doing their dirty work for them? Dragging them across the world to be their unwitting pawns, tricking them into believing that they are somehow involved in a 'great' and 'noble' cause – delivering 'civilisation'!

I am sorry for getting carried away, my dear Brother. It's just very painful when thinking about the tragedies that are happening here.

And yet, at times, I do wonder if I am losing my mind because of the inappropriately laughable and bizarre nature of some of what has gone on.

For instance, I heard only recently from a young student of history, who spent some time here on retreat, that when the border area between Kenya and Tanzania was being drawn up, our own Queen Victoria thought it would be a nice gesture at the time to give a German relative Mount Kilimanjaro! Apparently as a birthday present no less! The boundary on the map was then supposedly drawn up in such a way whereby the great mountain became part of the then German colony now known as Tanzania.

Whether what happened with Kilimanjaro is proved to be true or not – and could we honestly believe that this was not the case, given what has already happened in this continent? – what I would say, is let people make up their own minds. One only needs to look at the map to see the boundary that was drawn to separate these two countries – i.e. straight lines – drawn without any thought or consideration for the indigenous peoples.

Forgive me for digressing. Yet, when I reflect on these peoples' history and what is currently going on here, I can't help but wonder at how many other peoples have suffered similar fates, whereby they are pitted against their neighbours without even understanding the main reason why, or how it was done.

I suspect, in our supposedly *developed* world, the methods used by our governments and their elitist friends may now even be more subtle, almost subliminal perhaps – the media being a most useful tool. However, of course, this wilful act of continually spreading lies about people and dressing them up as the truth – a truth to be accepted and acted upon by the rest of the population – is diabolically evil.

And to think, Dom Leonard, that it was as far back as the sixteenth century that Machiavelli exposed the tricks of the trade on 'divide and rule', no doubt showing something to the rest of us of what was already known for centuries by those who held power, and also highlighting the fact that educating their offspring on these and similar strategies, generation after generation, was the thing to do.

Be that as it may, however, when I see the effects of divide and rule here in Kenya, I can do little but try to understand the why of it all, or rather try and make sense of its senselessness. Indeed, doesn't it become increasingly worrying when you think how often this ploy has been used by *leaders* throughout history, and how even today, it still manages to work every time on *ordinary* people?

In saying that, of course, I suppose the variants of this practice are continually reinvented and spun out by those who want to keep things just the way they like them – the status quo.

Perhaps, for now at least, moves towards true equality and justice are destined to come up against the countermeasures of those striving to keep their earthly power.

When we are divided like this, people can always be found to be the cause of the majority's ills, with the finger of blame almost certainly being pointed at our neighbours. I suspect it's then that we start to hear vociferous cries like 'this land is ours, and ours alone!' and before we know it we've become like greedy schoolchildren, wrapping our arms around our dinner plates, in case we need to share.

Tragically, seeing some of the attitudes we can see today, one would think that we've come so far that, in the womb, we are now capable of choosing where we will be born and what kind of life we will be born into! And it's the poor who make these cries, my dear

Brother, misled by those in power that it's the *other* poor who are sapping their already meagre resources.

It's so disheartening when I hear how we now believe that lands are ours, and ours alone, to be protected from our brothers and sisters who have nothing; brothers and sisters who are starving and dying daily from treatable diseases.

Have we become so self-sufficient that we've forgotten we are all but guests here? Have we forgotten too our own history in the West; a history of exploiting these poorer countries of their resources? And is it not still continuing today under the name of 'diplomacy'?

You would think, by now, we would at least be more aware. Yet somehow we continue to walk wide-eyed into believing the untruths we are told about our brothers and sisters. And before we know it, we've all become involved in the blame game.

Sadly, I suppose, if the elite can continue to propagate these divisive views and have them gulped down by the ordinary people, generation after generation, their positions will always be secure. Faces may change, and puppet dictators and governments may come and go, but it seems the dominant desires to take and hold on to power will remain, as will the strategies for keeping it.

I wonder is this not our *democracy* too, Dom Leonard? Ordinary citizens subtly conned by our leaders into indulging in some form of horizontal violence, whereby we see our neighbour or some section or group in society, as the very cause of our every problem?

Indeed, have we become so gullible, as to believe that we had a say in developing this type of 'democracy' that we now have?

If only we would reflect and think critically about our experience and stop believing the divisive lies that our elite-sponsored leaders and their media tell us. Perhaps then we would see that our energies were focused in the wrong direction.

By looking up, we would see who really had the cake, and how they were eating it! Maybe then we would be less likely to fight our neighbours over the crumbs that were tipped down to us from above. Maybe then we could think about bringing about peaceful change through dialogue, and truly it must be peaceful, for are we not brothers and sisters in Christ, made in His image and likeness? Is it not true that when we strive to hurt our brother or sister, we've moved out from our Christ likeness and are also hurting, damaging, and indeed dehumanising our very selves?

Indeed, are the elite not our brothers and sisters too? Are they not also in need of our prayers, love and support, sinners like us and tempted like us in everything, giving in to their disordered desires, as we all do, from time to time?

Forgive me, my dear Brother. I am sorry for getting carried away. All I can say is that what I have expressed here are only some of my observations on the social, political and, to some extent, the economic experience of Kenya – and my view of how I see it playing out today.

I have tried to be as objective as possible, but obviously frustrations are running high, and my time may also be running out, so please forgive any rash comments. It has not been my intention to judge anyone. I have, on the other hand, attempted to offer my evaluation of the situation.

There is, however, one final thing I feel compelled to share with you. I suppose you could say it's something of an *apologia*.

Yet, despite the fact that I've never written anything like this before now – and, indeed, have never really accepted these beliefs until recently – it's my humble prayer that I do not offend you with what follows, Dom Leonard.

I've been forever blessed by your wisdom and spiritual guidance in shaping me into a servant of God, and to cause you any embarrassment is truly the last thing I would wish to do.

Of late though, my mind has struggled to take in the evils that I have witnessed. And of course, they cannot be denied, for to do so would be to prevent any response in the Lord.

I should mention, before I go on to explain what I have come to believe, that despite what we've encountered here in Kipkelion, the Brothers and I have still observed our duties – Breviary, Daily Mass and Eucharist, Lectio Divina, Exposition of the Blessed Sacrament, the Sacrament of Reconciliation as necessary, and pastoral care for the community, which has included, of course, spending time with bereaved families after the death and burial of their loved ones. We continue to work the land and manage the cattle, but time spent on this has lessened.

CONSCIOUSNESS AND PERCEPTION

I will now try and relay my thoughts to you as I have come to understand them, and I apologise in advance for any confusion caused on my part. Again, if what I write isn't agreeable to you, please forgive me.

I sincerely hope that what follows doesn't shock you, my dear Brother, as some of the content, may, in fact, be controversial.

Paul placed the letter on the desk, and leaned back in the chair. He could no longer read over what he had written; not for now. He felt physically drained. Letting his head loll on his neck, he strained to gather his thoughts in the candlelit silence.

The malaria he knew would only worsen; eventually clouding his mind and deadening his sense of perception.

His eyelids were heavy, almost closing. But his need for rest was being disturbed by what was taking place outside in the cloister; a noise which dragged him from the haze. As the sound of bare feet pounding the concrete slabs grew louder, Paul sat upright in the chair. He took a deep breath in through his nose, filling his lungs, trying to focus, blowing out forcefully from his mouth.

'Father Paul! Father Paul!'

Pushing himself from the desk, Paul rose from the chair and headed towards the door.

The bells in the two church towers rang out incessantly. The alarm was being raised. The monastery was under attack.

9

Scene 1: *As long as it takes*

Opening the door, Paul, found Dominic out of breath and dressed in his civilian clothes. The young novice was carrying a small bundle of personal items in a cloth under his right arm. Looking beyond him, out, into the moonlit quadrangle, Paul could easily make out his Brothers in their distinctive white cassocks and black scapulars, running in all directions.

To his left, some were escorting the sick and the frail out from the church and into the cloister, walking gently with them and lying them down on the grass court, before returning to collect others.

Dominic shouted over the sound of the bells and the chaos around him. 'Father! The warriors have come! They are blocking the doors and windows of the church with the trees and branches that they have cut down! Father Paul, they will burn us alive!'

'Dominic, I need you to listen. Listen to me very carefully. Are the other novices ready to leave?'

'Yes, Father Paul, we are ready.'

'Good. I want you to gather all of them from the Novitiate and bring them out to the far side of the cloister away from the church,'

Dominic turned to leave, but Paul caught his right arm.

'Dominic, not yet. Listen, I haven't finished. Quickly,' he said, leading Dominic into his room and closing the door behind him.

He held Dominic's arms as he spoke directly to him. 'Listen carefully, Dominic. It's very important. When you gather all of the novices and bring them to the far end of the cloister. I want you to lead them into the visitors' wing. Here are the keys you will need,' he said, moving to his desk and taking a bunch of keys from the drawer.

Paul removed two keys from the bunch before continuing. 'This one is for the door that leads you into the visitors' wing. When you open the door, I want you, and all of the novices, to make your way into the reception area. Oh, and remember to lock the door behind you and take the key with you. Okay?'

Dominic grunted in response.

'Good! All of you will then need to pass through the corridor into the reception area, to the main door. Here is the key for the main door! Open it and lead everyone out. And again, lock the door behind you and take the key with you.

'When you're outside, move as quietly as you possibly can and make your way along the side of the building until you reach the clearing. When you reach the clearing I want all of you to run as fast as you can up the hill and into the forest. Do you understand, Dominic? It's very important.'

Dominic nodded; a look of terror on his face.

'Very good! When you reach the trees, I want you to lead your younger Brothers, Dominic! You know this area well! Lead them inside the edge of the forest and don't stop until you have reached a place of safety. Do you hear me? Do you understand me?' Paul said; unaware that he was shaking the young novice's arms as he spoke. 'You will need to have everyone prepared, Dominic. Have them ready to run as soon as you see the clearing and don't turn back, no matter what you hear, no matter what you see. Run! Run as fast as you can! You understand?'

'Yes, Father Paul, I understand.'

'Good!'

With his right thumb, Paul then made the sign of the cross on the young novice's forehead and whispered in prayer.

When he was finished, he kissed him on both cheeks. 'Now go, my young Brother.'

Dominic and Paul made to leave the room, before Paul turned back. 'Dominic! I almost forgot.'

Returning to the desk, Paul lifted the pages of his letter to Dom Leonard, his Brother General, in both hands, and placed them carefully on top of his *apologia*. He then picked up the small envelope containing the letter to his parents, and together, slid all of his correspondence into a large addressed envelope.

Sealing the envelope using Sellotape, he grabbed the money that he had set aside for postage and turned to Dominic. 'When you have led the others to safety and you yourself have reached home, I need you to post this letter to our Brother General, Dominic. Will you do that for me, please?'

'Yes, Father Paul, I will.'

Taking the coins from Paul, Dominic wrapped them in a handkerchief before stuffing the small bundle into his trouser pocket. Taking the envelope, he slipped it under his right arm, beneath his small roll of personal belongings.

'Thank you, Dominic. What I'm about to tell you is very important too. Please, do not come back to the monastery until you hear news from the Brothers, okay? Someone will contact you at your homes. Do *not* come back to this place until you hear from us that it is safe to do so. You understand?'

'Yes, Father Paul.'

'Good and remember… Tell the other novices the same thing. Do not come back to this place until we contact you at your homes. Will you tell them?'

'I will tell them, Father.'

'Okay.' Paul opened the door to the smoke that was now billowing down into the cloister. 'Stay safe, Dominic and move fast,' he said, giving leave to the young novice.

'Yes, Father,' Dominic replied, sprinting from Paul across the grass court to the far end of the Novitiate.

From where he stood in the doorway, Paul examined the scene. He realised that the sound of the church bells had stopped and was no longer drowning out the sound of the warriors' song and the war beat of their drums.

He ran to his Brothers, who were trying to comfort their terrified guests on the grass. 'Well done, Brothers,' he said to them. 'Is that everyone out of the church?'

'Yes, Father. We are all here,' Thomas replied.

Paul moved among the sick and the elderly. Some of them were sitting and others lay on the grass. 'Don't worry. We'll be okay. It will all pass soon.'

None of them replied.

Returning to Brother Thomas, Paul extended his right arm to show him the way. 'Thomas, can I see you for a moment, please?'

'Yes, Father.'

The two of them walked under the cover of the cloister, out of earshot of the group.

'I need to go into the church and see the situation. I need to see how the doors are holding up.'

'Yes, Paul, we can go now.'

Paul smiled at his friend and Brother. The two of them had been brought to the monastery in the same week, which now seemed like many, many years ago. Thomas had been brought from Uganda and Paul from Scotland.

Making their way from the cloister, they climbed the night stair which brought them out into the sacristy. They could hear the loud banging as they passed into church.

The Brothers genuflected and blessed themselves before hurrying through the thick smoke and a strong smell of paraffin. Reaching the altar, they stood and looked into the nave of the church.

With the acoustics of the building, the blazing trees and branches that had been forced through the windows on both sides roared and crackled with a ferocious intensity. Their flames raged upwards, licking over the helpless timbers of the roof. And with every soul-jolting batter of the ram, the burning main doors rattled violently on their hinges, sending flakes of glowing, charred wood into the aisle.

'They'll be in soon, Paul.'

'Yes, they will, Thomas.'

'What are you thinking, Brother?'

'I think we should leave the monastery to them, Thomas. I think we should carry our guests with us and leave. Young Dominic and the other novices should be well on their way by now. If we can reach the forest maybe we'll still have a chance. What do you think, Brother?'

'I agree. From what you have said of your meeting today and how far they've gone in carrying out their threat, it seems we have no other alternative, Paul. If they find us here, they will finish us.'

'I think so too, Thomas.'

They turned from the horror that was unfolding before their eyes and started to make their way back to the sacristy.

'Thomas, when we go back down to the Brothers, call them together away from our guests and explain everything. Tell them not to waste time taking anything from their rooms, just to leave everything. We need to move quickly. I'll speak with our guests and tell them the same thing.'

A loud crash made them turn around. One of the panels in the church's main doors had been breached.

'Go, Thomas, prepare the Brothers. I'll lock the doors of the sacristy and the night stair on my way out. Hopefully it will delay them and give us more time.'

10

Scene 1: The Initiates

As Thomas and the Brothers escorted and carried the guests to the far end of the cloister, to stand and wait outside the door leading to the visitors' wing, Paul raked through his room, looking for the spare keys.

The hot wax of the candle dripped on to his right hand as he tried to manoeuvre the light to see inside the drawer. In his frustration, he pulled the drawer out with his left hand, letting it fall and crash on the concrete floor, scattering its contents.

Kneeling down and pawing over the items, he finally found what he was looking for. He stood up and placed the candle on the desk. Holding the bunch of keys to its light, he removed the two he needed, before throwing the others to the floor on his way out.

Running across the grass, he made his way quickly through the waiting group and was soon unlocking and pushing open the door to the visitors wing and rushing further ahead along the narrow corridor.

Darting through the reception area, Paul finally reached the main door. It was solid mahogany: thick, sturdy, impenetrable. Unlocking it, he gripped the iron handle with both hands, fists one on top of the other, and pulled.

The heavy door opened slowly, and looking out, Paul found that the main entrance and surrounding gardens were clear. Closing the door gently, he slid the long iron bolt that was directly below the handle into its fixing, and hurried back to the group.

When he was sure that every guest and Brother had gathered inside the visitors' wing, and was making their way through the narrow passage way to the main door, Paul locked the door behind him and dragged three heavy hardwood chairs, and a bookshelf, into the narrow passageway. When he eventually reached the reception area, he found that it was empty. The main door lay open and the quiet, blue shade of night welcomed him, its light casting an elongated path along the floor before him.

Hurrying across the hall, and out through the open doorway, Paul steadied himself against the wall, before making his way gingerly to the end of the building. He could see the rest of his group in the moonlit clearing. It had reached almost halfway up the slope and they were about 150 yards from the edge of the forest. Paul burst into a sprint. The clearing was a mixture of straw and rough grass and crunched under his bare feet. But there was nothing he could do. He had to run.

When he was about forty yards from the group, he heard one of them scream out in agony. Paul came to a halt almost immediately. And, in that moment, he heard the flight of the arrows passing like a shallow breath high overhead. He closed his eyes on hearing their devastating effects as they fell on the group.

Opening his eyes again to look on the scene, he saw to his left, the young warriors coming into view. They'd been brought from the forest, fresh from their month-long initiation ceremonies. They had passed through the fire of circumcision and were now forged in the old ways of the tribe. From head to toe, they'd been smeared with the pale, yellowish ochre taken from the land. Animal skins only partly covered their naked bodies; they were painted, dressed and ready for war.

The older tribesmen had fired their arrows first and it was now for their younger counterparts to show that they, too, had come of age.

Paul looked on as, with a natural litheness, the young men covered the ground in seconds, confidently lashing out with their *rungus* (war clubs) and machetes.

Old game was being hunted anew, their tired hearts yielding to the inevitable spring. Screams of terror met with screams of delight.

Paul ran towards the carnage.

In the short time it took to reach them, most of the group had been beaten to the ground. Those who weren't already dead had their executioners standing over them.

The stench of sweat, blood, vomit and excrement filled the air around him.

To his left, he saw the hapless figure of Thomas between two warriors, stumbling around. His Brother had an arrow sticking out of the right side of his neck, its poison already doing its work.

The warriors laughed at Thomas as he fell to his knees. Taking hold of him, one held his head in both hands, above the ears, as the other took aim at the back of his neck with the machete.

Paul stumbled across towards them. 'No. Please! Don't do this, my young brothers! You don't know what you are doing.' However, before he could reach them, he too came under attack.

Instinctively, Paul raised his arms to block the blows, but the machetes hacked mercilessly through the sleeves of his white cassock, cleaving flesh and bone. Within seconds of the onslaught, his partially severed arms were hanging in an unnatural manner, no longer protecting his head and face. As Paul staggered around after further blows, it was then that a *rungu* brought respite; stunning him with a blow to the back of the head.

He fell flat face-down, on to the ground.

He lay there for some seconds then felt his body being turned over.

Lying on his back, Paul struggled to take in the light pouring from the countless stars glowing in the night sky. They seemed very close. He could see his breath rising up to meet them.

His body let out an involuntary groan and rocked slightly, as the warrior straddled his chest.

But it was the insufferable screams of those who had been set alight that brought Paul back to consciousness and with it, his own sense of heightened terror.

Struggling to breathe through his broken nose and badly disfigured and swollen lips, Paul's breathing was now a series of fast, short breaths. He was choking on the blood running into his throat when a reflex cough sprayed it upwards out of his mouth, as the warrior took charge.

With a tug on the skin, above his left cheek Paul's fractured and bloodied face, jerked in a spasm. But the warrior's grip was firm.

The thin, sharp blade slid in under the skin and was pushed and pulled in quick succession, as it made its way around Paul's left eye socket.

Paul could do nothing but try to hold on to the soil; try to clutch it with broken fists. The soil. The earth. Welcome it. Embrace it.

After his left eye had been removed, and made to hang by its optic nerve at the side of his face, the warrior started on Paul's other eye.

It was then, however, that Paul's body finally moved beyond pain.

In his mind it came to him that it was a cool but bright summer's day. There was a gentle breeze and the lower part of his gleaming white cassock rippled like silk above his ankles, as he walked barefoot over an abundance of lush, evergreen leaves that were somehow scattered on the ground along the way.

Yet, as he walked he came to realise that he was not alone; that the leaves he trampled underfoot were laurel leaves; that the feet of the one who walked with him were pierced.

As the warrior continued, a short burst from a police officer's AK-47 filled the air, bringing an end to the mutilation and slaughter.

PART IV

BOOK FOUR: ACCEPTED

11

Scene 1: Picking up

Friday 1st January, 1993, Kylemore Crescent, Forgewood, Motherwell, Scotland 8:00 p.m. (GMT + 0.00)

Ninian entered the off-licence on Kylemore Crescent. Walking up to the counter, he took a coin from the right-hand pocket of his dark brown cords and tapped at the metal grill.

'Alright, Norrie! Happy New Year!'

The middle-aged storekeeper smiled, as he turned from the shelf he was refilling with Buckfast. 'Happy New Year, Ninian! Aye, no bad, eh?' he said, walking over to the counter and giving Ninian the once-over. 'Where are you off tae, aw togged up?'

'No' far. Just a wee night doon in Gary's, Norrie.'

Ninian looked down, taking money from his pocket, counting it into his left hand. 'Ye can come down once ye finish if ye fancy it?'

Norrie cursed. 'Gary's! An Ah suppose that maniac Eldo'll be there tae! Are ye aff yer fuckin' nut? Whit the fuck makes ye think Ah'd…?'

Ninian looked up from his hands and smiled.

'Ha, ha, Aye, good yin, Ninian. Ye had me there for a minute,' he conceded, 'but anyway, mister, how long have ye been running about wi' they two?'

'Ah don't know, Norrie. I've known them since Ah wiz a laddie, through Paul, but, Ah don't know… a few years maybe?'

'A few years ye say, *eh*? Ah mind they boys when they were laddies, Ninian, comin' in here when it was ma Da's shop. That was when Ah got to know them. Ah had heard the stories aboot them before that right enough, but don't get me wrong, very, very kind boys, and they'd always be nice and respectful, and Ah'll tell ye, they'd dae anything tae help anybody in this scheme, but the two a' them. Huh,' Norrie shook his head. 'They're stone fuckin' mad, Ninian. Stone… Fuckin'… Mad!

'Did Ah ever get tae tell you aboot the time, *years ago*, when ma Da was getting bother in here aff some punters. *Huh*, and then they two came in tae the shop. By fuck they were only young laddies but I'll tell ye, they werenae long in getting it sorted oot. *And the men?* Pfft, they were fuckin' shitein' theirsells. *Huh*, and were even made tae apologise tae ma Da!

'Aye, but that wisnae enough, after they'd telt the men tae get oot the shop, they were ready follow the men ootside, and go right ahead wi' them. Ma Da had to run roon, from behind the counter, and tell them that it was aw just a misunderstanding, and that everythin' was alright, just tae leave it.'

'Och, they're no' the worst, Norrie.'

'Hey, hey, don't get me wrong. They're crackin' boys, hearts a' gold. I've got a lot of time for them masell. Just watch yersell, Ninian, that's aw I'm sayin'. They laddies are stuck in their ways noo, and if they're in bother and you're wi' them, well, ye know the score. Your Paul got a lucky escape bailing oot a' here when he did.'

'Aye maybe, Norrie. *Anyway*, are ye sortin' me oot wi' some swally or whit?'

'Whit ye wanting?'

'*Hmm* Geeza bottle a' Smirnoff for Karen, and whit dae Ah want? *Hmm* just geez two bottles a' Bucky an' forty Regal King Size, Norrie. Ah think that'll be okay tae take doon to the hoose.'

'Nae bother, ma son,' Norrie said, turning back to the shelves, and gathering the order.

Ninian paid for his carry-out, and wished Norrie all the best before leaving the shop.

Scene 2: *Wolf whistles*

Outside the shop, Ninian made his way cautiously down the partially gritted steps to the icy pavement. He was soon approached by Eldo's uncle, Frank.

'Awright, Ninian son, Happy New Year tae ye. Ye couldnae sort yer auld pal oot wi' a couple a' cans, could ye son?'

'Happy New Year, Frank How are ye getting on?' Ninian said, shaking Frank's hand.

'Aye, no' bad, son. Same auld, same auld, *heh, heh*… Whit am Ah like, *eh? Heh, heh.*'

Ninian smiled, and took what he had from his pocket. 'Listen, I never bought any cans but here's a couple a' bob. Sorry it's no' much.'

'Aw, yer a diamond, son. God bless ye. That'll keep me goin'.'

'Nae bother, Frank, aw the best. See ye later.'

'See ye, son.'

Ninian was ready to walk on further, but stopped, and turned around, just as Eldo's uncle was about to enter the off-licence. 'Frank!' he called out, 'mind and watch whit yer daein' the night. It's a cauld yin. Don't be hangin' aboot for long. Git yersell o'er the road.'

'Aye, Ah will, son, I'll get some cans and I'll go doon tae oor Shona's. *If she'll let me in heh, heh, heh.*'

Ninian smiled, and turned from the old man, and made his way towards Fife Drive. *Auld Frank. It was a fuckin' liberty for him.*

Walking down the street, with his carry-out, Ninian soon became aware that he felt ten times better.

In the windows, on either side of the street, coloured fairy lights flickered around Christmas and New Year decorations. Music, for all ages, blared out from living rooms. People were out on their verandas, smoking and singing, *some* calling out to him, raising their drinks, wishing him well.

Ninian smiled. He was smartly dressed, he had drink and fags. He was going to meet his girlfriend and his mates. He was part of things.

Nearing Gary's block, a taxi slowed down as it drove past, drawing into the kerb in front of the close entrance.

The door behind the driver's side opened, and a young, tall, slenderly built woman, stepped out. She had long, well-managed, light-brown hair. And her stylish, open, black leather coat, revealed a black, figure hugging, baroque styled dress, reaching down to just above her knees. In her black high heels, she was roughly the same height as Ninian.

Ninian let out a wolf whistle.

His girlfriend, Karen, smiled back at him, as she stepped away from the taxi, to wait at the entrance of the close.

Ninian hurried towards her. '*Wow*! You look absolutely amazin', Karen! What did Ah ever do right to get ye?'

In their embrace, they greeted each other with a long kiss on the lips. 'Thanks, Ninian. *Hey*, you look no' bad yersell, *Rock Star*.'

The two of them laughed, as Ninian released himself from her, and took a step back. 'Dae ye think so?' he said, pulling open his retro styled, dark brown, leather jacket, revealing a white, tailored shirt, before doing a twirl.

Karen gave him a wolf whistle back. The two of them laughed, and kissed again.

Gary, who had spotted them from his living room window, had come out on to the veranda of his top floor flat. 'Hey, love birds. Are yees comin' up or whit?'

Ninian raised the carry-out in salute, and, arm in arm, he and Karen walked into the close.

Scene 3: *Party on!*

Reaching the top of the stairs, Ninian smiled, as he walked with Karen across the landing. He could hear the music. Releasing his arm from Karen's, he reached out with his right hand and gently tapped the letterbox.

The bolts on the door were slid back, one after the other – four in total, evenly spaced from top to bottom. Gary eventually opened the door.

'How's Fort Knox?' Ninian asked.

'Ye can never be too careful, Ninian son. Ye know the score,' he replied, winking and smiling as he opened the door, welcoming them into the hall. 'That better no' be drink you've bought. Ah told ye not to bring anythin'.'

'Aye and you wouldnae have done the same, eh?'

Gary closed the door, and, with his back to Ninian and Karen, started sliding the bolts into their fixings. 'Yer some man, Ninian. *Whit aboot this laddie a' yours, Karen*, does he ever dae anything *you* tell him?'

Ninian smiled. The daftness had started.

'Aye! Aw the time, Gary!' Karen exclaimed, pretending to be surprised by the comment.

He slid the last bolt in, and turned smiling. The three of them laughed as they made their way down the hall.

'*Here*, put this wi' the rest a' the drink,' Ninian said; handing the carry-out to Gary.

'Thanks, Ninian, yer a good yin. Ye didnae need tae dae that though. *Oh* and thanks for coming the two a' yees. Me and Michelle really appreciate it, and *please* mind and make yersells feel at home and *pleeeease* enjoy yersells! It'll be a good night,' he said, opening the living room door.

The sights, the sounds, the smell, the smoke, and the warmth that bombarded Ninian's and Karen's senses, made them turn and look at each other. They then turned and looked at Gary.

CONSCIOUSNESS AND PERCEPTION

The three of them fell into a fit of laughter. Gary laughed at the expressions on their faces, as Karen and Ninian laughed with excitement.

Still laughing, Ninian put his left hand on Gary's right shoulder, and leaned in. 'It's like the fuckin' drug version a' Willie Wonka in here ya fuckin' headcase. *Fuck* aw that's missin' is the Oompa Loompas.'

'Heh, heh, heh, don't worry, Ninian *son*,' Gary laughed, raising his voice as he made his way into the kitchen. 'You'll see them later, when we start drappin' the acid *hee, hee, hee.*'

Standing just inside the living room, Ninian smiled at the faces that greeted them. *Eldo*, seated on the black leather couch, had a big grin on his face as he raised a bottle of Macallan, before pouring some into the crystal tumbler in his left hand.

Ninian smiled, and nodded back to him, giving him a thumbs-up.

Looking to his right, to the corner of the room, near the veranda door, it was then that Ninian saw *Michelle*, Gary's wife. Her eyes were closed, and she was dancing, in her bare feet, on top of a large speaker, that had been turned to lie on its side, on the floor. She wore, tight, black, leather jeans and her long, black, loosely curled hair reached down past *full* pale breasts brought together, and covered, ever so slightly, by a finely finished black lace bra. Her belly button was pierced and bore a large *sparkling* deep purple sapphire, the glittering centrepiece of an intricate silver chain that hung around her waist and captured an array of *smaller stones* as if droplets at the ends of silver threads. Her hands *almost touching the ceiling* writhed together, sensually entwined, as she elegantly swayed to the psychedelic rock of the guitar, at the climax of the song. She was part of the music, and what a symphony it was. Gary was strikingly handsome; of that there was no denying, but against Michelle even he seemed pale by comparison. She was truly, truly, something else. Ninian smiled, and let out a stifled laugh. She was also stone fuckin' mad into the bargain.

He was brought back to Karen, at his side, by an elbow to the ribs. '*Whit?*' he said, 'the lassie's only enjoying herself.'

'Huh, aye! No' as much as you, by the look a' it!'

'Here, settle doon!' Ninian replied, taken aback at the suggestion.

'Don't say things like that, Karen. What dae ye think Ah am? That's ma pal's wife for God's sake!'

Karen smiled back at him, giving him one of her *looks,* one that she knew he could never understand.

'Come oan, don't start. We're here tae have a good night,' Ninian pleaded, bringing her close, and kissing her on the lips.

'Ah know. *Ah know,*' she said, smiling, before cheekily sticking her tongue out at him.

Ninian smiled and shook his head.

Looking around the room, there were guys there that Ninian hadn't seen for a very long time. It was going to be a great night. The company was good. 'Nae bams', as Gary had put it.

At various places, black, Gothic styled candelabras adorned with evergreen climbing plants and lilies offered up the subtle flames of their ivory candles with an innocent benevolence. Understated, yet elaborately designed, snowy white porcelain vases openly gave birth to the sweet beauty of flowering violets: Rotating lights bled, cavorting, psychedelic coloured patterns through waves of sound to find expression on the white walls and ceiling.

And, on the floor, in the middle of the long rectangular mirrored coffee table that ran parallel with the couch, four silver bowls rested in a line at its centre. Two were half-filled with white powder: sulph in one; and coke in the other, probably. The third contained what looked like more than enough ecstasy, and lumps of dope and grass filled the other. All of it was, of course, on the house. Ninian smiled. Everything was produced freely for everyone to help themselves. It had always been that way. It was the way they'd been brought up.

Michelle spotted Karen by Ninian's side, and waved, as she rushed over to them. Her eyes were like saucers. And strands of her black hair stuck to her face. She kissed each of them on the cheek, and led Karen, by her right arm, over to the corner, where she had been dancing.

Ninian smiled as he watched Michelle help Karen out of her coat. Her dance partner had arrived, it was only that Karen hadn't realised it yet.

Moving from the doorway, Ninian was greeted by those in close proximity. He was hugged and kissed on the cheek by men and women alike. It was New Year and the drugs were kicking in.

Gary found him with a glass of Buckfast. 'Here, all the best, mate, and ye know the score: batter intae whatever ye fancy,' he said, gesturing with his head towards the table.

'Thanks, Gary,' Ninian replied. 'Ye're a good yin, and thanks for inviting us doon, mate.'

Gary gripped Ninian at the back of the neck with his right hand. 'Pfft, hey, settle doon wi' they ones. It wouldn't be the same withoot ye son. *Here*, do me a favour,' he said, releasing his grip, 'give this tae your Karen. I've another few drinks to bring in, then I'll be wi' yees.'

'Nae bother, mate,' Ninian said, taking the glass of vodka from his friend, before making his way over to Karen.

12

Scene 1: Fear

Saturday 2ⁿᵈ January, 1993, Fife Drive, Forgewood, Motherwell, Scotland, 3:00 a.m.

Ninian sat on the armchair, near the window, and looked across the mirrored table to Gary and Eldo, who were sitting on the couch.

To his left, Michelle and Karen shared the chair beside the doorway to the hall. The two of them, were face to face, in what looked like deep conversation.

All of the other guests had left, and the hi-fi played at low volume.

Gary was heating a piece of cannabis on the end of his lock knife with his lighter; preparing it for the tobacco and cigarette papers that he'd already arranged and placed on the table. Ninian felt wide awake. The voices rasped and whispered in his head. *The boy's here somewhere,* he thought, but he couldn't see him yet.

Ninian looked at Gary. 'He always has to be the centre of attention,' a voice, clearer than the others, told him. 'Look, look at the way he's staring at Karen. He's been staring at her the whole night. He always gets what he wants: Karen will be next. Grab the lock knife and stab him in the jugular. Grab it! Stab him! Quick, hurry! Plunge him!'

Ninian jumped up from the chair and rushed round the table. He was past the couch and in the kitchen in seconds. He stood over the sink and turned on the cold tap, letting the water run into his cupped hands, throwing it on his face.

He put his hands over his ears and closed his eyes. *Stop, please stop,* he repeated inwardly. *I need to get out a' here. Dear God, help me. Please Stop it. Don't let me do anythin'. Stop me, please!*

'Are ye awright, Ninian?' Gary asked, as he and Eldo came into the kitchen.

Ninian lowered his hands and held on to the sides of the sink. He didn't answer or turn around. His body was rigid with fear and his eyes were drawn to the chrome cutlery holder – to the handle of a large kitchen knife.

'Ninian, are ye awright? Are ye feeling okay?' Gary continued.

'I'm goin' up the road tae get some pills,' Eldo cut in.

'I'll come wi' ye Eldo,' Ninian replied, without turning around. 'Ah need tae get oot and get some fresh air.'

'Ah'll come an' aw then,' Gary said. '*In fact*, will we get the dogs, Eldo, and go doon the park a walk?'

'Aye, if yees want. Fuck it's no' as if we'll be sleeping anytime soon. We could get a fire going at the side a' the loch if yees want. I've got firelighters in the hoose.'

'Sound!' Gary replied.

Ninian turned from the sink when he heard his friends leaving the kitchen. He walked into the living room and returned to his seat as Gary and Eldo explained to Michelle and Karen what the plans were.

The two women were indifferent to what the men were telling them.

Gary briefly went to his bedroom. When he returned, he was wearing a vintage styled black leather jacket. He collected some of the drugs from the table, and checked his wallet to make sure that he was also carrying the LSD.

In the kitchen, Eldo placed the alcohol that was to be taken with them into a rucksack.

The three men said goodbye to the women and left the flat.

13

Scene 1: In keeping with appearances

Saturday 2nd January, 1993, Montrose Street, Forgewood, Motherwell, Scotland, 3:20 a.m.

As they reached and entered the close, they made their way to the door of Eldo's ground-floor flat. A dog began yelping.

'Quiet, Fredo! That dug's a nightmare, I'm telling ye. If it wisnae for the wean, I would've gave it away ages ago.'

Unlocking the door and pushing it open, Eldo turned on the light as they entered. The Jack Russell continued to bark excitedly and began jumping up to Eldo's waist, as he and his friends made their way down the hall towards the living room.

Leaning down slightly, Eldo caught the dog as he jumped up, holding him under his right arm. On entering the living room, he gently threw him on to the couch. 'Stay, Fredo! Stay!'

Seeing his master, Laddie, his old black mongrel, raised his head and beat his tail on the rug at the veranda door.

Stepping over toys on the living room floor, and making his way past the Christmas tree, Eldo knelt down beside the old dog and patted him on the head while scratching under his neck.

'You done well with the wean, Eldo,' Gary said, looking around at the new toys scattered around the room.

Getting to his feet, Eldo turned around. '*Aye*, Ah suppose. It could've been a lot worse. Linda seemed happy with what we managed tae get the wean and she seemed happy wi' whit I gave her for her ain Christmas tae. So *aye*, it went awright, thank God.'

'Good, Eldo,' Gary acknowledged, nodding.

'Wire intae they sweeties there if yees want,' Eldo said, gesturing with his left hand to the chocolates and selection boxes that lay on the wooden coffee table. 'There's some turkey in the fridge tae fae

CONSCIOUSNESS AND PERCEPTION

the day's dinner *and some bread* if yees want tae make up some sannies?'

'Naw, yer fine, Eldo, thanks,' Gary said.

'Aye, I'm awright tae, Eldo, *cheers*,' Ninian added.

Eldo, got down on to his knees, to the hi-fi speaker that lay on the floor beside the couch. *Well*, yees know the score. If yees change yer minds, just help yersells. Sit doon the noo while I get the pills.'

Gary sat on one of the armchairs at the kitchen door, and Ninian sat on the other.

'How much gear are ye hawdin' for yer man, Eldo?' Gary asked.

'I'll show ye the noo.'

Taking the speaker in both hands and turning it around, Eldo removed the back cover and rested it against the fireside wall. He then pulled six, white, cylindrical plastic containers from inside the speaker, and sat them on the floor.

Moving to sit on the couch, he picked one of the tubs from the floor and reached over, handing it to Gary.

Gary screwed the lid off the container and looked inside.

'There's another six tubs in the other speaker as well,' Eldo told him. 'In total, there's eight tubs a' Temazepam and four tubs a' Palfium.'

'How many pills does a tub haud, Eldo? A thousand?' Ninian asked.

'Aye.'

'Twelve thousand pills?' Gary nodded. 'That's instant porridge if ye get caught wi' these. Ye know that, don't ye?' Gary smiled thoughtfully.

'Ah keep some loose tae,' Eldo said, 'purely for medicinal purposes, of course.' Reaching into the speaker with his right hand, he brought out a small, clear polythene bag.

Standing up from the couch, he loosened the knot and tilted the bag, letting the Temazepam and Palfium slide into his left hand. 'Here. How many are yees wanting?' He spilled some on to the floor.

Fredo leapt from the couch in an instant and began trying to eat the pills that had fallen, causing Gary and Ninian to roar with laughter in their chairs.

'Nae wonder they fuckin' dugs a' yours arenae right in the nut,' Gary hollered, as he watched Eldo trying to shoo the Jack Russell from the pills on the carpet.

The saliva fell from Eldo's mouth as he sniggered at his own foolishness, crawling around the floor and trying to pick up the pills before the dog could get to them.

Sensing defeat, he grabbed the dog by the scruff of the neck, and lifted him from the floor, making his way to the open doorway of the hall, where he released the dog and prevented him from re-entering by closing the door.

Pulling his jeans back up around his waist, Eldo stepped forward to take the plastic tub that Gary held out to him. 'Ah telt ye that dug was a nightmare, *didn't Ah*? Nae wonder I take a wee soda water to get me through the day, *heh, heh, heh*.'

'*Aye* Blame the dug..!' Gary replied, nodding his head towards Eldo, who was, once again, on his hands and knees, picking up the tablets. '*Pfft, whit aboot yer man, Ninian, eh? It's the fuckin' dug's fault hee, hee, hee!*'

Ninian, who had his arms crossed, held his ribs in laughter.

Gary tilted his head back, licked his lips, and blew out from his mouth as he leaned back into the chair. Reaching into the right-hand pocket of his jacket, he removed a wrap and threw it over to Ninian, before slipping back into *his proper English accent*. 'Sorry, my dear Ninian, would you be ever so kind as to decorate the table? I fear my attempts at drug induced nirvana *are,* for the want of a better expression, in need of some maintenance. *Hmm,* such a preposterous proposition, of course an oxymoron indeed. Yet oft-times we do like to indulge ourselves in the ridiculous *wot wot?*'

'*Quite so, sir, quite so*!' Ninian replied, in keeping with his friend's tone.

Ninian emptied the contents of the wrap on to the coffee table as Gary withdrew a bank card and then a ten-pound note from his wallet. 'Jolly good, my young prodigy! Two bumper lines each should suffice. How do you see, my dear Eldo? Will two be enough to encourage greater dexterity?'

CONSCIOUSNESS AND PERCEPTION

Ninian could only laugh.

Eldo raised his right index finger and waved it to Gary. 'You know, my learned friend I think you might just be on to something there.' Taking the ten-pound note from Gary, Eldo began rolling it for the task at hand.

Ninian and Gary put the Temazepam and Palfium that Eldo had given them into their pockets, and helped to ensure that all of the pills that had fallen had been removed from the carpet.

Then Eldo returned the six tubs and the polythene bag to the speaker, and fixed the plywood panel into its rightful position. Satisfied that it was closed properly, he turned the speaker around to face out into the living room – the way they had found it when they entered.

When Eldo had collected the firelighters and lighter fluid from the cupboard in the hall, the three friends, accompanied by the two dogs, left the flat.

14

Scene 1: Level crossing

Saturday 2nd January, 1993, Bellshill Road, Forgewood, Motherwell, Scotland, 4:10 a.m.

The main road was fairly quiet, apart from the odd taxi taking revellers home from nights out. There were no other people to be seen walking around. The skies were clear, it was cold and the pavements were covered in what was left of a thin layer of snow that had turned to ice the day before.

The three friends were roughly 30 yards away from the level crossing when they heard the siren. The barrier was coming down and a train would be approaching soon.

'Come oan. We'll make it. *Run*!' Eldo shouted. Giggling with excitement, he set off, running ahead of Gary and Ninian, his two dogs chasing after him

Gary and Ninian watched anxiously, as Eldo, who very nearly lost his footing on several occasions, eventually came to a halt.

'Here! I'll take the rucksack!' Gary called out, shaking his head as they caught up with him, 'or we'll end up reaching the park wi' a wet bag full a' broken glass.'

Eldo was now jogging on the spot. 'He's just jealous, Ninian. He could never beat me at the running even when we were weans, at the school. He knows he just cannae handle the pace! Cannae handle the pace a' the Eldo Boy! The Undisputed Forgie Gala Day Championnaaaay!'

Eldo picked up speed and was soon running at full pelt on the spot. He had a look of total concentration on his face. His arms pumped like pistons as he blew out, making a whooshing sound, as though the sound was coming from the speed of his movement.

Fredo, his Jack Russell, barked excitedly, and was jumping up to his waist, while the old mongrel, Laddie, stood, unfazed.

CONSCIOUSNESS AND PERCEPTION

Gary turned to look at Ninian and shook his head. They couldn't hold it in any longer: the two of them buckled with laughter.

Gary had his hands on his thighs and tears in his eyes. '*Hee, hee, hee,* don't laugh, *hee, hee, hee*! Eees poor Mammy's heart's roasted wi' him, a constant source a' worry tae her, *hee, hee, hee.* God love the poor, fucked-up, crazy bastart, *hee, hee, hee.*'

Eldo, encouraged by the effect he was having on his two friends, was trying to run even faster.

Seeing Eldo was getting out of breath, Gary winked at Ninian, before turning to Eldo. 'Right, come oan then. I'll race ye.'

'Right, come oan then. Come oan then!' Eldo said, taking the backpack off and passing it to Ninian. 'A sprint! Fae here tae the level crossing!'

'Nae bother, son. Prepare to lose your title,' Gary told him, getting into position down beside him on the imaginary starting blocks. 'Ninian will give us the shout. Awright, Ninian?'

'Aye.'

In their starting positions, Gary nudged Eldo, causing him to laugh and lose his balance slightly.

'Mind noo!' Eldo told him. 'Don't start yer greeting when ye get beat like ye used tae dae when ye were a wean.'

'Whit the fuck are ye oan aboot?' Gary laughed. 'Don't listen tae him, Ninian. E's talking pish.'

'It's the truth!' Eldo said, turning his head to look up to Ninian. 'Honest, Ninian, when he got beat, he used to run home tae ees Mammy greetin' and girnin', tears and snotters trippin' him, bawling and wailing. *Mammy, Mammy that bad boy Eldo beat me again! Mammy, Mammy how can Ah no' be the best? Mammy, Mammy how can Ah no' be brilliant? Mammy, Mammy can Ah sook the milk fae yer diddies pleeeeeeaaaase?* Heh, heh, heh. Then you'd see the daft bastart *half an hour later* aw smiles *wi' that stupit toothless grin*, runnin' back oot tae play, *wiping ees maw's diddy milk aff ees face heh, heh, heh.*'

'Whit the fuck is wrang wi' your tattie, ya fuckin' maniac?' Gary said, laughing. 'You're really quite a fuckin' disturbed individual, int ye? *Right*, come oan Ninian, *get us started* so Ah can pull the drawers right aff this real yin.'

Ninian was still laughing. 'Right then, are yees ready?'

'Aye!' the two of them replied.

'On yer marks, get set... go!'

Eldo and Gary set off together, trying to be serious but laughing at the same time. Fredo, the Jack Russell, ran with them

Gary knew he had no chance of winning, even before the race. But he knew his friend Eldo wouldn't be beating him either

At the first sign of Eldo pulling away, which was only some few yards into the race, Gary pushed him hard in the direction of the Jack Russell.

Eldo sniggered as he tried to avoid the dog but the dog *somehow* got caught under his feet. Losing his balance, Eldo fell headlong and slid along the icy pavement, hurling obscenities at Gary.

Gary continued to run, laughing and shouting: 'And the undisputed champ is down. He's lost his title. A distinguished career lies in tatters!'

When Gary reached the level crossing, he raised both arms and jumped up and down in celebration. He started shadow-boxing, making the same *whooshing* sound that Eldo had made earlier. Hearing a car's engine revving up, he turned towards the sound.

Across the barriers, on the other side of the level crossing, the driver of the police car was letting Gary know that they were watching him.

Gary stopped and immediately started assessing the situation. He knew he would be out of earshot of the police, who were about 30 yards away, and called out to Ninian and Eldo as they walked towards him. 'Here! The bizzies are o'er there. Quick, but don't run. It'll look suspicious. We'll need tae go over the bridge. It'll give us a chance tae stash the gear.'

'*Fuck*!' Ninian exclaimed. 'That's aw I'm needin'... getting' captured wi' pills.'

'Don't worry, we'll be awright,' Eldo told him. 'As soon as we're oan the bridge an' oot a' their sight, we'll ditch everythin'.'

The three friends crossed the road, passing the red and white barrier on their right, and made their way to the pedestrian bridge that would take them over the railway tracks to the North Motherwell side.

When they were on the bridge and hidden from view, Gary spoke up, removing all the drugs he had in his possession. 'Right, we can throw the gear or we can hide it. It's up tae yersells.' He bent down and took off his right shoe. Pulling down his sock, he slid the wraps, the pills and the LSD under the arch of his right foot. He quickly pulled up his sock and forced his foot back into his shoe.

'I'm ditching mine,' Ninian said. 'Ah cannae take the chance. Are any a' yees wantin' them, before Ah throw them?'

'Aye, I'll take them, Ninian,' Eldo said, removing his own pills from his pocket.

After taking the Temazepam and Palfium from Ninian, Eldo followed Gary's lead and slipped the drugs inside his right sock, sliding them under the arch of his foot, before pushing his foot back into his shoe.

'Right! Are we ready?' Gary asked. 'Mind! Just try and act normal. Quick... we better move, or they'll be wondering whit we're up tae.'

When they had crossed over the bridge and stepped down on to the pavement, they had only walked a few yards when they heard the police vehicle reversing.

In less than three seconds, it had skidded into the side of the kerb in front of them.

The window on the driver's side was already rolled down. 'Haw, MacGregor, ya numpty. How many times have Ah tae tell you aboot keeping they dugs a' yours oan a leash?' Craig Munro, the young police officer, shouted.

'Oh,' Eldo began, 'I'm very sorry, Ossiffer. Ah mean orifice. Ah mean *Cunt*stable.'

'Do you want tae spend the night in the cells, ya fuckin' arsehole? And whit are you sniggering aboot Jamieson?' he said, focusing his attention on Gary.

The young officer turned to his companion in the passenger seat,

Sergeant George Miller. 'Look at whit this yin's wearing, Sarge.' He turned back to Gary. 'Who the fuck do ye think ye are? Dorian Gray? Aw, sorry, you'll no' know who that is, will ye, coming fae that shithole o'er there.'

As if on stage, Gary pushed his hair back from his face, before striking an imaginary match in his cupped hands, giving the impression of lighting and puffing away on a large pipe, held firmly in his right hand.

Continuing with his act, he bent forwards slightly, looking into the vehicle, beyond the young policeman, before addressing the commanding officer directly in his *most proper English* accent. '*Ahhhhhhh*! Good morning, Sergeant Miller. *Ha*! How novel! By blazes you uttered those words without the slightest movement from your lips! What infernal trickery indeed. *Ha*! How the devil did you do it? *Hmm, hmm,* let me see, sleight of hand, a trick of the light, smoke and mirrors perhaps? Hmm, hmm, or, dare I say, could they have come from this docile appendage protruding from your weeping anus?'

Ninian and Eldo laughed uncontrollably.

'Bravo, Holmes! Bravo!' Eldo exclaimed, in character.

Gary curled the fingers of his left hand, and scrutinised them. He blew on his fingernails and started to rub them on the lapel of his jacket. 'Trifles, Watson, mere trifles, a simple deduction of reason nothing more, nothing less. The aura of idiocy is exposed in such parodies of urine.'

Sergeant George Miller tried to disguise his snigger with a cough, and turned to look out of his side window. His shoulders moved up and down. Constable Munro's look of confusion turned to one of rage. In an instant, he was out the vehicle, drawing his baton.

Sergeant Miller hurried out after him. 'Stand down, Constable Munro!'

'But, Sarge...'

'Stand down, I said.'

Walking round the vehicle, Sergeant Miller stepped on to the pavement. 'Right, you three. I don't know where yees are goin' and I don't care, but if I find yees on these streets in the next half an hour, yees'll aw be up in cells for the rest of the weekend and taken tae

CONSCIOUSNESS AND PERCEPTION

Hamilton Sheriff Court on Monday morning. Is that clear?'

'Aye,' Gary answered.

'Right! Now on yer way,' he told them, before turning to the young officer. 'Constable Munro, join me in the vehicle, please.'

When the two policemen got back inside the car, Constable Munro spoke first. 'What was that aw aboot, Sarge? We never even searched them!'

'You could be a good officer, Craig,' Sergeant Miller began, 'but if that's the way you're addressing people, you've got a lot to learn. How do you expect people to treat you with respect if you don't treat them the same way? And I'll tell you something else, if you keep that approach up, you'll make life very, very difficult for yourself and your partner. So, if I ever decide to join you for a night out on patrol again, I'd better not witness anything like what I witnessed here tonight. You not only embarrassed yourself, you embarrassed me also. And not only that, your perception of the people in these schemes is way off the mark. The people in these places are just the same as people everywhere else. If my years of service have taught me anything, they've taught me that it's only that the methods of survival and the behaviours associated with that survival, are sometimes different. There are two reasons why we didn't search them: the first is that the drug squad is already involved in an operation that is gathering intelligence from all over the west of Scotland and the north of England, and Gary Jamieson is only one of many small-time dealers being monitored closely, along with his friend Eddie MacGregor. Their doors'll go in; it's only a matter of time. However, it will happen *only* when it's the right time. The second reason – a lesser reason given the first – is that even though the three of them were clearly under the influence, it's the early hours of the morning. If they had any drugs on them, they'd be minimal amounts. In searching them we might've got a small result, but it would have let them know that we were on to them and they'd have changed the way they do business, which would have a negative impact on the work of the DS.

'In addition to this, before it sank into their skulls to go over the bridge, rather than wait for the train to pass by and for the barrier to go up, they saw us. So, the questions now are: what made them decide to go over the bridge? And what do you think they were doing while on the bridge?'

The young constable, all the while facing the front, looked out through the windscreen and nodded. 'They went on to the bridge to hide the drugs.'

'Okay. Now let's get up tae the station and get ourselves home.'

The train had already passed and the barrier had been raised when Constable Munro started the vehicle.

With the green light giving him the go-ahead, he drove through the level crossing and made a right turn on to the Bellshill Road heading up to Motherwell Police Headquarters.

After leaving the officers, the three friends walked a short distance along the pavement before crossing the road on to Watling Street on their way to Strathclyde Country Park.

PART V

BOOK FIVE:

THE OLD NEW DAWN

15

Scene 1: Resolutions

Saturday 2nd January, 1993, Strathclyde Country Park, Motherwell, Scotland, 5:40 a.m.

When they reached the pebbled area at the side of the man-made loch, Gary, lowered the rucksack on to the ground. Taking control, Eldo, asked his friends to find logs that they could use as seats, while he found the broken twigs and branches that he would use to make a fire.

With the help of the firelighters and lighter fluid, in less than ten minutes Eldo had the fire started. And after twenty minutes, it was blazing.

The three friends sat around its warmth smoking, drinking, joking, laughing.

Eldo's older dog, Laddie, lay close by the fire. But Fredo, the Jack Russell, barked at the water's edge, excited by the movements of the wild waterbirds, and was jumping every time one flew close by.

The fire greedily ate into the wood, crackling noisily as it spat burning splinters around Ninian's feet, but, like the near-empty bottle of whisky resting between his legs, he took no notice.

Flames roared upwards, in yellow orange green lilac purple red *altering shape and vitality within the enchantment of their embrace,* radiating splendour, bronze *now* gold, *rising lengthening, the towering pipes of a magnificent church organ, reciprocating the gift of nature's song to the heavens.*

Ninian slid off the log to change position; not once taking his eyes from the fire. He lay down on his left side, stretching out, contemplating the golden flames disappearing upwards into the night sky.

He then gazed into the heart of the fire, and began reaching out with his right hand.

'Niniaaaan! Niniaaaan! For fuck's sake!' Gary screamed.

'What?' Ninian said, drawing his hand back.

'Whit?' Gary shouted. 'You were nearly sticking yer hand into the middle a' the fuckin' fire!'

'Naw, I wisnae, I was just going to…' Then it dawned on him. Ninian kicked out forcefully with his legs, his feet dislodging the pebbles in his struggle to get away from the fire.

Gary looked over to Eldo. The two of them sniggered.

'Please tell me yees are fuckin' jokin'?' Ninian said angrily.

'Hey, don't blame us. We're trippin' an' aw,' Eldo laughed.

'Aye, very fuckin' good! Yees are some mates! I told yees Ah didnae want any acid. Dae yees want me back in the fuckin' asylum? Cause that's what'll fuckin' happen!'

'Ninian, geeza break here! We'll talk aboot it tomorrow,' Gary told him. 'If ye talk about negative stuff like that, you'll only end up talking yourself and us intae a bad trip. Just go wi' the flow. We love each other. And we're thegither and we won't let anything bad happen tae any a' us. When they start wearing off in a few hours, we'll go up the road, take a couple a' temazzies, and sleep it all off.'

Ninian felt disgusted with himself, but he knew Gary was right. If he kept thinking bad stuff, he could end up with a real nightmare on his hands.

Gary walked round the fire and knelt down, hugging Ninian and ruffling his hair. 'I'm sorry if ye got a fright there. If any rubbish comes intae yer heid, just tell yersell it's a lot a' pish and laugh it off. Don't dwell on any of it, Ninian. It's fuckin' nonsense.'

Gary turned to Eldo and smiled. '*Huh*, remember when we were aw doon here when we were weans, Eldo. When I had just got my first ever lock knife. *Mind!* Me, you, Paul and Ninian, the four a' us. *Huh. We aw slashed our right thumbs and then, when they were bleeding, we pressed them together. Mind!* And that was us blood brothers. *Ha! Then we carved our names under the Clyde Bridge.*'

'*Pfft.* Aye, how could Ah forget? Ye nearly cut the thumb right aff me ya fuckin' real yin. *Dae ye mind a' that?* Then I got slapped aff the auld dear when I got up the road, *heh, heh, heh.*'

Gary laughed with Eldo, before turning to Ninian. 'Do you mind that day, Ninian? *God! We* were young, *but you were right young.* It was even before you got yer callipers. *Huh,* and ye were greetin' for ages tae 'cause we said you were too wee tae get yer thumb cut *heh, heh, heh.* Your Paul ended up giving in, and let ye dae it, jist tae stop ye fae greetin'.'

'Aye, Ah mind, Gary,' Ninian replied, breaking into a smile and a snigger.

Gary adjusted his position to sit beside him. 'Whit is it?'

Ninian smiled. 'I was going to tell ye something. Och, it's nothing. It's just daftness.'

'Whit? Tell us whit it is?'

Ninian laughed, shaking his head. 'It's just as well you shouted when ye did. I thought the fire was a massive church organ and that the flames rising up were its golden pipes.'

Eldo joined in with the laughter. 'Nice one, *heh, heh, heh.*'

Gary fell silent *as he looked around at what was before him.* 'As it gets nearer first light it'll be absolutely beautiful down here. Believe me lads. *Honestly.* It's really something. Wait till yees see,' he said, opening his left hand out to the mist on the loch. '*Once it lifts* you'll see an amazing sight, *swans, geese, ducks, gulls, and all,* making their effortless descents to land on the water. And hearing their cries and calls above.' he continued, raising his head. 'And following their flight, who knows where they've come from? Who knows how many miles they've travelled? Hundreds, thousands, through time and space, overcoming countless struggles, to come and share their majestic beauty, just with us,' Gary's voice was cracking with emotion. '*Honest,* I'm telling yees. See when ye see them flyin' in formation, frantically beating their wings, ye can almost feel yer heart racing with theirs.'

Gary stood up, and slowly walked a few yards from where he had been seated.

He slipped his hands into the pockets of his leather jacket and, raising his head, gazed up into the starry night sky.

After some seconds, he closed his eyes and spoke out *softly* almost in a whisper.

'Soar high
and sing
immaculate friends
Of the Love
that never ends
Of the Rhythm
and the Song
Of the Light
that we belong
And of the blazing
heart's desire
And The Flame
within its fire
And of
the day
that turns to night
The
restless
beauty
of the flight
To the Home
within the Heart
Where we live
and ne'er depart.'

CONSCIOUSNESS AND PERCEPTION

Gary's lips trembled. And tears were in his eyes when he opened them. 'And the trees!' he exclaimed, as he again moved position, gesturing with his open right hand to the area behind Ninian. 'Just before the sun comes up, you'll see them, *caressed by the breeze*.

The leaves, shimmering and swaying, the revelry of ethereal shoals at play... Stirred by Love, and awakened to bliss, deep beneath the waves of an azure firmamental sea.

Dear God *the trees* I swear it! If you look with an open heart you'll see the glory of All Life radiating from beyond their leaves and branches. Each one of them a Cinderella just before for the Ball, glowing virginal purity that's to return to the humdrum of the everyday, *Infinite splendour* that's to remain hidden, until that day when the mystery behind the miracle, *fully blossoms*, in the humble *willing heart* of every man.'

The three friends were quiet.

The only sound was the crackle of the fire.

Gary moved back to take his seat beside Ninian, as Eldo, with a solemn expression, spoke up. '*Hey*, that's some deep beautiful shit, bro,' he told him. 'Geez another one a' they acid tabs. Ah think I'm the only cunt that's missing oot here.'

Gary and Ninian looked at each other. And then both looked at Eldo.

All three roared with laughter.

The hilarity was so infectious, that it continued for some time, until Gary, *eventually*, brought them back. 'Give it some time, Eldo. It'll come oan ye shortly. It's no' hit me yet either,' he explained, with regret in his voice; a regret of wishing, like Ninian, that he too hadn't taken any LSD.

'Ye know, boys,' Gary said, as he gazed beyond the flames, 'one day I'm gonnae chuck aw this. Awright, it's a bit a' fun and it's not as if we take ourselves too seriously, which is a good thing, but...' He looked down at the black frill of his shirt, sticking out from the sleeve of his black leather jacket, 'let's be honest. It's aw fantasy world stuff, int it? The drink, the drugs, the clothes, the image! One day, it's coming.' He raised his head to look again through the flames. 'Don't get me wrong, it's good to look after yersell and keep yersell lookin' smart, but, there's so much, much more tae life. Put it this way, if as they say you only get one crack at it, why dilute the experience? Why no' live fully aware, fully conscious, wide awake? Naw, Ah mean but seriously, look at aw the fuckin' nonsense that people fill their lives wi? Is it any wonder that there are so many of us walking aboot in a fuckin' daze? Sleep-walking our way through most of our lives? Paddin' aboot like fuckin' robots? And for what? We're caught up in so much shite that half the time we don't even know we're fuckin' alive. Stuck in our own wee worlds in our own wee hooses like fuckin' battery hens, fed and bombarded wi' aw the shite a' the day, so that we'll keep buyin' intae aw the shite a' the day. Aw the shite that we're told that, "we must do, we must have! That we can't possibly live without!" And all the while the unsaid threat hangs over us all: "You must have it! You must get it! You must be this way! Or else!" Aye, *or else*! Or else you'll just be seen to be one of society's losers, an outsider, a useless bastart. And that's the irony right there. We swallow aw that pish and then end up spending our whole lives runnin' aboot like fuckin' idiots, trying tae keep up wi' it aw. Kiddin' ourselves on intae believing that if we have this or that, we'll feel more secure, more alive. Aye, we'll show everybody else that we're in control, we'll show them aw that we're on the ball, that we've got it aw sorted. But inside? Inside we're runnin' on empty; runnin' on the fumes of fear and loneliness.'

Gary shook his head before continuing. 'But, *of course*, we don't want to dwell on any of that, do we? *And so* we keep goin' *keep runnin'* faster and faster on our wee hamster wheels, *oblivious*, living the way that we're "supposed to live" continually allowing ourselves to be conditioned *more and more*, bred to consume, '*You are what you have*'. That's our mantra. If you've got fuck all, *well*, you're simply of no value. You're just seen to be an arsehole "*You are what you have*" Huh. It'd be funny.

'It'd be fuckin' hilarious, if it wasn't so tragically fuckin' sad. Is this the culmination of humanity's wisdom? Is this the world that untold millions have worked so hard to create? Whit a fuckin' joke that is. We've lost sight a' everythin.'

'Every real beauty *within and around us*. Huh. *Familiarity breeds contempt so they say*, and what fuckin' contempt there is when everything that is sacred, everything that is pure, every real and perfect beauty *is seen to be so familiar.* Everything! Hidden from our view. Because of our own *unadulterated* pig fuckin' ignorance.' Gary blew out through his mouth in something like a heavy sigh, before adding, 'awright, it can be hard at times, but life, huh, and I mean Real Life! It's so, so fuckin' beautiful. The wean's growing tae. God, she'll be four this year, and Michelle, *huh.*' he smiled, looking into the fire.

After a few seconds, Eldo spoke up. 'Don't sweat it, bro'. It's coming tae us aw,' he told him. 'We're only having a bit of fun. It's no' as if we'll be sitting here like this when we're aw auld age pensioners, is it? Surely no', for fuck's sake!'

'Aye,' Gary laughed. 'Ah suppose, Eldo.'

Gary felt, at that moment, a deep sorrow for Eldo. He believed that *he* himself could play around with alcohol and drugs, every now and again during the weekends, in a recreational way. There was no problem. *He* had no problem. He could take them or leave them. Ditching the cannabis might be a problem, right enough, but that would probably have something to do with the craving for the nicotine in the cigarette tobacco. But Eldo... *his* personality was one a' they addictive ones; the drink was there in the family. His auld uncle Frank was an alkie but he wasn't the only one. Eldo's maw and da had bother wi' *it* tae. *Was it in their genes? God*, poor Eldo. *Huh*, he'd been caught drinking when he was eleven, that was how he got ees name, got caught drinking his Uncle Frank's bottle a' Eldorado. *Poor bastart*: it wisnae only the name that had stuck. When he'd become old enough to drink legally, he'd already been drinking nearly every night a' the week for aboot a year and a half. His complexion was changing noo tae. He was still a good looking laddie, still managed tae keep himself smart fae ees *mod days* a' smart suits and cropped hair, but the broken veins, and the reddishness wi' the drink. *Aye*, it was now there for everyone tae see: *A misguided notion of a badge of honour.*

Gary came to realise that he wasn't the only one who wasn't talking. Each of them was with their own thoughts.

Ninian had been the first to start tripping, probably cause he wisnae expecting it. When he'd got drunk fae the whisky, that's when he started pestering *us* for ages before we gave in. The other drugs had eventually been drowned out and the whisky had come tae the fore. That was what had happened. He didn't even know. He'd forgotten he'd taken the acid. He only recognised the effects when it started to take him on a different journey. He'll be awright. We'll watch him. I shouldnae have gave him it though. Fuck. Whit was Ah thinkin'? He's still in a fragile place *mentally*. *Hmm* it's a fuckin' shame, a great boy, just like ees brother, Paul. Crackin' laddies. Diamonds. Ah'll sort it after today. *Aye*, I'll start doing it right. I'll take care a' him properly. It's New Year, a new start. *Aye*, that's what I'll dae. We'll just get this session o'er wi' then that'll be it. Me, Michelle and the wean tae, a new start, for the lot a' us.

Scene 2: 'See'

Long periods, or what felt like long periods – no one knew – of conversational silence were broken, only occasionally, by one of them uttering something that was only relevant to the complex yet inane themes running through their own heads.

A low buzzing sound started to fill Ninian's perception *VWOOM VWOOM VWOOM VWOOM.*

Unnoticed, the wind crept up on the fire and pushed back the flames, forcing them to lie down at its behest.

In the distance, Ninian heard the low ascending sound of a dog growling and the sound of something scurrying over the pebbles away from the fire.

Turning to the sound, Ninian watched as the old mongrel rushed to the side of the Jack Russell. The dogs barked rabidly at the water's edge. Looking beyond them, out, into the mist, Ninian saw what had caught their attention.

'Ninnnniaaan!'

Getting up from where he was seated, Ninian began walking over the white, ice-covered pebbles. The wind forced him to take a step backwards, throwing open his jacket as he pushed forward. On the loch, the water raged beneath the eerie stillness of the mist

'Join me, Ninnnniaaan. Commmmme,' the breathless voice called.

In a trance-like state, Ninian walked past the dogs, ignoring their warnings, and continued straight into the ice-cold water.

'Ninian! Ninian!' Gary shouted.

Eldo soon realised what was happening, and scrambling across the pebbles, was up on his feet in seconds. He ran straight into the water, and caught Ninian by his right arm, just as the water reached past their waists.

The dogs continued to bark in a frenzy, moving close to the water, only to crouch down, and leap back at its approach.

Ninian acknowledged Eldo by his right side but not in the way Eldo had hoped. Looking straight ahead, Ninian was still trying to move forward, out into the mist, as the deep blackness of the water came up to meet them. 'Are you coming too?' he said to Eldo. 'That's good. We'll be with him, together.'

'Ninian, it's no' real. There's nothing there. Come oan. We need tae get out a' here. Ye're freakin' me oot,' he told him, as he struggled to hold Ninian's right arm. 'Gary!' Eldo shouted, 'you'll need tae help me here. Yer man's heid's away. Ye need tae get us oot a' here!'

At the water's edge, Gary was already quickly removing his clothes. 'I'm coming. Hawd oan tae him for fuck's sake! Don't let him go, Eldo!'

Stretching out to keep a hold on Ninian's arm, Eldo could feel the underwater currents pressing against his legs, *only* it didn't *feel* like underwater currents. The pressure around his ankles around his thighs felt like hands. The fog too was moving differently; parts of it were breaking free, swirling around them at speed; misty cloaked and shrouded figures, with solemn yet beautiful veiled angelic faces, flowing gracefully in and through the spaces between them, up and around them, tenderly acknowledging them with the kindness of their eyes; but changing, becoming anxious, becoming distressed, inconsolable…

weeping in agony

screaming in terror

shrieking with malevolent delight

Letting go of Ninian's right arm, Eldo cried out, struggling to take in the evil entities that raced around them, above them, between them, diabolical whispers consuming his mind.

Ninian stood motionless. He continued to face straight ahead, seemingly unconcerned by the demonic entities encircling them.

'Since I was a boy I've tried to tell anyone who would listen. But no one would believe me. But now you believe me. Now you can see, see that they're real. See that?' His voice was suddenly replaced by another; a low, breathless, penetrating whisper.

'Heeee's heeeere.'

Ninian's head seemed to flop forward, his chin, held by his chest. His eyes were closed and something else had taken over; something else was in control, forcing him to turn, to turn around to Eldo.

Looking on in terror, Eldo cowered with dread. Coming into view, he could see the two, small, pale white hands clinging to Ninian's left forearm. They belonged to the thin, drenched figure of a boy – a schoolboy; ashen-faced, deathly white with jet-black hair. His head was lowered. His eyes were closed, the water cascading from him.

Without warning, the boy scrambled up and across Ninian's chest, around his back, hiding, until slowly the pale white hands appeared once more, the fingers curling and pulling on Ninian's left shoulder, the dripping wet head emerging slowly, still lowered, now brushing against Ninian's face.

Eldo fought to escape, but the hands that gripped his thighs tightened with each movement. Instinctively, he looked down into the water only to see the pale evil faces grimacing back at him. Screaming wildly, Eldo raised his head, looking to Ninian and the boy.

With a rapid and otherworldly ease, their rigid bodies glided through the water towards him, their heads flicking upwards in a lifeless glare. 'Seeeeeeeeeeeeeeeeeeeeee!'

Their eyes were totally black, black glistening pools of pure evil.

Eldo fell backwards, screaming in the water.

Gary grabbed hold of him. 'Eldo, it's awright! It's me! It's Gary. I've got ye! Ye're awright.'

'Keep them away! Keep them away fae me!'

'Eldo, it's awright. Come oan, it's freezing. We need tae get tae the fire! Come oan.'

'Ah seen them! Ah seen them, Gary! They're there! Ninian's wi' them! Keep them away fae me. Please, keep them away!'

Ninian, in a trance-like state, walked past his friends on his way out of the water, passing the dogs, to sit once again by the fire, and gaze into its flames.

When Gary eventually managed to get Eldo up near the fire, he unzipped his friend's dripping wet wax cotton jacket and started to undress him.

Leaving Eldo to stand naked beside the fire, Gary rushed to the water's edge and collected his own clothes, then hurried back to the fire, dried Eldo down the best he could and helped him into his leather jacket.

When Gary himself was dressed, he quickly wrung out Eldo's clothes and hung them on some of the broken branches that he had placed around the fire.

He then approached Ninian, and convinced his friend to allow him to help him do the same.

For the remaining hours before daybreak, the friends sat around the fire in relative silence.

Initially, Gary had tried to calm Eldo by trying to convince him that what he had seen had come about as a result of knowing Ninian, and so too knowing the history of Ninian's delusions. Continuing with this line, he had even dressed it up further, telling Eldo that it had all been possible because of 'the power of persuasion and nothing more'.

Yet, somehow, deep down, Gary knew he was telling Eldo these things not just for Eldo's benefit but for his own too.

Something had happened in the water. There were things moving around in the mist. He too had seen them. He had seen them when he was undressing at the water's edge. He had seen Ninian and the boy, their bodies rigid, standing upright, heads hanging to the side, gliding through the water towards Eldo. It was at that moment that Gary had charged into the water with eyes closed, in Eldo's general direction, and was relieved to have barged into him.

It was with these realisations that Gary then talked his friends into taking some of the Temazepam. He told them that the pills would quickly dull the effects of the LSD, and would soon return them to something like normality. However, what he didn't explain, was that he was hoping for something else; hoping that the sedatives would quickly blank out the immediate memory of what they had seen.

When their clothes were partly dry, Ninian and Eldo got dressed, and when the sun came up, the three friends headed out of the park.

16

Scene 1: Never again

Saturday 2nd January, 1993, Kylemore Crescent, Forgewood, Motherwell, Scotland, 9:50 a.m.

Ninian unlocked the door to his flat and entered the hallway. Closing the door, he fixed the latch, turned and was about to head down the hall, when he suddenly stopped himself.

As he stood, with his back to the door, Ninian proceeded to assess the state of his jacket, his shirt, his cords and his now wrecked light-brown suede moccasins. 'Whit a fuckin' arsehole!' he said aloud.

Kicking the shoes off in disgust, Ninian walked down the hall and entered the bathroom. Leaning over the sink, he looked into the mirror resting on the windowsill. Ninian barely recognised the face looking back at him. There was something like a dirty green, purplish tinge to his complexion. *Comin' off acid was always the same*, he thought. *Ye always look exactly the same way as ye feel – absolutely fuckin' filthy, inside and out.*

'Why the fuck dae ye keep daein' this tae yersell?' he snapped, shaking his head in rage. Pushing himself from the sink, he put the plug in the bath and turned on the hot tap. Taking the bottle of shampoo, he poured some into the running water.

Walking into the bedroom, he removed his coat and hung it on the front of the wardrobe, then moving to sit on the edge of the double bed, he started to undress.

Ninian's eyes caught the framed picture of Karen on his bedside cabinet and the brass crucifix beside it; the one Paul had given him before he had left for the missions.

Taking his clothes, he walked over to the corner of the room and launched them forcefully into the washing basket. Leaving the bedroom, he passed through the steam that was now gathering in the hallway, and entered the bathroom. Checking the water beneath the foam with his right hand, he turned on the cold tap.

When he was content that the water temperature wasn't too hot, he turned off the taps and stepped into the bath still disgruntled and *still* deeply mortified.

Leaning back in the bath, he pinched his nose and closed his eyes as he slid under the water, fully immersing himself for a few seconds. When he came back up, Ninian rested the back of his head against the surround and slowly pulled both hands down over his face.

With eyes still closed, he lay like that, and when his body could no longer keep up with his mind, he fell asleep.

BOOK SIX: TIME

17

Scene 1: Decorations

Saturday 2nd January, 1993, Montrose Street, Forgewood, Motherwell, Scotland, 12:30 p.m.

Eldo, *sprawled out in his double bed*, let out a groan, as he pulled a pillow over his head at the competing sounds of the phone ringing in the hall, and the dogs barking outside his bedroom window. Through the din, he picked up on the voices of his wife and daughter, as they made their way into the close. Linda, Eldo's wife, pushed the key into the lock and opened the door, allowing Chloe, her six-year-old daughter, to run ahead of her, down the hall.

'Daddy! Daddy!' she cried out, running into the bedroom, and climbing on to the bed.

Eldo pretended to be asleep. 'Daddy, Daddy, wake up!' she persisted, trying her best to shake her father's dead weight.

Unexpectedly, Eldo quickly swung round and grabbed her by the waist, pulling her close and nuzzling her neck, growling like a dog, causing Chloe to tee hee with laughter.

Smiling, Eldo, continued to hold her and tickled her ribs, as she tried to wrestle free, giggling in hysterics.

'I'll get the phone!' Linda said sarcastically, picking up the handset from its fixing on the wall.

'Hello?'

'Hiya, Linda, it's me, Michelle. How are you getting on? And how's yer mam?'

'Aye, fine, Michelle, thanks, that's me just in the door this minute. *Aye*, she's doing a lot better thank God. She'll be back on her feet and out and about in a couple of days, I think.'

'That's great, Linda, glad to hear it.'

'Aye, it's good to see her picking up. Chloe kept her going. *Huh*, that wean, I'll tell ye, she's never stopped playing with that nurse's set that you and Gary gave her for her Christmas. She absolutely loves it! That's aw she keeps saying, '*When I'll be a nurse like Aunty Shelly, I'll help her with the sick people. And we'll make them better.*'

'Aw, the wee soul.'

'I don't think she's had that nurse's apron off once! *Huh*, and she's walking about with the plastic stethoscope around her neck, and then taking the toy thermometer out her nurse's case and sticking it in everybody's mouth *every five minutes*! I think ma poor mammy was glad to see the back a' us this morning. *God*, she'll probably be sleeping it off as we speak, the poor soul. *Oh*, and how did yer night go last night? *Was it good?*'

'Aye, it went well, Linda, *too good*! *Pfft*, I've been up aw night and no' slept. Karen has just left about ten minutes ago.'

'Oh, oh sounds like you're in for a sore one the day, lady!'

'*God*, tell me aboot it! I'm still oot it the noo. In fact, that's what I'm phonin' aboot Linda. I'm on tae ask you if you could do me a massive, if you could help me oot.'

'Aw aye, here we go,' Linda replied, teasing her friend, before thinking better of it. 'I'm only joking! *Sorry*, I know you'll be suffering. Whit is it?'

'I think ma mam's a bit pissed off with me the noo. She was watching wee Kelly last night and she's brought her back this morning *aboot an hour ago* and then left straight away. I was hoping she'd watch her for the weekend. I've no' mentioned to Gary yet *but* I was hoping to surprise him by taking him out for a meal tonight. It's ees birthday on Wednesday but I'm back on nightshift from Monday.'

'Look, it's no bother I'm here anyway and won't be going anywhere. Bring Kelly up the now if ye want. Then you and Gary can get a few hours' sleep, and go out later.'

'Thanks, Linda, yer a star!'

'No bother, I'll see ye when you come up.'

'See ye soon, Linda, cheerio.'

'See ye, Michelle, cheerio.'

Linda hung the phone back on its fixing on the wall, and walked into the bedroom, removing her coat, and throwing it on to the bottom of the bed.

'Mammy! Daddy's not well, but I'm going to make him better,' Chloe said, taking a toy thermometer out of her dad's mouth, and pressing the plastic stethoscope against his bare chest.

'Good luck wi' that one, darling,' Linda said. 'I'm sure it'll be a scientific breakthrough.'

'Ha, ha, yer mammy's very funny isn't she, darling?' Eldo said, smiling at Linda, who was now crawling on to the bed to embrace her husband.

'God, you stink!' she said, drawing her head back to look at him, 'I don't know what's the worst: the smell of the smoke or... what have you been doing?'

'Don't even ask,' Eldo replied. 'You've no idea!' he exclaimed in relief; knowing that he was once again safe and sound back at home, with his family around him.

'That good, eh?' Linda smiled, kissing him on the lips.

'Aye! Tremendous! Nightmare a' nightmares disnae even come close. Quick, talk aboot something else. I'm still raw at the thought a' it.'

Linda sniggered at her husband's discomfort. 'Naw, tell me? It sounds interesting.'

'Please, darling, I'll tell ye later. Just pray ma mind disnae snap in the meantime.'

'Huh, whit mind?'

'Please, darling, don't. Come oan under the covers. I'm no' well. Nurse Chloe, tell yer mammy to be nice to yer sick patient.'

'Be nice, Mammy,' Chloe said, as she opened her white plastic medic's case.

'Hell, mend ye! It's aw self-inflicted!' Linda retorted.

'Don't be like that, darling. Can ye no' see yer poor loving husband's in need of some TLC. C'mon in under the covers. Me, you and the wean'll get a long lie, and then we'll aw get up later oan and watch a film or something.'

'We cannae, Michelle's bringing Kelly round for me tae babysit and I want to get this house tidied and get they stinking clothes a' yours oot a' this room and washed!'

Eldo let out a groan, and closed his eyes at being reminded, once again, of his earlier escapade.

Linda pushed herself from her husband, and, taking a pillow in her hands, sniggered as she dropped it on to his face, covering it. 'Right, c'mon, Chloe,' she said, as she sat on the edge of the bed, 'you told Mummy that you'd help to tidy up the living room today and that you'd put the toys that Santa brought ye into your own room, remember?'

'Mum, but Kelly's coming to play.'

'Yes, and yees can play in your own room. Mummy's to take the decorations down today.'

Linda stood up and walked round the bed, starting to pick up Eldo's dirty clothes from the floor.

'Go and help Mummy, darling. That's a good girl,' Eldo said, before smiling to his wife and sticking his tongue out at her. 'And close the door quietly behind yees like good girls.'

'Don't push it, boyo,' Linda replied, smiling, as she flicked two fingers up to him.

'*Darling! Now, now!* Is that any way to behave in front of our beloved child?'

Linda laughed as she threw the clothes to the floor and leapt on to the bed.

Eldo cried out as he pulled the quilt over his head, cowering and laughing, as Linda tried to punch his thighs, hoping to give him at least one dead leg.

Eldo laughed at her feeble attempts. 'Ow, ow, stoap it. Ow, ow.'

'And let that be a lesson tae ye *fool*,' Linda told him, as she stopped to catch her breath, rolling off the bed, and standing up.

Eldo peeked over the quilt, happy to see his wife, once again, picking his clothes from the floor. 'Love yoooo,' he said, sheepishly, puckering his lips and making a smooching sound, causing Linda to turn and smile at his foolishness.

Linda left the bedroom, and closed the door and walked into the living room to find Chloe fixing her tiny white nurse's hat on her head. 'Mammy, is the red cross straight?'

'Yes, it's perfect, sweetheart,' she replied, walking into the kitchen.

Linda put Eldo's clothes into the washing machine, and put his wet, wax cotton jacket on the worktop. *He'll take care of washing that one*, she thought.

Taking the soap powder from the cupboard under the sink, she poured some into the tray in the machine and started the cycle. She then turned on the kettle and walked back into the living room, wondering where to begin.

'Okay, Chloe, let's start moving the toys into your room, so Mummy can get space to take down the decorations.'

The dogs started to bark outside, as the chimes of the ice-cream van came within earshot.

'Mammy, can Ah get sweets from the tally-van, with the money ma Granny gave me?'

'You've got plenty sweets, Chloe. Look at yer selection boxes, not even opened.'

'Ah know, Mammy, but I want to get mix-ups and some juice for me and Kelly.'

Linda remembered that she needed cigarettes. 'Come oan then, quick, put yer jacket on.'

Linda collected her own jacket from the bedroom, and noticed that Eldo was *now* sleeping soundly.

Closing the bedroom door quietly on the way out, she found Chloe already waiting at the front door.

Linda reached over her daughter, and turned the latch, opening the door.

When they made their way outside, she put her key back into the lock and turned it, closing and locking the door gently.

Outside the front of the close, they walked out into the street, and headed for the ice-cream van. It was parked at the side of the road, three blocks down.

'Mammy! There's Aunty Shell and wee Kelly coming!'

'So it is, darlin'.' As they approached each other, Linda sniggered. 'You look like a burst couch,' she said to Michelle.

'Huh and don't Ah feel like one,' Michelle laughed. '*Here*, I got some bacon and some rolls for yees from the shops on the way up. Thanks again for taking the wee one for me, Linda.'

Linda took the carrier bag from her friend. 'Thanks, Michelle, it's no bother. I'm just rushing to catch this van the noo, for some fags.'

'Aw listen, Linda, I don't mean to be a nightmare, but is it awright if Ah get some Temazepam so I can get a few hours' sleep when I get back doon the road?'

Linda pulled the keys to the flat from her coat pocket. 'Aye, here,' she said, handing them to Michelle. 'The mortise isn't locked. It's just on the latch. The pills are in the speaker at the side a' the couch, the one near the fireplace. Just get them yersell. Eddie's out for the count, in bed.'

'Thanks, Linda,' Michelle said. 'I'll no' be long. *Here*, give me that bag and I'll put it in the kitchen for ye.'

'Thanks, Michelle,' Linda replied, handing over the shopping. 'Alright, Kelly, are ye coming tae the van wi' me and Chloe, and we'll get some sweeties?' Linda asked, taking four-year-old Kelly by the hand.

Kelly smiled at Chloe and nodded.

On the way to the ice-cream van, the police vehicle approached and slowly passed Linda and the children. Linda pretended to take no notice and continued on her way, holding the children's hands, then turned casually, following it with a glance as it passed Michelle, who was heading into the close.

The driver of the ice-cream van revved its engine, and the last customer was already walking away. Linda called out to the young man: '*Sammy*! Tell him to wait.'

Sammy turned and walked back to the van, leaning over the counter and calling in to inform the driver.

Turning once more from the ice-cream van, Sammy waved to Linda. 'It's okay, take yer time, he's waiting. Watch the pavements. They're bad wi' ice there.'

'Thanks, Sammy.'

Reaching the ice-cream van, Linda and the children, were met by John, who stood behind the counter, waiting. 'Hi, Linda, hi, Chloe, hi, Kelly. What can I do yees for today?' he said, smiling.

'Hi, John, thanks for waiting. Can I have twenty Regal King Size, please? And what are yees wanting, Chloe?' she said, turning to the children.

'Let me see, Mammy,' Chloe replied, raising her arms up to her Mum.

'You'll have to be quick, darling, it's very cold and wee Kelly's waiting,' Linda told her, as she took her up in her arms.

'Can I have two ten pence mix-ups, John, please, and two wee bottles a' Fanta?'

'No bother, ma wee darling, is that you now?' John asked as he gathered the order, and placed it on the counter.

'Yes, John. Thank you,' Chloe said, causing her mum to smile.

'*Okay*! Since you and Kelly are my very, very, very, very, *very bestest customers, ever*! Here's two Lucky Bags for yees. *Is that okay*?'

'Mammy!' Chloe exclaimed, full of excitement, as she took the gifts from John.

'Thanks, that's nice a' ye, John,' Linda said, lowering Chloe to stand beside Kelly.

'No bother, Linda, how are yees all getting on, *awright*?'

'Aye, we're doing fine, John, thanks,' Linda replied, as she handed John a ten-pound note, 'and what aboot yersells? You and Sheila, is it going okay wi' the van?'

'Aye, no' bad, Linda, ye always get chancers right enough, *other vans*, comin' intae the scheme tae try and steal the business fae ye, *but* the people here have been good with us, *people like yersell*. Most of them wait until me or Sheila come round before they come out and buy what they're wanting. After a wee while, the guys in the other ice-cream vans get fed up, and bail oot.'

'That's good, John,' Linda said, taking her change, the cigarettes, the sweets and the small bottles of fizzy orange. 'I hope it's a good year for yees.'

'Aye, thanks Linda and yersells tae.'

'Aye, here's hopin,' *Right*, we'll get away up this road and get back in the hoose, John. See ye later.'

'See ye, Linda, thanks, *see ye, Chloe, see ye, Kelly, bye, bye*,' John said, waving to the children.

'Bye, bye, John, thanks for our Lucky Bags,' Chloe said.

'Bye, bye,' Kelly added.

Turning from the van, Linda handed Chloe the mix-ups and the drinks, and helped her daughter to put them into her jacket pockets. For a second, Linda thought of taking little Kelly and carrying her in her arms, but the pavements were still treacherous with patches of ice. Instead, she again took each child by the hand, and slowly and carefully, walked back with them.

As they neared the close, Michelle, stepped out of the entrance and made her way towards them.

Looking beyond Michelle, Linda saw the police car turning from Breadalbane Crescent, into Montrose Street. Once again, the car slowly passed Michelle and made its way past Linda and the children.

Linda walked with her head down, trying to engage Chloe and Kelly in conversation.

She reached Michelle. 'Where is it now?'

'It's just turning right on to Dalriada. Hopefully that'll be it heading back out the scheme. Right, I'll get down the road, Linda. Ah got they pills, but I couldn't manage to force the cover on to the back of the speaker. I've left it at the fireplace for ye tae sort when ye get in. Sorry. I hope that's okay.'

Linda took the keys from Michelle. 'No bother, Michelle. It's hard tae get the cover on that speaker. Look, hurry up and get yersell home, and I'll see ye the morra.'

'Thanks, Linda. Is five o'clock tomorrow okay?'

'Aye, that's fine, Michelle.'

'Thanks, Linda,' Michelle said, as she crouched down to Kelly, her young daughter. 'Okay, ma wee honey, Aunty Linda's goin' to take you to her house so you and Chloe can play together, like we said, and then tomorrow, Chloe can come to play with you in our house, isn't that right?'

'Uh-huh,' Kelly replied.

'Give Mummy a kiss and you'll be a good girl, won't ye?'

Kelly nodded at her Mum. Michelle kissed her daughter on the cheek and gave her a cuddle. 'Love you, Kelly.'

'Love ye, Mammy.'

Michelle turned to Chloe, and held her arms out.

Chloe ran into Michelle's outstretched arms, almost causing Michelle to lose her balance, and making Linda and Michelle laugh.

Michelle smiled as she rocked Chloe from side to side in her arms. 'Love you, Chloe,' she said, kissing the child on her left cheek, before releasing her. 'You'll look after yer wee sister, Kelly, won't you?'

'Yes, Aunty Shell.'

'That's a good girl, and I'll see you tomorrow, and bring you down to our bit, *okay*?'

'Yes, Aunty Shell.'

'Okay,' Michelle said, standing up.

Linda and Michelle stepped towards each other. 'See ye, Linda.'

'See ye, Michelle.' They gave each other a hug and a kiss on the cheek before parting.

As Michelle walked away from the group, she continued to wave to Linda, Chloe and Kelly, until they had reached the entrance, and walked into the close.

As they entered the close, the dogs hurried in after them. *Fredo*, running around their feet, was barking excitedly. 'Keep the dogs out of the house while Mammy's tidying, darling we'll let them in later.'

Linda told Chloe, as they approached the door to the flat.

As Linda put the key in the latch and turned it in the lock, opening the door, the telephone was on its fourth ring. Letting the children go in ahead of her, Linda closed the door and made for the phone, lifting the handset from its fixing on the wall.

'Hello?'

'Hello, is that you, Linda? It's Phil Murray, here. How are you getting on?'

'Hi, Phil, not bad, thanks. How's yersell?'

'*Aye, okay, Linda, thanks I was down last night and Eldo was telling me you were up at your Mam's. How's she doing now?*'

'Aye, she's a lot better, Phil, thanks, she'll be okay.'

'*That's good, Linda, and what aboot that man a' yours, is he in?*'

'Aye, ees in, Phil, *but* you'll be lucky to get him. I think he only got into the house a couple of hours ago. He was in bed, wakened, when me and the wean got in *at the back of twelve*, but he's now sound asleep.'

'I'm sorry to be a pest, Linda, but could you see if you can wake him, please? I really need to talk to him about something.'

'Okay I'll try.'

'Thanks, Linda.'

Linda let the phone hang on its cable; the handset almost touching floor.

Opening the door, she walked into the bedroom, and started shaking her husband. 'Eddie, Eddie! That's Phil Murray on the phone.'

Eldo groaned. 'Can ye no' tell him I'm sleeping hen, and that I'll phone him later?'

'I already said that, but he said he wants to talk to ye.'

'Can ye take a message for me, hen? Ma heid's burstin'.'

'You're a nightmare!' she told him, and turned and walked out of the room, leaving the door open.

Linda lifted the handset by its cable. 'He's still a bit knackered, Phil, and he's asked if ye can leave a message, and he'll phone ye later.'

'Awright, sorry aboot that, Linda. Can ye tell him I'll be down about six o'clock? And can ye tell him that I'll be taking aw the pills wi' me, and to have them ready to go? There should be twelve tubs. I've got a guy in the toon who's looking to take the lot aff me.'

'No bother, Phil, I'll let him know. If he's not up in a few hours, I'll wake him and make sure he has the stuff ready for ye coming down.'

'Thanks, Linda, that'd be great, I'll see ye later.'

'See ye later, Phil. Oh, and Phil… '

'Aye?'

'There's been a polis motor slowing down as it's been passing the house twice in the last hour, just to let ye know.'

'Thanks for that, Linda, I'll keep an eye oot for them when I'm coming down. I'll maybe park the car up on the main road and walk down and come into the close through the back way.'

'Okay, Phil, see ye later.'

'Thanks again, Linda, see ye after, cheerio.'

'Cheerio, Phil, bye.'

Linda hung the phone on its fixing, and walked back into the bedroom.

'What was he saying?' Eldo asked.

'He said he's coming down at six and has asked if ye can get aw the pills ready. He said there should be twelve tubs, and that somebody in Glasgow wants to take the lot. He must be taking them in there tonight.'

'That's good. I'll get a few hours' sleep, and then I'll get up and get them ready for him,' Eldo replied. 'Listen, I was going say to ye, hen, maybe I'll no' keep any more pills for him. Whit dae ye think? We've managed to get Christmas and the New Year over wi'. Do ye think we'll be awright tae a get a job?'

'Aye, we'll be fine. We'll manage, Eddie! It was good we had some money to get things for Christmas, but I don't feel good aboot having stuff like that in the hoose. It's too risky. You could end up getting the jail, and the polis have been slowing down as they've been driving past the hoose.'

'Ye're joking!'

'Naw I'm no'. I saw them doing it twice today when I was out at the ice-cream van wi' the weans.'

'Aye?' Eldo asked, trying to concentrate, 'just another few hours. When Phil comes down, I'll tell him that that's it, no more, that he'll have tae get somewhere else tae stash them.'

'That's good, Eddie. It's for the best. Right, I'll away in and get started on the decorations.'

'See ye, darling,' Eldo said, pushing his neck out and puckering his lips in anticipation. Linda laughed at the stupid face he was pulling and made her own as she bent down to kiss him. Leaving the bedroom, she closed the door and turned to find Chloe holding a doll against her chest with her left hand, her white plastic medic's case in her right. Kelly walked beside her as they made their way into Chloe's bedroom.

'Good girls!' Linda told them. 'Is that all the toys from Santa in your room now, Chloe?'

'Yes, Mammy.'

'Well done, and are yees going to play in your room until Mummy finishes taking down the decorations?'

'Uh-huh.'

'Okay, that's good. We'll watch a film when Mummy's finished and then yees can help Mummy make the dinner, okay?'

'Yeah!' Chloe cheered, turning to face her Mum. 'Can me and Kelly make the custard, Mammy?'

'We'll see,' Linda smiled, heading up the hall, to the cupboard, near the front door.

Opening the cupboard door, Linda checked the electricity meter. There was less than three pounds credit left. It'd last another day, she thought, as she started to remove the empty boxes that had held the Christmas decorations.

Scene 2: A few hours

Entering the living room, Linda tried to clear her throat and realised that she was feeling a bit flushed; she was running a temperature. She sighed as she put the boxes on the couch, and entered the kitchen, opening a cupboard door, above the worktop.

She found, and removed, the bottle of Benylin cough syrup that she had used to treat Chloe the week before. Chloe was the first to get the flu and then Linda's mum. Linda hoped she wouldn't be next, as she opened the bottle and took a swig.

Walking back into the living room, on the floor, facing her, Linda noticed the open hi-fi speaker, its back cover resting against the fireplace wall, just as Michelle had said.

Kneeling down beside it, Linda quickly looked over each of the six large white tubs, standing in two columns of three. The lids were firmly fixed in place.

Taking the cover for the back of the speaker, she tried to force it into position.

After a few attempts, she was successful and turned the speaker round to sit in its proper position, facing out, into the living room.

Getting to her feet, she started gathering the Christmas cards that were spread out on top of the mantelpiece.

Linda smiled as she picked some at random, and re-read them. Some of the cards were old, from previous years, and some were new.

That's it for another year, she thought, as she began placing them into one of the cardboard boxes resting on the couch.

BOOK SEVEN: RIPPLES

18

Scene 1: In the wake

Saturday 2nd January, 1993, Bellshill Road, Forgewood, Motherwell, Scotland, 4:50 p.m.

As the telephone rang in the hall, John folded the newspaper, and threw it on to the coffee table, before pushing himself out from his chair in the living room. Entering the hall, he turned on the light, and answered the phone.

'Hello?'

'Hello, John, is that you?' asked the softly spoken Englishman, in a gentle, southern accent.

'Aye, it's me. Is that you, Dom Leonard?'

Immediately realising who he was speaking with, a feeling of dread welled up inside John but he fought his initial instinct. 'Happy New Year to ye, Dom.'

Dom Leonard didn't return with the customary greeting. 'Thanks, John.'

This response and the silence told John their own story. Now he was forced to be quiet.

'John, I'm afraid I've got some terrible news for you and the family.'

John found himself having to sit down on the seat attached to the small phone table. 'Dear God save us, Paul!'

'Yes, John. I'm very sorry. He's in a very bad way. I'm very sorry, but it's not looking good at all.'

'Bring him home, Dom Leonard. Bring him home! I'll bring the money up tae ye the now. Get him on a flight. I'll get the money fae somewhere. We'll bring it up tae ye the now. Andrew's got the car. He can drive us up to see ye right away.'

'I'm sorry I've had to tell you this over the phone, John. I'd rather have come through to Motherwell to see you and Agnes. And I will, of course, as soon as I know more. We'll definitely bring him home for you as soon as we can.'

John was quiet as Dom Leonard continued. 'I know you'll be aware that there was a presidential election in Kenya last week?'

'Aye, we've been waiting on news for months, Dom Leonard.'

'Yes, and I can only apologise about that too, John. I've only, within the last hour, had a brief update from one of our Brothers, a Brother David, who took another of our Brothers to a hospital in Nairobi.'

John remained silent, letting Dom Leonard continue.

'Apparently, there have been pockets of violence in the South Rift Valley region for a number of months, and the telephone lines in the area around Kipkelion were brought down. Brother David was telling me about our sick Brother, Dom Stephen, who is terminally ill. He explained that when they left the monastery yesterday to travel to the hospital, they were so concerned for the safety of those that they had left behind that they travelled to the nearest administration police station, in a town two hours' drive away, to raise the alarm. David said that when they reached the station, they expressed their fears to the officer in charge and left, only after receiving assurances that the officer would take action by sending a *division* up to the monastery, to check the situation.'

John sat motionless in full concentration as Dom Leonard continued.

'It turns out our Brothers' worst fears were realised, John. I'm just off the phone to the police officer who was in charge of the operation. He told me that when they reached the monastery, part of it was already burning and other parts were being ransacked.

'However, something much worse, awaited them. Apparently the Brothers had been sheltering people who had been chased from their homes during the build-up to the elections, and it seems that the indigenous tribesmen had had enough. From what I've been told, it seems that Paul and the Brothers had tried to escape into the nearby forest with those they had been sheltering, but were caught, out in the open.

'Information is still sketchy, but it seems it was merciless: sixteen of our Brothers were murdered, along with twenty-two civilians, with only Paul and another civilian still alive, but critical in hospital.'

John rested the phone on his thigh and wiped the tears from his eyes with his left hand.

'John, I'm terribly sorry. John, are you there? *John?*'

John picked up the phone. 'Aye, I'm here, Dom Leonard.'

'I'm sorry I don't have any more information, John, but as soon as I hear more, I'll call immediately. I'm trying to get the number for the hospital that Paul's in and I'll call you when I get it. We're praying that they pull through.'

'Okay, Dom Leonard, thanks I'll get off the phone and let you get back to it.'

'I'm really sorry, John. I'll call you as soon as I speak to the hospital. God Bless.'

John struggled to respond. 'Thanks, Dom.'

John put the phone down, and sat in silence, praying that God would return his son alive. How could he tell this to Agnes, he thought?

John picked the phone up again and started to dial his daughter Margaret's number, only to put it back down. He couldn't tell them that over the phone. He'd wait until he saw them. John looked at his watch. Margaret would be driving Agnes back home shortly.

He picked up the phone once more and dialled Andrew's number.

John listened as the phone rang four times, before it was finally answered.

'Hello.'

'Hello, Andrew?'

'Alright, Da. How are ye getting on?'

'No' too good, Andrew, son. Can ye come down for a wee while? I need to talk tae ye.'

'Aye, nae bother, I'll be doon right now.'

'Thanks, son,' John replied, sniffling through the tears.

'Da, are ye alright? Whit's wrang? You've got me worried.'

'It's Paul. He's in a bad way, Andrew.'

Andrew cursed. 'I'll be down right now.'

'Thanks, son. Yer mam disnae know yet. She'll be back home in a wee while with Margaret. It would be good if you could be here tae help me, son.'

'Aye, nae bother, Da. I'll be doon in the next five minutes.'

'Watch yersell on they icy roads, Andrew. Don't be driving fast.'

'I'll be awright, Da, don't worry see ye soon, cheerio.'

'Cheerio, son.'

Scene 2: Held

Saturday 2nd January, 1993, Kylemore Crescent, Forgewood, Motherwell, Scotland, 5:30 p.m.

The dim, yellow glow from the streetlights seeped in through the white roller blind of Ninian's window, finally perishing in the darkness of the bedroom. In his bed, Ninian, lay naked, face-down, the left side of his head resting on a pillow. Despite the coldness of the room, his duvet lay in a crumpled heap, having been pushed to the side.

Disturbed by something, Ninian's eyes, suddenly sprang open.

The room was ice cold. Breathing out, he could see his breath pass from him and with that he became fully awake, fully alert to the evil that he now sensed within the room.

Out of the shadows, the boy slowly emerged, his head lowered.

Ninian watched as the boy walked up by the side of the bed. Suddenly, the boy scrambled up on to the dressing table, and, upwards still on to the wall. Almost at the ceiling, he turned his head to look down on Ninian. The light glinted off the blackness of his eyes and his mouth raced in silent conversation, filling Ninian's mind with a cacophony of low, demonic bellows.

Making to rise from the bed to escape, Ninian found that he was unable to move. He willed every fibre and sinew to respond, but he was trapped.

His body was being *held*, face-down, by something unseen. An overpowering evil was pinning his arms and legs.

Unable to scream out, Ninian screamed within. The entity that held him seemed to be trying something. It was pushing itself down on to him. It was only then that Ninian realised what it was trying to do. It was trying to rape him.

In his mind, Ninian cried out: *Dear God, help me! Don't let this happen. Jesus! Pleeeease! Stop this!*

In that moment, the attack stopped.

Ninian leapt from the bed and fell against the dressing table, scurrying along the floor to the doorway

Standing up, he turned to look at his bed. Nothing. Around his room. Nothing. He turned on the light to confirm. Nothing. The boy was gone and there was no sign of anything untoward within the room.

Ninian quickly grabbed clothes from the wardrobe and hurried into the living room.

He threw on his clothes and rushed out of the house. He'd call Karen from the phone box and ask if he could stay at her place for the night.

Scene 3: Darkness

Saturday 2nd January, 1993, Montrose Street, Forgewood, Motherwell, Scotland, 6:10 p.m.

In darkness, Eldo woke to the sound of the letterbox being rapped. He looked at the red light from the digital alarm clock on his bedside cabinet, and pushed himself from the bed. Adjusting his boxer shorts, he opened the door, and walked out of the bedroom.

Reaching the front door, he turned the latch and pushed down on the handle. Pulling the door open, he found, Phil Murray, holding two rucksacks.

'Awright, Eldo. Did ye get ma message?'

'Aye, Ah did, Phil. C'mon in.'

Eldo flicked on the light switch, and walked down the hall, opening the living room door. The living room was in darkness, with Linda, asleep, on an armchair.

Eldo turned on the light as they entered.

'Have a seat the noo, Phil, and I'll get them for ye.'

'Cheers, Eldo.'

Linda stirred in the chair and woke up, stretching her arms out with a yawn. '*God*, is that the time?' she said, looking at the clock on the mantelpiece.

'Aye, were you sleeping for long, hen?' Eldo asked.

'Naw, I don't think so. I'm no' sure. I never slept much last night at ma mam's. God, I remember noo, I took some a' that Benylin earlier. It must've knocked me out,' she said, rubbing her eyes.

'Aye, it can make ye right drowsy that stuff,' Phil said.

Eldo had already removed the white plastic containers from the first speaker, and was in the process of removing the others from the speaker at the fireplace.

When all of the tubs were resting on the living room floor, Eldo walked into the kitchen and returned with a damp dishcloth. He began wiping down each container, removing any prints, before placing them *inside* Phil's rucksacks.

'Did ye see any polis on the way in Phil?' Eldo asked.

'Naw, Linda was telling me aboot that on the phone earlier, so I came in the back way, just in case. I've left the motor up on the main road.'

'That's good,' Eldo replied. 'You've helped us oot, Phil, and I don't know how to put this tae ye, but we were thinking, that'll dae us. That this'll be the last lot that we can keep for ye, mate. I hope yer no' offended, but it's just getting a bit risky. We got a pull last night as well, up at the level crossing, but they never searched us, which we thought was a bit unusual.'

'Aye?' Phil asked, raising his eyebrows. 'Listen, it's nae bother, Eldo. I understand totally. And, ye know, if this guy that's wanting them tonight turns oot to be okay, I'll be able tae offload the pills tae him, as soon as I get them, and I'll no' need tae keep them hanging anywhere.'

'That's even better for ye then, Phil.'

'Aye, hopefully, Eldo, and thanks for keeping them for me. Yees've done me a turn.'

'Aye, nae bother. You done us a turn tae,' Eldo replied. 'By the way, you don't need to give us anymore dough. We used some a' the pills ourselves, about fifty, I think: twenty-five Temazepam and twenty-five Palfium.'

'Nae bother, Eldo. Thanks for letting me know. This guy and 'es pals will want tae count them, no doubt.'

Linda rose from the chair and entered the kitchen, turning on the light. She sniffled as she turned the switch on the kettle. 'Are yees wanting a cup of tea?'

'Naw thanks, Linda, I better get moving,' Phil said, zipping up the second rucksack, and grabbing the two of them by their straps.

'Aye, I'll take one, hen,' Eldo answered.

'Right, Eldo, I'll see ye again. Thanks for hawdin' these for me,' Phil said, raising the rucksacks slightly.

'Ye're sound, Phil, nae bother.'

As they walked down the hall to the front door, Phil took a twenty-pound note from his pocket and handed to Eldo. 'Here,' he said quietly.

'I'm awright, Phil, honest.'

'Look, I'm gonnae make a few quid aff a' these. They junkies in the toon go mad for this kit. Here, come oan, take it, it's only a score. If I had mair oan me, I'd give ye it.'

Eldo took the money. 'Cheers, Phil.'

'Nae bother.'

Eldo opened the door to let Phil out. 'Mind and watch what yer doin' in there, Phil. Some a' they cunts in the toon think they're wide. Too wide for their ain fuckin' good! Ye're no' goin' in there yersell, are ye?'

With this question, it was as if Eldo had picked Phil up, *bodily*, and thrown him naked, into an ice-cold bath. The sudden realisation actually frightened Phil, and made him turn to Eldo, and smile. 'Yer a good cunt, Eldo, d'ye know that?' Phil said, offering Eldo his right hand.

Eldo smiled. 'Ye're no bad yersell,' he replied, shaking Phil's hand. He watched as Phil left the close via the back entrance.

Before he had a chance to close the door, his two dogs hurried past him, and entered the hall, causing him to smile.

Closing the door, he followed them into the living room.

'How ye doin', darling, are ye awright?' he asked Linda. 'Ye don't look too well.'

'Ah think I'm getting that flu.'

'That's a nightmare,' he said, walking over and giving her a cuddle; rubbing her back with the palm of his right hand.

'Thanks,' Linda replied, giving him a kiss on his right cheek.

Releasing her, Eldo smiled as he handed her the twenty pounds that Phil had given him.

'Where did ye get that?'

'Phil gave me it as he was leaving.'

'Aw, that's great. That'll get us some electricity,' she said, as she looked at Eldo, who had now turned his attention to the hi-fi speaker, near the fireplace.

'What is it?' Linda asked.

'Aw, nothing. I'm no' sure. I had a bag a' pills in that one, separate fae the tubs. I must've dished them oot last night tae Gary and Ninian.'

'How many was in it?'

'Aboot fifty, I think: twenty-five and twenty-five.'

'Yees couldnae have taken aw a' them?'

'I know, that's what I was thinking. There's no way. We already had plenty a' drink as well.'

'Saying that, Michelle was in earlier, when I was at the ice-cream van wi' the weans. Maybe she's took them, or maybe she put them into one a' the tubs when she had finished taking some.'

'Aye, maybe, hen. Where are the weans anyway?'

'They're in the room playing.'

'They're awfy quiet, are they no'?'

Linda looked up at her husband, and immediately, the two of them knew what the other was thinking.

Linda rushed into the hall. She opened Chloe's bedroom door, but it would only open so far. Something was preventing her from opening it further. The room was in total darkness.

'Chloe, it's yer mammy. Open the door, hen.'

Chloe didn't answer.

Eldo stepped forward, gently forcing the door, opening it further. He flicked the switch on the wall, turning on the light in the room. Squeezing his head through the space, he looked in.

The two children were sprawled out on the floor, unconscious. Kelly's body was blocking the door and Chloe was slumped over her plastic medic's case. The empty polythene bag that had contained the pills lay on the rug, between them.

Eldo began to whimper. 'Naw, naw, naw.'

Linda's look of horror turned to one of sheer panic. 'What is it? What is it?' she screamed. She knew, but there was no way she was letting it sink in.

Eldo ran to the front door, pulled it open and rushed out into the close and out of the back exit.

He broke Chloe's bedroom window with his elbow and reached in, opening the window by the handle, on the inside.

Climbing in, he clambered over the chest of drawers, knocking over toy figures as he dropped to the floor to kneel down beside Chloe.

'Wake up, darlin'. It's yer daddy. Wake up, sweetheart.'

Picking Chloe from the floor, he carried her gently and laid her across her single bed, before quickly turning to Kelly.

He lifted the child from the doorway. It was as though she weighed a ton in weight. Eldo's legs were buckling. 'Please, please, please. Naw. Naw. '

Linda was squealing as she entered the room, tears streaming down her face.

'Phone an ambulance, hen,' Eldo told her, as he laid Kelly on the bed beside Chloe.

Linda couldn't function. In her agony, she let out an almighty cry and fell to her knees.

Crawling helplessly to the children, she lay over their bodies wailing.

Eldo rushed from the room and picking up the phone, dialled 999.

BOOK EIGHT: SEARING

19

Scene 1: Pain

Saturday 2nd January, 1993, Fife Drive, Forgewood, Motherwell, Scotland, 6:40 p.m.

In the bathroom, fully dressed, Gary, clapped some aftershave on to his face and neck as he looked into the mirror that rested on the windowsill. Moving in closer, he put the fingers of both hands on to his cheek bones, and pulled down – *pish holes in the snow*, he thought. Moving from the bathroom, he walked into the hall and turned left, entering the living room.

Michelle, sitting on the edge of the couch, was bent over, snorting one of the two lines of cocaine that she had prepared for herself.

'Michelle, whit are ye doin'?' Gary asked, showing his annoyance.

Michelle tilted her head back, sniffed and pinched her nose. 'What?'

Gary shook his head. 'Nothing. Forget it.'

'What's wrang wi' you?'

'What's wrang? You got me up. You invited me out for a meal, and now you're firing that gear up yer beak!'

'And whit aboot it?' Michelle answered.

'Nothing. Just forget it! Have ye phoned the taxi?'

'Aye, I've phoned it, Gary. Whit's wrang wi' ye?'

Gary rubbed the palms of his hands up and down both sides of his face. 'Och I'm sorry. I'm just a bit tired. It's just when you said dinner, hen, I don't want to go up here and be sitting eating on my own cos you're right oot yer box and don't have an appetite.'

'I won't, darling, I promise. It's only a couple a' lines.'

Gary knew she was already high as a kite, but thought better of pushing her any further. 'Okay, I'll go and stick ma jacket on.'

'You look lovely, darling,' Michelle said to him.

Gary turned back from the hall, feeling guilty. He hadn't commented on Michelle's new outfit. 'I'm sorry, hen. I love ye,' he said, walking over to her and bending down to kiss her forehead. 'You look gorgeous and your outfit's beautiful. I'm a lucky man,' he said softly, as he kissed her once more.

Michelle stood up so he could see her properly. 'Is it okay? It's not too much, is it?' she said, turning side on.

'No, you look amazing, hen,' he said admiring her in her new outfit, which consisted of black leather platform boots that reached up to her knees, a ruffled black lace mini-skirt, and a dark green Goth styled corset made of silk, visible underneath the black lace of a floral blouse.

'We'll just go for a meal and come back home and have a quiet night together, *how's that?*' she told him, taking hold of him round the waist and pushing up on her tiptoes to kiss him.

'Are you sure?' he said, knowing that any time they went out together, Michelle wanted to party.

'Uh-huh. We've already had a few heavy nights.'

Gary smiled. 'Are you sure you're sure? We know what happens, when we get out there and the drink and the drugs and the blah blah blah...'

Michelle laughed. 'Am I that predictable, sweetheart?' She kissed him again.

'Did I say that now, darling?' Gary replied, joining in with her laughter. 'Right, I'll go and get ma jacket while you finish powdering your nose, dear!'

'Be sweet, honey,' Michelle said, grinning as she sat back down, picking up the rolled-up note that lay beside her next line of white powder.

Gary walked into the bedroom, and opening the door to *his* side of the wardrobe, took out his black velvet, Goth styled coat. Examining it closely, front and back, he removed it from the coat hanger, and pulled it on over his white frilled shirt.

He walked over to the full-length mirror and bent down, adjusting the hang of his black denims, partly covering the laces of his black leather ankle boots.

Standing up, he gave a reluctant smile, slid his hands over and down his long black hair and let out a groan. He turned and headed for the door, switching off the light, on his way out.

As he walked into the living room, outside in the street the horn of the taxi sounded. Reaching the veranda door, Gary opened it, and signalled down to the driver with a thumbs-up.

'Right, is that us?' he said to Michelle, who was pulling on her black leather coat.

'Yep, that's me, honeee!'

Turning out the lights, they left the flat and locked the door.

Reaching the taxi, Gary opened the door behind the front passenger seat for his wife, then walked round the back of the vehicle to the other side, opened the door and climbed in.

'Alright, Gary!'

'Alright, Mark, it's yersell. How's things?'

'Fine, mate. Where are yees off tae the night?'

'*Aw*, just oot for something to eat, Mark then back doon the road,' he answered, turning to Michelle and giving her a wry smile. '*Well*, that's the plan anyway *but* who knows? I suppose it could all change.'

Michelle raised her eyebrows. '*That's ma boy!*' she exclaimed, smiling back at him and squeezing his left thigh in the full knowledge that dinner would be the start of a night out on the town. She knew he'd come round. *He loved a night out just as much as she did. She'd work on him, more, during dinner, and before long they'd be on the train and on their way to one of the nightclubs in Glasgow.*

The taxi pulled away from the close and headed up Fife Drive, turning left at the roundabout on to Kylemore Crescent, making its way past the shops. Passing Braidhurst High School on the left, Gary looked out through the window on his right. Looking up Montrose Street, he caught the brightness of the ambulance parked directly outside Eldo's close. Its back doors were wide open.

'Dae us a favour, Mark, wid ye? Can ye stop the now and reverse back a wee bit, please?'

'Aye, nae bother, Gary son.'

'Whit is it?' Michelle asked.

With his right hand, Gary began winding down the handle of the window, as the taxi started reversing. 'There's an ambulance parked at Eldo's close.'

As the taxi stopped at the entrance to Montrose Street, Gary and Michelle looked out through the side window at those caught in the ambulance's light, flurrying around its frightening presence.

'Dae ye want us to go up, Gary?' the taxi driver asked.

'Aye, Mark.'

'Whit dae ye think? Dae ye think it's…?' Michelle couldn't bring herself to say it.

Gary didn't answer.

The taxi stopped two vehicle lengths from the back of the ambulance, but by then Gary and Michelle had seen enough.

In no time, they were out either side of the taxi and running.

'Naw, please God!' Michelle called out, falling to her knees some yards from the ambulance.

Eldo stood outside its back doors, holding up Linda, who was wailing in hysterics at the sight before them. Two paramedics were working on the two small bodies lying on the stretchers.

Gary ran past Eldo and Linda, taking the steps at the back of the ambulance in one leap.

'Look, ye need tae get oot a' here, son. We're trying to save these weans.'

Gary fell against the side of the open doorway, his open left hand partly covering his nose and mouth. Tears welled up in his eyes as Michelle, catching up to him, clung on to his legs, looking into the ambulance.

The children were white, pale white.

Michelle let out a primordial scream of unbearable pain and tried to throw herself bodily into the ambulance.

Gary bent down to his wife.

The senior paramedic who was working on Kelly called in to the driver, who was seated at the wheel. 'We need tae get them up to the hospital, Jim.'

The driver immediately responded by putting the ambulance into first gear.

The paramedic who was working on Chloe, finished putting the oxygen mask over her nose and mouth, and turned to the back door. 'Right, folks, there's only room for two of yees in here, so make yer minds up quickly who's coming.'

Gary held Michelle. 'You go with Linda,' he told her. 'We'll follow yees in the taxi.' He kissed her forehead and guided her to sit at the bottom of Kelly's stretcher. He then jumped out of the ambulance to make room for Eldo, who was helping Linda to walk forward.

Gary hurried to the taxi, oblivious to the people around him and the two young policemen, who were now getting out of their car to approach him.

'Looks like yees'll aw be goin' tae the jail, eh?'

As soon as Gary realised what Constable Craig Munro had said, he flew at him. Two men from the scheme, rushed in front of him, physically holding him back.

Gary looked over the men's shoulders and was pointing at the officer. 'I'll gladly dae aw the time in the fuckin' world for putting you doon right now, ya sick bastart! That's fuckin' weans lyin' in there!'

The police officer stood smirking until an empty Buckfast bottle whizzed past the front of his face, missing it by inches, and smashing on the road.

'Whoaaaaa, unlucky lads!' Gary shouted, to the group of young men he now noticed, standing close by, with their carry-out bags.

He turned to the policeman, who was now radioing for assistance. 'Aye, that's it. That's your fuckin' usual! Cause the bother and then call for back-up when yer arse collapses. Ya fuckin' arsehole!'

Eldo rushed to Gary's side and took him by the arm. 'Come oan. Fuck him!' he called out, looking over to the distressed policeman. 'He'll get 'es day that fuckin' bam!'

The two of them left the group and ran towards the taxi.

Mark, the driver, who was waiting, started the engine as they approached. The taxi raced directly behind the ambulance, the flashing blue and red lights searing through the car's occupants.

Leaving Motherwell, they entered, and passed through Craigneuk, and then Wishaw, on their way to the Law Hospital.

BOOK NINE: PRETENCE

20

Scene 1: Prep

Saturday 2nd January, 1993, Glasgow, Scotland, 7:15 p.m.

Entering the East End of Glasgow, Phil Murray, who had earlier collected all of his stash of drugs from Eldo's flat, smiled as he turned from his friend in the passenger seat, to look in the rear-view mirror, tilting his head to smile at his two other companions.

Moving down the gears, he felt much, much better, and smirked wryly as he considered how events had caught him off guard.

What the fuck was I thinkin' aboot? But, of course, he already knew the answer. He'd been too busy thinking about the money: the money that would come from offloading all the pills in one go; the money that would then pay off the guy from the West End – the guy who had supplied the pills up front. 12,000 withoot taking anything. No deposit. Fuck all! That was either real trust or some cunt that knew he had any amount of bad endings for a poor bastart that messed up. Phil found himself smiling. *Thank fuck for Eldo! Fuck! If he never put me right when he did, I'd be driving in here on my own like a fuckin' novice. Whit the fuck was Ah thinkin' aboot? And anyway, whit the fuck did it matter that the guy came oot tae Motherwell tae discuss the deal? At the end of the day did Ah know the cunt fae Adam? Naw! And did he know me? Naw! The cunt had been name-dropping aw day tae. Aye, and I had bought it aw like a fuckin' starry-eyed lemon! Whit a fuckin' idiot! I should've known he was acting the cunt when he told me to come with the pills masell. Whit a fuckin' idiot!* 'Aye, just come yersell, Phil. We'll have a few drinks and chill oot 'n' that. We can even listen tae some sounds. Aye, that's whit we'll dae. It'll be great.'

Aye, that's whit we'll dae. Phil sniggered, and shook his head at the thought. *Aye, it'll be great. It'll be absolutely fuckin' tremendous! We'll just get ye in here yersell, and then we'll just wait, wait till yer aw nice and comfy, maybe a bit stoned. Aye, we'll just wait, wait until you're tellin' yersell that everything's kosher, that everything's brand new, no probs, and then when you're least expectin' it, right oot the blue, we'll just batter yer cunt in, there and then, nae fuckin' aboot. Aye, that's what we'll really dae. And then, efter that, when we've taken the lot aff ye, we'll jist fuck ye right oot the door, wi' fuck all; battered tae fuck, wi' the blood pishin' oot ye, like a fuckin' bam!*

Phil laughed out loud and punched the steering wheel, before gathering himself and addressing his friends. 'Aye, so hopefully it'll go okay, lads, but at least we'll be ready for the cunts if it goes pear-shaped.'

'Aye, we'll be ready, Phil,' his friend in the passenger seat murmured, as he gazed out through the side window at the tenements and the dreary shops below them. 'It's funny,' the man continued, raising his voice, "these cunts" in here, dae yees know what they think? They think that people like oorsels, people that live outside the city, in places like Motherwell 'n' that, they think we're aw fuckin' mugs, they dae! That's what the stupit cunts think. They think we've aw got straw hangin' oot our fuckin' ears. Fuckin' bams!'

Phil moved forward in his seat, and tilted his head to look in the rear-view mirror, raising his eyebrows at his two friends in the back seat.

The three of them burst out laughing.

The man in the passenger seat was brought back by the laughter and turned casually to his friends. He smiled at them with a look of surprise on his face. 'Whit? I'm telling yees. That's whit some a' these cunts think in here!'

'Aye I know,' the passenger sitting behind Phil started, 'it's fuckin' no' real, int it? Have ye seen the state a' the cunts tae? That fuckin' talk oot a' the side a' the mooth brigade, and their stupit fuckin' swaggers that you could dry a week's washin' oan.'

Phil joined in with the laughter. 'Aye, it's fuckin' no' real awright. *Huh, wait tae yees hear this yin.* It's a fuckin' topper!' He cleared his throat before continuing. 'Ah mind, I came in here, *one Saturday*, tae the Barras. Ah cannae mind what I was coming in tae buy but, *anyway*, I seen this cunt *who was one a' that division that yees are talking aboot.*

Honestly, I nearly fuckin' pished masell laughin'. The *cunt*, was swaggering aboot the stalls talking oot the side a' ees mooth tae these other cunts'. *Yees know the types*, loud as fuck *so everybody can hear the pish that they're talking. But, anyway,* that wisnae the best bit. You could see this cunt didnae have two bob tae rub thegither, but dae ye know what the daft cunt done next? *Huh,* as he swaggered aboot the stalls. *The Cunt, as calm as ye like,* started *whistling* the *fuckin'* Godfather tune *heh, heh, heh*!'

'Now that is the fuckin' icin' oan it,' the man sitting behind Phil acknowledged.

'*Ah know*, it's no' fuckin' real int it? What a fuckin' almighty whalloper a' a man! The daft cunt thought that he was some millionaire gangster, like Don Corleone, *hee, hee, hee*. Pfft, and walking aboot the Barras for fuck's sake! I mean, come oan tae fuck. It's no' exactly fuckin' Belgravia is it? *Honestly*, I'm no joking. See when I seen that cunt that day, I felt like running o'er and just drawing ma boot right aff ees plums, just tae bring the laddie roon, fuckin' bam. Whit dae ye make a' it?' Phil said, turning to his friends, and blowing out through his mouth, shaking his head.

'Aye, *well*, that's what yer up against son, *heh, heh, heh*,' the man in the passenger seat laughed.

The laughter in the vehicle continued for a brief moment, before the silence resumed.

Phil started to slow his metallic gold Rover 3500, as they passed the streams of people entering the public park on his right. 'The place is just up here, lads. I'll drive past it first. It's the flats on the left-hand side, the ones wi' the scaffolding goin' up them. They're getting done up. It's the top flat on the right, I'll be goin' tae. Dae yees see it?' he asked as he passed the block.

'Aye, nae bother, Phil. We've got ye,' his friend in the passenger seat replied.

'Good. As I said, I hope it goes smoothly, but, if I'm honest, I think it looks as shady as fuck.'

Phil turned the car full circle at the roundabout, heading back the way they had come, passing the flats once more. He now had a better view.

Apart from the light coming from the top flat on the right, the one he would be visiting, the only other visible light appeared to be the dim light coming from within the close. It looked as though there were no other lights on in the building. Phil smiled, excited by the sudden rage that welled up inside him. *Every other flat in the block's empty.*

Having passed the flats, Phil drew the car into the side of the kerb just before the entrance to the public park, and turned the engine off. 'Right, lads, I'll drop yees here. I won't be stayin' in the flat for long. Whatever happens, I'll be half an hour max. Take aw the tools wi' yees and, here, hawd oan tae this one for me,' he said, discreetly drawing a twelve-inch, stainless-steel kitchen knife from the inside of his leather jacket, and handing it to his friend in the passenger seat.

'Are ye sure ye don't want us tae come wi' ye the noo, Phil?'

'Naw, honest. Yees are alright, lads, thanks. I've had a good think aboot it. Wait in the park for fifteen minutes and then walk down and wait outside the flats for another fifteen. If I'm not out and yees see some cunt coming oot the close carrying the rucksacks or anything else, just do them there and then. Don't fuck about wi' them. Just do them, and take whatever they've got, then yees can come and get me.'

'Nae bother. Watch yersell.'

'Thanks, lads. See yees soon,' Phil replied, shaking hands with his friends. 'I'll drive this up and park it a couple a' blocks away fae the flat.'

'Okay, Phil.'

'See ye, Phil. Watch what yer doin' wi' they cunts.'

'Aye, see you soon, Phil,' the men in the back told him, as they opened the doors of the car.

Phil smiled. 'Cheers boys and don't enjoy the fireworks too much that yees forget to come and get me!'

The man in the passenger seat took hold of Phil's left forearm with his right hand. 'Don't worry, Phil. We'll be there,' he said, gently patting the khaki canvas holdall that was resting on his lap, with his left hand.

'Ah know, mate, cheers.'

'See ye shortly,' the man told him, as he left the vehicle, taking the holdall with him.

Closing the door, the man walked round the back of the vehicle and, stepping on to the pavement, soon caught up with his friends who were waiting for him at the entrance of the park.

Starting the engine, Phil pushed the car into gear. Doing a U-turn, he headed back along the road, towards the flat.

Indicating, and drawing into the side of the kerb, around fifty yards from the scaffolded tenement, Phil turned off the engine and stepped out of the car. He walked to the back of the vehicle and opened the boot. As he took hold of the two rucksacks by the straps, his eyes caught sight of the two, five-gallon, jerry cans, filled with petrol. Phil smiled. For once he was glad that his car was a petrol guzzler. He had an idea though that tonight it wouldn't be the car that would be swallowing the petrol.

Removing the rucksacks, Phil closed the boot and checked that all the doors were locked. He made his way along the poorly lit street, which suited him just fine.

By the time he had reached the start of the scaffolding, Phil, was totally focused. *If they're expecting a novice, that's what they'll get, a gullible, gibbering, fuckin' idiot.*

Reaching the close entrance, he stopped, and looked at the building. He filled his lungs with a deep breath.

He walked the four yards to the door, and found and pressed the buzzer on the wall.

After a few seconds, 'Aye, who is it?'

'It's Phil. I was to come and see Jamie. He's expecting me.'

'Are ye just yersell, like Jamie agreed wi' ye?'

'Aye, I'm jist masell, like he said.'

'Ye fuckin' better be.'

'I'm jist masell. That wiz part a' the deal.'

The connection went dead. Some moments later someone pulled the close door open from the inside.

The man looked at Phil and then stepped out of the entrance, letting the door close and lock automatically behind him.

Walking past Phil, the man headed out on to the street. He stopped and looked left and right, and crossed the road and did the same on the pavement on the other side.

Ees in ees early thirties a few years older than me, Phil thought.

Making his way back across the road, the man stepped on to the pavement. He looked left and right once more and then walked towards Phil, who waited by the scaffolding.

'Where's yer motor? Whit are ye drivin'?'

'The gold Rover. It's just up there oan the right.'

'Wait here,' the man replied, setting off in a jog up the street, towards Phil's car.

Phil walked out on to the street, and watched as the man reached the car and started to peer in through its windows.

When he was finished, the man turned and started to jog back.

Walking into the close entrance, the man passed Phil and pressed the buzzer to the flat.

'Aye?' the voice asked.

'It's right enough. He's just here 'esell.'

'Good. Has he got the gear?'

The man looked at Phil, who, in turn, held out the rucksacks.

'Aye, 'es got it.'

'Right, bring him up and make sure you lock the door.'

As they entered the close, Phil saw that the place was just as he had thought. The front doors on the two opposite ground-floor flats had been removed, and the insides were bare, some of the floorboards had been ripped up.

The smell of dampness and wet plaster hung heavily in the air. 'Wow! Yees run a tight ship in here, don't yees? I'm Phil by the way. What aboot Jamie? He's some man, int he? He's got some patter, int he? Was he telling ye that he came aw the way oot tae Motherwell tae see me. It ma bit!' he blabbered, holding his right hand out to the man as they headed up the stairs.

'Eh?' the man asked, taking no interest in Phil's hand.

Phil continued, encouraged by the man's response. 'This is the first time I've been in this part a' the toon. It's some place, int it? I normally just do ma business fae roon aboot ma bit, but when Jamie phoned me oot the blue and then said to me that he wanted tae meet and talk aboot us working thegither, I thought, fuck, ye cannae knock that back, Phil, and then, when I finally met him and well, you know yersell, he's just a bang-on guy, int he?'

Phil noticed the man picking up speed and heading up ahead of him, which caused him to smile.

As they reached the door to the flat, another man in his thirties held the door open. *Smack heid*, Phil thought, *and ees already right oot it.*

'Staun there a minute,' the man at the entrance of the door said. He looked at the man who had escorted Phil up the stairs and nodded his head to the side, gesturing towards Phil.

'Drop the rucksacks and hold yer arms oot tae the sides,' the man who'd led him up told him.

'Aye, nae bother, lads.'

The man then ran his hands over Phil's arms and patted his body down, before running both hands down Phil's legs.

He nodded to the man at the door.

'Right, come oan in.'

'Nae bother, big man,' Phil replied as he picked the rucksacks from the floor. 'How ye doin? I'm Phil, Jamie's mate.'

'Aye, good for you.'

Phil could now feel the adrenaline rush even more. He already knew everything he needed to know. He was focused and smiled, as he acknowledged his thoughts, thoughts of what he was going to do to these men.

As he walked in through the open doorway and on to the bare floorboards, Phil took it all in. Moving forward, he passed the two bedrooms, one on either side. He heard the door being closed behind him, the latch clicking into place.

Walking into the living room, he mentally recorded the small wooden table with the dope, the ashtray, the white powder, the tin foil and the machete; four wooden chairs close by, two black leather holdalls near the window, the light in the kitchen, and the shadow of someone on the wall – Jamie, standing by the fireplace, listening to a small radio device that was tuned into a police frequency, and another machete beside it, on the mantelpiece.

'Jamie! How are ye getting on, mate?' Phil said, putting the rucksacks on the floor, and briskly walking over to his host, with open arms.

'Phil! Glad you could make it,' Jamie replied, his body rigid, as he embraced Phil. 'Have a seat. Is that the gear?'

'Aye, that's it there, mate: 8,000 Temazzies and 4,000 Palfium, just as we agreed. So, whit's the score wi' this place? Are yees doin' it up? How many bedrooms have ye got? It's some place. Great potential!'

'Aye, it has, Phil. We're just doin' up a wee bit at a time. Have a seat.'

Lyin' bastart, Phil thought. *This place has fuck all tae do wi' them. It belongs tae some cunt though; the cunt behind these fuckin' joeys. They'll only get tae use it so they can rob cunts like me, then they'll fuck off sharpish.*

'Sorry, I'm just a bit excited wi' it aw. I've been looking forward to doing business wi' yees since we met, Jamie,' Phil said, as he sat down, pretending not to notice the man taking the rucksacks into the kitchen.

'Aye, us tae, Phil. In fact, I want ye tae meet somebody else, a business partner a' mine.'

The guy in the kitchen, Phil thought, *the snidey cunt on the intercom.*

'If he's anything like yersell, then that'll be sound, Jamie. Is that the ten grand in used notes, as we agreed, o'er there in the holdalls?' Phil said, motioning with his right hand to the black leather bags at the window.

'Aye, that's it there, Phil. We'll just need tae check the gear first. Ye know the score.'

'Aye, fine mate, nae bother. Try some the noo if yees want. They're the real deal. I just wish I could join yees, but I need tae keep sober, for a while, anyway. It's ma mam's birthday and we're havin' a wee do for her in ma aunty's later oan. I cannae let her doon, Jamie.'

As Phil was talking, a man that he hadn't met walked out from the kitchen, carrying an unopened six-pack of bottled beer.

'Talk a' the devil!' Jamie said, smiling. 'Phil, this is Clarky, my *associate*.'

Phil rose from the chair and extended his right hand. 'Pleased tae meet ye, Clarky.'

'Aye, you tae, Phil. Jamie was telling me aw aboot ye. Thanks for coming in tae see us,' he replied, shaking Phil's hand. 'Sorry, if I was a bit nippy there, when I was talking with ye earlier. I get a bit stressed wi' these kinna things.'

'Aw that was you on the intercom? Nae bother. Don't worry aboot it. Ye're fine.'

'Dae Ah look fuckin' worried?' Clarky cut in, strolling up to Phil and standing directly in front of him, their faces inches apart.

'Naw, I'm just sayin'…' Phil answered.

'Aye, is that right? Ye're just sayin'. And whit the fuck are ye sayin'?'

Here we go, Phil thought.

Suddenly, Clarky burst out laughing. 'Ha! Ah got ye there, Phil, *eh*?' he said, turning to Jamie. 'Did ye see 'es face?'

Jamie laughed too. 'You're a fuckin' psycho!'

Phil smiled as he fought the urge to lift the machete from the table. 'Aye,' he laughed. 'Ye got me.'

'Have a seat, Phil. Ye're a good cunt,' Clarky said, taking a bottle of beer from the pack and handing it to him.

'Cheers,' Phil replied, moving his chair to make space for Jamie, who walked from the fireplace to take a seat beside them.

'And help yersell tae the powder,' Clarky continued, motioning to the table. 'I've been cutting the rest a' it in the kitchen for the last couple a' hours. It's good gear,' he told him, removing the lid from his beer with a bottle opener. 'And that's something else we were wanting tae talk tae ye aboot, Phil, int it, Jamie?'

'Aye,' Jamie began, 'we see this as being a good opportunity, for aw a' us, Phil. We've got a good business relationship with a guy we know and he's able to provide us with a steady supply a' coke. We were seeing that if you were interested we could supply you, and you could sell it at whatever price ye wanted, oot in Motherwell. We'd add a bit oan tae the price at this end for ourselves, of course, before selling it tae ye, but nothing extortionate. You could call it a *handling fee,* just like what you're doing for us wi' the pills. You don't need to give us an answer the noo, but it's something we'd like ye to think about, Phil.

'When we get the coke, we cut it but not so much that it fucks it up, and you could easily cut it again when ye got it back to Motherwell. The profits are phenomenal, Phil, as long as ye don't develop a habit for it, like some cunts I know,' he said, gesturing with his head towards Clarky and smiling.

'A wee line here and there for fuck's sake! Everythin' in moderation. What's wrong wi' that Phil, eh?' Clarky asked.

Phil smiled at Clarky, who was dragging the machete over the white powder, separating it into lines on the wooden table.

'Here, Phil, give me yer bottle and I'll open it,' Jamie said. 'My partner here's a bit preoccupied as ye can see.'

'Cheers, Jamie.'

'So, what do ye think about whit we're sayin', Phil? Is it something ye might be interested in?'

Phil took the opened bottle from Jamie. 'Aye, it sounds good. Cheers,' he said, raising the bottle to the two men before taking a drink. 'Aye, we'll definitely talk more. Yees can come out to Motherwell or I can come in here. I'm a bit stuck for time tonight wi' the auld dear's party but, aye, I'm sure we'll be able to sort something oot.'

'Good. If we play this right, it can be win-win for every cunt.'

The conversation was interrupted by the sound of Clarky trying to snort a long line of cocaine through a shortened drinking straw.

'For fuck's sake! Are ye trying to get the table in as well?' Jamie shouted, showing his frustration.

'Whit the fuck are ye oan aboot? I've been in that kitchen aw night doin' the biz, while you've been in here fuckin' aboot wi' a stupit fuckin' radio!'

Jamie looked at his watch while shaking his head. 'Anyway, Phil, as I was sayin'… working together we can aw make a right few bob. The pills are a good earner as well, as ye know, and I'm sure you've got an idea of the profits ye can make selling them in here.'

'Aye, I know they're probably worth double the amount in here, Jamie, but I don't mind. I'm doing alright oot the deal and, to be honest, I'd rather move them on quickly.'

'Well, as I was saying to ye in Motherwell, Phil, we'll move these aw day long in here and we'll get rid a' them as quick as you can supply them.'

Scene 2: Clocked

Phil's three friends approached the block from the opposite side of the road, behind a row of parked cars.

The man, who had been sitting in the passenger seat, led the way, carrying the khaki canvas holdall.

When they were about thirty yards from the close entrance, the man put his right arm out to the side, halting his two friends. He watched, as, across the road, four men, wearing black ski masks, rushed into the entrance of the scaffolded building.

As he continued to watch what was taking place, the man smiled. 'And there you have it, lads. The double bluff. Plan the deal and plan the robbery, making it look as though you've had fuck all to do with it. Fuck, if yer clever enough, ye can even blame the robbery oan the poor cunt ye invited, in this case, Phil.'

The man seemed to become unaware of his friends beside him and started to mumble 'So that wiz it? Steal ees gear and blame him at the same time? Pity they never thought a' something else. Aye, that wiz their biggest mistake. Stupit cunts. They never thought a' that. They never thought that Ah'd be here, tae blow their fuckin' heids aff.'

Scene 3: Business

'Right, lads, I better get moving,' Phil said, rising from the wooden chair.

Jamie looked at his watch. 'Hawd oan a minute, Phil. Fuck! You've not even checked the money,' he said, standing up himself.

Jamie walked over to the window and picked the two black leather holdalls from the floor, returning to drop them at Phil's feet. He looked to Clarky. 'Is everything in order wi' the pills?'

'Aye, sound. We never counted them aw obviously, but aye, they're the real product alright. No generic.'

'Good,' Jamie replied, checking his watch as he sat back down on his chair. 'Count the money just tae be sure, Phil. I wouldnae want ye leaving here and then finding oot it was short. It's mostly in bundles a' tenners, as ye asked, but there's some fivers and twenties tae. I hope that's okay.'

Phil pulled the zips back on the holdalls, one after the other. 'Nae bother, lads. Aw, Ah meant tae say, the guy who was holding the pills for me took fifty for 'esell, so that's fifty I owe yees, or do yees want the money?'

'Naw, ye're fine, Phil. We'll get them on the next round. Thanks for letting us know,' Jamie replied.

Phil started to take some of the bundles of notes from the bags at random and began counting. At the sound of the living room door creaking, he raised his head.

The door was slightly ajar and opened a little further, pushed by a gentle breeze. Someone had opened the front door.

Phil turned to Jamie and Clarky, who seemed to be readying themselves.

The living room door was kicked and swung fully open, revealing the masked men rushing into the living room.

The first had a revolver in his right hand and raised it steadily, shifting his aim from Jamie to Clarky to Phil. 'On the floor now!'

Jamie and Clarky complied immediately, lying face-down. Phil, continued to look on.

The gunman walked over and pointed the pistol directly at Phil's face. 'Get oan the fuckin' floor!'

Phil dropped the money and raised his hands slightly. 'Awright, awright, take it easy!' he told the man, slowly moving to lie face-down on the floor, just as the other masked men carrying machetes, brought the other two members of Jamie's group from the kitchen.

The first man was forced to lie beside Jamie. The addict, who by now could hardly walk, was dumped beside Clarky.

'Don't try anything stupit,' the gunman told them, before turning to his accomplices. 'Okay, Number Four, take whatever's in the kitchen, Number Three, check the rooms and, Two, if any of these cunts as much as breathe the wrong way, you know what to do.'

The gunman walked forward to the holdalls containing the money and picked them up with his left hand. Keeping his eyes on the men, he took four steps backwards, and dropped the holdalls in the centre of the living room.

Moving to take the machete from the table, he then took the other from the mantelpiece and returned to the centre of the living room to shove them inside one of the open holdalls.

'That's everything oot the kitchen,' Number Four said, as he entered, carrying the two rucksacks and another black leather holdall.

'Good,' the gunman replied.

Number Three entered the living room from the hall. 'The bedrooms are empty.'

'Okay.'

Lying on the floor, Clarky strained, to look over towards Phil. 'Haw, cunt, this isnae finished by the way!'

'Whit the fuck are ye oan aboot?' Phil roared back at him.

'You know whit Ah'm fuckin' oan aboot,' Clarky answered. 'You've set us up, ya cunt!'

Phil laughed sarcastically. 'Dae ye think it's a fuckin' mug ye're talkin' tae, eh? This is your pitch, ya fuckin' bam! Did ye give them a key before I got here, *ya fly bastarts?* Aye well, I'll tell ye, ye're right aboot one fuckin' thing: no way is this fuckin' finished!'

The gunman rushed over and forcefully kicked Phil in the face. 'Shut the fuck up or maybe I'll just finish you the noo!' he said, leaning down and pressing the gun against Phil's temple.

One of the gunman's accomplices spoke up. 'That's us, boss. Let's go. It's time!'

The gunman came back to his senses. 'Good,' he replied, standing upright. 'Right, youse cunts! Any of yees try 'n' follow us oot and it'll be the last thing yees dae. It's only business. Nae use getting yersells killed o'er it. Let it go.'

His accomplices were already making their way out of the living room as the man with the gun leaned down to pick the remaining two holdalls from the floor.

Backing his way steadily out of the living room, he closed the door and walked the short distance across the hallway, heading through the open doorway, where his friends were waiting.

Closing the front door of the flat, the gunman stuffed the revolver into one of the bags carrying the money and held it open for his friends to do the same with their machetes. 'Right, let's get oot a' here.'

The four men hurried along the landing, removing their ski masks and heading down the stairs.

Walking briskly, they reached the close door, and opening it, made their way out with the holdalls and the rucksacks.

Phil's friend, the man who had led the others, stepped out from the street and straight into the robbers' path, pulling the trigger on the sawn-off, double-barrelled shotgun.

The blast blew the first man off his feet, and the spread of the pellets caught the two behind.

The fourth robber slipped and fell against the close door, pushing it open with his body, and scurried his way inside along the floor, before finally staggering to his feet.

The man with the shotgun hurried after him.

Stepping over the bodies of the wounded men, he turned to see his friends with their blades at hand, ready to finish the job.

Catching the door before it closed, the man with the shotgun pushed it open further and sprinted towards the stairs.

The robber, who was halfway up the first flight, was fumbling around with his right hand inside one of the holdalls.

Reaching the bottom of the stairs, the man with the shotgun came to a halt and smiled as he looked up at the robber.

With the shotgun at waist height, he raised the barrels.

The robber cowered, instinctively, as the man with the shotgun pulled the trigger.

The majority of the pellets from the blast caught the back of the robber's head, throwing fragments of skull and brain on to the wall and ceiling behind. His body crumpled in a heap, and falling lifelessly down the steps, he dragged the holdalls with him, coming to a halt at the feet of the killer.

Breaking the shotgun open, the man removed the spent cartridges, slipping them into the front right pocket of his wax cotton jacket. He took two new cartridges from his front left pocket and pushed them into the tubes.

Locking them in place, he headed up the stairs.

'Don't shoot, *it's Phil!* Don't shoot, it's Phil!' Phil called out as he made his way down the stairs.

Coming to meet his friend at the top of the first flight, Phil saw the glistening mess on the wall and ceiling, and looked down at the body, lying at the foot of the stairs.

'That's the cunt that had the revolver,' he said, as he rushed past his friend holding the shotgun.

Reaching the body, Phil untangled the holdalls. Resting them on the steps, he pulled them open.

He soon found the gun and, hearing the gentle knocks, turned to the close entrance.

Through the glass in the door, Phil could make out the face of one of his friends looking back at him. With the revolver in his right hand, Phil walked to the door and pulled it open. 'In yees come, boys. Good tae see yees. Where are they other cunts?'

'We just fucked them under the scaffolding. We've got yer gear in the rucksacks and there's a load a' powder in a holdall. Are we ready tae move?'

'Aye, shortly.'

Phil let his two friends enter and closed the door, making sure it was locked.

As they made their way towards the stairs, an enormous blast from the shotgun made the three of them duck down.

Continuing, Phil took the holdalls containing the money in his left hand, as they quickly climbed the first flight. On reaching the second, they found another body: the man who had met Phil when he had first arrived. They hurried past him, and, on reaching the landing for the flat, they found their friend waiting, standing outside the door.

'It's locked. Have they cunts got any other guns in there?'

'Naw I didnae see any,' Phil replied, 'it was only yer man at the bottom a' the stairs and he was the one who took their machetes.'

'Right then. Staun back,' the man said, raising the shotgun and aiming at the lock on the door.

Turning his face to the side, the man pulled the trigger, blowing a hole in the door where the lock had been.

'Leave the bags here,' Phil said, walking forward and kicking the door open, as the man with the shotgun quickly reloaded.

Walking into the hallway, Phil gestured to his two friends, who carried their blades, to check the two rooms.

Moving forward, Phil booted the living room door open and entered. 'Where the fuck dae yees think youse're goin'?' he shouted, pointing the revolver at Jamie, who was pushing Clarky out through the open window on to the scaffolding boards, to freedom.

Jamie, with his back to Phil, stopped and raised his hands, but Clarky continued, and was getting on to his feet escaping.

Rushing past Phil, the man with the shotgun ran up to the window and pulled the trigger, blowing out the glass and Clarky off the scaffolding. He was dead before his body bounced off a parked car and hit the pavement, on the street below.

Phil walked into the kitchen, and found the addict, sitting spaced-out on a wooden chair, a crack pipe, some rocks, a spoon and a needled syringe on the worktop beside him.

Walking back into the living room, as well as being filled with the smoke from the blast, Phil's nostrils also contained the smell of singed skin.

Looking at Jamie, he soon realised where the smell was coming from.

Jamie was kneeling on the floor with his hands in the air. His lips were wrapped around the burning hot tubes of the sawn-off shotgun.

The man with the shotgun stood over him. 'That's it. Stick yer tongue in as far as it can go. Roll it around. That's it. Taste it. Savour its walls of death.'

'Okay, we'll need to be quick,' Phil told the man holding the shotgun. 'Take it oot ees mooth so we can get some answers.'

Jamie rolled his eyes to Phil, pleading in terror. The man with the shotgun wasn't responding.

'We need tae get some answers, mate,' Phil told him again.

The man removed the gun from Jamie's mouth.

'Phil, don't dae this. Please. This was fuck all tae dae wi' us! We got set up tae.'

Phil immediately pistol-whipped Jamie, causing him to fall to the floor.

He stood over him. 'Right now, be smart here. Who owns the flat and who owns the coke?'

'That's what I'm sayin', Phil!'

Phil stepped forward and quickly booted Jamie in the mouth, sending him sprawling once more, on the floor. 'Names, cunt!' he shouted down to him.

'Terry Patterson. He put us oan tae ye. He told us tae set up the deal then rob ye.'

Hearing this, Phil cocked the revolver and leaned in, pointing the gun directly at Jamie's face.

Terry Patterson, the man from the West End. The same man who had given Phil the 12,000 pills had set up the robbery, thereby ensuring that Phil would be the new recruit, the new mug, that would be forever in his debt, forever under his control; the new mug that would be made to do the same things that Jamie had done.

'Hurry up and do this cunt so we can get tae fuck,' the man with the shotgun said. 'I'll do him for ye, if ye want.'

'Phil, for fuck's sake don't!' Jamie pleaded.

'It's okay, don't worry,' Phil told him in a whisper.

'Please, Phil! Don't dae it, I've got a wife 'n' weans.'

Phil pulled the trigger, shooting Jamie in the head, killing him instantly. He turned and walked towards the kitchen. Walking in, he found that the addict was now slumped in the chair. 'Geeza a hand in here boys,' Phil said, calling out to his friends.

Lifting the addict from the chair, Phil's men frogmarched him into the living room, to stand some feet away from Jamie's body.

The man with the shotgun was in the process of removing the live and spent cartridges from his pockets and was wiping them on his jumper, before returning them.

When he was finally ready everyone stood back from the addict as the man with the shotgun took aim.

He pulled the trigger, and the addict was thrown like a rag doll against the wall.

Phil and the man with the shotgun quickly wiped down their guns.

After they had put Jamie in the wax cotton jacket, they put his hands on the shotgun at various places, before finally placing it in the grip of his right hand.

They then placed the revolver in the right hand of the dead addict.

Phil quickly grabbed his empty bottle of beer from the table and the small radio device from the mantelpiece. It had already warned them once, and now warned them again: *'Reports of gunshots in the East End. Officers to proceed with caution. Armed Response Units have been notified.'*

Hurrying from the flat, Phil and his men picked the rucksacks and holdalls from the floor, before running down the stairs.

They left the close via the back exit and made their way quietly in the darkness, along the back of the tenements.

Trying the back doors as they went, they were successful on the fourth attempt. The lock was broken and the closed door lay open before them.

Phil told his men to wait in the darkness while he collected the car.

When he walked out through the front of the close and into the street, Phil knew by the distance that they had travelled at the back of the building, that he would've passed his vehicle. He was relieved to see, however, as he walked towards it, that the car was only twenty yards away.

Phil started the car, and drove down the road.

Passing the scene of the crime, he turned the vehicle full circle at the roundabout and headed back. He continued as calmly as possible, and indicated as he crossed over to the other side of the road, coming to a stop near the entrance of the building where his friends were waiting.

With the engine running softly, Phil reached over with his right hand, and pulling the handle, pushed open the back door.

To the sound of police sirens, one by one his friends emerged from the close, carrying the goods.

When everyone was in the vehicle, Phil indicated and crossed over to the correct lane. He told his friends to keep their heads down, as made their way slowly through the East End.

BOOK TEN:

PARTING WAYS

21

Scene 1: Passing

Saturday 2nd January 1993, somewhere between Bonkle and the Law Hospital, 7:15 p.m.

Gary and Eldo sat in silence. They hadn't spoken since they'd entered the taxi, and Mark, the driver, knew it was no time for words.

As they passed through Bonkle, on the outskirts of Wishaw, the ambulance that they were following started to slow down on the country road and eventually stopped. Mark pulled the taxi in behind. Gary rushed out from one side, as Eldo hurried out from the other.

Reaching the back of the ambulance, Gary gripped the handle pressing it down and pulled the door open. The senior paramedic was counting out as he pushed down on Kelly's small frame before leaning down and administering mouth-to-mouth. Michelle had gone into shock minutes earlier and sat in silence, the mental anguish overwhelming her. She knew from her training as a nurse that her daughter was already dead, that the paramedic was only going through the motions.

When the paramedic eventually stopped, his colleague checked his watch mentally noting the time.

'Naw. Keep doin' it,' Gary mumbled as he stepped into the ambulance.

'She's away, son. I'm sorry.'

'Ye can dae it! Please, mister. Ye can dae it. Just dae it, mister.

Please, Ah beg ye. Please, mister. Please try. Ah beg ye. Please. *Please.*'

The paramedic put one hand on top of the other and again began pumping Kelly's chest as he counted out, following on with mouth-to-mouth.

The tears streamed down Gary's face as he knelt down on to the floor of the ambulance. He took Kelly's cold hand and rubbed it in his own. 'Come oan, ma wee darlin'. It's yer daddy. Come oan, ma wee honey.'

Linda, who had been talking out loud to herself, eventually broke down and began wailing.

After almost two minutes had passed, the paramedic stopped and blew out softly.

Gary, on his knees, with his head lowered, was now silently planting kiss after kiss on the small lifeless hand that he clasped between his own.

'I'm sorry,' the paramedic spoke up. 'She's away, son. She wasn't in any pain.'

The junior paramedic signalled to his senior, telling him what he already knew. The other child, Chloe, was in a coma and barely breathing. They had to get her to the hospital if she had any chance of surviving.

The senior paramedic nodded back to his junior in acknowledgement, before calling to the driver, 'Okay, Jim.'

The driver turned in his chair to confirm his colleague's signal and returned to his position behind the wheel, sliding the ambulance into gear.

Eldo, had stood, all the while, watching from the back of the ambulance. He had never known such pain or suffering was possible. His body soon responded. Lurching sideways, he threw up on the grass verge at the side of the road.

At the feet of her daughter, Michelle, sat motionless, staring vacantly, her mascara and make-up all but washed away by the earlier flood of tears.

Linda's eyes continued to take in everything and nothing as she reverted once more to babbling in madness.

The senior paramedic caught Eldo's attention. 'Do you want to get into yer taxi and follow us up, son?'

Eldo nodded. He closed the door of the ambulance and walked back to the taxi alone. The ambulance pulled away, just as Eldo reached and entered the front passenger seat of the taxi. Struggling to breathe, Eldo held his head in his hands and wept inconsolably.

Mark, the driver, checked his rear-view and side mirror before setting off again, following the ambulance.

When the ambulance had reached the hospital, the two families were parted. Gary and Michelle were escorted with their dead child to the mortuary. And Eldo, Linda, and Chloe, were rushed to Accident and Emergency.

PART VI

BOOK ELEVEN: HANGING ON

22

Scene 1: Out in the open

Friday 8th January, 1993, Kylemore Crescent, Forgewood, Motherwell, Scotland, 7:45 p.m.

The snow had turned to sleet and was now falling steadily on to the frozen pavement. Underneath the yellowish glow of the streetlights, Ninian hurried, but couldn't escape the voices or the boy, who flittered in and out of his peripheral vision on the opposite side of the road behind the row of parked cars.

'Just get tae the shop, get fags, pick up Paula, drap her at ma maw and da's, then back to the flat,' Ninian said aloud.

Gathering pace, he pushed his right hand into the right-hand pocket of his black denims and pulled out all the money that he had, counting it into his left hand.

He found that he had enough change to pay the exact amount. 'Thank fuck! In and out. As quick as.'

The voices in his head were relentless and he blinked unconsciously as he strode out. He had to concentrate to put them out of his mind, had to break the visualisations and the mockery: *Where will you get yer drugs fae now? Now that yer pal's wean's deid. Pity it wasn't you tae. You'd be as well toppin' yersell. Look at the fuckin' state a' ye.*

And so the taunting continued, despite his best attempts, and was accompanied all the while by the sound of the boy's hurried footsteps.

With the money for the cigarettes in his left hand, Ninian started to run the short distance remaining. He never slowed down as he reached the steps outside the shop and stumbled at the top, falling against the glass doors, forcing them to open with a loud bang.

Norrie, the shopkeeper, was in the front aisle, arranging the boxes of potato crisps. 'For fuck's sake, Ninian! Ye nearly smashed that glass!'

Ninian caught his breath. 'It was an accident, Norrie. I'm sorry. I slipped as I was coming in. Dae me a favour, wid ye? Geez twenty Regal King Size? Here,' he said, handing Norrie the money.

'Are ye in a hurry or something?' Norrie asked, making his way to the other side of the counter.

Ninian lowered his head and rubbed his eyes with the index fingers of both hands. He could still hear the voices and the sound of the boy's footsteps. Removing his hands from his eyes, Ninian looked around the shop and caught a glimpse of the boy disappearing behind the far aisle, as the crazed laughter came again.

'Ninian? *Ninian*! Here's yer fags. Ninian, are ye alright?' Norrie asked. 'Do ye want me to phone someone, Ninian?'

'Naw, I'm fine, Norrie. Ye're alright,' Ninian replied, walking over to the counter, still trying to hold himself together, but visibly shaken.

'Are ye sure yer alright? You look as rough as fuck. Have ye slept since New Year?'

'Aye, I'm okay, Norrie.'

'I'm sorry aboot Gary's wean,' the shopkeeper said. 'It's terrible. Tell him I'm askin' for him. I've never seen him in the shop yet and I wasn't sure what to do, whether tae go to the hoose or no'. And Michelle, is she oot the hospital yet?'

'Naw, she's still in the hospital. I don't know when she'll get oot.'

'And what aboot the wean's funeral?'

'Maybe another week or two. I don't think anybody knows when they'll release the wean's body,' Ninian replied.

'And what aboot Eldo's wean, Chloe? Is she still oan life support? Is Linda still staying at the hospital wi' her?'

'Aye.'

'Whit a tragedy, God! And your Paul tae. Fuck, I nearly forgot. How's he doin'? Is he coming home?'

'He's getting brought back tae Scotland on Monday and the monks are collectin' him from the airport and taking him up to the monastery. We're goin' up tae see him on Tuesday or Wednesday.'

'Is it true he's lost 'es arms and had 'es eyes cut oot?'

The voices whispering in Ninian's head were indiscernible, before one resounded above all the others. *'Tell this cunt tae fuck off!'*

'Eh, I'm no' sure whit's happened, Norrie. We don't know aw the details.'

'Ah see, and whit aboot you, Ninian?'

'Aye, I'm okay. Can I get they fags noo? I need tae hurry. I've to collect Andrew's daughter, Paula, fae the youth club, up in the community centre.'

'Aye, here,' Norrie replied, handing Ninian the cigarettes. 'I didnae mean tae bombard ye wi' questions. I was just worried.'

Just worried? Whit a dirty lying bastart a' a man. 'Nae bother, Norrie, see ye later,' Ninian said, trying to interrupt the onslaught going on in his mind. *Aw these cunts wi' shops are aw the same, wanting to know aw yer business so they can tell every other cunt behind yer back, then they can aw laugh at ye and make a right cunt a' ye when ye're no' there. Fuckin' arsehole!*

Ninian blew out from his mouth, unconsciously expressing his anxiousness and headed to the glass doors, pulling one open by the handle and walking out of the shop.

'See ye, Ninian.'

Scene 2: Keeping it civil

Ninian had his head lowered as he attempted to make his way through the crowd of people standing directly outside the shop.

Eldo's uncle Frank caught sight of him and gripped his left arm as he tried to pass.

'Alright, ma best pal.'

'Alright, Frank.'

'It's no' half cauld, int it no', son?'

'Aye, it's some night,' Ninian replied, trying to continue on his way.

'Ye hivnae got something for yer auld pal, have ye, son? I'm choking for a can.'

'I'm skint, Frank. I'm oot the game. Sorry.'

'Whit aboot a wee fag? Could ye spare one?'

Ninian lowered his head as he reached into the right-hand pocket of his black fleece jacket.

'Can I get a fag aff ye tae, Ninian?'

'And me tae, Ninian?'

'Me an' aw, Ninian?'

Ninian lifted his head and looked up to the sky letting out a groan as he wiped his eyes with his left thumb and forefinger. *Beggin' bastarts!* one of the voices cried out above the others. *They'll work for no cunt. Give them fuck all.*

Taking the cigarettes from his pocket, he opened the pack and started handing them out.

'Thanks Ninian, son. Yer one a' the best.'

'Aw cheers, Ninian.'

'Yer a good yin, son.'

'Thanks, Ninian.'

'Nae bother,' Ninian replied, taking a cigarette for himself. He lit the men's cigarettes with his lighter before lighting his own.

'Right, see yees later, lads.'

'See ye, Ninian. Aw the best.'

'Cheers, son. Aw the best.'

Ninian walked along the pavement and crossed the road, on to Dinmont Crescent. Reaching the short path leading up to the community centre, Ninian flicked the cigarette end on to the road as he took the right turn. He hadn't even known that he had smoked it.

With his eyes still stinging, he rubbed them with his right thumb and forefinger.

In and out he thought as he pulled open the graffiti covered steel door.

Scene 3: Cycles

Squeezing his eyes closed at the brightness of the fluorescent lights buzzing on the ceiling, Ninian pushed his right hand out to the side, finding the wall.

'Ah hope you're no' drunk, cause see if ye are, ye can just turn right aboot and go back tae where ye came fae,' Martha, the caretaker, told him, before taking a draw on her cigarette.

Ninian opened his eyes, straining to see her sitting behind a small table at the entrance to the main hall.

'I'm no' drunk, Martha. I'm just here to pick up oor Paula,' he told her, looking beyond her to the wire-glass doors, and the boy scowling back at him from inside the hall, the whispers escalating almost immediately.

'Okay then, in ye go. It's just finishing up.'

'*Please stop, please stop, please stop.*'

'What?' the caretaker asked. 'Did you say something?'

Ninian walked past Martha and opened the door to the hall and the wall of sound.

The excitement was palpable. It was Friday and the youth club was drawing to a close and the weekend was just starting.

Stepping inside, Ninian lowered his head and held his hands over his ears. He couldn't differentiate between the noise inside his head and the noise outside. The voices, the laughter and the sound of running footsteps merged into one.

Ninian slumped back against the doors, almost collapsing.

'Hi, Uncle Ninian!' Paula called out, as she rushed over. 'Are you okay, Uncle Ninian?'

'Paula!' Ninian replied, straightening up. 'Aye, I'm fine, hen. Are we ready to go?'

'Aye, Uncle Ninian. I've just to help put the badminton stuff in the cupboard.'

'Okay, hen. I'll just be here, waitin'.'

'Thanks, Uncle Ninian.'

As fifteen-year-old Paula made her way over to help her friends, Ninian noticed two boys of a similar age standing to his right. They were acting suspiciously, looking at him and then looking away. When they had finally built up the courage, they approached him.

'Alright, Ninian,' the taller of the two said. 'We're goin' tae a party tonight and we've got our Buckfast stashed outside, but we were wondering… could ye get us a bit a' draw? We've got the money.'

Watching them from the side, and overhearing what was going on, Billy, a man in his forties, who was helping out at the youth club, stepped in. 'Right, youse two, youse are barred fae the youth club for a fortnight, okay?'

'Aw for fuck's sake, Billy!' the smaller youth replied.

'Well, yees know the rules!'

'Ah suppose you never took anything when ye were young, eh?' the taller youth said angrily.

'Aye, ye're right. Ah never. They things took me!'

Ninian wiped his brow, hearing one of the voices in his head clearly above the others: *Here comes the lecture fae the arsehole.*

'Aye, they took me,' Billy continued, 'tae places that I thought were great, but realise now were fucked-up big time! Come oan over here for a minute, and we'll have a seat wi' Ninian and talk aboot it.'

Ninian felt himself zoning out of everything going on around him. The assault from the voices was overwhelming. Before he knew what was happening, he was following Billy and the two youths, who were walking towards a wooden bench placed against the wall below a window.

Sitting down, Ninian somehow came back to his senses to find the two youths sitting between him and Billy, who was continuing with his story.

'Let me ask yees something. In fact, tell me something,' Billy said, addressing the two youths. 'Do yees think yees are doin' anything any different?'

The two youths smirked at each other.

'Think aboot it,' Billy continued. 'Dae yees think yees are doin' anythin' any different from yer das, yer grandas or yer great-grandas? Or anythin' any different from any of the other men that have lived in schemes like Forgewood, North Motherwell, Jerviston, Craigneuk, eh? Dae yees? When is that light gonnae come oan in they nappers a' yours, eh?

'The only thing that changes in these places is the type a' drink and drugs! But the consequences, they never change! Listen, I'm probably aboot the same age as yer faithers,' he said, focusing on the teenagers. 'Why dae yees think that some aulder people, like masell, try and tell yees to watch what yees are doin'? Eh? I'll tell yees why: 'cause see everything yees are doin', they've already done it maybe a hundred times over, or they know some other cunt that has.'

The boys looked at each other, smiling uneasily as Billy continued. 'And dae yees know another thing? Dae yees think that they'd be telling yees to screw the nut if they thought whit yees were doin' was good for yees? Have a good fuckin' look at some a' the people in these schemes, lads: young men in their thirties hobblin' aboot wi' fuckin' walkin' sticks, their bodies fucked-up wi' drink and drugs, faces rid raw, and stomachs rotted to fuck wi' cheap booze, lungs clogged up wi' so much shite that they've to cough their cunts up every twenty yards they've tae walk, jist tae get a fuckin' breath! But here's the thing. The *Young Team*, like yersells, whit dae youse see? I'll tell yees whit yees see. Youse only see the cunts that hivnae reached that stage yet. Youse only see the ones that are just a wee bit aulder than yersells; the ones that still seem to be in their prime, doing the biz, Jack the Lads, ones that yees look up tae 'n' then say, "Aww, look at him. He can take some amount a' drink. Look how red ees face is", or "aww, look at him. he can smoke some amount a' draw, dae ye hear 'es cough?" or "aww, look at him, see the chib marks on 'es face. He's even done the jail. He's as hard as fuck!" And dae yees know something else? Dae yees know how Ah know yees think like that? Dae yees? I tell yees how. It's because I'm fae this place tae and that's what I used tae think when I was your age.

'But listen, dae yees know whit's really fuckin' sad aboot it aw, lads? It's this. See if yees had tae ask any of the aulder men in this scheme, the ones who've come through aw that; *well*, the ones that have managed to come through it aw withoot their heids being too fucked-up. See if ye'd to really ask them tae really tell ye aboot their ain lives and asked them whether they'd change anything if they could, what do yees think they would say? Eh? I'll tell yees whit they would say: they'd say, "Don't be the next generation tae fuck yersells up, lads!" That's what they would say! Yees need tae start usin' your fuckin' heids, boys, cause I'll tell yees, see if yees don't, yees'll just be living the same life that some a' the other poor bastarts that have lived here aw their days have lived. And do you know whit, see before yees know it, yees'll just be part a' another cycle: another cycle a' drink, drugs, jail, drink, drugs, jail: addiction, broken marriages, broken families, yer weans stayin' wi' ye one weekend, then staying wi' yer ex the following weekend, and then, one day, youse'll be the ones – if yees live that long and yer heids arenae too fucked-up – to tell yer ain weans when they grow up, "Don't dae the same as me!" Screw the nut for fuck's sake, lads, please! Come and see me during the week if yees want, oan Wednesday before the fitba' training, and yees can talk to people who are mates a' mine, crackin' people, men who've had it rougher than me, and they'll tell ye aboot their ain lives. And dae ye know whit? They were the Jack the Lads tae, *men* who were once young boys just oot to have a laugh, just like yersells. They only lived for the weekend tae come as well, but here's the thing: they'll tell yees the score, straight, nae bullshit, and they'll no' be braggin'. They'll only be tellin' yees in the hope that it'll stop youse fae making the same mistakes that they did. And dae yees know something else, boys? Some poor bastarts don't get another shot at it. They don't get aff the road a' drink and drugs that they wandered oantae when they were young. It becomes aw they know, and so they continue like that until they're dubbed up in jail, or fucked intae a care home, or planted doon Airbles cemetery.

'And dae yees know whit? See before it gets tae that stage, deep doon the poor cunts want tae change, but they think if they do try and change that they'll be somehow letting the side doon… their mates. It's so fuckin' sad. I'm tellin yees, boys, that's whit happens. The poor cunts continue to follow one another, with the idea that they know who they are, but see if they'd to really admit the truth tae themselves, they'd see that they didnae have a fuckin' clue, not one fuckin' scooby aboot who the fuck they are, or whit the fuck they're doin', and so the drink and drugs misery goes on. Relationships with family, partners, and the rest of society ootside their own wee world a' security, totally fucked-up!

'And what happens then? I'll tell yees whit happens. They then stick two fingers up tae everybody else and say, "Fuck yees!" But do ye know what? They're only fuckin' theirsells! Nobody else ootside their ain families gives a fuck whit happens tae them. And dae ye know why they don't give a fuck? I'll tell ye why: because everybody else believes that it's their ain stupit fuckin' faults. They say, "They were the ones that chose tae live that way." They say, "They were the ones that chose tae fuck their ain lives up!"

'Listen boys, I'm only telling yees this cause Ah care aboot what happens tae yees. There's absolutely fuck all romantic aboot fuckin' yersells up. There's absolutely fuck all romantic aboot choosing tae stick tae a life a' self-destruction, as if it somehow makes ye look like a fuckin' hero.

'That whole *"work hard, play hard"* is the biggest load a' total fuckin' pish that I've ever heard in ma natural! It's an absolute fuckin' joke I'm telling yees.'

The two youths were silent, looking at the floor.

Billy hoped that they had taken at least something in. He looked at Ninian and tilted his head to the two boys, hoping that Ninian would follow his lead.

Ninian wiped the hair across his brow with his right hand. 'Lads,' he started, 'whit Billy's telling yees is spot on. It's a fuckin' mug's game. Honest. It's aw fantasy world stuff. Yees'll think yees are missing oot oan something, but see if yees really look at it, yees are missing oot on nothing.' Ninian looked over to Billy, who nodded back his approval.

'Right, lads, that's it for this week,' Billy said, getting up from the bench. 'Come and see me doon here on Wednesday, if yees want, and we'll have a talk. If yees come on Wednesday, yees can come tae the youth club next Friday as usual, that's the deal. Otherwise, I'll see yees in three weeks. It's up to yersells.'

Billy held his right hand out to the boys and Ninian as they rose from the bench. All four shook each other's hands in turn, before the boys turned and walked away, making their way towards the exit. 'Mind and watch whit yees are doin' oot there,' Billy called out to them. 'Mind, yees are still ma mates. Use the nut!' he smiled, tapping the right side of his head with his right index finger.

The boys turned, smiled and gave him a wave back.

'Thanks for helping me wi' they boys, Ninian. Experiential learners, just like the rest of us, eh?'

'Aye, I know what yer sayin'.' Ninian smiled, as they both watched the youths walk on. 'It's good what yees are trying to do with them, Billy.'

'Aye, it's funny. It's only when ye get a bit aulder that ye see the ones in yer ain life who tried to do the same for you when you were that age. For me, it's only now that I really appreciate it. Fuck, tae think a' the nightmares that I gave ma own family. God and the nightmares that I gave tae the people who ran youth clubs like this.' Billy laughed. 'We know it aw at that age, don't we? We believe auld cunts like masell are just oot to spoil the party.

'Ye know some day some a' them will find oot, as they get aulder, that they didnae get the same chances as the other kids in wealthier places, but can ye tell them aw that at this stage? I don't know. Sometimes you wonder if you had to tell them aw that the noo, whether the fuck you'd be driving them tae the drink. Fuck, and oursells along wi' them.'

Ninian laughed and smiled as he looked to the floor. 'Aye, ye're no' jokin'.'

Billy smiled as he shook his head. 'It's hard. Ye want tae let them know the score, but at the same time, you don't want tae batter that hope oot a' them.

'Here, I meant to say to ye, Ninian,' Billy continued, offering Ninian his open right hand, 'I was really sorry to hear aboot yer pals' weans. What a fuckin' tragedy that was, and the families. God.'

'Aye, thanks, Billy,' Ninian replied, shaking Billy's hand, but unable to say more.

BOOK TWELVE:

ONGOING

23

Scene 1: Day to day

Wednesday 13 January, 1993, Sancta Maria Abbey Guest House, Nunraw, Scotland, 8:00 a.m., Dining Hall

After celebrating morning mass with the guests, made up of mainly recovering alcoholics and drug addicts, and after joining them for breakfast, Dom Leonard was now standing at the sink, helping with the washing-up.

'Have I missed the boat this morning, Dom?' Shuggie, the postman, called out, as he entered the dining hall carrying the mail for the monastery in his hands.

Dom Leonard looked up from the sink and smiled 'No, as always your timing is impeccable, Shuggie. There's a couple of sausages left, some rolls over there in the basket and the urn's still on, so, "wire in ye ken" as they say in this neck of the woods,' Dom Leonard smiled.

'You've been up here for too long, Dom Leonard,' Shuggie laughed, 'in fact, I think we might just be able tae call ye an honorary Scotsman noo,' he said, placing the letters on the table before picking up a plate, and heading towards the stainless-steel buffet trays

'*Really,*' Dom Leonard answered, 'an old Sassenach like me? What's the world coming too indeed?'

With his back to Dom Leonard, Shuggie smiled as he filled his plate. 'Ah ken ye're a good man, Dom, but dinnae get too ahead a' yersell noo. Ah wouldnae want ye tae get aw disappointed, ken.

You'll mind Ah was sayin' we might just be able.'

Dom Leonard laughed, as he dried his hands on a dishtowel, and walked over and picked up the letters, immediately recognising the Kenyan stamps on the brown A4-sized envelope.

'Shuggie, when you're finished, can you drop me off up at the monastery, please? There's something very important here that I need to look over.'

Seeing the concern on Dom Leonard's face, Shuggie rose from his chair at the table. 'Aye, no problem. C'mon, Ah can eat this oan the way up,' he said, lifting his roll from the plate.

'Are you sure? I can wait till you finish.'

But Shuggie was already heading for the exit. 'C'mon, it's no bother. I was goin' tae ask ye if ye were wantin' a lift anyway. It's still bitter cauld oot there. We'll be up at the monastery in no time.'

With Paul's letter and the other mail in his hands, Dom Leonard followed Shuggie out of the dining hall, down the stairs, and out of the main door, to the post van.

Scene 2: Shell

Wednesday 13th January, 1993, Law Hospital, 8:30 a.m.

Carrying Michelle's clothes and personal items in a rucksack that hung from his right shoulder, Gary steadied his wife with his left arm around her waist, as he continued to lead her gently, her right hand gripped firmly in his own.

Michelle was still in her nightdress and slippers and shuffled along, heavily sedated.

The dark rings around her raw eyes told their own story. She had barely slept since her daughter's death and, in what seemed like every waking moment, the tears were continuous.

As they made their way out of the hospital, Mark, the taxi driver, was waiting. He nodded to Gary and rushed towards him, taking the rucksack before quickly heading back to the taxi, opening and holding the door, allowing both of them to enter.

When they reached Forgewood, Gary tried to pay Mark for the journey, but the taxi driver would hear nothing of it, and left, after telling Gary to call him should there be 'anything' he could help with.

PART VII

BOOK THIRTEEN: EVERYTHING

24

Scene 1: Something of an Apologia

Wednesday 13th January. 1993, Sancta Maria Abbey Monastery, Nunraw, 9:00 a.m.

Sitting behind his desk in his office after reading Paul's letter about the tragic events prior to the slaughter, Dom Leonard, picked up the remaining pages of what Paul had written: his final comments that he had referred to as his 'something of an *apologia*'.

Apologia

I have prayed deeply about the events that are taking place here, Dom Leonard. It's true that we have witnessed many things. And while some have been hard to take, others have filled us with hope, in places where there looked to have been none.

Indeed, throughout this period, in times of solitude, there have been moments when my mind has been brought back to the following concepts: identity, desire, sin, pleasure, power, status, responsibility, division, guilt, fear, repentance and, reconciliation.

I suspect this will have something to do with the way I've seen things unfold here, my dear friend. Yet, despite this probability, I was never quite able to grasp how these ideas/beliefs, although apparent, were held together within the environment so to speak. In other words, I couldn't really see how these *situations* could seem to manifest, as it were, and then seem to change, only to find out sometime later that no real change had taken place at all. Perhaps what I'm trying to say has something in common with a negative reading of the saying, 'the more things change, the more they stay the same'.

But thankfully I was brought to a greater understanding of this, Dom Leonard. Indeed, the moment of revelation, which helped bring about what could be described as my perceptional shift, came to light, as it were, during my silent retreat with the Benedictines, at their monastery in October.

For it was there that one evening after supper, on retiring to my room and sitting at my desk, I found myself once again, considering Kenya's current predicament, and I suppose how *we*, humanity as a whole, have come to this.

Yet recalling this moment when I first sat down, my dear Brother, I remember that it also came to me that I was, once again, considering the same questions that man has asked from the dawn of time.

Indeed, from our history we can see that we've been offered all manner of suggestions, from the various fields, as to the how and why of life.

Today, of course, science gives us the Big Bang; our religions give us their Creation stories; and for those of an open mind, it would appear, for now at least, that both are compatible.

In terms of our ongoing evolution, however, as we ventured into the considerable undertaking of learning to stand and walk upright, we are told today, with some confidence, that our senses too were also sharpening in new ways.

Yet, although, of course, they were not merely functioning in isolation – and all play a vital role in helping us to understand our world – current evidence suggests that at certain stages we were certainly depending on some senses more than others, in what was seen to be our fight for survival.

Indeed, within this process, science is informing us that we shifted from what had been, to a greater extent, a dependence on our sense of smell, to a slightly more tactile existence – touching and feeling the external world around us.

But we would again move on from here, my dear friend, to our position today, where it is said that of all the information gathered into our brains, from the five senses, the majority – around seventy per cent – is brought to us through the eyes and our ability to *see*.

Yet remarkably, Dom Leonard, science has also found that the information we take in through the eyes is not what we might at first have imagined. Incredibly, it has been proven that at the back of our retinas, for instance, the images in and of our external world are actually, upside down. Seemingly it's the case that it's different parts of the brain, taking in light, colour and movement, that converts this information, supposedly in much the same way as a computer does, to symbol or code form, which is then *collated*, and used to provide us with an *image* that we have learned to understand in our world.

This ability of the brain to function in this way is also said to have been vital for our survival, my dear Brother. For in those moments when some of the visual information is missing from our sight, the brain through time – or so it is believed – developed the capacity to fill in the gaps; for example, enabling us to recognise predators lying in wait, camouflaged in their natural habitats, and, similarly, helping us to spot prey that would become our food.

It's with modifications such as these over millennia that are said to have helped us gain an advantage over other species, Dom Leonard. Indeed, in another fascinating example there is evidence to suggest that we were even hunting and killing animals for food, long before we developed the ability to make spears or other weapons, like bows and arrows.

Amazingly, despite the fact that prey or predators of the four-legged variety are generally faster, anthropologists are telling us that through our evolution to stand upright, we had, to a certain extent, freed our lungs; that is, in the sense that they were no longer restricted, or compressed in the way that other animals' lungs were, when they ran quickly on all fours.

In addition to this, however, during the hunt, being hairless, and able to sweat, enabled us to cool down a lot quicker, which helped us to recover faster than the animals that we were chasing over long distances. This is said to have allowed us to track and kill animals that we had chased to the point of exhaustion, through what anthropologists called *persistence hunting* – a technique that is still used here by the Maasai, and some of the other tribes living on Kenya's plains.

Yet at some point, within all of what could be described as some of the earliest developments in our evolution, something else emerged that would really make man, in a sense, man.

I am of course referring to the suggestion, from scientists and theologians alike, that our early ancestors experienced a Big Bang of their own: the Big Bang of *consciousness* – the event that made us capable of abstract thought among other things; our 'great leap forward' as it were.

When and how consciousness was experienced within our ongoing evolution is, however, still open to discussion, Dom Leonard. But in spite of this, it appears that there is now a general consensus on the idea that our earliest forms of communication would've still consisted of nothing more than simple gestures and gruntings, etched images and symbols, all made in an attempt to inform and describe what we felt, needed or saw.

Yet, although it is difficult to know how effective these initial communications would've been at the time, we can say at least that they were nonetheless vital for our survival, especially when we consider that, over time, a number of the first humans are said to have spread out across this great land mass, which we now call Africa, some sixty to seventy thousand years ago. And from here proceeded to explore and populate the furthest reaches of the globe.

Indeed, according to this analysis, in different parts of the world, our predecessors would come to experience new and varied climates and environments. They would go on to adapt to these new surroundings over time, and their bodies would change accordingly, most notably, in physical appearance.

At some stage too within this process of course, our utterings would also develop into something more structured and coherent. But we would still continue to firm up what were effectively our earliest oral traditions by using what we would find within our surroundings, transforming them into the teaching aids that our archaeologists would come to discover millennia later: our primitive effigies and sculptures, cave paintings and glyphs.

And all while of course time would continue to lead us on.

Our languages and alphabets would become more refined, and the written word would soon emerge. And so it would be that, with ongoing developments such as these, we would become more and more exposed to new experiences. New learning opportunities would arise that would continually push the boundaries of our existing knowledge, values and beliefs, changing our ideas about life, and how we live.

Our communities, societies and civilisations would emerge from within this seemingly continuous state of flux, with our more common understandings recognised and accepted by all – our 'cultural universals'.

Time has certainly played an enormous part in the sense that this pattern would seem to continue, my dear friend, and we can see from what has been recorded through the centuries that our ideas and levels of understanding have, to a certain extent, undoubtedly changed, with what was seen to be acceptable in one period being developed further, or, completely rejected in another.

Indeed, when considering our history from our vantage point, we can also see the times when it's looked as though we've been taking a step forward, only to find out, at a much later date, that we had sadly taken further steps backwards.

I am sorry for rushing over so many of the specifics relating to the history of humanity's ongoing development, my dear Brother, particularly my omission of how we are told that slight changes in our genetic make-up, the physiology of the brain, and conditions such as synaesthesia, and mental illnesses, can also greatly affect how we might come to understand life and our world – not forgetting of course the whole nature versus nurture debate and all that it entails – and how these factors too are also said to influence the growth and specific functioning of our brains, further influencing our behaviour. For leaving out all of this and more, I can only apologise.

Yet, perhaps for now at least – in considering the above letter on Kenya's current predicament – and, from our own experience of today, we can tentatively suggest that whatever humanity deems to be 'acceptable' or 'unacceptable' can be seen to be dependent on any number of variables; not only within our own people's lives, values, customs and beliefs, but also within our own individual understandings of these, and again, not forgetting of course the constricts of a given time and place.

However, it becomes clear that humanity, when we use our minds correctly, is certainly capable of some truly marvellous and beautiful things, my dear friend.

Yet sadly, of course, the opposite is also true. Through using our minds incorrectly, it's fair to say that we've come to make some tragic decisions, not only to the detriment of our own lives, but to the lives of our neighbours, and to the life on and of our beautiful and blessed earth.

It seems we are truly capable of greatness and at the same time of great catastrophe, Dom Leonard.

Learning and understanding no doubt have important parts to play, yet sadly, it appears that even this doesn't always guarantee that we will come to know, or indeed, follow, what is true.

But why does this have to be the case?

Why are we still capable of such inhumanity?

Why are we still so content not only to let our history repeat itself, but also to continually involve ourselves in filling it with the same and similar horrors?

In being given over to contemplation, my dear friend, I believe now – as I hope to explain – that the reasons behind the continuous and seemingly countless possibilities for human tragedy, lie in the fact that *we* – humanity – are prone to losing ourselves, individually and collectively, in some of the more destructive *suggestions* that run through our minds. Indeed, perhaps unsurprisingly, given what has been said above, this is a problem I see now that can be traced back to humanity's beginnings; that is, in how we came to draw and so construct our understandings of life – our reality – from the information we received from the senses. And, more specifically, how this led to confusions arising within our own particular experience of consciousness.

But what do we actually mean by this often relative and vague term 'consciousness', Dom Leonard?

Perhaps, for our purposes, we can describe consciousness as being our particular, and relative, state of awareness that enables us to *know* and *see* all that we might then come to believe to be true and real within ourselves, within our fellow man, within our environment; and of course includes the way in which we live and interact with the same.

In other words then, Dom Leonard, we can say that, in general terms, our individual and collective state of being conscious refers to our particular and relative way of knowing, seeing, and living, within whatever we might believe 'our true reality' of life to be – if I can explain...

It goes without saying that our science of today is showing us many new and very different, additional ways, in which to see life, my dear Brother. Indeed, for example, we hear now that the chemical elements found within our world – often referred to as the building blocks of life – whose specific combinations make up the varied forms of life on earth and, everything of it, are also – as this would suggest – the very same elements that make up our physical bodies.

Absolutely everything, ourselves and all that is around us, from the mountains, trees, the ground we walk on, the air we breathe and the water we drink, is made from a variation of the very same materials.

Remarkably, these very same elements are not only found on earth but are also found within, and indeed, help make up our universe.

Incredibly, science is able to tell us that the elements are produced in the unimaginable temperatures and energy generated during the life, gradual implosion, and exploding death of stars, like our sun. Yet, in this process, even more amazingly, absolutely nothing is lost, as it is only the form that changes. Indeed, over time, new forms of matter can emerge to become new stars and planets.

In addition to this, however, there is now evidence suggesting that even some of the fragments from these exploding stars – for instance, meteorites, like the ones that often enter the earth's atmosphere and land on the surface – may also carry life, so much so, in fact, that some scientists believe that life as we *see* it can begin and evolve on planets in this way too.

Yet, however difficult all of this may be for us to take in, so to speak, the information being presented to us from the scientific investigations at the atomic and sub-atomic levels can really only be described as being 'something else' entirely, my dear friend.

Indeed, for here, mind bogglingly, those who are working in this area, are now telling us — at these levels — that every physical or solid object, absolutely everything that we can see and touch in our world, our environment, our home — from the bricks we use to build them, to the chairs and beds we relax on — and even our very selves; in other words, all things, <u>everything</u>, can be seen as being one, great, limitless sea, of moving particles.

Of course, the very universe is included within this sea, as it too is made up of these particles. And even here we are told that some of these, for example, neutrinos, have such little or no mass, that they can even pass through what we know as physical matter, undetected. Indeed, it's believed that these tiny particles not only enter the earth's atmosphere and pass straight through the planet itself, but that around seventy trillion of these very same particles are passing through our physical bodies, every second, without our knowing.

Science is really showing us some incredible and fascinating things about these materials, my dear friend. Indeed, even now it's being said, that, the very atoms of our bodies, once belonged to other things; i.e., other things that existed, long before we came to be; for example, prehistoric trees, pieces of rock, and so on.

It's almost as if we've reached the stage where scientific fact sounds stranger than science fiction. It's truly amazing when you consider that absolutely everything, from our bodies to everything within the world around us, and everything within the entire universe, is not only made up of the same things, but all of these things themselves are now coming to be seen by some as being integral, unitive parts, of one, natural, system of life.

These are really wonderful discoveries, Dom Leonard. And new breakthroughs will undoubtedly emerge, which will hopefully further encourage humanity, as a whole, to come to accept, and so consider the implications and possibilities of such information, that is, in terms of how we might now come to see life, our reality, both within and around us, from this more holistic perspective. Indeed, and how, in adopting this way of seeing, we might also someday overcome the often difficult task of *living* with ourselves, with our fellow man, with our environment, with everything.

Yet, perhaps strangely, Dom Leonard, despite the fact that all of this wonderful information is being brought to light now, I can't help but feel that it somehow makes something else appear even more amazing.

For although they would be ridiculed during their lifetimes, and some branded heretics, and even murdered, remarkably, albeit using a different type of language, some of the teachings of the saints and mystics of old, had already been telling humanity this truth about the unitive and all-inclusive oneness of life.

Indeed, with this being the case, perhaps the questions then become: How were these often ordinary, everyday, simple people from the ancient past, able to come to such knowledge? How was it possible that they were able to *know*, to some extent, what our science is only now coming to discover?

Moreover, when we bear in mind the numerous factors and variables which have an impact on our ability to *see* life and reality, are we suggesting then that the lives of the mystics were somehow less *troubled* by such hindrances?

Perhaps consolingly for the rest of us, Dom Leonard, we find that, in this regard, we are not so different after all. At particular moments in their lives, the mystics themselves were also faced with similar challenges.

And it is precisely here, my dear Brother, within these 'similarities' and within these challenges that the lives of the mystics can assist us. Indeed, for in reviewing their 'experiences', we find once more, that it is our own particular and relative state of consciousness, at any given moment, that tells us something about the way in which we are consciously experiencing, seeing, and so, living out, our everyday lives – which I will now try to explain further...

Interestingly, although we could say that it is a gross generalisation, given the complexities and stages of life, and what it means to be human, it's often been said in the past – and, to some extent, even today – that some of us see the glass half-empty, while others see it half-full; that is, some have a pessimistic outlook on life and reality, whereas others are seen to have a more optimistic outlook.

These points of view, as Evelyn Underhill states in her *magnum opus*, *Mysticism*, were also 'perspectives' that were evident in the lives of the mystics, although, in their case, it was generally evidenced that some were pessimistic about the human condition and their own particular sense of imperfection.

Yet, significantly, Dom Leonard, these different ways in which even the mystics at times saw themselves, their neighbours and all life, 'their reality', was also of great interest to the mystics' contemporaries.

Indeed, for when these scholars from the fields of philosophy and theology studied the written personal accounts of what the mystics were saying about how life, and reality truly was, from their 'experiences', these academics would then not only use this information to try and develop their own understandings, and shape religious doctrines, they would also, in a sense, then go as far as labelling each mystic – that is, as someone who held to a pessimistic world view, or as someone who held to a more optimistic world view.

And so it would be that, over time, these simple terms of 'pessimistic' and 'optimistic' would come to be used to sum up the slightly more complex theories of Emanation (associated with transcendence) and Immanence, respectively – two particular ways of seeing life, which can tell us something more about our human experience of consciousness, and why we must look at both very briefly.

In order to help us understand how the mystics who came to be associated with Emanation theory perceived life and reality, Underhill quotes, among others, St Thomas Aquinas at a particular moment in his life, who suggested that:

'As all the perfections of Creatures descend in order from God, who is the height of perfection, man should begin from the lower creatures and ascend by degrees, and so advance to the knowledge of God. And because in that roof and crown of all things, God, we find the most perfect unity, and everything is stronger and more excellent the more thoroughly it is one; it follows that diversity and variety increase in things, the further they are from Him who is the first principle of all.'

Those who held to this pessimistic theory and saw life in this way were said in general terms to perceive God as *separate* from the material universe, and so separate from humanity, but illuminating Creation with life from far off; that is, as in life emanating from what was to them the Absolute or Source of All Life.

Man, according to the proponents of this view, can, however, somehow ascend or, more specifically, transcend 'upwards and outwards' from the more prevalent sense driven reality of the 'human condition' – to a 'higher level of consciousness', from where he can then come to 'experience' True Reality, and, whereby, in being united with 'It' once again, can 'perceive' life, as how the mystics would claim 'It' truly is.

And so, as Underhill reminds us, this way of 'seeing' life 'comes naturally to the temperament which leans to pessimism, which sees a 'great gulf fixed' between itself and its desire, and is above all things sensitive to the elements of evil and imperfection in its own character and in the normal experience of man. Permitting these elements to dominate its field of consciousness such a temperament constructs from its perceptions and prejudices the concept of a material world and a normal self which are very far from God.'

At the opposite end of this, what would seem to be an apparent continuum, those who are said to hold to the theory of Immanence – which Underhill suggests is prominent in today's theology – can be seen to be of a more 'optimistic' temperament. Indeed, for those holding this view, 'the quest of the Absolute is no long journey, but a realisation of something which is implicit in the self and in the universe: an opening of the eyes of the soul upon the Reality in which it is bathed. For them, the earth is literally 'crammed with heaven'.

With these two examples, we can hopefully see again the differences in states of consciousness, and how these influence perception – God is perceived to be outside of man, and so too the material universe, but somehow illuminating it with life which passes from Him, in Emanation theory, whereas God, as perceived by those holding to the Immanence theory, is believed to be within man, and so too, within everything.

In another interesting example used by Underhill to express this idea of Immanence, she mentions to us that, 'God,' says Plotinus, 'is not external to anyone, but is present with all things, though they are ignorant that He is so.'

And, expanding on this by way of her own description, she suggests that, 'the Absolute Whom all seek does not hold himself aloof from an imperfect universe, but dwells within the flux of things: stands as it were at the very threshold of consciousness and knocks, awaiting the self's slow discovery of her treasures. 'He is not far from any one of us, for in Him we live move and have our being' is the pure doctrine of Immanence: a doctrine whose teachers are drawn from among the souls which react more easily to the touch of the Divine than to the sense of alienation and of sin, and are naturally inclined to love rather than to awe. [Creation], the universe, could we see it as it is, would be perceived as the self-development, the self-revelation of this indwelling Deity. The world is not projected from the Absolute [as in Emanation theory], but immersed in God. The world process, then, is the slow coming to fruition of that Divine Spark which is latent alike in the Cosmos and in man.'

And, again, using another exponent's example, 'God,' says [Meister] Eckhart, 'is nearer to me than I am to myself; He is just as near to wood and stone, but they do not know it.'

Interestingly, Dom Leonard, despite the fact that those in the past, studying these two theories, would see a very clear distinction between Emanation and Immanence, Underhill, from her research, concludes however, that, in truth – by way of their explanations – many of the great mystics were often drifting in and out of, or touching on, both notions.

Yet with these 'features', which were associated with both theories clearly evident, Underhill claimed that this did not dilute the truth of the mystic's account, but rather, actually proved its absolute validity, stating, '[these accounts] do not contradict, but complete each other. They form, when taken together, an almost perfect definition of that Godhead which is the object of the mystic's desire: the Divine Love which, Immanent in the soul, spurs on that soul to union with the transcendent [Emanating] and Absolute Light – at once the source, the goal, the created light of all things.'

Here then, 'when taken together', according to Underhill, was the sure sign within the mystic's 'experience' that the mystic was continuing on the right path.

With this very brief retelling of the Emanate and Immanent nature of life – from the mystics' perspective – perhaps we can then clear up any of the misconceptions that we might have regarding the term 'mysticism', my dear friend – and who better to explain this to us than Underhill herself, who states,

'Mysticism, in its pure form, is the science of ultimates, the science of union with the Absolute and nothing else. Under the spur of this love and will, the whole personality rises in acts of contemplation and ecstasy to a level of consciousness at which it becomes aware of a new field of perception. By this awareness, by this 'loving sight', it is stimulated to a new life in accordance with the Reality which it has beheld.'

With this definition, here we see again from Underhill the underlying Emanate and Immanent of Reality 'at work' in the suggestion that humanity can indeed rise within 'consciousness' – to a higher "level" – from where we are then able to 'experience' and so come to 'know' and perceive the 'True Reality of Life'.

And so, as one might expect, Dom Leonard, it was this 'conscious experience' of union with the Absolute which was of paramount importance to the mystics.

Indeed, for it was here, within this experience of union, where the True Nature of Reality could be 'known' and 'confirmed': knowledge of man's true self, and knowledge of God, all of which, when realised, naturally brought about a True Relationship with All Life. For the mystics, this 'experienced' True Knowledge of Reality was worth infinitely more to humanity than any philosophical or theological ponderings, musings, or postulations on 'Reality' – no matter however 'useful' they appeared to be.

Yet, crucially, my dear Brother, as the mystics would also tell us, as was almost always the case, this 'True Reality' could only come to be 'experienced' and 'known', as it were, first and foremost, through a conscious meeting within the 'heart': that place, in our human experience, so described by Thomas Merton, as 'the deepest psychological ground of one's personality, the inner sanctuary where self-awareness goes beyond analytical reflection and opens out into metaphysical and theological confrontation with the Abyss of the unknown yet present.' The place – he tells us, using a quote from Augustine's *Confessions* – where we encounter the 'one who is 'more intimate to us than we are to ourselves'.

And so it was here, in the 'heart', according to the mystics, where this meeting was realised: a meeting that was Willed by Love; their Beloved's and theirs. It was essentially 'a call' to a 'conscious rest' in union with Perfect Love, as well as being 'a call' to participate in an outpouring of 'conscious action' in the world, in union, with Perfect Love.

And so, hopefully, we can now come to understand a little more why the mystics – from their point of view – would tell men of science, philosophy, and theology, over and over again, that the True Reality of Life could never be approached through the 'senses' or indeed through the intellect's logic or reason alone; and, that, if they continued in this way, they would never find, or 'experience', Life, as it truly is.

Indeed, Aldous Huxley – writing some years after Underhill's 'Mysticism' was first published – tells us something similar from his studies on the mystics in his 'Perennial Philosophy', suggesting,

'But the nature of this one Reality is such that it cannot be directly and immediately apprehended except by those who have chosen to fulfil certain conditions, making themselves loving, pure in heart, and poor in spirit. Why should this be so? We do not know. It is just one of those facts which we have to accept, whether we like them or not and however implausible or unlikely they may seem. But it is a fact, confirmed and re-confirmed during two or three thousand years of religious history that the ultimate Reality is not clearly and immediately apprehended, except by those who have made themselves loving, pure in heart and poor in spirit.'

And again, 'no amount of theorising can tell us much about divine Reality as can be directly apprehended by a mind in a state of detachment, charity and humility. The self-validating certainty of direct awareness cannot in the very nature of things be achieved except by those equipped with the moral 'astrolabe of God's mysteries'. If one is not oneself a sage or saint, the best thing he can do, in the field of metaphysics, is to study the works of those who were, and who, because they had <u>modified their merely human mode of being, were capable of a more than merely human kind and amount of knowledge.</u>' (I have underlined part of this comment for a particular reason, Dom Leonard, and will explain in due course.)

Speaking of Aquinas's life also, Huxley tells us that the saint – at a later moment in his life – came to a similar understanding himself, when 'after his experience of infused contemplation he refused to go on with his theological work, declaring that everything he had written up to that time was as mere straw compared with the immediate knowledge which had been vouchsafed to him' – that is, immediate, True Knowledge of Reality, which he had received during his 'experience of infused contemplation'.

Indeed, to the mystics themselves, as Aquinas came to understand, it seemed that some of those who were seen to be the studious intellectuals of the day – if I can use an analogy – were continuing to ask the same question: that is, where is the forest?

And, for the mystics?

Well, for their part, they kept giving them what was the same, and, indeed, their only answer, that man was not only standing among the Trees, but was actually, in all truth, an eternal, living, unitive part, of the Great Forest Itself.

Yet, of course, many mystics would use language that would sound insane to the intellect: for instance, they would call for the 'leaving behind of all attachments', tell people to 'live in the world, but be not of the world' etc., when journeying towards the Absolute. They saw wisdom in Christ's 'lose your life to find it' and his call to 'deny yourself, pick up your cross, and follow me.'

But as developments in psychology are shedding more light on what the mystics meant when they were telling men that True Reality could not be approached through 'the senses' and 'intellect' alone, we find that it is also shedding light on what Christ was really teaching us, my dear friend; which also, I see now, comes back to the way in which we began using our minds in the beginning, which I hope to explain.

When 'man' began to experience 'consciousness', Dom Leonard, as we have said, he was indeed exploring, and discovering, all that was around him.

However, what we tend to forget, or fail to really accept, is that, while he was doing all of this, 'man' was also, for the first time, freely, coming to explore, experience, and discover, his own mind.

And it is here, my dear Brother, I wonder whether 'we' – humanity – for the most part, may have, somewhat unwittingly, wandered into a horrendous nightmare, and believed it to be true. For, in trying to survive, use, and understand his environment, and, through trying survive, use, and understand his mind, 'man' would tragically – as the ancients would later describe – 'fall' for the temptation.

And what was this temptation that man 'fell' for?

Some of the sages and prophets of old would see it as man chasing his fantasies of 'power' (and this is of course a very important part of the story, of how we used, and, sadly, continue to use, our minds to this day).

But the mystics believed that man 'fell' for an even more tragic temptation, my dear Brother; indeed, one, that would not only set in motion his desires for 'power' but one that would effectively go on to 'form' and, to some extent, 'set in place' humanity's now predominant state, or level, of 'consciousness'.

Indeed, for when 'using' and 'taking in' his information from his environment, man, <u>for the most part</u>, would surely soon come to 'see' and so believe that every piece of information that he received was from the <u>external world</u>: that is, for the world, and everything else, was external to him, it was on the 'outside'. For man, 'saw', 'touched', 'heard', 'smelt', and 'tasted' <u>everything</u> that was 'outside' his 'physical' body.

As a result of this interpretation – from what would seem to be this overpowering evidence – man would begin to 'interact' and 'develop' in a way, whereby, he would be continually reinforcing a 'view' of reality that would go on to become our more prevalent understanding. In other words, my dear friend, the 'consciousness' of man for the most part, would become concentrated around the notion that we were 'separated' from our environment, from our neighbour, from All Life, from Everything.

Indeed, by continually reinforcing this 'view' of the world, we would soon come to 'believe', 'feel' and 'accept' more and more, that we were alone, isolated, cut-off, abandoned.

We'd get used to this way of 'seeing', this way of 'thinking', and 'see' it, as our 'reality'; a reality in which we felt and believed we were 'separated' from nature, from our environment, from our neighbour, from All Life, from God.

Yet, according to the mystics and contemplatives, we weren't finished there, my dear Brother, for in accepting 'separation' and 'isolation' as our 'reality', we soon came to consider, and so too 'believe', that, if we could then, eventually, gain enough of what we 'understood' to be 'power' in our environment – acquiring 'it' whether it be through acts of violence: stealing, defending and hoarding 'wealth', being given 'status', being seen as 'knowledgeable', and so on – we, as individuals, and communities, would then, no longer, feel 'afraid', would no longer, live in 'fear', would no longer, feel 'empty', would no longer, feel 'alone'.

We would become 'self-sufficient'. And so, accordingly, and in order to be as such, 'our world view' would become one in which we 'saw' that we had to compete with each other. We believed we had to compete and 'win' in order to have more 'power', in our environment – and so too our world – than those around us.

Huxley again brings us the contemplatives' perspective on this, stating, 'For, as all exponents of the Perennial Philosophy have constantly insisted, man's obsessive consciousness of, and insistence on being, a separate self, is the final and most formidable obstacle to the unitive knowledge of God. To be a self is, for them [the mystics], the original sin, and to die to self, in feeling, will and intellect, is the final and all-inclusive virtue.' (This use of language, i.e., what Huxley and the mystics mean by the 'self', as we have said above, is cleared up for us through recent understandings in psychology, which we will look at shortly, my dear friend.)

From the mystic's point of view – and what science is now showing us – we can say then that they would tell us that 'man', for the most part, tragically fell for the temptation 'to believe' that he was somehow able to exist outside of, and, indeed, was separated from, the Absolute – in other words, 'separated' from the Very Essence of All That Exists. They would suggest that he failed to recognise, at the very core of his being, that he was, already, a living part of Everything.

They would say that he was unable to 'see' that this Life who made, lived, and moved, within Everything around him – the Seen and the Unseen – was the very same Life who made, lived, and moved, within man himself. 'Man', for the mystics, was, already, an eternal, living part, of what they called the Unitive Life. He was, already, and forever, a unique part, of All That Is.

CONSCIOUSNESS AND PERCEPTION

But what can we then say about the mystics' experiences and their lives, Dom Leonard?

Firstly, according to Underhill and Huxley, people of this nature were, and are, evident, in all religions of Love. And they tell us that, although the mystics themselves would say that words were inadequate in terms of trying to describe their 'encounters', all would speak of their 'experience' or 'meeting' with the Absolute in the same way – a union with Perfect Love.

They were (and are) undoubtedly human beings, perceiving reality in a different way from the majority.

Yet, if we are talking about 'perceptions' and the mind, we are of course also talking about psychology, my dear friend.

Today, our current psychology tells us that the ego, in general terms, is the part of the mind that presents us with notions of ourselves, i.e. 'suggestions' on who we are, or who we can be – propositions that we can choose to believe in and test out, i.e., through acting them out in our physical world; thereby creating a self-image, from where we can go on to create a sense of self – <u>our identity</u>.

But, with further developments in this field, particularly from psychologists now recognising the evidence from physicists working at the sub-atomic and quantum levels – as we have touched on above – we are coming to understand, that it is also, this very way of 'seeing' that the mystics would claim that humanity had entered into, in the very beginning. Indeed, for the mystics, it is in this 'consciousness' – which 'we' have created – where we continue to 'experience' and 'believe' that we are separated from Everything.

So, how can we 'see' it today?

For all of us today, we could say, that, in one way, it is observable in those moments – within our minds – when we experience those many puffed up suggestions of how 'we', ourselves, would be 'seen' by others in 'our world', if we were somehow 'successful', 'famous', 'wealthy', 'prestigious', 'perfect', and, similarly, in those 'moments' when we would 'show' everyone else how 'knowledgeable' or how 'right' we are, in any given situation.

However, what we don't often 'see' in these 'suggestions' is the undercurrent that runs through all: the ego's desire for 'power'. For the ego offers us the illusion of 'power' within the illusory self-images that it presents us with, the 'power' we are tempted to believe will take away our fears, our loneliness, our emptiness, etc.

Indeed, as we have indicated above, throughout the development of our communities, societies, and civilisations, being 'powerful' has always depended on our egotistical understandings of 'power'; which has included our ideas on what it means to have it, and, how we can get it, which, in turn, further shapes our ideas on who we think we are, who we think we should be, and, what we need to do, in order to be 'powerful'.

With these new understandings, my dear friend, we can see then, that when Underhill and Huxley share with us what Christ and the true mystics within all religions of Love were imploring us to do, that is, to 'leave the self and find Life' that all were, undoubtedly, telling us to leave and 'deny' what is really this <u>false self</u> or <u>false selves</u> that the ego consciousness presents us with – these many fantastical self-images that we unconsciously identify with, and, sadly, often believe to be the truth of who we are.

This of course begs the question, however, that if we are not these false selves that the ego consciousness presents us with, what are we?

Here, I have added the words in brackets to Huxley's quote from William Law's writings, who presents us with a similar question in a rather more enlightened fashion, when asking, 'What could begin to deny [this false] self, if there were not something in man different from [his false] self?'

Christ and the mystics, of course, had their own view as to what was 'in man' that was different from his false selves. However, perhaps we can say for now, that, when man accepts these false suggestions as the truth of who he is, and tries to make an identity to suit (essentially, making up, and identifying, with an illusion) that this was, undoubtedly, to Christ and the mystics – speaking from their 'experience' of the Unitive Life, which, to them, was the highest level of human experience and consciousness; literally, the Fullness of Life – nothing more than man, unconsciously, opting to believe and accept a heartbreaking and diabolical abomination in place of Truth.

But, if Christ and the mystics are correct – and we see now from quantum physics and psychology what they meant by 'leaving and turning away from the self', is, today, what we know to be a turning away from these 'false selves' of the ego consciousness – the next step they appear to take is to say that if 'we' have identified with and live our lives believing that we are this false image, this 'suggestion' from our ego consciousness. And, if we have accepted this image as the truth of who we really are, i.e., a false identity, it follows that we must be 'perceiving' not only ourselves, and everything in our world, incorrectly, but that we are, first and foremost, <u>living our lives in what is essentially a false consciousness.</u>

With this in mind, perhaps we now have an additional reason as to why the mystics would tell the 'intellectuals' of the day that they would never 'experience' True Reality. Indeed, for if the majority of men are living in the false belief of a false self as the truth of who they are, then it not only follows that they are thereby living in a false consciousness, it becomes clear that the faculties of the mind – the will and the intellect – are being governed and controlled, by a man, whose perception of his own reality is false. If the starting position, i.e., of, and from, his own perspective is false, then these faculties cannot possibly function at anywhere near the optimum level. Furthermore, if his 'consciousness' and 'perception' of his own reality is false, what 'darkness' will he 'see' in the world. In other words, how many other false selves will he see all around him?

Indeed, for if he doesn't 'know' his true self, how can he possibly 'know' what is true, in anyone, or anything else?

Underhill, in her later work, 'Practical Mysticism' offers us something similar to this when she explains, 'It is not merely that your intellect has assimilated, united with a superficial and unreal view of the world. Far worse: your will, your desire, the sum total of your energy, has been turned the wrong way, harnessed to the wrong machine The surface [false] self, left for so long in undisputed possession of the conscious field, has grown strong, and cemented itself like a limpet to the rock of the obvious; gladly exchanging freedom for apparent security, and building up a defensive shell of 'fixed ideas'.

And, again, if this is man's predominant level of 'consciousness', 'his mind is full of little whirlpools, twists and currents, conflicting systems, incompatible desires. One after another, he centres himself on ambition, love, duty, friendship, social convention, politics, religion, [false] self interest in one of its myriad forms; making of each a core round which whole sections of his life are arranged. One after another, these things either fail him or enslave him.'

Why?

Because, accordingly, when we take and shape our identity – cultural, social, religious, political or otherwise – from either one, or 'any mix' of these ever changing false images that the ego consciousness presents us with, we not only unconsciously come to build up, shape, and reinforce our 'opinions' and 'tastes' of 'everything' to suit, we 'genuinely' – and falsely – go on to 'think', and so 'believe', that we really 'know' and can therefore, really 'judge', what is true, and, what is real, within ourselves, within our fellow man, and, within our world; all of which, only results in further failure, disillusionment, suffering, and enslavement.

Of course, throughout our history, all of this has had truly devastating effects on us, my dear friend

In formulating his understanding around the notion that he was 'separated' from Everything, man, 'entered' into the 'kingdom' that Christ said was 'divided against itself', the kingdom that is not of Love, the kingdom where man experiences 'separation' and 'division' both within and outwith.

Indeed, for the mystics, the ego's 'images' of 'power' are in no way, never have, or ever will be 'part' of our true identity. They are illusions. The only power that they have is the 'power' that we unconsciously give them i.e., each time we tragically live within the conflict zone of trying to be 'like' them; and so, continuing to strengthen, within us, our false belief and 'experience of separation', separation within ourselves, separation from our fellow man, and separation from All Life, our man-made prison, where every self-pride, self-hatred and self-punishment reign.

And so, to those who were given to 'experience' moments of True Knowledge and Wisdom, humanity's predominant 'consciousness' and 'belief' that we are separated from All Life was, and is, our greatest tragedy.

Indeed, for in their view – from their experience of Union with the True Consciousness of Life – they recognised that absolutely nothing, no-thing, can exist outside of, or, indeed, apart from, What Is. For the mystics, this Wholeness of Life Itself, is, All That Is. It Is Everything That Exists; It is the Seen and the Unseen, of the Unitive Life.

To these people of faith, Life, in this context, is as Complete as it is Whole. It is inclusive of, and is, Everything, which of course, includes every person. It is the True and Only Reality: Perfect Oneness, with no 'separate parts': and no opposite, of any kind, whatsoever: Perfect Love, Perfect Consciousness, Perfect Existence, of which, we, all of us, are unique, inclusive, and unitive parts.

Interestingly, Dom Leonard, when we look at Underhill's and Huxley's illustrations and descriptions, based on the experiences of the mystics and saints of various religions, it is perhaps important then to point out, as they remind us, that they were not talking about people who were experiencing or touching 'something' somewhere far off in the distant future, millennia from now, or this 'something' that man's 'consciousness' can somehow evolve to. (Nor, as Underhill points out, was she talking of any notion of 'pantheism' or 'the doctrine of deification' – in which a person holds his transfigured self to be identical with the Indwelling God. Indeed, she was also, for that matter, not speaking of becoming stuck along the way, i.e., in seeking only what is really the false self's over indulgence in quietism, where the individual seeks only to experience and bask in the ineffable peace often received in moments of contemplation; as though this was some kind of end in itself.)

They were, however, relaying the facts of the mystics' lives' and the possibility for the rest of us of a life experienced now, in the present, fully conscious – operating at our optimum capacity – as an integral part of the Unitive Life: The Only Reality.

Indeed, for it was only in this 'Life' that, according to the mystics' accounts, all senses and mental faculties are brought to their fullness, that Life may be actively experienced in all its Fullness.

And so, this Life was not something that was just for some and not for others. Indeed, the mystics saw that this Reality was for everyone, because, for them, it was the Truth of humanity's existence. In a sense, it was more than a destiny – for it was, already, the Living Truth; now, here, in the Present. (Yet, it was also – within time and space – 'man's' becoming, knowing, being; all three, which were integral to the 'experience'; all three, included along with other tell-tale markers or illuminations that would confirm to a person that they were following the correct route: the discipline and the accompanying grace of the mystic way.)

Indeed, as well as being confirmed by Underhill's research, this importance of 'a lived experience' of Immanent and Emanate Reality was also confirmed by Huxley, who stated that, 'the sincere worship of God changes character as well as conduct, and does something to modify consciousness. But the complete transformation of consciousness, which is 'enlightenment', 'deliverance', 'salvation', comes only when God is thought of as the Perennial Philosophy affirms Him to be – immanent as well as transcendent [Emanate], supra-personal as well as personal – and when religious practices are adapted to this conception.'

The story of the mystics, saints, and other great contemplatives, then, could be said to be the story of men and women, like us, who were perhaps more sensitive to – and aware of – the false consciousness, and the false selves, that are often the everyday reality for the rest of us.

Where we continue to stay, however, they choose to leave; i.e., leave the false selves and deny the 'identities' that the ego consciousness offered them.

Some continued in this struggle over the course of their lives, their crosses, with even the slightest flashes of grace and illuminations of Truth, being enough for them – enough for them to continue in the purgation of the false selves that they had unconsciously clothed themselves with; thereby allowing grace and faith to lead them on, that they may live in harmony with All Life.

Indeed, for they knew what Ansari of Herat meant – again, quoted by Huxley – when he said, 'know that when you learn to lose your [false] self, you will reach the Beloved. There is no other secret to be learned, and more than this is not known to me.'

With science providing humanity with the concrete evidence it craves, perhaps the time will come when this Wholeness of which we are in, will no longer be dismissed as the ramblings of a hermit, or a peace lover's utopian dream, Dom Leonard.

And as Christians, of course, we know that Christ told us that He is the Way, the Truth and the Life. And this too is interesting, Dom Leonard, for in St Thomas's Gospel He tells us,

'I am the Light that shines over all things. I am Everything. From Me all came forth, and to Me all return. Split a piece of wood, and I am there. Lift a stone, and you will find Me there.'

And what did St Paul tell us about Christ?

'There is only Christ: He is Everything and He is in Everything.'

The suggestion here again of course is that there is only Life. And that Everything Is Life.

And so, although the terms Christ and Life are sometimes used in different contexts, or used to express different things, I see now that they are in Truth, also one and the same, my dear Brother. Indeed, although we could say that this has always been the case, I have never really experienced this Reality until recently.

If the truth be told, perhaps I was hesitant to write and believe such things as these before now. Perhaps I was afraid to accept them; perhaps I wasn't ready for them. However, I came to realise that, even if I do close my mind to Truth, it doesn't mean that Truth Itself ceases to exist.

And so, from reflecting on my experience here in Kenya, Dom Leonard – and from what I've found out about its regrettable history – I've seen the problems we encounter when we try to create another world; 'our world' separate from Love. I've seen the problems we encounter when we live in our false identities and try to fulfil, at any cost, our desires for false power, wealth, pleasure, and a life of irresponsibility.

Today, poor men, who've had little material wealth all their lives, are now drunk on a false sense of what power is, and are going around wide-eyed, looking drug crazed, killing their neighbours, all because someone says it is okay to do so 'this is your tribe', 'this is your identity', 'this is who you are, take what is yours!'

And isn't it the same for so many around the world, living a way of life that's 'expected of them' in communities and societies that tell them, 'this is who you are', 'this is what you do', 'know your station', 'do what you've to do!'

And how strange it is, Dom Leonard, that when we see a vulnerable infant living in poverty, or an African child malnourished and starving, that we find our heartstrings being tugged, yet when we see an adult living this way, we are told that they are just another drain on 'our resources'; just another waste of space from the dregs of our world, sponging an existence.

Yet, who made the world this way? Who put in place the boundaries that lock people into places where war is often the everyday? Who put in place the boundaries that lock people into places where famine and drought are possible? And who made the unjust social and economic structures and then tried to convince us that these things were 'natural'; falsely justifying them through the misuse of science?

I am of course thinking of the poor and long-term unemployed at home too, Dom Leonard. Those in our society who are made to feel 'worthless' by what it tells them; a tag that establishes itself so well, indeed, that it becomes a self-fulfilling prophecy, a damning indictment to continue in the self-destructive behaviours that destroy their lives and the lives of their families, making themselves deaf to the Love inside, Who tells them, 'My child, this is not who you are!'

Will we continue, my dear friend, to let the world or the societies that we have created from the ego consciousness define who, and what we are, by what it tells us? Is this the identity we choose from it, or, is it the identity we are given by it? Sadly, either way, it is an identity that we try to live up to; yet deep within our hearts, we feel uncomfortable, for we know, that all is not well; we know, somewhere, deep within, in Truth, that it isn't truly us.

And the 'elite' too, Dom Leonard, with their 'earthly power' and 'wealth', orchestrating their war plans well in advance, bringing about further perversions of Hegel's dialectic, creating ever greater instability in the world, covertly or otherwise, that they may then bring about their pre-planned outcomes, and so manipulating the 'ordinary peoples' of the world, throwing them into situations whereby they then cry out for the only solution, 'more war', the 'saving grace' – unaware that their so- called 'rescuers' were also the very same manufacturers of their doom.

And for what reason?

None other than to 'take more', go beyond the 'maintenance' of their status quo; that they may garner even more 'power', 'wealth', 'status' and 'control'.

Yet, in spite of this, Dom Leonard, these 'elite' brothers and sisters of ours, are they too not in need of Christ the physician? Are these gross excesses, in part, not similar to the uncontrolled desires that we may find, say, in a person with psychopathic tendencies, or, someone, say, struggling with an addiction? For truly, is this behaviour not the result of some form of illness also?

And for what reason do we continue in this destructive vein, but to try and live up to a false identity, to try and fill the imaginary void inside, to try and blank out the guilt and pain of separation, a gap within, that isn't truly there?

And isn't it ironic that in all of this we believe ourselves to be in control? But have we not handed over the responsibility for our very own lives to the 'things' of the world, creating, worshipping, and enslaving ourselves to the false images of our egos, as we struggle to be 'like' them?

And so I see now, Dom Leonard, that the proverb, 'the more things change, the more they stay the same' can be seen to be a summary of humanity's 'experience' of the ego consciousness. For nothing will ultimately change until every single one of us is brought out of it

Yet, in spite of our unconsciousness, His Mercy is greater still, for even if 'we', as yet, do not know and have not experienced our Truth, He is continually at work doing Our Father's Will, gently drawing us by the Spirit to Himself, that we may come to know ourselves as we are known by God.

Taking me by the hand, together, we approach the tree of Life.

Here, He gently raises me upon His shoulders.

Here, He shares with me, the fruit from its branches.

With each mouthful, just as the scales begin to fall from my eyes, so too, the shambolic mutterings of the ego fall from my mind.

I begin to realise that I have been brought to a forgotten, yet somehow, familiar place;

to a place where I re-encounter the Vastness of Existence;

to Clarity, beyond thought;

to a place where the Peace of His Reality, within me,

is at once, made known;

to a place where I acknowledge,

in the Stillness within Movement,

in the Silence within Sound,

in the Love That Is All Life,

I Am.

For through His Providence, all live, and are brought to Love: His Love, Perfect Love, where we are once again consoled, and once again made Whole.

And so, as we take the humble steps to trust in the Truth of his infinite love and mercy, His grace gently guides us from fear to understanding. 'Our' mistaken belief in the separation is exposed to His Light, and the Spirit Himself, and our spirits, bear united witness that we are children of God. In Love, we freely return, that, which was freely given, and as we naturally come to embrace Our Father's Will as our own, so our minds are healed in their return to Wholeness; free once more to carry out our true purpose, that purpose we had from the beginning, that purpose of enabling the Way, that purpose of ensuring that Divine Love is known, is received, and is shared, in the physical realm, with each and every one of our brothers and sisters. Unbound from their chains of self-punishment, and self-hatred, our minds are truly resurrected from their clouded egoistic tombs to a perfect dawn; freed from all consequences of the human tragedy of the lie, forever. Here, our Holy Innocence is revealed to us within the Home that we have never truly left; in the LOVE gushing forth from the Wellspring of Eternal Life, the Perpetual Light that bathes and flows through the sanctuary of our very souls, the True Dignity and Joyous Beauty of All That Exists, and continues to make All Things new. Glory be to the Father, and to the Son, and to the Holy Spirit.

When we awaken to the Reality of the Love that courses through our very being, and is naturally extended into the world, we not only see through eyes of Love, but we see the Love That Is Life Itself. We see again what is Holy and Sacred, and know once again the Love that spoke to Create, spreading and sharing His Glorious Majesty Forever.

We see with Him, all that He has made, and we know Him, in all that He has made

> Ineffable Love
> Looks through
> Ineffable Love
> At All
> That Is
> Ineffable Love

'There is only Christ: He is everything and He is in everything.'

'If we live, we live in Christ. If we die, we die in Christ. Whether we live or die, we are in Christ'

There is no death. There is only Life. There is only Christ. There is only Love.

I have now come to the end, my dear Brother, and I pray I have not caused you any anxiety with what I have written. I hope I have not failed you as your student. I am truly grateful for everything we have shared throughout the years.

Thank you, my dear friend. You have been a true model of

Christianity throughout my life.

God Bless,

With love and prayers,

Your dear friend and brother in Christ,

Paul

Order of the Divine Servant

Dom Leonard removed his bifocals with his right hand, and leaned back in his chair.

After some moments, he picked the remaining pages from the desk, and walked over to the window.

Standing there, he savoured what little heat the winter sun provided. And, looking out, through the glass, *out* at the partly frosted gardens in the cloister, he became conscious of his breathing. Sliding his spectacles on to his face, he turned sideways. And, holding Paul's reflections in the light, he drew them in slowly; word by word, sentence by sentence one by one.

Scene 2: Reflections

Emblems of a distant land
            radiate Love
                      before my hand

                    Till in my heart
                    I come to know...

                  He
                    Who
                      dressed
                        these
                          flowers
                              so...
                  He
                    Who
                      moves
                        these
                          birds
                            to
                              sing...
                  The Light
                    Who
                      Shines
                      in
                        Every
                          Thing

***

Life's Sacred Beauty burns to find
       recognition
           in my mind...
Immaculate
    Love
      Enshrined
        How long
           must I stay blind...?

For what can I see without Thee...
        Pain...
         Death...
           Misery...?
A life without meaning
    to a hole in the ground...
A scatter of days
    where shadows abound...
A treasure trove of tears
    my only bouquet for the years...
   A casket from a tree
      holding
        what
         remains
           of
            me...
What a murderous view of Life
      Man's empty reason
         and its knife...

     ***

CONSCIOUSNESS AND PERCEPTION

Who
    can
        speak
            of
                The Light
                    carried in The Breeze?
                  Seeking
                    out
                        His Father's treasures
                          in
                            the
                              depths of stormy seas...

Gathering
    every
        diamond...
            dreamed to have fallen
                from
                    The Chest
                        Re-establishing their honour
                            with
                              finest
                                robes
                                    and royal crest

Who
    can
        speak
            of
                The Light
                    carried in The Breeze...?

Who can speak of Our Brother...Carried in The Spirit...In The Will of Our Father...?

***

Nature's
    sentinels
        in bloom
           line
              the
                  route
                      to Our Father's House

Soft and silken
        fragrant petals
            bear
                each step
                    with
                        Our True Spouse

For
  The
    Bridegroom
      leads
        the
          SOUL…
            WHERE THE MARRIAGE FEAST AWAITS

Each cup filled
        and running over
                in the Love
                      It Celebrates

***

CONSCIOUSNESS AND PERCEPTION

Teeming
  tumbling
    crystalline tide

      nurturing life
        beyond the gates of my pride...

          Flood
         me
          with
            Light
              as the break of the day

              Purging the darkness
              with effortless sway

                Oh
                 burst
                from
                 our
                  hearts
                    with Your Food for the world...!

                    Immanent
                    Love
                        as banners unfurled

***

TONY MCKAY

Flashes of Eternity
        catch
                my vacant eyes

The portraits of my destiny
                in sight
                      but yet
                            disguised

Cry out to me oh mirror
And tell me what is true
The Union that beholds us
One Body
Seen
Anew

Oh what if Your whispers could be loud?
What if Your image could be proud?

But then
        You
                would be like me
                        with eyes that cannot see
                        with ears that cannot hear
                        a voice of ignorance and fear

                    ***

CONSCIOUSNESS AND PERCEPTION

Life
    is
        Love's
            Rapture
                in time

                    Emanating
                          yet Immanent
                                Divine

Love
    is
        Life's
            Heartbeat
                through space

                    Re-birthing
                          of
                          Infinite
                              Grace

***

Our Father
> I adore You
> > I prostrate
> > > myself
> > > > before You

Your Will
> Is Done
> > The Mystical Body
> > > of Thy Son

Your Word of Truth
> in sacredness
> > and beauty

The breath of life
> returns
> > as
> > > is
> > > > its
> > > > > duty

And so as the tide exhales
> so the tide inhales

Present
> yet still to be
> > the emergent whisper
> > > of The Sea

***

CONSCIOUSNESS AND PERCEPTION

Silence bleeds
        within my heart

Yet in fear of Stillness
        I must
            depart

To run away
        far from Thee
            to where
                I see
                    myself
                        to be

A place
    I'll build
        in toil and strife
            My vision
                of
                    the perfect life

And with the world
        and all its wealth
            I'll shroud my differing
                state of health

Till when night comes
        upon my bed
            to
                find
                    me
                      weary
                        from all I've said
                        from all I've tried
                        from all I've done

TONY MCKAY

                                                        We'll watch it
                                                        pass
                                                        before the sun

Then once again You'll have my hand
                            to lead me from
                                          my dreamed up land
And bring me Home
               to Life Complete
                           where Mercy Reigns
                                          and children meet

                         ***

CONSCIOUSNESS AND PERCEPTION

Breath of the tide
        that
            unfolds
                on
                    the
                        shore

A symphony borne
        of
            a
                heavenly
                      score

The heartbeat of One
            in
                the
                    heart
                      of
                        all
                          things

Whispering beauty
        from
            the
                silence
                    It
                      Sings

A Love that goes forth
            while
                an
                    echo
                        returns

To be filled once again
            with
                the
                    Fire
                        it
                          yearns

***

Dom Leonard smiled solemnly as he looked up from the papers.

He thought of his Brothers; indeed, all who had lost their lives and he thought of Paul, 'Young Paul', as he called him; what he had come through; where he was now and the work of healing and rehabilitation that lay ahead.

In silent prayer he asked that his young Brother be given the grace to see his predicament, his current crisis, clearly, for what it now was: an opportunity that, through time, if he submitted, would allow for his continued growth; an opportunity whereby, on reaching that place through, with, and in Him, he would come to "see" once more that, together, they had risen, risen indeed, high above what the world had decided, once more, to throw at Him.

PART VIII

BOOK FOURTEEN:

FORGETTING AND REMEMBERING

25

Scene 1: Prognosis

Wednesday 13th January, 1993, Sancta Maria Abbey Monastery, Nunraw, 9:40 a.m.

Making his way in the shade of the cloister, Dom Leonard saw Sister Mary ahead of him, closing the door, leaving Paul's room.

As she started to walk towards him, he noticed that she was carrying the dirty dressings that had covered Paul's wounds.

'Good morning, Sister.'

'Good morning, Dom Leonard.'

'How are you today and how is our patient?'

'I'm okay, but Paul… For a start he's too weak to be trying to move around, yet he's still trying to practise walking with that walking stick, up and down the room. How he got hold of that in the first place I'll never know, but I've got a fair idea!' she said, showing her annoyance. 'He's nowhere near that stage yet, Dom Leonard! His body not only has to get stronger, but needs to get used to the fact that the weight of his left arm is no longer there. In his current frail state it's going to take time. He can't force this! He has to give himself time to adjust, to balance.'

Dom Leonard kept quiet, listening intently, letting Sister Mary continue with her report.

'It seems he's responded well to the anti-malarials. The fever has left him. This morning I've removed as much of the pus from the stitched wounds around his right eye as I can, and managed to clean the stitched wounds on his face and left eyelid, but his head and face are still very badly swollen and still bright red from the infections. The fractures to his nose and cheekbone won't be helping. And another thing… I think he's pretending that he can see a lot more out of his right eye than he's letting on. It's like a slit, almost shut from the swelling, as you know.

'I told him he'd be better letting his family come to the monastery to see him in his room, but he's adamant that he wants to see them down in the Guest House. When I first entered his room I found him out of bed trying to walk, and despite the obvious pain and the stitches on his swollen lips, he was trying to talk!

'It then occurred to me what he was really doing: he was rehearsing, rehearsing his greetings for his family! Can you imagine, practising greetings for your own family? God only knows what's going on in that poor boy's head,' she said, looking at the ground.

'Yes,' Dom Leonard replied thoughtfully. 'I think somewhere inside he feels as though he's put them through enough, and wants to show them that he's okay, that he's on the mend.'

The nurse quickly turned her head and looked up at Dom Leonard, a look of total disbelief on her face.

'*I know, I know,*' replied Dom Leonard, realising just how crazy his comment must have sounded; given the extent and truly horrifying nature of Paul's injuries 'We just have to try and support him through this, Sister. All we can do is be there for him. Our Lord is there in the mire with him,' he told her, putting his right hand on her left shoulder.

Sister Agnes nodded her head. 'I'll just take these to the laundry room and I'll be straight back. Paul's sitting on the edge of his bed ready for you to collect him.'

'Thank you, Sister.'

Scene 2: Lost and broken

Dom Leonard knocked and entered the room, finding Paul smartly dressed, in a new white cassock and black scapular, sitting straight up on the edge of the bed, face forward, as if to attention, the walking stick in his right hand.

'Good morning, Paul. I see you're all set.'

'Good morning, Dom Leonard,' Paul slurred, rising eagerly from the bed, but losing his balance, and falling, striking his face against the bedside cabinet, knocking it sideways on his way down, causing the water jug and glass to topple and smash on the floor beside him.

Lying flat, face-down, Paul was hurriedly sweeping the floor above his head with his right hand, trying to find the stick that he had lost in his fall.

'Forgive my clumsiness, Dom Leonard,' he gasped. 'I'll, I'll be with you directly, and we'll, we'll be on our way.'

Dom Leonard, who had rushed over to Paul but was unable to catch him before he'd fallen, knelt down beside him. 'It's okay, Paul. It's okay. It's okay,' he whispered, taking hold of Paul's shoulders.

With Dom Leonard's words, and physical contact, Paul, still face-down on the floor, abandoned his attempts at trying to find the stick, and lay motionless.

Struggling for breath, through his broken nose and badly swollen and disfigured mouth, Paul was making something of a snorting, slurping sound. However the sound soon changed, changed to a deep aching and sorrowful sobbing, the sound from a pain that was not physical in nature. And so it ascended; a wail of agony, of desperation, of total, and absolute grief. The dam had finally broken and the magnitude of Paul's suffering was now laid bare.

'Sister Mary! Sister Mary!' Dom Leonard called out.

Despite the older man's frailty, Dom Leonard struggled and eventually managed to help turn Paul on to his right side on the floor.

Blood and yellow pus oozed and trickled from the now opened stitches on Paul's mutilated face, running together with the tears from the raw puffy slit that was his right eye.

'I killed them!' he roared forcefully, grabbing and shaking Dom Leonard's left arm. 'I killed them, Brother! I killed them! All of them! Dear God, what did I do? Their broken families! Their broken families! What did I do? What did I do? Did I know, Dom Leonard? Tell me! Tell me, Brother!' he pleaded. 'Surely I didn't know. How could I have known? Surely I didn't, I didn't mean it, Brother! Rather me than them, isn't it so? That they should live, not I? Not I. Isn't it so, Brother? That they should live, that they should live, not I. No, it can never be! Never! Never!'

'Sister Mary! Sister Mary!' Dom Leonard shouted towards the door.

Seconds later, Sister Mary rushed into the room.

26

Scene 1: Journey - Looking back, looking forward

Wednesday 13th January, 1993, Sancta Maria Abbey Guest House, Nunraw, Scotland, 10:00 a.m.

The talk among the family members had steadily reduced during what they knew to be the last few miles of their journey and their reunion with Paul. Andrew, taking the final bend on the road, afforded himself a discreet smile as he brought the car out from the woods and into the stately, sunlit grounds of Nunraw Abbey Guest House. 'God, the auld goalposts are still there, Ninian,' he said aloud.

'Aye, Ah see them,' Ninian replied, already absorbed in memories of their shared childhood, visiting Nunraw during the summer holidays when he, Andrew and Paul had played football all day on the lush green grass.

Ninian smiled. 'Even when you fall, it isnae sore, int it no'?' Paul would tell him each time he picked him up from the ground.

Up on the roof, their father had worked through the list of repairs, fixing the slates that had been dislodged during the winter months. The roof of the old, yet still stunning, fiery red, sandstone building, with its turrets and battlements 'the monks' castle' as they'd called it. 'I wonder if yer slates are still in place up on the turrets, Da.'

'Aye, it takes ye back, dint it?' John answered from the front passenger seat, shaking his head as the car drew nearer.

In the back, beside Ninian, Margaret gave her mum's hand a reassuring squeeze.

Agnes nodded her head, smiling through quiet tears that she discreetly dabbed with the handkerchief in her left hand.

It had been eight long years since she had last seen her son Paul, and she was afraid to think what had happened to him. What state she would find him in. What would be left of him? But that didn't matter now. He was back home and he was alive! Thank God, he was alive.

Scene 2: Regrouping

After Sister Mary had cleaned and re-stitched the wounds on Paul's face, she made all agree that there would be 'no more walking around with the walking stick' for the time being, and that Paul would use the wheelchair from now on, accompanied by the young seminarian, Brother Gerald.

When Brother Gerald arrived at Paul's room, Dom Leonard led their introductions. And, with that, the young seminarian expressed that he was only too glad to be of assistance.

Soon after, the three men left the monastery on their way to the Guest House, with young Gerald, pushing Paul, in the wheelchair.

Scene 3: Time out

Wednesday 13th January, 1993, Sancta Maria Abbey Guest House, Nunraw, Scotland, 10:10 a.m.

Ninian and his family were led to the dining hall by Brother Aloysius, as they waited for Paul to arrive.

On entering, they were met by members of the visiting drug and alcohol support group, who were already ten minutes into their tea break.

Ninian was quickly becoming increasingly anxious. 'Look at the state a' these cunts,' one of the voices in his head told him. 'It's like the fuckin' caper hoose in here.'

Realising that he would soon be overwhelmed, Ninian struggled to hold on as he accompanied his family over to one of the dining tables.

When he had seen to them being seated, he made his exit, heading out of the dining hall, running down the stairs and out into the grounds, to the back of the building. Impulsively, he lit a cigarette and exhaled with relief, his back against the wall.

When he had regained his composure, several cigarettes later, he headed back inside to re-join his family.

BOOK FIFTEEN:

HOME

27

Scene 1: As you go As you are

Wednesday 13th January, 1993, the road from Sancta Maria Abbey to the Guest House, 10:30 a.m.

Making their way along the country road, with its frosted trees and glistening fields on either side, Dom Leonard was now, in his own way, venting his anger, and coughed gently, clearing his throat before continuing. 'Of course, although we are led to believe that the "powerful" of this world couldn't possibly behave in such a way today and even foolishly tell ourselves that they wouldn't do such and such a thing in this day and age and that today we are all ever so much more "advanced" and "civilised" and so on, if we would only take the time to look, we would inevitably come to see that throughout thousands upon thousands of years of human history, that they have not only, almost always, invaded, murdered, stole lands and enslaved, but have also, as part of their modus operandi, done whatever they deemed was necessary to ensure that everyone else would come to see the world exactly how they wanted them to see it. And let me tell you my young brothers, don't be so naive as to assume that this pattern has miraculously changed, or indeed is going to change anytime soon. For in their case, this behaviour is related to a state of mind, and, it is purely pathological at that.

'*Pfft*, indeed, even with the relatively recent advent of Darwin's theory of evolution they were soon proposing that their status at the top was, in itself, merely "natural selection" playing out in the world of men. It was simply social Darwinism at work, their positions of "power" a result of the "natural order" being established! Blatant lies and utter nonsense of course, and indeed a pseudo-scientific theory adopted by themselves that has been comfortably disproven by modern science. But these are some of the more subtle ways in which they try to justify and so too brainwash us into accepting their positions of power; thereby making the unsuspecting populations of the world their "doers" in the maintenance of the "status quo" which, undeniably, only serves to show a further example of the characteristic psychopathy at play; the tragic condition underlying their behaviour.

'Yet, it's been with this view of reality that they've self-imposed themselves on our world, overseeing and, thus shaping, the "development" of our communities, societies and "civilisations", putting in place and orchestrating the monetary system, and every other system and institution for their own ends, to a place where we find that what they have made by design, is all now seen as perfectly "normal". Perfectly "normal" that ordinary people should be trained in competing against each other, from childhood onwards, in "education", "sports" and whatever else the unjust society demands, so as to guarantee that they will be ever more accepting of the same in their lives as adults, automatically continuing in the same vein within a poisonous structure that says they must blindly compete against each other in order to provide food and shelter for themselves and their families, all the while unknowingly doing their all in maintaining the positions of the "powerful".

'And we need only look at our very own relatively recent history to see a plain example of this my young brothers. For the monarchs and nobles of Britain not only did what they did in Kenya. *Oh no!* In days gone by, when they had their very own private armies at their disposal, long before their "empire", they were also dividing and ruling, and everything else that goes along with it, right here! Killing those who rejected their self-imposed "authority" all the while terrorising and chasing the rest off the land, only to bring them back again at a later date.

'*Huh*, yes, bringing them back again at a later date and ever so kindly giving them tiny plots of land to live on, as long as they provided their free labour, effectively turning them into slaves on the very fields that had been stolen from them, which, of course, also started the ball rolling in terms of getting people to pay rent and tax for the land on which they lived.

'Incredible, really, *imagine*, not only being made to pay rent and tax to live on the land that you once lived on for free, but to *"work it"* in competition against your neighbours, that you may then give its produce to those who have stolen it from you. *Huh*,' he sighed, shaking his head.

'But, again, from our history, we can see that, before long, well, *pfft*, at least until sometime after the mass murder and random killings are no longer required, as is almost always the case, the poor, become compliant and, eventually, become programmed into accepting these arrangements and, sadly, it must be said, through time, are then all too keen to readily and "joyfully" live under them, feeling "honoured", indeed "privileged", to have "received" their special "title", the title of "subjects", following their masters' every command, being told what to do and where to go, and even marching with great pride to fight and die in illegal wars that will enable their masters to gain even more of the same, blind to the very fact that crimes are being committed against them, blind to the very fact that their rights are not only being violated against, but are continually being constrained.

'And so we are left with a manufactured situation whereby the opposite of the golden rule becomes the reality, "Do whatever has been done unto you unto others."

'Of course, not only are these crimes and violations against humanity, they also run contrary to the very essence of Natural Law; which, again, should not be confused with any Darwinian theory, social or otherwise. Indeed, for in Natural Law, in the true sense, we are talking about the immutable Laws inherent within the universe, those that are in place to guide and govern the behaviour of beings who are capable of experiencing heightened states of consciousness, and so, outwith the "animal kingdom", those same Laws that are likewise known within other traditions and practices as Moral Law, Universal Law, Cosmic Law, God's Law, Spiritual law, Karmic Law and so on, all of which is similarly discussed in consequentialism. And it is precisely these Laws my young brothers which assist man that he may come to a true understanding of right behaviour from wrong behaviour, in order that he may live in harmony and in accordance with all of nature, as it truly is.

'But, of course, when we take the time to look at the injustice within our world, the question that inevitably springs to mind is that, if there are truly consequences for our behaviour, why then are those who orchestrate such evil in the world seemingly unaffected? Why is it that there seems to be no apparent consequences for them? Well, the answer, and the fact of the matter is, is that those in "power", while knowing the Laws, have learned how to lessen the consequences for themselves. In other words, they have learned that it's better to get those who are uneducated in such matters to carry out their dirty work for them. In this way, the powerful do not experience the full consequences of the chaos and disorder that inevitably follows from going against the grain of Natural Law. Indeed, for although they are deceitfully instructing people to commit heinous acts on their behalf, they are not physically committing these acts themselves, and so, it is the ones who carry out the acts who are more culpable. Thus, the major share of the karmic consequences are accrued by the countless unwitting pawns who do their bidding without question, and so, it is these "order followers" if you will, committing acts of evil on behalf of the "powerful", that take on the brunt of the consequences. And yes, in this they do learn the hard way! For they soon find that the statement of "I was just following orders", or "I was just doing my job", doesn't cut it with Natural Law. And you see an example of this in the lives of the poor soldiers who have found themselves doing unimaginable things to their brothers and sisters, and are then afterwards left to endure a lifetime of psychological and physical torment, looking on with regret on how they were used, and the sickness they were a part of, indeed, and only coming to find true healing in their return to the Lord, whose consoling grace and loving mercy makes all things new.

'And the "powerful" who give the orders, you might ask? Well, they themselves do not get off entirely scot-free of course, and there may very well be something else coming their way after physical death, but whether they really care about this, or have the capacity to truly see, or understand, is another question. For it would appear, for the most part, that, in their sickness, they are quite happy and content to live and rule in the living hells that they have created, living in open rebellion against the Laws and doing whatever they can to remain and hold on to life here, for as long as humanly possible.

Dom Leonard nodded and let out a sigh. 'Yes, it's a very sad state of affairs my young Brothers. And of course, within this rather bleak picture of the way our world has been ordered by those who have held power, we have to recognise also that we would have to be somewhat naive to assume that the original teachings of what would then become the world's religions would have somehow been sacrosanct. Indeed, for the sad truth of the matter is, is that these teachings have also been interfered with. And you see a blatant example of this in the "teachings" within our own bible, informing us that those in power have received their positions from God, that they have been "divinely ordained" and therefore must be obeyed. This is plainly ridiculous of course. And Christ, in obedience to the Will of the Father who wants nothing less than man's true freedom, did not entertain such nonsense. Indeed, in his life, who do we think he spoke out against, was it not precisely the very "powers that be" which, let's not forget, also included the religious leaders, and the money changers?

'But, if we are still not convinced, we need only look to see how our religious institutions have played, and continue to play their role. I mean, *please*, let's be honest, who do we think gave them all the lands, wealth, and "power" they possess, and what do we honestly believe they were given it for? Payment for some kind of plenary indulgence? My young brothers, they received it for continuing to do what they were meant to do at any given time, which often meant appallingly turning a blind eye at the crucial moment, and saying and doing absolutely nothing at all.

'*Imagine*, and we were told to let Caesar have what belongs to Caesar, and give to God what belongs to God, but, sadly, we have given Caesar both!

'Thus, man, who was made free, has made himself a slave.

'Yes, all in all, Einstein was close to the truth when he said that humanity's problems cannot possibly be solved by the same level of consciousness that created them.

'*Oh*, which reminds me, I meant to say to you, Paul, the apologia that you included along with your letter, also reminded me of a story I once heard, some years ago, from an old friend. And it's a story you may also find interesting, young Gerald.'

'Yes, Dom Leonard,' Gerald replied enthusiastically.

Dom Leonard paused for a moment, and coughed once more before continuing 'My friend's name was Father Raphael Nissi, God rest him. Indeed, he was such a remarkable old man.

'At the time when I first met him, he was leading a mostly enclosed life, but would, on occasion, take classes of seminarians – and priests for that matter – and lead them in all sorts of wonderful discussion. I was a young seminarian myself when I first met him, many, many, moons ago,' he smiled. 'Anyway after me and my classmates were ordained, we, like your own group, were all sent to our various posts overseas. And, it was perhaps, say, around twelve years or so later, before we saw old Raphael again, here, at the monastery. If I'm not mistaken, I think we had all been called here, for a few days, to attend some meeting or other.

'In those days, of course, the numbers of vocations were nothing like what they are today. Indeed, we were forty-eight in total; all, more or less, straight out of school. So young, in fact, that we were all still relatively fresh when we first returned, still full of the vitality and excitement of youth.

'Anyway, with not having seen, or, for that matter, having heard from each other, for a number of years and not being ones to miss an opportunity, each night, after supper, we would all make a point of gathering together in one of the common rooms. *Goodness*, our chats would oft-times continue long into the early hours. *Huh*, come to think of it, I think we were boring the living daylights out of everyone else. *Ha!* Driving them to the nearest exits!' he sighed, 'But, *anyway*, it was during one of these late nights, when old Father Raphael joined us, that was to really stick in our minds.

'Looking back, I suppose I never realised it at the time, but, interestingly, although he had spent decades in various countries himself, what he told us that night, was not of something that happened to him overseas *but*, from a time when he had lived in London, where he had spent a year's sabbatical, at a parish, in Knightsbridge.

'Specifically, so the story goes, the event itself, he said, occurred during a glorious summer's evening, where he, and the parish priest he was assisting, had just received the body of a prominent dignitary, into the church, for burial, the following morning.

'As is common, of course, as you know, shortly after these pre-burial ceremonies, the sacrament of reconciliation is made available for those who wish to partake. And so, with this being the case on this occasion also, old Raphael explained that he was to be the one who was to hear the mourners' confessions, thereby allowing his colleague more time to prepare for the funeral mass the following day.

'Anyway, it was in coming to this agreement, my young brothers, that, you could say, the story, really begins. For, as things transpired, and, in keeping with what they had discussed, after the short service, Father Raphael quickly changed in the sacristy and, without further ado, made his way out to the confessionals.

'On the face of it, he said that, as he approached the row of compartments, the scene *was* as you would expect, a number of people were leaving the church, and a smaller number were arranging themselves, in orderly fashion, in the adjacent pews. *Greeting them*, he asked to be given some few moments to prepare and, with that, opened the door, and entered the confessional.

'And so it was, that with the sun's rays still filtering in through what he described as this awe inspiring multi-coloured plate glass window, making the environment suitably warm and comforting, he then sat down on the chair, opened his prayer book, and began preparing for the penitents.

'According to his account, the earlier service apparently went as well as can be expected, given the circumstances, and now that he was in the confessional, things there too, he said, appeared to be moving along rather smoothly. Indeed, if I'm not mistaken, I believe he told us that he'd heard around seven or eight people's confessions in relatively quick succession.

'Anyhow, after some time, sitting in prayer, it came to him that it seemed as though there would be no one else. And that perhaps all might have left the church.

'*Yet*, not wanting to deny anyone, he decided to wait a little longer. And so, continuing in prayer, he waited and waited.

'With the time continuing to move along though, *and no one else having entered the adjoining compartment,* it then came to him that he would finish his prayers for the time being, and go out into the church, and check that all was in order, before locking up, and retiring for the night.

'*And so,* in coming to this conclusion, it was here that our old brother then closed his prayer book, admired the retreating rays of coloured light penetrating his surrounds for a final time, and stood up. However, here, my young Brothers, strangely, as he turned, and reached out to put his hand on the door knob, apparently, out of nowhere, came this sharp, scraping sound, so strange, in fact, I remember that he said it sounded something like the sound of a stiff wooden door being quickly and forcefully, dragged, partly open, across a concrete floor.

'*Anyway,* still standing, *and,* I suspect, a little puzzled, old Raphael then told us that he then paused for a moment, to listen more keenly.

'Yet, as he stood, and so, coming to feel that there was nothing untoward, he said that he was then just about to leave once more, when, suddenly, this sharp, scraping sound, came again, this time, louder, and longer.

'Deciding now to sit down, our old brother slid to the edge of his chair and leaned forward and, with that, began to peer in through the tiny spaces in the small, wooden, lattice window, into the adjoining penitent's compartment.

'*Huh,* oddly enough, however, much to his surprise, he told us that he couldn't really say for certain whether or not there was anyone there.

'Yet, despite being quite bewildered by all of this, little did he realise at the time, that this was, really, only the beginning. Indeed, for as he began to draw his face back from the lattice window, he said that he then heard the faint sound of these whispering, breathless voices.

'As you might imagine, he was quite startled by this development. *Huh,* and indeed, promptly drew himself back, to sit fully in his chair, where I believe he was rather relieved to find that the whispering had stopped.

'Recalling his description of this part of the story, I remember him informing us that, at this point, he genuinely didn't know what to make of it and, indeed, that he was still struggling to find a rational explanation when all of a sudden, out of the quiet, *the whispering* could be heard again, only to suddenly stop again.

'Pondering on all of this a little further, old Raphael said that he then went from being initially unsure as to what to do, to finally deciding that enough was enough.

'And so, pushing his superstitions aside, he said that he then leaned forward, or, should I say, in closer, to the lattice window, and immediately went on to address those in the adjoining compartment with something like, "I'm sorry, but the compartment simply wasn't built for such purposes".'

'However, strangely, there was no reply forthcoming. Indeed, a few seconds must've passed, for Raphael explained that he found himself, once again, gazing in through the lattice window, at the light passing in through the darkness.'

'Was he not afraid, Dom Leonard?' Gerald, the young seminarian, asked, with a confused smile.

'*Well*, wait till you hear, young Gerald, wait till you hear,' Dom Leonard replied, 'for soon after, old Raphael heard the whispering again! Indeed, ascending this time. And not only this, but the voice of one, speaking out, above the din, who seemingly quite forcefully interjected with something like, "Forgive me, Padre, my younger siblings can be a tad unruly at times, *especially* if they don't get what they want, and are left unattended. Don't worry," the voice continued, "they won't understand what we are talking about".'

Dom Leonard paused for a moment. 'Yet perhaps more disconcerting than this, my young brothers, was the information that old Raphael went on to share with us. For he then went on to say, that the one speaking, started to tell him that "it" came from a Principality.'

Young Gerald turned quickly to Dom Leonard, '*Demons, Dom Leonard?*'

Paul smiled instinctively at his younger brother's excited response; only to be stopped by the onset of extreme pain, stabbing across his badly swollen and disfigured face. Acknowledging the discomfort, Paul tried to let the thoughts pass, and was relieved to return to thoughts of young Gerald. His young brother had reminded him of how *he* was, all those years ago when *he* was a seminarian, how *he* was,

CONSCIOUSNESS AND PERCEPTION

all those years ago, when he was around his old formator, the now *Dom* Leonard; especially, when listening to one of his stories.

'Well,' Dom Leonard replied, 'who can say, young Gerald? Who can say? I'll let you decide. What I do know is that old Raphael, for his part, went on to tell us that the voice then said to him, "*Padre*, I find your commitment and perseverance quite amusing. *You*, being an educated man, must surely know that Christianity is made up of, indeed, has stolen, a large number of different elements, symbols, and practices from a wide variety of different religions, pagan and otherwise for that matter, and so too, of course, traditions and values from a wide range of different cultures, not to mention those of ancient Egypt, Greece, Persia, need I go on, assimilating whatever was found to be useful, and cunningly using the same to bring about its own dominance."

'Old Father Raphael sat quietly, listening intently, as the voice continued.

"And what of the various denominations you have within it?! Did your own Lord not inform you that a kingdom divided could not possibly stand? Ah, but alas, it seems here, at least, that this anomaly isn't solely confined to Christianity, or any of man's other religions for that matter. *Indeed*, would you be so surprised to learn, that, even of those following my own master, those taking the left-hand path, that there are some, who serve him spiritually, others, who desire to be their own gods, and others still, who serve him in the worship of their own egos, actively pursuing, and indulging, in its every whim? All of this, of course, is much to the disdain of some of the aforementioned followers might I add, indeed, who refer to this last group – and so too, of course, the rest of humanity – as 'the mundanes', 'cannon fodder', if you will. 'Dregs' to be used abused and culled every once in a while, until such times, of course, as and when, they can, almost naturally, be wiped out, totally eradicated, by each other of course.'"

'Good heavens,' young Gerald murmured, shaking his head.

'Indeed, Gerald, indeed! Yet it wasn't finished there for the voice continued to taunt old Raphael still, with, "And again, my dear Papaaaa, would you be so surprised to learn that of those who hold to these beliefs and practices act in such a manner that they may tear themselves away completely from the Life that is within them, that they may 'become' their own masters, a new species, independent from what is, and, what has gone before, creators of a new dawn, makers of their own truth, following their own will, in the physical, and, in the spiritual. Interesting, wouldn't you say? And," it went on, "moreover, oh wise one. Would you be even more surprised to learn that in order to bring about this breakaway, that some, albeit the lesser minions, receive instruction on how to disguise themselves? For example, let's say, by taking on the persona of 'the extremist' that is, that they may become 'acquainted' with such groups, religious, political or otherwise, not that it matters which of course, that they may then 'infiltrate' these groups, that they may ever so 'subtly' rise within their ranks to positions of influence, let's say, from where they can then be used to 'manipulate' more effectively, from where 'we' can then stoke the fires with an increasing intensity, harmonising, if you will, the perpetual regurgitation of whatever the group's slogans happen to be, hypnotising its members with their own mind-numbing mantras, their blinkered doctrines, their hilarious 'justifications', thereby exquisitely swirling the melting pot, until such times, of course, as and when, 'it' almost naturally, erupts. Erupts! Revealing beyond all doubt, man's true nature, showing him what he is in plain sight, for all to see. And so, finally, once and for all removing every pretence, finally, once and for all, releasing in him the magnificent raw unadulterated evil which he has so foolishly tried to hide, which he has so foolishly fought to contain, but which can now no longer be denied. For that to which he has given birth, was nurtured, and carried, within the heart, indeed, from the beginning. And its name? Well, its name, none other than Annihilation of course. *Ha*, what a delight!

"*Yes* only one of the many methods used. Ah, but alas, if it all adds up to helping to bring about their end at the appropriate time *then* so much the better. And how fortunate, wouldn't you say, that even if the numbers of these devotees and their luminaries might appear small that we can, of course, always depend on the ordinary people of today – and indeed, throughout history – who are dedicated to this mission, indeed wholeheartedly. *Ha*, requiring no motivation from, or, having any notion of, the insidious among them.'"

'Diabolical, Dom Leonard! What did Father Raphael have to say?' Gerald asked, wide-eyed.

CONSCIOUSNESS AND PERCEPTION

'*Well* old Father Raphael was silent,' Dom Leonard replied. 'It was the voice that continued and went on to challenge and abuse him further, with something like, "So, what have you to say? What are you, *a charade?* Are you a man of your convictions or not?"

'Our old brother Raphael, as if gathering himself, waited for a further moment before responding, and then finally replied, by going on to say, "When men believe the 'suggestions' inside their heads instructing them of all that is evil to be a part of who they are, or, worse still, their own voice, they have truly wandered far. Indeed, so far, as to have become 'lost'. 'Lost' in the unreality of all that is the ego, 'lost' in all that they have derived from its unreal interpretation of the subconscious, 'lost' in an unreal world that they have built in time, a psychological construct, a sinister maze of illusion and madness".

"Padre, my dear fellow,' the voice chuckled, "surely you're not suggesting that my master does not exist? Perhaps you've spent too much time in that cosy solitude of yours. *Ha!* Why not try opening that tinted window every once in a while? Look out at the world. Breathe in some of its smelling salts. *Wouldn't you say?*"

"Despite the many temptations thrown up by the ego," old Raphael began, "there have been true mystics and contemplatives, of all times and places, who have found something of the True Reality. Indeed, for they have received glimpses of the Truth within themselves, within their brothers and sisters and, so too, of course, within nature. I suppose one might say that these people, are, at times, in some ways, more receptive and, therefore, with humility, able to recognise that Truth Itself walks with them, spoon feeding them if you will, gradually revealing Itself, gradually letting Itself be found and known.

"Indeed, for it is here, in this awareness, that these humble souls soon come to recognise the inherent directive written within their hearts, man's moral code, the law guiding him on how he should behave with regard to himself, his fellow man, and, all Creation, and, so with it, the ability to understand and know the laws that govern the natural phenomena, in occurrence, all around him, that he may live in harmony with his environment.

"With information such as this, it's fair to say then that these human beings were and are able to act in ways befitting people with

True Knowledge, in other words, able to act, as intended, in and with Wisdom, so as to live in true freedom.

"Of course, in service to the Will of Love, they would then do whatever they could and use whatever they had at their disposal to share this True Knowledge with everyone, for the benefit of all things.

"However, sadly, just as there are, and have been, those, who have worked to assist in bringing humanity to the Truth – and so, playing their part in raising the consciousness of humankind – there are, and have been, again, in all times and places, those, for whatever reason, whether it be partly psychological, neurological, physiological, sociological, pathological, cultural, or any possible combination of the same, or, for that matter, whether it be a case of what some have described as left-brain imbalance or, indeed, something to do with the way our thought patterns are said to influence the development of the brain, who have, by all intents and purposes, actively sought to 'encourage' man's stagnation and enslavement.

"Indeed, from ancient times onwards, we could say, for the most part, that those who have sought to hold power in the world have behaved in such a way. Tragically, through operating from an unnatural state of mind and by continuing to focus, solely, on what their erroneous world view has 'taken in' and 'understood' about 'power', they too, in their own way, have done whatever they could. They too, have used whatever they've had at their disposal, 'imprisoning' not only themselves, but those seen to be under their control. Yet, perhaps the saddest thing of all is that they have done this, in the main, by misusing the very knowledge that was given to enable man to live in freedom. Indeed, for in acquiring the knowledge of the true mystics – which is essentially made up of two interconnected components which form one body – rather than seeing that they now had the keys to unlock many of life's great mysteries for the benefit of all, the rulers themselves, from their disordered state of mind, it must be said, saw how this information could be used, or rather misused, to maintain and further strengthen their positions of power.

"The information explaining that Natural Law was a real phenomenon in operation within Creation was of course one component, indeed, and one in which they would do their utmost to defy during their lifetimes, but their prime area of concern lay in its complimentary component. For it was here, in their distorted way of thinking, where they soon came to recognise that they had found all that needed to be known on how to effectively manipulate, divide, control, and ultimately govern, human beings. Indeed, for they now had, within their possession, not only some of the earliest understandings of the human psyche, including information on its drives, its fears and, how it operates, but information on man's experience and associated behaviour within his 'lower' and 'higher nature', which, essentially, defined levels of consciousness, and which, to the powerful, when 'understood', was the equivalent to their finding the proverbial pot of gold.

"Indeed, for it was in this knowledge which was common to numerous mystical traditions across the globe that the powerful came to learn that human beings were, without the shadow of a doubt, made with the capacity to consciously experience life on what was ordinarily recognised by the ancients as 'five planes of existence'. The terms used to describe these planes of course varied from tradition to tradition, however, importantly, the identified and given understandings of each tradition on the specific characteristics common to the human experience and behaviour at a particular plane was essentially the same.

"In ancient Greece, for example, the terms used to categorise and describe the human experience at each of the five planes were known as 'earth', 'water', 'air', 'fire' and 'good mind' or 'quintessence'. Yet, although I do not claim to know the unique workings of each person's mind, or indeed the specifics of a given individual's personality and their traits, what I can say, in the very simplest of terms, is that 'earth' in the Greek system was said to describe man's lowest state of consciousness; which is why even today we hear the terms earthly or worldly being used to describe a particular person's way of life. Indeed, for here, 'earth' captured all that was seen to be base, and was characterised by a life directed by the sensually driven or carnal mind, which had little or no interest or understanding of the principles of morality that were alive in Natural Law.

"'Water', the second plane, was seen as being a slightly higher state of conscious experience. Indeed, 'water' was believed by some, particularly those interested in the esoteric teachings of Christianity, to be evident in the symbolism associated with the life of John the Baptist, who, you will remember, called people to leave behind their earthly/worldly ways to experience this higher conscious state of 'repentance' where there was, to some extent, a recognition, a recognition within man that all was not well, and that he was indeed 'called' to a life or existence 'above' that which he currently lived. And so, the baptism with 'water' was said to have also symbolised this slightly upward movement in consciousness – from 'earth' to the higher plane of 'water' – where man came to recognise that he should indeed leave behind his previously 'earthly' ways and move towards attempting to lead a more righteous life. However, such are the subtle intricacies of 'earth' and 'water', and despite this recognition within man that a movement from 'earth' to 'water' was necessary, together, both these terms were also seen by some mystics as being representative of the experience of the enduring battle common to man's experience when 'trapped' in what was described as his 'lower nature'. Indeed for it was here, within this 'lower nature', man's consciousness was said to be 'caught' within a kind of to and fro movement, where, on the one hand, the solely self-centred interests associated with the earthly/worldly lifestyle were still to some extent driving his desires and actions, and yet, in spite of this, were also subsequently followed afterwards by the feelings of guilt, shame, remorse, and thus repentance, associated with 'water', and so, it was this experience of internal conflict within man, or this typically lived state of dualism, which the mystics believed provided the evidence that man was still operating from within his 'lower nature'.

"However, importantly, from here, if humble and persistent in his efforts in trying to leave behind his former 'earthly' way of life, and in spite of his many falls, the mystics also knew that if he responded wholeheartedly, the 'inner call' would, and could, lead man higher still, higher still, out of 'water' to 'air'. 'Air', a 'higher level' within the Greek system, was understood to be indicative of man's experience within a state of mind that was free from the almost default and disordered psychological dual state of constant chatter that was common to his 'lower nature', and, it was here, in 'air' where man would meet the One whom John the Baptist had said would come after him; the One Who led the call, the Christ, the One Who, in our Bible, calls His followers to meet Him in the 'air'.

Once here, in the conscious state of 'air', and in receipt of His

Peace, Christ would then lead man higher still – essentially deeper and deeper in Truth – and baptise him with 'fire' – the fourth plane – symbolic of The Holy Spirit, where it would be revealed to man the true reality of his own life, and where he would see in his 'higher nature', what he truly is. Knowing now that he was a unique, unitive part, of the Whole, and thus now knowing True Reality, here man, now awakened, had indeed been lifted up by Christ to the plane and state of 'Good mind', where, having now encountered, known, and now entered into a true relationship with Truth Itself, understands that the Life that lives within and shares His Life with him, is also the very same Life that lives within and shares His Life with all things. Sadly, though, in what can only be described as their sickness, the 'powerful', in spite of this knowledge, continued to see what they could do to benefit themselves. Indeed, for them, they saw plainly that all that needed to be done to ensure that they would remain in power was to use whatever they had at their disposal to keep the masses in the lowest planes of existence/states of consciousness possible. For they now knew that when man lives his life in the 'lower states'/or his 'lower nature', he is, in essence, in a state of mind where internal conflict and division is, for the most part, already his everyday experience. And so, if an individual could be kept in this state, where he is already internally divided, how much easier would it be to keep him divided from his neighbour, and how much easier would it be to keep the community in which he lived divided among themselves, and, from other communities?

"And so, when we reflect on these truths that have been present and known for millennia we see the sickness of those who have worked to keep humanity from coming to experience True Reality, and how, as a consequence of adhering to this course of action, man's life on earth has, in the main, been one of manipulation and conflict, resulting in widespread chaos and disorder.

"As Christ Himself expressed, shamefully the powerful have taken the key of knowledge, but have refused to enter into True Knowledge, baulking at the prospect, and preferring instead to dance around in illusion, all the while using every means they have at their disposal to ensure that those beneath them are kept in darkness, and so stifling humanity's entry into Truth."

"Well, well, Padre. It seems even you can sketch a neat and tidy little picture," the voice then stated, "and you're sure that this isn't part of a greater strategy *a ploy* or, indeed, one of the many wonderful deceptions of my master? Surely you'll be aware that the greatest trick he ever pulled was convincing people that he didn't exist?"

"Yes," old Father Raphael answered, "so we are told, and perhaps the most dangerous trick we ever pulled on ourselves was accepting his reality and believing him to be true. You do realise that there was no mention of a devil or demons in the earlier Hebrew text and that, historically, a great deal of this thought, and, subsequent doctrine, which found its way into a number of religions, is first said to have been suggested in ancient Persia; indeed, in the Zoroastrianism religion, which, although monotheistic, suggested dualism, and again," old Raphael continued, "within Judaic thought also, I'm sure you'll be aware that scholars suggest that these and similar ideas were also incorporated, and evolved, well before and during the time of Christ, to provide some kind of explanation as to the why of difficulties experienced in life, particularly the great why of the Roman invasion, and the subsequent occupation of the Jewish lands.

"However, if you are asking as to what led to the belief in this form of dualism and man's many other tragic beliefs, well, they undoubtedly have their foundation in the diabolical first error, the acceptance of the false belief that humanity is, or somehow can be, separated from Life."

"Ah, Padre but surely you see the serious flaw in your reasoning. How would you know light if there was no darkness? How would you know what was good if there was no bad? How would you know love if there was no hate?"

"My dear friend," old Raphael said, "where do you believe all of *this* to be taking place?"

"What do you mean?" the voice asked.

"*Well*, I'm sure you'll be aware by now that even some of the enlightened occultists of the world are now showing their hand. Indeed, and so coming to shout out from their elitist societies and orders that absolutely nothing, no-thing stands in opposition to All That Is.

"And, moreover, like other practices, are also showing an increasing interest in the study and findings of psychology, with some even going so far as to advise their students to first undertake some form of psychotherapy before becoming involved in the 'Great Work' – so described by Regardie as 'nothing more or less than the total transformation of man from a sense-oriented creature to one who is conscious of his being a vehicle of the One Universal Life, a human being illuminated by gnosis, the knowledge that God exists within as well as without him."

"In this way, of course, these 'light' occultists – as opposed to those deluded with the 'dark' – are coming to terms with the idea that these 'things' these 'evil spirits' these 'demons' that they have been trying to 'evoke' and 'commune with' during their magical ceremonies – and so bring under their control before banishing – are, in fact, none other than their very own egoic 'interpretations' of what are essentially their very own egoic 'personal', multi-layered, and often deeply intertwined, psychological complexes.

"In other words, the resultant mishmash of all that we 'experience' when we live our lives from 'within' the false reality of all that is the ego consciousness, all of the misconstrued destructive and harmful emotions, feelings, memories, suggestions, and so on, that we attempt to 'suppress' and forget about, but merely push to the back of our minds to our subconscious, to a place in which, through time, they become even more indiscernible, metastasising, if you will, to become our very own 'living' demons, leaping in and out from their pit, to further 'deceive', 'manipulate' and 'haunt' our very own particular 'experience' of ego existence, all the pains and sufferings we inevitably bring about – and endure – as a result of our adherence to our disastrous and fictitious belief that we are separated from Our Source, all the pains and sufferings we accept when we identify with the 'suggestion' of a false self-image; not forgetting of course, all of the misdirected energy of trying to live up to, and defend the same.

"Yet, as Regardie rhetorically asked, how does knowing all of these things about these psychological complexes really help me?

"And the answer, of course, is that – when we are within this level of 'knowing' – it does not; not in the real sense. For although we may come to 'know', at this level, that these complexes are 'there', floating around in our experience, it still doesn't mean that we are relieved of them. *Why?* Because we are, in all truth, still 'operating', as it were, within 'our' predominant state of ego consciousness, and *here* – in our association with this consciousness – no healing, as such, can take place.

"And so, we can say at most that this level of 'knowing' is just that, just another piece of information; just another textbook to be read, and studied, by our ego governed intellects; nothing more; for, as a 'true experience', it is incomplete. Indeed, we can even read every holy book on the planet, but unless we have an 'experience', or an 'encounter' with the living Truth Itself, then we are dancing around in illusion.

"However, when we 'truly' seek and 'truly' put ourselves into the hands of the True Healer, in all humility, we find that True Knowledge, and True Healing, are One. For in our 'experience' of being raised up to share in His Consciousness, we not only come to Know and See through His eyes, but we are 'shown' – in 'experiencing' our true identity in Him – that these complexes, etc., are not who we are; we see that they are not our Truth. We come to know, within this experience of Union, that we are not the contents or sum total of these 'madnesses' that, at times, seem to flash from nowhere into our more common, everyday reality of the ego; and so, we come to find, that it is only here, in experiencing True Reality – in this 'true experiential knowing' – where our true healing not only begins and takes place, but *is*.

"So remember, we only come to truly 'know' Reality, from our experience of Union, where we are shown our true identity in Christ, for He is the one who reveals this True, Consoling, and Healing Knowledge to us.

"Our wedding garment is Truth, and, as such, we are all called, and are already present at, 'the wedding feast'. But the ego is not. For it is not part of our True make-up. We cannot 'consciously' be at the wedding feast, or, indeed, 'consciously' enter the sheepfold, on the false self's terms.

"And, again, when we indulge ourselves in such false states, do we honestly believe that we can come to 'know' and 'experience' that which is True?

"Surely, if we continue in this 'mindset', the practices that we are involved in are essentially only 'another thing', 'another label', another 'I am this', or 'I am that', or another, 'I am doing this', 'I am doing that' scenario, further nonsensical exercises designed to massage our egos.

"Indeed, Regardie said as much when saying, 'Nor do we find Him by a belief in any religious, metaphysical, or occult doctrine. At best these are intellectual constructs for the expansion of our minds – but later come to have profound meaning as useful constructs only after we have found Him.'

"Why, why should this be the case? Because all doctrines have elements of man's unconsciousness within them and, if we are in our 'predominant state of unconsciousness' when we look at these doctrines, we will inevitably accept and believe that which is false within them to be true, and we know where that has led unconscious men in the past, to follow the instruction of their unscrupulous leaders, themselves, of course, wholly unconscious, the blind leading the blind.

"Only when you truly experience Him can you come to Know the Truth and when you are shown what is True, you will see what is True within the teachings themselves, for the Truth sees and Knows Itself, all of which is brought about, purely, by Divine Grace.

"*Yes*, Divine Grace. Or are you still of the impression that it was you, by setting your alarm clock, who woke you from sleep this morning, and gave you another day on this blessed earth?'

'The voice remained silent, and again old Raphael continued. "And what of the Trappist monk, John Jacob Raub, commenting on Thomas Merton's view regarding the devil, and explaining that Merton hardly mentioned the subject and that, on the occasions when he did, that he approached the matter in a very 'balanced' way? Indeed, according to Raub, Merton maintained that whether this 'it' was a 'force' or, whether 'it' was proved sometime in the future to be a projection, was, and is, indeed, irrelevant. The main problem is, however – as was the area of concern for Merton – is that 'man' is somehow susceptible to being drawn into, or becoming involved in, carrying out his own destruction.

"But the challenge for Raub and Merton of course – as is the same for all who have received and experienced a moment's Union with the Divine – is that, if anything evil existed, 'it', would have to have Him, Who Is All Life, at 'its' source, and so, in effect, 'it' or 'evil' per se, would have to be in Him, so as to have been created, so as to be able to exist.

"This is why the proposition, or reality, of evil, somehow being 'in' what the true contemplatives and mystics have experienced in Union is utterly abominable to them. For even though they would admit that what they have experienced in Union, could never, effectively, be put into words, any notion, or suggestion, of evil being a part of what they have 'experienced', is totally unacceptable.

"Yet, with having some, let's say, somewhat spurious and conflicting ideas within their theologies and doctrines, they are left in a quandary.

"For they 'know' from their own experience of Union with the Life that breathes within them – at the very deepest level of their being – that no such thing as evil can possibly exist in Reality. And so, here, they are left with the question, where can this evil that is present in the world of men come from? What is this evil that man is capable of doing to himself, to his fellow man, and, indeed, to all that is created?

"And here, it is why, that in trying to understand this, that we find the terms 'non-existence' and evil, being a 'privation' – an absence of good – being brought into theology to accommodate, or rather, to try and explain, why 'it' is 'there' in the world: They obviously recognised that in Union with Christ, in His reality, in other words, in Truth Itself, duality does not exist.

"However, in our predominant current state – in other words, 'our experience' of our earth bound existence, 'our current ego consciousness' – we must, at the same time, recognise that conflict, duality, plurality and the many multiplicities in our everyday lives, are, indeed, 'our reality'. For this, after all – as 'our' predominant egoic state suggests – *is* 'our world'.

"Yet, even so, this doesn't mean that we should simply sit back and accept things the way they are. For in Life, we cannot simply be observers, or bystanders, letting evil have its way in the world. Indeed, we have a duty, a moral obligation, to act, in Conscious Union with the Truth. For, in Truth – True Reality – we stand in the physical, and, in the spiritual. And, as such, are called by Truth to participate in bringing about the change that is required in 'our world'. In other words, we are called to become the vehicles for 'That' which is to be done on "earth", as it is in heaven.

"Indeed, this is why, where, like the mystics, who believed wholeheartedly that man's false belief in the separation was the initial problem, that Merton and Raub are forced to take this more 'balanced' view; with Raub, suggesting, that we must continue to renounce all sorts of 'devils' or 'demons' of 'any kind', that we must leave the false selves of the ego, in order that we may, at once, through that same grace, come to see 'our' illusion of separation, in and through, His Loving Mercy and Consolation; that we may, at once, come to 'live' in conscious awareness of the Truth, the Truth of our True Union, in and with Christ, Who, with the Father, and the Spirit, *is* All That Is.

"So you see my dear friend, whether we talk of Life on other planets, or Life in other dimensions, we are, ultimately, talking of precisely that, Life! All forms of Our Father's Will. All forms of the same essence, That Which Is One, which no-thing, nothing is separated from. Of course, there are 'different', 'unique', 'forms', but this should not delude us. For in Truth, all life, lives, in Life Itself. Talk of 'other' 'separate', exclusive, forms, and accepting a false egoic belief in the same, is harmful to our physical existence, and interferes with our movement towards a lived experience of Union, Our Truth. So you see, my dear friend, Light casts no shadow, for no-thing, absolutely nothing, stands in opposition. Yet Simeon of course said to Mary that Christ would stand as a sign of contradiction.

"Why..?"

"For He stands as a 'contradiction' to our ego consciousness and its duality, a state of 'consciousness' that does not, and cannot, understand Him. Yet He of course knows our contradictory experience and continues to draw us out from it to the Truth, to Himself.

"Indeed, if you believe that Love has an opposite, or any sort of contradiction within Itself, be assured that what you experienced was, and is not Love. Rather, it is the duality of your ego consciousness, of course, which, in His Reality, is no consciousness at all, false witness trying to speak to you of truth, truth of which it cannot comprehend, and has no knowledge of.

"So, do not imagine, or accept, that Love is not in the world; it is only that you have never experienced Its undeniable Reality and are unconscious of Its Presence. And so you see the clarity of the Son when he asked rhetorically, what Father would give His child a stone when he asked for bread, or a snake when he asked for a fish, or a scorpion when he asked for an egg?

"The Father did not plant a devil in our heads or leave us like the cartoon characters we often see in popular culture, with a devil on one shoulder, and an angel on the other, and 'us' somewhere in the middle, with a dazed and confused look on our face. This is our experience of the dual nature of 'man's' egoic consciousness, the plane where all of the expressions of moral relativism in the world reside. Indeed, here, any sense of morality is relative to the egoic 'life' experience of the individual and their community, leaving human beings in a quandary, where no one actually knows what is really true or, what is right or wrong. And we see examples of this all over our world, with laws in one country different from those of another country, with what is legal here, different from what is illegal there, and so on. The True Reality of Truth Itself, however, is High above this expression of duality, and It has no opposite, for as Truth, It is the Perfect Guidance which is given to man and which is poured out from Divine Love so that that which is done in heaven maybe received, brought down, and done on earth, thus redeeming the lower nature.

"Yet in 'our world', the world which unconsciousness men have created it must be said, we, as human beings, have also heavily influenced our environment, which, in turn, has shown to have an effect on human life, not only from birth, but even, within the womb.

"Throw into the mix the 'influence' of our genetic make-ups and the suggestion that we might very well be predisposed to certain behaviours as a result of 'favourable' social/environmental conditions at any given time, and we have a complex soup of stimuli – internal and external – that can have different bearings on how we might then come to experience life as children, adolescents and adults.

"Yet, even so, in coming out into the world, the newborn baby has no concept of the ego's version of 'good' or 'bad', 'right' or 'wrong'. The child radiates the pure Holy Innocence of the Life it represents. For He Who Lives Within, is there for all to see. The newborn exemplifies the Openness and All-Embracing Acceptance the Uncreated has for all of us, because what He has made, in His likeness, has, no ego. Indeed, is it any wonder then that He should tell us that unless we receive the kingdom of God like a child we shall not enter? Is He not telling us that when we are lost in our ego consciousness that we can have no notion, or clue, of His Kingdom, no notion or clue of Truth, true consciousness?

"Yet, still, the ego consciousness will come to be 'visible', according to psychologists, around the 18 month stage of the infant's life.

"By now the child is said to be able to differentiate between its own voice and image and those 'other' voices and images in its vicinity. And so the building of the 'identity', or, should I say, the many 'identities', it will take in, and shape, during the course of its life, begins in earnest.

"From this early stage, the separate selves of the ego slowly begin to emerge, in accordance with the child's development in time, place, community, and interest.

"Yet the remarkable thing in all of this is that, despite the many 'identities' he or she will then go on to take, and shape, from the ego, over a lifetime, should he or she then become, or take on the role of a parent themselves, they will then have the opportunity to 'see' in their own newborn 'That' which is in them, 'That', which they are in Union with, 'That' which no-thing, absolutely nothing, can separate us from. For That which Is *Is* our very essence, the Unchanging Truth and Reality of All Life – LOVE.

"Love does not try to possess. For It Is, It Has, and It Gives, Everything With In and Through Itself.

"And so you see, my dear friend, in Truth, each breath you take into your lungs and exhale out into the atmosphere is taking place within What Is. It is taking place within Christ.

"And again, the heart you feel, beating in your chest that pumps blood through the arteries of your body is doing so, within Christ.

"Each step you take along this blessed earth, is taking place within the Reality of All Life, The Reality That Is Christ.

"The piece of soil that you take up into your hands and 'break' with your thumbs and forefingers, and watch as it crumbles and falls between them to the ground, is in Christ.

"*You*, my dear friend, every part of you, is firmly rooted in, and lives within the Reality of All Life, and That Life is Christ, and if it were not so you simply, would not exist! One day it will be given to you to know, that even in those times in which you were unconscious, that your soul has, and is, and will always be, in a constant state of prayer, adoration and grace with and in Him.

"Indeed, as you stand on this earth it may be given to you to ask where you 'think' your feet end, and the earth begins, such is the nature of Him. The One Whom the true mystics of every age have said Is in, and Is, Everything, and is yet nothing (exclusively). The Knowable and The Unknowable Abyss. The Seen and The Unseen. The Immanent and The Emanate. That, Which Is, The Unitive Life, All That Is, at once, shared in Love, the Created and the Uncreated, The Absolute."

"Padre?" the voice then spoke up in a condescending tone, "and what role has the will in all of this? Where is the free will that man was supposedly given?"

"My dear friend," old Raphael replied, "if you have not experienced, and therefore, do not know, the Real Truth of who, and what you are, if you are living the life of a dreamed up image, a separated false self, an illusion, presented to you from your ego consciousness, please explain to me, how is it possible for you to *truly* have free will? What is your 'consciousness' grounded in? Where, and what, are you choosing from? A series of 'suggestions' of ever changing 'images' or 'descriptions' of whom or what you 'think' you can, or might be. Are these not more of the same – *illusions*? Indeed, do you actually even 'know' what is true around you? Please believe me, what you believe to be 'free will' in your lower nature, which is essentially egoic, is nothing more than freedom to choose insanity over insanity. Yet the remarkable thing in all of this is that – as we have seen from childhood to adulthood – when man's life is socially engineered by the powerful to the extent that for the duration of his life he operates from within these lower states of consciousness, he not only becomes unable to recognise the insanity that has become his life experience, he comes to see that his way of life and the lives of those in similar states around him as 'just the way things are'. And conversely, of course, within this world view of his, those who try and speak to Him of Truth, these are then the very ones whom he sees as living strange and unreal lives, and who have even 'lost the plot'.

"So, please, leave the false selves, surrender to Love, or rather, let the Love that is together, with, and in you, turn in union with you, towards Itself. Indeed, for when Truth is encountered, and known, free will is now truly operating as intended, and here, in Truth, one can only assume that if one were then to reject It, having at once experienced and known It – and here we are not speaking of our moments of weakness and falls into sin, repenting and resolving to start again – then that person's mental health must surely be called into question.

"For there can be no doubt that when Truth is encountered, It cannot be passed off as some kind of hip or cool random experience. For when you encounter the Living Truth, the Truth that is Alive and Is Life Itself, you will find that in this Life, Love's Will has been awaiting Its discovery by you, and as you become awakened in that LOVE, it will be given to you to know, that this Will, that you have received, is also, in reality, who you are. For the true you *is* your Father's Will, and that in this Union, That It Is One, and you will know, when that moment is given to you, what your free will really is, and what it means. For it is knowing this True Knowledge which gives you your True Conscience, true understanding of how to behave in the world, in accordance with the Truth of The Divine Unity, a Unity that holds All Things together, a Unity that Serves, a Unity that Loves in, with and through All That is, Its Very Self.

"Indeed, moreover, please enlighten me. What is it that you 'believe' that you actually own? For truly, in giving you what you perceive to be your own life, He is, in Reality, already sharing with you, what is already His. You came into this world 'owning' nothing. And when you leave this world, you will leave it 'owning' nothing, and what happens in between is of course precisely the same. It is this way for a purpose, and when you come to know this, you will also understand that herein lies your True Freedom.

"All of these ideas of 'owning' 'things' 'images' 'identities' of who we think we are, and, of course, the similarly ludicrous ideas of 'owning' other people – thus perceiving ourselves as having 'power' and 'control' over the very same – shows, not only that we are living in illusion, but that we have accepted the fundamental error as our truth – the abomination that we are separated from all things."

"Padre, my dear fellow, if you believe all of this to be true how do you know that you are not merely changing one system of thought, for another?"

"The ego consciousness and the Consciousness of the Unitive Life cannot be compared for only one is True. In Reality, only one Exists, and it is the consciousness of your being, as it is, in Truth, in Union with All Life: a Union which is inseparable which Is, your True Reality.

"For in Him you live, move, and have your being just as in you, He too lives, moves, and has your being, forever safe and secure.

"When you are brought to conscious awareness of this, where you then see your true freedom, you will understand what St Paul meant in that moment when he said that it is not he who lived; in other words, not his false self, but Christ, who lived in, with, and through him."

"And how then do you know this Truth," the voice asked, "and what if you are mistaken, and after death, you find yourself in the company of my master?"

"My dear friend," old Father Raphael began, "man, for too long, has lived in a false consciousness and assumed it to be his reality. He has run around within his ego experience using its false light as his guide, and what has he brought back? He has brought back 'suggestions', formed and re-formed, over centuries, indeed, millennia, of all sorts of ancient devils, demons, realms of this or that, guardians or gatekeepers to be manipulated and placated, to allow further passage, with further promises of 'secret knowledge' lying ahead, visited all sorts of ancient hells and heavens, and all that lies in between, unconsciously projecting the 'worldly' usage of hierarchical power structures into the unseen, all the while giving 'birth', 'power', and 'strength' to a belief in illusions, illusions that have held humanity in their grip for too long. And where have all of these remarkable visions and journeys emerged from? None other than from his first dreams of separation, a life lived in a false consciousness, and all his subsequent desires for what he believes to 'power'. So, you see, my dear friend in all seriousness ask yourself, how can you 'imagine' anything about Truth? How can you 'imagine' anything about Reality? Surely, when you do this, you are, already, wandering in illusion. Indeed, do you seriously believe that what you 'imagine' is, or can be, true? And, if so, true in what? Your own illusion?

'Truth is revealed within your experience of Union, all of which is given, and received, as a gift; with, in, and through, Divine Grace. Truth is not something that can be 'imagined' and then dressed up by 'us' – our false selves – who try to convince ourselves, and others, of what Truth 'really' is. So, whatever you 'imagine' about Truth, about Reality, be assured, that it is 100 per cent false.

"Indeed, if there is anything to be consumed by the Fire of Holy Spirit after death, it will surely be the many false ideas, thoughts and feelings that I've had about Truth, about Reality, about who, and what I am, and the life that I have unconsciously lived, the times when I've unconsciously let an imposter – a false self – pose, and speak, as though it were the real me.

"But why should we wait till then, when Eternity is now? For in Truth, with our conscious participation, we can work with Love in purging these non-entities from His temple; expunging all that we falsely value; all that we falsely identify with; all our false attachments, every false perception; indeed, all the fallacies that we have made up in our minds and accepted as truth. For we have, in our unconsciousness, turned His home into 'the robbers' den'; filling it with all that robs us of our 'experience' of Life; all that blinds us to the Reality of His Divine Indwelling, all that robs us of consciously experiencing our shared Life, The Reality of our Union in and with Love.

"And please know, it is only through Love that He clears His temple, that we may 'see' with His true clarity, thereby drawing an end to all the gnashing of teeth, at ourselves, and our brothers and sisters, freeing us from the living hells that we have unconsciously created here on earth.

"And who can say that He is for some and not for others. The notion is so ludicrous that it is almost laughable, had we not caused so much of the suffering that we see now in our world, suffering brought about by the many false beliefs that we have made up and accepted about Him, the One Who Is Love, the One Who draws all things through, with and in Himself."

"So," the voice interrupted, "how do you know this Truth, this Love that you speak of?"

"Surrender everything and repent in all humility and love! For in doing so," Raphael went on, "you present and offer yourself to God, free, from any egoic desire. And so the prodigal returns, and, made still, soon comes to know, what the prophets of Love within all religions have said.

"Indeed, for what a wonder it is, when man first encounters the Divine. In the process of leaving behind all that is false, he comes to find in his encounter that the language he has used previously, to name, define, categorise, and describe all things is now, magnificently, insufficient; indeed, is totally useless and inadequate.

"Why?

"Because, having been brought forth by Divine Grace – which you will later understand was in, with, and through, Christ and the Holy Spirit – man, in his humble 'yes', can now do no more, than simply 'be' as he truly is, and so come to experience, for the first time, that, which he truly is; his true self, fully conscious, open, pure, and free.

"Indeed, here, man, in his first conscious encounter, resembles those same disciples who innocently asked Him, 'Where do you live?' to which He replied, 'come and see'.

"And so, just as they, each man is truly brought by the Son to where He lives.

"Yet, miraculously, as they enter into that boundless, Holy, Sacred Space, man finds that Truth Itself reveals, something, even more astounding, for here man finds that his own truth is also revealed: The Truth that he is assimilated within the Immensity of the Divine, complete, in the Absolute's Oneness, at Home, in, and with, Christ, in Infinity Itself.

"However, although we might imply that some sort of journey has been made, we are of course stretching 'language' beyond its limits. Indeed, despite the fact that we know words themselves are inadequate, we still, nonetheless, try to relay a sense of our 'experience', whether it be by using metaphors, or, what could be described as metaphysical descriptions.

"Indeed, we come to realise that, although we may use phrases such as 'rising upwards and outwards', or even 'journeying inwards', in Reality, there is no movement at all. It is, in truth, Revelation. Revelation whereby we come to the unquestionable Realisation of His reality, True Reality, in which we find our own, find the place where we already are, find the place where we have always been, and have never left, Our Home, a place void of all duality, void of all, and any sense of separation.

"Yet within this experience of Unitive Wholeness, the child, it is true, gently becomes cognisant of another, and it is here that the Father presents Himself as being the very essence of His child. Divine Love, in that moment, makes it known to His child, forevermore, the Truth of who the child is, forever, Alive In.

"And in that moment of communicated Stillness, in that moment of communicated Silence, the name of God reverberates in, with, and through, the child's whole being, in with, and through, the child's whole experience. And so, in, with, and through, All That Is, expressing in simple, humble, glorious majesty, I AM, and so, revealing, once again, in the present, and so too in time and space, The Unitive, Ultimate, and only Truth, wherein all other words are unnecessary.

"For now the child knows and understands, beyond all doubt, that all exist, and truly live, in, I AM, that all exist and truly live, in Love, and that that Love Is Holy, Sacred, Pure, Divine Life. The same Love that is the lifeblood of you, and all things, All That Is Unitive, Perfect, Oneness.

"And so, through this experience, we come to understand how St Paul can say, 'there is only Christ' and so too, understand, why the Son is able to say, 'I am the Way, the Truth, and the Life' and how when you 'see' Him, you have seen the Father. For Father, Son, and Spirit, are merged in, and are, LOVE, the LOVE in which those who have been 'awakened', throughout history, in different times and places, have known: that same LOVE, that same Christ, that same Life, in which All Things Are One.

"And know that this Truth is not old age or new age, it is the Eternal Truth of every age, The Truth of the Unitive Divine Life.

There is no, and never has, or ever will be, any separate 'other' life, The Unitive Life is, All That Is.

"And how will this experience be possible, you might ask? It's possible, simply, because it's not your false self's doing, or 'the work' of one of your false gods. It is the work of Divine Grace. The child is wholly dependent on the Father. And it is Your Father's Will that none will remain lost in their unconsciousness.

"As the Spirit re-establishes His Peace in our minds, His Love flows with our conscious participation, out, into our world, where we then 'experience' that same Love, in All Things.

"We pray for our enemies, not because we have enemies, but because 'our' perceptions, that is, 'ours of them' and 'theirs of us', are false. Indeed, Christ goes even further telling us that if we come to Him without being ready to give up our 'love' for our 'father' and 'mother', our 'spouse' and 'children', our 'brothers' and 'sisters', and, indeed, 'our very selves', that we cannot be His disciple. *Why?* Can He really be telling us not to love? No, He is telling us in Truth that when we live, individually and collectively, in a false consciousness, that even our 'interpretation', our 'understanding' of what 'love' is, even our 'understanding' of who and what 'we' and our 'loved ones' are – even our 'understanding' of how, and the way we should, 'love' – is incomparable with what is True and is why He tells us to 'give up' these false understandings that we have made up and accepted about Love, 'give up' these false understandings that we have made up and accepted about ourselves, about our loved ones, about all peoples, about Him, these false beliefs, these attachments to false perceptions.

"But to do this, He tells us that we must pick up our cross and follow Him, follow Him out of our lives lived in unreality, bearing with Him, all the while, as we go, the pains and temptations that accompany this movement; enduring, with Him, all the while, the mental anguish, the psychological, and physical turmoil.

"But do not be dismayed, for its time is limited. So, never give up in your journey with Him, out of your false consciousness, no matter how many times you fall, or, how many times you think you fail; or, indeed, no matter how painful or worthless the 'movement' seems to be. For, despite being awakened to a Love that courses through and is the lifeblood of All Things, a Love which simply *Is*, man never ceases to amaze himself by continuing to fall into illusion, and all its subsequent madness and wastefulness. So, hold on, and never deny the Truth within, for that Love is the Living Truth, the One Reality, and, being so, *It*, is infinitely greater, than any of your mishaps. Indeed, to believe otherwise, is to believe in a false God, making a mockery of Love and What Is.

"And what Love it truly is, that It should honour us with its breathtaking beauty; allowing us to share in Its awareness breathing with, in, and through us, enveloping Its Creation, nurturing and covering it in selflessness.

"So, never give up, for your perceived trials can be seen as the birth pangs preceding 'That' something, which, in Reality, is already your Truth, where you truly live, the place from where you know and experience His True Compassion, His True Love, His True Light, in which you, and All Things, are bathed. For it is only when we return, with Him, to the True Source within, that we may, in Union With His Love, encounter, again, what is True, what is Real, where we 'see' the Reality of ourselves, 'see' the Reality of our loved ones, 'see' the Reality of all peoples, indeed, of All life, as it is, in Him. For it is only when we return and 'experience' our Union with the True Love Within that we can 'see', 'experience', and share, in our Union with the True Love Outwith, only then, can we Love, and be Loved, truly, as Our Father Wills. Only then can we live as what we are: Our Father's children, His Son's disciples, only then, do we know, understand, and share, in the Reality of what Love Truly Is.

"So please, let us make no mistake, only 'good seed' was, and is, ever sown, and you, my dear friend, are one of those wholly, unique, precious and miraculous gifts, Loved by Him into being, and so born, into Eternity.

"Find the Truth in Him and Live.

"His grace is wholly sufficient for you. His power, made perfect, in what 'the world' 'sees' as weakness.

"As you journey in the way of His grace, you will grow in Humility, Love and Patience. You will come to see that there are no more desires or seeking of the pleasurable ecstatic moments of bliss that were often found in your earlier moments of contemplation. This is given to protect you from trying to search out these grace filled moments as a means only to this end, that you do not become stuck in your movement away from your false lives and the selfishness of the ego consciousness. For all that is given to you, is to be shared in the service of all. It will be enough for you to be carried by the way of other graces, graces that will be given, that will remind you of the gift of faith He has given you, the Wisdom and Knowledge to know that He is in, and together, with you, always, and cannot – ever – possibly leave you.

"Yet, as I have said, there will, undoubtedly, be moments of 'darkness', what the mystics called 'the dark night of the soul' moments that seem to last for days, weeks, months, years, moments, that seem endless, moments, where you feel as though God is no longer there, no longer with you. But take heart as you pass through this; indeed, no matter how many times in your earthly life that you pass through this, for you will become aware of these moments, and, will come to know them for what they are. For the True Physician will show them to you. He will let you know that these sufferings are 'features' of your cross, and He will ask you once more to trust Him, to hand over all that you 'perceive' in each moment of suffering to Him. And so, you will come to realise, once more, that He is the One who is your strength, He is the One who is carrying you through your unconsciousness and, indeed, taking on each 'burden' gently relieving you of them one by one as He gently heals you, and leads you Home.

"Indeed, contemplatives often referred to God as being like a Magnet, drawing us by the Divine Spark, at the very core of our being, to Himself, and be of no doubt, He is drawing you through these periods of 'darkness' also.

"Yet, the usage of the word 'darkness' can, of course, be misleading, for in truth, darkness, in this sense, was used by the mystics to mean the darkness of the intellect; that is, that the intellect was unable to comprehend what was happening during these moments. However, it becomes clear that they meant that the false consciousness was still present, and, in a sense, still governing our attention at some level, still manipulating, still tempting us.

"For even at this stage in our 'journey', although we may not be aware of the fact, we are still being tempted to hold on to its false images, its false suggestions about ourselves, others, and, of course, God; indeed, these moments of 'darkness' can be seen as challenges thrown up by the ego consciousness in its attempts to keep us tied to its false truths, in other words, temptations thrown up to prevent us from leaving, that we may continue to feed it, by accepting its falsities, and believing them to be true.

"But, again, remember your faith and remember, that, in spite of what you are going through, whatever illusion you are experiencing, you are, still, and are always, in Christ, so do not behave like the Pharisees, who kept asking for signs, crying out in their own unconsciousness to a God that they alone had made from their own false selves, a God that they hoped would respond to whatever their false will demanded, thereby encouraging and confirming their own false beliefs about Him, and so reinforcing their false desires for more of the same, more of their much sought after 'power'.

"So, always try to be patient and gentle with yourself, as Christ is patient and gentle, and try and hold on to the fact that in coming through these dark moments, you are, in truth, continuing to grow in faith, maturing, strengthening your ability to stand firm in and with Christ, so that when further challenges arise, you will not be so easily swayed to give in to what is false. And remember too, that no matter the anxiety you face, it will ultimately pass, for you will not be left here; for grace, as always, will see you through, and such will the outcome be, that you will, in your experience of Union With Him, 'see' that the 'questions' and fearful moments of, 'oh why, oh why, oh why, oh Lord?' which you cried out and asked countless times during the 'dark nights', through time, become 'questions' that are turned in, and on, themselves. Indeed, for when you come out of from your 'dark nights', you will undoubtedly look back with joy, and laugh, laugh at why you could even begin to ask such ridiculous questions.

"For once again, in that moment of your ineffable experience of Union, even though this too will pass, you will, truly know, that He is with you always, and can never leave you, and that no matter what happens to you in this life no-thing, nothing, not even death, can remove us from Him; can remove us from Love; can remove us from That Which Is, Uncreated.

"And so, it is perhaps wise for us to recall and reflect on these moments in our lives, for they will not only encourage us to remain attentive they will help us to see all that He has done in untangling us from each and every false image that we have ever adopted and lived by, all the while gently helping us to recognise what still needs to be discarded. For, ultimately, this is the work that must be done in every human being, and it will not be complete until even that 'favourite' image of each of us is also cast aside.

"And what image is this you might ask?

"It is the one that has been hiding in plain sight all along. The one in which you see yourself as this 'seeker of Truth', this 'spiritual person', the one who is 'giving up' and 'surrendering everything to God', this image you have unconsciously designed from your imaginings of how such a person would and should be, and soon bought into 'wholeheartedly', and soon foolishly believed to be who you 'really' are, this person living their life in the 'higher planes' of consciousness, this idea that you held so firmly, the notion of you being this observer on high, aloof from your fellow man, this untouchable idol, which all along was nothing more than your ego's latest best suggestion for you to believe in. But even this image must go! Surrender all means surrender all, until even this false identity finally becomes consumed by Divine Love, revealing to you once more and completely that there is no you that is separate from It, reminding you that the true you is only knowable in Union with Christ. Indeed, for as the psalmist explained wherever you 'think' you can go there is no escape from Life. The work He has started will not go unfinished. For in the True Reality of the Mystical Body of Christ, He speaks for all of us when He says, 'I and the Father are One'.

"Of course, it goes without saying, that because of this truth of the Unitive Life, we are not suggesting that it doesn't matter what we do, or suggesting that we should desire to carry out any other will than our Father's Will of Love. Indeed, and in no way are we suggesting a descent into nihilism or solipsism for that matter. For in the Reality of Life, the more you receive, the more you will be called and driven by Love, to give.

"Yet, you will, naturally, still be a part of this world, and may oft-times still be ruffled by its illusory images. However, ask for His help that you may acknowledge your illusion; that you may respond in Truth, obliterating the lie by the Light of His Love.

"For through grace, when you are prompted to reflect on what you are, and what is before you – and of course, what you are a part of – your understanding, your awareness of All Things, as they are in

Truth, are now held in Light. For you now know that in that Truth, and in that Light, is Life; and that in this Life is Love. Now, in your true consciousness of Union, all that you take in through the senses is brought directly to Christ within, so that, together with Him, you, using the faculties of the mind correctly, may perceive and 'see', clearly, Christ outwith, a realisation of Truth in which you find and deliver, in union, your only response, Love. For love knows and sees Itself, and reciprocates the same; a Perfect Communion of Love. For the Kingdom within is also the Kingdom at hand, and the Kingdom has come upon you.

"The Unitive Life is no dream or illusion, my dear friend, It is Reality.

"When we believe we are hidden, or can hide ourselves from His Light, does not make 'our belief' to be true, or mean that His Light is not in us.

"We can, however, tragically misuse our gift of life, and make, and 'live' in our own fantasy world, turning our life experience into a living hell, where only madness and insanity reign. And please, let us be clear, the experience of Union cannot be manufactured or made in a laboratory. It is a gift in and from Absolute Humility, that Love may be known, and shared, throughout His Kingdom.

"And please know also, that man can never experience Reality in a life 'lived' in the identity of a false self; that is, by the false self's doing. Why? Because He who made and lives in the true you, did not create your false selves; 'we' men created them, and they became the false rulers of this world.

"Indeed, men in this false state cannot 'consciously' relate to Him who is Life Itself. They are like Pilate, in that moment of unconsciousness, when he asked Truth Itself, standing, directly in front of Him, 'what is Truth?' For when men live out the lives of false selves, 'men' 'live' unaware. Their false selves become their false cells, yet they are unaware, unaware that they are caged. They cannot 'see' that they too are a part of that very same Truth. They cannot 'see' nor comprehend that they are a part of That which Is The Reality of All Life.'"

Dom Leonard then turned to his brothers. 'And with that, old Raphael told us that he then sat in peace. There was no more discussion and so he said a final prayer of thanksgiving then left the confessional, and so too the church and retired for the night.'

After some moments, young Gerald spoke up. 'But, Dom Leonard, before he left, surely he must've checked to look inside the penitent's compartment?'

'When we first heard this story from old Father Raphael, we too asked the same question, Gerald. We too asked whether he checked inside the penitent's compartment before leaving and to this he simply smiled, and replied, "No."

'*But why?* Why didn't he check?' young Gerald asked.

Dom Leonard smiled. 'For he said that there was nothing there to see. And told us that, "if there is only Christ, and that if Christ is everything, and is in everything, and that if I, my true self, and all that exists, is, in truth, part of What Is or, in other words, part of this Wholeness of Life Itself, namely, the Mystical Body of Christ, where then is the devil? Where then are the demons? Where then is the darkness, when darkness to Him is not dark, and night is as clear as the day?

"And know this," he said, "He who sees 'power' in evil, lives in illusion. Indeed, in such instances, one might be so convinced as to believe that he honestly 'knows' what he is doing, but, in truth, he is, in all actuality, perceiving himself as being separated and so, is unconscious, in other words 'lost' in unreality.

"And similarly in those moments when you look at the world and are tempted to ask where is God in all its suffering, ask, instead, whose face is looking back at you. For the Transfiguration is not the story of Christ being transfigured before His apostles, it is the story of the apostles' 'perception' being transfigured before Him.

"For they were given the Divine Grace to know and 'see' in Union with the Light within, the Light that was before them, the Light that He is, and that same Christ is the Light of All Things.

"So, follow Him, for just as they, you too will know, you too will 'see'. For Truth will be revealed to you, and when that moment is given to you, you too, just as they, will 'look around' and you too will 'see' that there is 'no one else'. There are no such things as false selves. There is only Christ the beloved.

CONSCIOUSNESS AND PERCEPTION

"He is the True Light in and with you, and so too your brothers and sisters, and is the same Love that bears and overcomes the cross, the same Love that makes the suffering in this life as nothing; nothing compared to That Which is Revealed, the Truth of your True and Eternal Life in Union with Perfect Love.

"And remember, the suffering we experience in this life is not something that should be held aloft, or paraded, and clung to, like some perverse trophy. It should only be embraced with Patience, that we may, through that same Divine Grace, not only gain the courage to face our sufferings, but that we may in Union with Perfect Love, come to transcend them, allowing ourselves, to be brought forth out of them, resurrected, in and with Christ, that, together, we may rise above them, no longer letting them steal away from us the experience of our true identity, our true existence, no longer, allowing our sufferings to have 'power' over our lives. For in Truth, we are infinitely more than all our sufferings. So, never divert your line of sight from your positioning in Christ. For it is in that True Reality where you not only come to see and know your own, but where you come to see and know the One Who Is With you, Who Is in you, Who is All around you.

"Yet, some might continue to argue that there is a place for the ego consciousness in our lives, in our shared world. However, this is total folly, for as all advocates of Wisdom have said, the false self and its false life must be left behind where, ultimately, of course, it is consumed by the Fire of the Holy Spirit, that Fire of Love that Christ told us He had come to bring to the earth, the True Consciousness of the Kingdom of Heaven that consumes the 'earthly' egoic consciousness, and how He wished it was blazing.

"Indeed, for if the ego consciousness is still prevalent, what will it matter if even the whole of humanity were to gather round a particular philosophy, a particular religion, a particular ideology?

"With man's consciousness, and so perception of himself – and thus of any of his particular notions – clouded in unreality, we are surely destined to continue in uncertainty, condemned to repeat the same tragic mistakes over and over, re-enacting the same history, from the same fantastical illusions. Indeed, our so called 'human progress' will continue to remain the 'human fantasy' that it is, absent of Love, Truth and Wisdom.

"And so, humanity, as a whole, must come to 'see' that its challenge lies in helping man 'in part' to awaken, and to stay awake.

"Yet why 'in part', you might ask?

"Because, it is, in the main, the work of Our Father.

"Yet as His children, brothers and sisters alike, we all have our part to play. For just as we are all dependent on Him, so too, are we called by Him, in Christ, that we may share in the Light of His Love, and share it with one another: One Light, One Life, One Body, One Spirit. The Living Bread that comes down from Heaven. The Living Bread that gives, and Is, True Life Itself, The Living Bread That Is Love.

"Indeed, for just as the lightning flashes in one part of the heavens lights up the others, so it will be with the Son of Man, when His day comes. For in that day, all will be awakened. The work of His Hands will truly become the Hands of His Work. For man will know himself, as he is known by God, and we will truly know, 'That' which we behold is 'That' which we are in Union with 'That' of which we are a part 'That' which is One.

"And what a gift it truly is! Not only to be driven by Love but to be given the grace to 'see' that we are, already, where our hearts longed to be. My dear Brothers, we are already Home!"

When they reached the Guest House, Dom Leonard and Gerald helped Paul out from the wheelchair. Supporting him on each side, they made their way through the small foyer, up the stairs and into the sunlit sitting room, where his family were waiting.

When the McLeods were finally reunited, all earlier fears were forgotten.

The tears were there as was the laughter.

The love that held them together showed its strength, and before long, it was as though they'd never been apart.

Agnes and Margaret said they would stay in the Guest House at night and help with Paul's care during the day, at the monastery, then return home with him, so he could spend some time with the rest of the family, when his strength had increased, and his immediate medical issues were showing signs of improvement.

BOOK SIXTEEN:

MOVEMENTS

28

Scene 1: Stuck

Thursday 14 January, 1993, Fife Drive, Forgewood, Motherwell, Scotland, 7:20 a.m.

Gary opened his eyes to the ceiling and immediately felt the raw, excruciating pain of loss.

His wife, Michelle, lay in bed, next to him, but far, far away. She too was awake.

For Michelle, another night had passed without sleep, and lying on her side, with her back to him, she continued gazing at the photograph she had placed underneath the lamp, on the bedside cabinet – a picture of her daughter, Kelly, smiling happily with her birthday cake, on the day of her third birthday.

Gary turned gently to Michelle, and put his left hand on her arm, rubbing it softly. Michelle was unresponsive but for the tears welling and flowing from her vacant eyes.

After a moment, Gary, struggling with the solitude of her grief, gently pushed himself out from under the covers. Quietly leaving the bedroom, Gary crossed the narrow hall into the bathroom.

Closing the door, he urinated in the toilet bowl, and flushed the cistern, before washing at the sink.

Returning the bath towel to the radiator, he opened the door, left the bathroom, and entered the kitchen, heading towards the cigarette packet that lay beside an ashtray, and disposable lighter, on the worktop.

Taking it in his hands and finding it empty, he walked over and pushed the packet inside the plastic carrier bag hanging on the handle of the cupboard door, on his way out.

Walking into the living room, he glanced at the mirrored table, then at the mantelpiece. No cigarettes.

Walking back into the bedroom, he picked his items of clothing from the floor one by one, and was soon dressed. Moving round to Michelle's side of the bed, he sat down beside where she lay.

With the palm and fingers of his right hand, he lovingly caressed her face and head, gently arranging the straggled hairs, softly pushing them together; sweeping them behind her left ear. He then leaned down and kissed her left temple.

Michelle, despite her love for him, was *still* unresponsive.

Gary, trying to remain strong, continued, silently, in his attempts to soothe her. 'Try 'n' sleep, Michelle, *please*,' he whispered, unable to hold himself back any longer.

After a few more painful minutes had passed, Gary told Michelle that he was going to the shop to buy cigarettes, and that he would prepare their breakfast when he returned. He gently kissed her again on the side of the head, before collecting his leather jacket from the wardrobe, and pulling it on.

Reaching the dressing table, he picked up the notes, coins, and house keys that were lying next to his lock knife, and pushed them into the pockets of his black jeans. Leaving the bedroom, he headed down the hall.

Sliding the bolts from their fixings, he opened the door and let himself out, closing it quietly behind him.

Scene 2: Out

Thursday 14th January, 1993, Fife Drive, Forgewood, Motherwell, Scotland, 8:30 a.m.

When Michelle heard the door close, she reached out with her left hand and stroked the glass in the picture frame. After a moment, she took the picture frame in her hand and drew it closer. The tears came again.

Pushing herself out from under the covers, Michelle, still holding, and gazing at Kelly's picture, got up and out from the bed, and walked, in a trance-like state, out of the bedroom and into the bathroom. She leaned into the bath, and, taking the plug on its chain, fixed it in the plug hole and turned on the hot tap. She then left the bathroom, walked down the hall to the door, and began to slide the four bolts into their fixings, one after the other.

Walking back into the bedroom, she sat down on the bottom of the bed, holding the picture on her lap, her silent tears falling on the glass.

When Michelle felt that enough time had passed, she moved from the bed. And taking the lock knife from the dressing table, she walked into the bathroom, immediately stepping into the running bath still wearing her nightgown, and still holding the picture and lock knife in each hand.

Scene 3: Chance

Thursday 14th January, 1993, Kylemore Crescent, Forgewood, Motherwell, Scotland, 9:20 a.m.

In the shop, Gary took the eggs, bacon, milk, bread, and a large glass bottle of Lucozade from his shopping basket. He rested them on the counter, in front of Norrie, who was at the till.

Hearing the tinkle of the bell on the shop door, Gary, with his back to it, looked beyond Norrie to the mirrored glass on the wall. The first man entering was one of Phil Murray's associates. And, sure enough, Phil came in after him.

Gary, still watching Phil in the mirror, wrapped his right hand over the neck of the Lucozade bottle and, in an instant, swung round to his right.

The bottle exploded on contact with the side of Phil's head, knocking him to the floor. Gary then lunged forwards with his body towards Phil, but was immediately rugby-tackled by Phil's burly friend, their bodies sliding along the tiled floor coming to a stop near the shop entrance.

Pinning Gary to the ground, the man soon had a blade at Gary's throat.

'Go for it, ya fuckin' bam. Dae it!' Gary roared at him.

Phil pushed himself up. Blood was trickling out from the three-inch split on the right side of his head. He steadied himself by holding on to one of the shelves, before walking over to stand next to the two men, who were still on the floor.

'Leave him. Let him up,' Phil told his friend.

Phil's friend continued to hold Gary, unsure of Phil's current state and his judgement of the situation.

'Look, Gary,' Phil started, looking down at him. 'Ye need tae listen tae whit Ah hiv tae say tae ye here, an Ah mean really listen. I'm sorry aboot whit happened to yer wean, really sorry, but ye hiv tae realise that that was fuck all tae dae wi' me! Youse were the cunts that were fuckin' aboot wi' they pills! No' me!'

'Whit the fuck are ye oan aboot, ya fuckin' idiot?' Gary screamed. 'Whit the fuck dae ye think's gonnae happen when you've got a fuckin' alkie hawdin' drugs for ye, eh?'

Phil didn't have an answer.

'Right!' Norrie shouted to them from behind the counter. 'That's enough! The three a' yees oot the shop now, or I'm phonin' the polis.'

'C'moan,' Phil said to his friend, opening the door of the shop.

Phil's friend took the knife from Gary's throat, and shoved him hard on the chest, as he got up off him, leaving him there as they left the shop.

Scene 4: Gone

Thursday, 14th January, 1993, Fife Drive, Forgewood, Motherwell, Scotland, 10:20 a.m.

Gary, carrying the shopping, entered the close and headed up the stairs.

On the second landing, he found Gail, the young woman that lived in the flat directly below his. 'Gary,' she began, 'Ah know yees've got enough goin' on, and I'm really sorry tae bother ye, but have you left a tap runnin', or is yer washing machine leakin'? There's a lot a' water comin' fae yer flat and it's running doon ma walls.'

Gary rushed past Gail, up the stairs.

Reaching his flat, he put the key in the lock and turned it, putting his weight against the door, but the door wouldn't open.

Dropping the shopping on the floor, he lifted the flap on the letterbox. Looking in he began desperately calling out Michelle's name.

He started kicking the door with all his strength, thrusting the sole of his right boot below the lock, but it wouldn't budge.

Gary ran down the stairs straight past his mother-in-law, who had just entered the close.

'What's goin' on?' she asked, following him out.

Gary ran to the drainage pipe that ran from the gutter on the roof down past the right side of the three verandas to the ground, and started to climb.

When he had passed the first two verandas and reached his own, he climbed over the railing and tried the handle on the door. It too was locked.

Gary smashed the window on the door with his elbow and, reaching in through the space in the broken glass, turned the key in the lock, opening the door.

Rushing through the living room and across the water-soaked

carpet in the hall, he entered the bathroom and found Michelle's lifeless body, the picture of their daughter on her lap under the water that flowed, pinkish-red, over the side of the bath. His lock knife lay open on the floor.

'Jesus Christ! Please, Michelle, pleeeease,' he pleaded, taking hold of his wife's body in his arms, deaf to the pounding on the front door.

'Let me in! Let me in, Gary!' his mother-in-law screamed through the letterbox.

Gary whimpered as he held on to Michelle, rocking her from side to side as the banging on the door continued.

He eventually let go of Michelle's body, turned off the tap and sat on the floor beside the bath.

His mother-in-law was now screaming through tears. 'Let me in, ya bastart! Let me in. Let me in tae see ma wean!'

Gary's eyes caught the lock knife on the floor and the look on his face changed from one of sorrow, to rage. He wiped his tears with his right sleeve and grabbed the lock knife in his right hand.

Standing up, he walked out of the bathroom, down the hall and slid back the bolts, opening the door.

'What have ye done, ya bastart? You and yer fuckin' drugs!' his mother-in-law screamed, lunging at him.

Gary stood motionless, as she clung to him, dragging her fingernails down his face before pushing him aside to rush down the hall, calling out Michelle's name.

Gary left the flat, carrying the lock knife in his right hand.

The screams of his mother-in-law filled the close as he ran down the stairs.

BOOK SEVENTEEN: CLOSURE

29

Scene 1: *Joy and Sorrow*

Thursday, 14th January, 1993, Montrose Street, Forgewood, Motherwell, Scotland, 11:10 a.m.

Eldo opened the door and was about to leave his flat, when the phone rang.

Walking back down the hall, he lifted the phone from its fixing on the wall. 'Eddie, she's woke up! She's gonnae be awright. The wean! Chloe! She's jist woke up!'

Hearing the news, Eldo broke down.

With his back against the wall, he slid to a seated position on the floor, still crying, with the handset held against the right side of his face.

Hearing the dogs barking in the close, Eldo turned to see Gary standing in the open doorway.

'Okay, Linda,' Eldo said into the phone. 'I need tae go, Gary's here. I was just oan my way up tae the hospital when ye phoned. I'll see ye in a wee while. I love ye, hen. Cheerio.'

Eldo got up from the floor and placed the handset back in its fixing. He walked to the door towards Gary, who was still standing in the doorway, his arms by his sides.

As Eldo took in Gary, he stopped some feet away from him. Eldo didn't know what else had happened to Gary, but he understood, Gary, was done.

CONSCIOUSNESS AND PERCEPTION

Eldo caught a glint of the knife and then looked again at his friend, his brother… the pain, the suffering, the agony.

Eldo silently nodded in acknowledgement, wiping his own tears with his right arm. 'It's okay, bro',' he said quietly. 'I understand. Ah love ye, Gary. Ah know the score. It's okay. Dae it. Ah deserve it,' he said, walking towards Gary, his arms outstretched to embrace the inevitable.

Through his own tears, Gary, looked at Eldo, and then looked down at his lock knife.

He was immediately struck with horror. Alarmed by this sudden realisation, with a look of confusion and disbelief on his face, Gary let go of the knife, letting it fall to the ground, and then turned from Eldo, and ran.

Eldo called out to him, but Gary was already on the street, and running towards the Bellshill Road.

Scene 2: Chase

Thursday, 14th January, 1993, Bellshill Road, Forgewood, Motherwell, Scotland, 11:30 a.m.

Leaving his mum and dad's, Ninian, caught sight of Gary, to his right, running along the pavement, on the other side of the road.

Hurrying out through the open gate, Ninian kept sight of him, as Gary ran through the open traffic in a diagonal direction, crossing over to Ninian's side, but now roughly forty yards ahead of him.

Instinctively, Ninian sprinted after Gary, calling out to him. Coming within earshot, Ninian could hear the siren of the level crossing.

Running alongside, and past the gates of the level crossing, Gary took the stairs of the bridge two at a time. When he had reached the middle point of the bridge, Gary looked over the five-foot high parapet, saw the train approaching, and pulled himself up.

Climbing up, and over the parapet, Gary hung by his arms above the tracks.

Ninian lunged forward and grabbed Gary's arms. 'Hawd oan, Gary, for fuck's sake. *Please*. We'll get through this. Hawd oan. I've got ye.'

With raw, tired eyes, Gary looked up to Ninian and smiled. 'I'm sorry, bro',' he said. 'I'm goin' home.' And with that, Gary pushed himself free, dropping directly in front of the oncoming train.

BOOK EIGHTEEN:

SIGNS AND SIGNALS

30

Scene 1: Yes or no

Friday 28 January, 1993, Braidhurst Industrial Estate, Forgewood, Motherwell, Scotland, 5:00 p.m.

After Gary's funeral, Ninian stayed sober. He slipped away early from the mourners' gathering at the Motherwell Miners' Social Club and now walked through Braidhurst Industrial Estate, making his way to the Glenisla Kilt factory, where he knew Karen, his girlfriend, would be standing in line, waiting to clock out. He needed to see her. He needed to ask her. It was time.

Stopping underneath one of the streetlights, Ninian unzipped his black mackintosh, and reached inside, removing the ring box from his pocket and prising it open.

He smiled as he looked at the engagement ring that he had only just started paying in instalments the day before. *Hope she likes it. Fuck, and hope she says aye.*

Pushing the ring box into his right trouser pocket, Ninian started to walk, wondering whether now really was the right time.

He remembered that Karen had told him, only last night on the phone, that while she loved and missed Gary, she couldn't attend his funeral, not after going through Michelle's and their daughter's. It was 'too soon'. She just couldn't 'deal wi'' anymore'.

When he was almost thirty yards from the factory, Ninian saw Karen walk out of the building and get into a car. *Probably getting a lift home.*

The car drove off down the road, which Ninian knew was a dead end. He'd wait for the car to do a U-turn and wave it down as it as it drew nearer.

As Ninian waited for the car, he came to realise, that from the distance it had to travel to make the turn, it should've made its way back before now, so he set off, walking towards the dead end.

Parked underneath one of the streetlights, Ninian could see the car's red brake lights and exhaust fumes as he approached and, through the back windscreen, two figures in a clinch.

Ninian started to run towards the car, heading for the driver's side.

Pulling the door open, he grabbed the driver by the shoulder, to drag them out of the vehicle, only to find that the driver was a young woman.

Ninian stepped back from the car in a state of confusion

Karen got out of the passenger side. 'Ninian!' she started, unsure of what to say next. 'It's not what you think. It's nothing serious, it's just…'

But by then Ninian was already walking, and when Karen called out after him, he broke into a run.

Scene 2: Siren

Friday 28th January, 1993, Bellshill Road, Forgewood, Motherwell, Scotland, 5:45 p.m.

When he reached the off-licence, Ninian bought a bottle of Macallan whisky, twenty Regal King Size, firelighters and lighter fuel, and when he had left the shop, he found Eldo's old Labrador, Laddie, standing at the railings looking up at him, wagging its tail.

The dog accompanied Ninian across the road and onto the footbridge, where Gary had taken his own life. On the bridge, Ninian crouched down beside the half dozen or so bunches of flowers, and began relighting the candles that had been blown out by the wind.

Standing up, he cracked open the lid on the bottle of whisky and poured some out on to the spot where Gary had climbed up. Ninian screwed the lid on to the bottle, and returned it to his pocket, before moving closer to the parapet.

With his chin resting on his interlocked fingers, Ninian unconsciously followed the shiny tracks below, to where they were swallowed up by the darkness.

Lost in his thoughts the siren rang out and the gates on the level crossing slowly started their descent.

With tears in his eyes, Ninian climbed up onto the edge of the parapet, positioning himself on its narrow ledge, his legs dangling roughly thirty feet above the tracks below.

Laddie began to growl and barked loudly, looking up at him. Ninian drew the sleeve of his right arm across his tear-filled eyes.

He could see the light of the train approaching and heard the rhythmic drone of its wheels on the tracks, the tired, hypnotic sound steadily increasing.

The ledge of the parapet was vibrating and Ninian responded by moving to a standing position. The train sounded its horn as it bore down on the level crossing, drowning out the sound of the dog barking.

The narrow ledge was now shaking violently. Ninian's body

swayed in his struggle to keep upright as he waited for the right moment.

Filled with rage, Ninian removed the bottle of whisky from his pocket and hurled it directly at the oncoming train, watching it explode on contact with the roof of its engine.

When the train had passed underneath, Ninian climbed down from the parapet. He crouched down beside the old dog and stroked its head.

'Okay. Let's go, Laddie,' he whispered.

Stepping down on to the North Motherwell side, Ninian and Laddie wandered down Watling Street, before entering the darkness of Strathclyde Country Park on their way to the loch.

Scene 3: Asunder

Friday 28th January, 1993, Strathclyde Country Park, Motherwell, Scotland, 7:00 p.m.

When he reached the pebbled area at the side of the loch, Ninian charged around in a frenzied state; spending almost an hour gathering, and arranging the firewood.

By the time he was finished he was soaked with sweat.

The bonfire stood, almost eight feet high. And, when it had eventually *caught*, its golden flames crackled and roared wildly.

Ninian paced around and was soon talking out loud. He laughed. He cried. He shouted. He screamed.

And then the voice: 'Ninnnniannnn.'

And again, 'Ninnnniannnn.'

The boy was there in the water, somewhere in the mist, calling out to him.

Ninian, with tears of fury, tore off his black tie and scrunched it into a ball, hurling it into the heart of the fire. He then wrestled his way out of his black mackintosh, almost falling, before launching it too into the flames.

Turning from the fire he made his way briskly across the pebbles towards the water, straight past Eldo's dog, deaf to his rabid barking, and straight into the freezing cold water.

The evil entities soon engulfed him, fluttering in and through the mist as he pushed forward. Looking down, he let the water pass between the fingers of his open, outstretched hands, and smiled wryly at the evil faces that grimaced back at him beneath the surface.

'Ninnnniannnn.'

Responding to the call, Ninian looked directly to where the sound of the voice came from. The boy was suspended in the air, almost hovering three feet above the surface, his arms open, reaching out to him.

The water now reached up to Ninian's chest, yet he was still ten feet away from the boy. But with his next step, Ninian was pulled under.

Struggling in the grip of the entities that clung to him, Ninian's mind was suddenly filled with light, and, in that instant, brought to *the sight and experience of another.*

He felt the gasp for breath, the struggle, the racing heartbeat, the panic of one being chased – a child, a boy, a schoolboy, running for his life on a bright autumn day, through the woods, the golden leaves crunching underfoot, and the voices of evil, louder, as they drew nearer, his fellow pupils behind him, calling out to him their harmful intentions. And suddenly, without warning, the fall, the fall off the edge of the cliff, forty feet or more, plunging downwards, straight into darkness, the darkness of depths of the river, the strength of the current, pulling him down, deeper, sweeping him along further and further still, only to be caught, caught by the legs – his tired legs tangled in the branches of a submerged tree, the skin of his bare knees tearing in the struggle, fighting to break free as he looked up through the water, clawing towards the surface, at the children standing at the cliff edge, the girl with the red hair, until the struggle was no more.

Ninian saw the seasons pass quickly and the lifeless body eventually being dislodged by the current and carried again, further still into the depths of the loch.

With his own death steadily approaching, Ninian's mind was now shown moments from his own life passing by: his first and only day as an altar boy; the day that would change everything. He saw the boy at the edge of the middle pew, talking to the woman – the woman with the red hair; the woman who had once been the young girl who had helped chase the boy. Yet now, something had changed. Ninian was made to see what the woman had seen on the day of the funeral, to hear the voices that the woman had heard, in her head… all that had plagued her.

'Forgewood, look at the state a' these people. Fuck they've even got a spastic on the altar.' Then the manic laughter and the battle within, the woman biting into her tongue, drawing blood that trickled out of her mouth and down her chin; pain, self-inflicted in an attempt to prevent her from venting *that* which was trying to take over, *pain* self-inflicted in an attempt to keep the voices at bay, to hold back the madness from being disclosed.

And so now to the altar, and Ninian with the boy standing next to him, the boy gripping him by the arm, and the subsequent roar of the multitude rushing deep within. And so receiving the revelation, the boy's gift to Ninian; the gift that became his curse; the gift that would allow Ninian to hear *them;* hear *them* in the minds of other people.

The replays continued and the events of Ninian's life flew by: moments when he'd experienced the many diabolical and destructive thoughts and feelings that he had believed were his own demons were now shown to be the torments which those in his surroundings had struggled to contain within themselves.

He was shown his Community Psychiatric Nurse outside his block of flats arguing in the car with her husband before visiting him on New Year's Day.

The boy beside her as Ninian opened the door to his flat to welcome her in. The boy, sitting beside her on the chair, in his living room, and what was really running through her mind.

'Nothing major, he says! Who the fuck does he think he's tryin' tae kid? Look at the fuckin' state a' this place. It's fuckin' stinkin'. Thank fuck that window is open or I'd be spewin' ma fuckin' ring by now. The daft cunt doesn't even know. He's that fuckin daft he doesn't even know he'll be back in the asylum within a fortnight. He'd be better on 'es meds, and taking the lot a' them in one fuckin' gulp. Whit the fuck am Ah doing here? And New Year's Day as well. Whit a fuckin' waste.'

And then his Community Psychiatric Nurse leaving, 'Thanks, Ninian, I hope you have a nice time too. Cheerio.'

Flashing forward again, Ninian was shown the New Year's party in Gary's flat: how he'd felt wide awake, with the voices relentless in his head.

His focus had been brought to Gary. *He always had to be the centre of attention. Look at the way he's staring at Karen. He's been staring at her the whole night. He always gets what he wants. Karen will be next. Grab the lock knife and stab him. Stab him in the jugular Grab it. Stab him. Quick. Hurry. Plunge him.*

Ninian had jumped up from the chair and rushed round the table and was past the couch and in the kitchen in seconds. Standing over the sink, he turned on the cold tap, letting the cold water run into his cupped hands before throwing it on to his face.

Putting his hands over his ears, he closed his eyes. *Stop, please stop,* he inwardly repeated. *I need to get out a' here. Dear God, help me. Please, Stop it. Don't let me do anythin'. Stop me. Please!*

Then Gary entering the kitchen – 'Are ye awright, Ninian?' – followed by Eldo.

It was here that Ninian was shown that the voices he had heard were the voices that Eldo was experiencing; what was going on in Eldo's head. It was Eldo's eyes that had been drawn to the lock knife in the living room, and so too, in the kitchen, where he'd looked at the handle of a large kitchen knife.

And how Eldo had struggled, struggled within, he wanted to escape, to get out of there, out of the flat, and away, away from Gary, in case he did anything. Eldo was in danger of losing his battle, and he knew it, but was fighting *inside*; yet, trying not to show it, trying to keep it together, but terrified of what he might do, and so, taking, what, was to him, his only opportunity for a way out: 'I'm goin' up the road tae get some pills.'

And so later, that same night, to the loch, where Eldo had joined Ninian in the water and where Ninian knew now, the boy had shown Eldo his own demons, the horrors that were holding Eldo in their grip, the demons that *he* had battled and had fought to contain throughout his life.

Onwards once more, Ninian was now making his way to Norrie's shop, where the voices and visualisations had so overwhelmed him that he had started to try and outrun them, the voices that had told him, *Where will you get yer drugs fae now? Now that yer pal's wean's deid? Pity it wasn't you tae. You'd be as well toppin' yersell. Look at the fuckin' state a' ye.*

But now he was shown that these attacks directed at him had come from a woman, a neighbour, out walking her dog, looking over to Ninian from behind the row of parked cars on the other side of the road.

And so to Norrie's shop at the counter, where a voice in Ninian's head had cried out in response to Norrie's relentless questioning: *Tell him tae fuck off!*

And Norrie later explaining, 'I didnae mean tae bombard ye wi' questions. I was just worried.'

And then, the voice again, *Huh just worried! Whit a dirty lying bastart a' a man. Aw these cunts wi' shops are aw the same, wanting to know aw yer business so they can tell every other cunt behind yer back, then they can aw laugh at ye, and make a right cunt a' ye when yer no' there. Fuckin' arsehole!*

But now Ninian, for the first time, *saw* the *other* customer, the man who had been in the shop with him; an older man of a similar age to Norrie, who had been standing behind Ninian, waiting to be served, and who had overheard their whole conversation, and who had been *carried away with what was running through his head.*

And so the events continued to replay themselves.

Outside the shop to the meeting with Eldo's uncle Frank and the other men: Ninian giving out cigarettes, and then the *'Beggin' bastarts! They'll work for no cunt. Give them fuck all.'* And the young woman he now noticed getting out of her fancy car to go to the shop, the scowl, on her face as she looked over to them on her way past.

And so onwards to the community centre, where he had to collect his niece, Paula, and had been confronted by the two youths, who had been challenged by Billy, the youth worker. 'Right, youse two, youse are barred fae the youth club for a fortnight. Okay?'

The smaller youth's response: 'Aw, for fuck's sake, Billy!'

'Well, yees know the rules!'

And the taller youth showing his annoyance. 'Ah suppose you never took anything when ye were young, eh?'

'Aye, ye're right, Ah never. They things took me!'

And then one of the voices heard clearly above the others: *Here comes the lecture fae the arsehole,* and seeing the glare on the smaller youth's face.

Bringing the replays to a close, he saw a scene from the Abbey Guest House, where he and his family had been led by Brother Aloysius as they waited for Paul, and the increasing anxiety that had swept over Ninian on seeing members of the drug and alcohol support group, a voice once more rushing to the forefront of his mind. *'Look at the state a' these cunts. It's like the fuckin' caper hoose in here.'*

And Ninian now seeing one of the group members, one who believed he didn't need to be there, one who believed he didn't have a problem, annoyed by the very presence of those around him, lost in his own denial.

Scene 4: *Anew*

Saturday 29th January, 1993, Strathclyde Country Park, Motherwell, Scotland, 8:30 a.m.

The driver of the police car flicked on its siren as it drew up to the edge of the car park.

Ninian, who was lying face-down with his head resting on his arms beside what was left of the fire, raised his head wearily and let out a groan.

Sergeant Miller and the younger officer got out of the vehicle and approached Ninian.

'So, what the fuck was it this time? A dip in the moonlight?' the young officer asked.

Ninian rolled over on to his back and looked up to the clear blue sky and before long was smiling at the birds flying overhead, what Gary had been telling them about, and what a truly beautiful and breathtaking sight it was.

In the back of the police vehicle, Ninian could hear the whispering voices begin to ascend. The boy was sitting beside him.

The young officer turned from the driver's seat and making his right hand into the shape of a pistol, he pointed it at Ninian, before raising it slightly to the sound of '*bang, bang, bang*'.

With the back of his right hand, Sergeant Miller swiftly slapped the young constable on the back of the head. 'Start the engine and get us up the road, clown!'

Ninian smiled and looked out of the side window. It was a beautiful morning.

Sergeant Miller instructed the young officer to drive to Forgewood. When they had reached Ninian's block and parked the police car, Sergeant Miller spoke to Ninian at length. He spoke of the time when he and Ninian's dad had had a 'run in', as he called it, and how it was something that he had regretted all his life; something that he definitely wasn't proud of.

He concluded by telling Ninian that, while life could be tough, he had a good family and that he should take care of himself, for their sake also.

EPILOGUE

One month later

Strathclyde Country Park, Motherwell, Scotland, 10:00 a.m.

Ninian pushed Paul in the wheelchair, to the edge of the car park and, fixing the brakes, leaned into his brother, taking hold of him in an embrace and helping him out of the chair.

Together, they walked slowly across the pebbles.

Reaching the water's edge, they stood for a moment in silence.

'It's interesting, Ninian,' Paul started, 'in ancient times, vast expanses of water like lakes, seas, and so on, were believed to hold all kinds of monsters and demons. And, as you know, even Legion entered the water.

'Yet, for some today, the stories surrounding the biblical Sea of Galilee, and Christ's miracles there, can also be seen as allegories. For example, with the sea and all the monsters and demons that it contains, providing us with a picture, a picture of our reality, our 'lower nature' our predominant egoic consciousness – and how we experience it, with all its illusions, ignorance and fears.

'And so too, of course, our difficulty in walking with, and in, the higher consciousness of Christ, who walks *on* the water, and continues to reach down to us – at once, a willing, trusting, but then floundering, Peter – who He takes by the hand, up, and out of the water, unto Himself, and so out of our false consciousness to The Truth, The Truth, which, ever present, calms all storms; calling out and waiting, patiently, for its Creation, nurturing It, to True Reality, The Unwavering and Unopposed Divine.'

Ninian opened Paul's prayer book, found the pages that Paul had requested and held it open.

When Paul could just about make out the text, he made the sign of the blessing over the water and began to read aloud prayers for the dead.

'God will wipe every tear from their eyes; there will be no more death, no more weeping or pain, for the old order has passed away.'

Jesus answered them: 'I have told you all this so that you may have peace in me. In the world you will have trouble, but be brave; I have conquered the world.'

A SPECIAL THANKS FROM THE AUTHOR

Thank you for purchasing *Consciousness and Perception: A part fictionalised reflection on humanity's struggle to know Reality*. This work has and is part of what I realise now to be my life's vocation. As such, it is my sincere hope and prayer that in reading it you will have been encouraged not to lose hope or ever give up, but to also take up the challenge daily and in all humility and patience turn inwards in prayer and contemplation that through Divine Grace you may come to know True Reality, that is, 'That' which is to be done one earth as it is in Heaven.

Indeed, for He Who started this work in you will not fail you. He will get you back on track when you stray, and pick you up again and again when you fall. And remember, the more you receive the more you will be called and driven by Love to share. For we all have a role to play in sharing what has been revealed to us; and so playing our part in removing the unnecessary suffering caused by adhering to a life lived in a false consciousness.

If you have a few moments, please feel free to add your review of *Consciousness and Perception: A part fictionalised reflection on humanity's struggle to know Reality* to the online site for feedback. In addition, if you would like to contact me regarding anything at all with regards to the book you can reach me on anthonytmckay@yahoo.co.uk

It would be great to hear from you.

Yours sincerely,

With much love and prayers,

Tony

SELECTED BIBLIOGRAPHY

A wide range of material was researched and considered in the development of *Consciousness and Perception: A part fictionalised reflection on humanity's struggle to know Reality*. Below is a brief selection which some may find useful. These works are by people like us – human beings – and their interpretations and attempts to help us come to know and understand Reality and Truth.

As such, their interpretations are of course flavoured by their own uniqueness in time, place and community of interest.

Jacob Boehme:

— *The Signature of All Things* (2008), Evinity Publishing Inc. Santa Cruz, U.S.A: Kindle eBook

Dietrich Bonhoeffer:

— *The Cost of Discipleship* (1995), Touchstone, New York, U.S.A

Oliver Davies

— *Meister Eckhart: Selected Writings* (1994), Penguin, London, U.K: Kindle eBook

Fyodor Dostoevsky

— *The Brothers Karamazov* (2004) Vintage, London, U.K

Louis Evely:

— *That Man Is You* (1964), Paulist Press International, U.S.A

G.A. Gaskell

— *Dictionary of All Scriptures & Myths* (1981) Gramercy Books, New York, U.S.A

Aldous Huxley:

— *The Perennial Philosophy* (1947), Chato & Windus, London, U.K

Jean-Yves Leloup:

— *The Gospel of Thomas, the Gnostic Wisdom of Jesus* (2005) Inner Traditions, Vermont, U.S.A

St John of the Cross

— *Dark Night of the Soul* (2003), Dover. Thrift. Editions. Dover Publications Inc. New York U.S.A: Kindle eBook

Chris Mathews

— *Modern Satanism: Anatomy of a Radical Subculture* (2009) Praeger Publishers, U.S.A

Ralph McInerny

— *Thomas Aquinas: Selected Writings* (1998), Penguin, London, U.K: Kindle eBook

Thomas Merton:

— *Contemplative Prayer* (1971), Image Books, Doubleday: New York, USA

— *New Seeds of Contemplation* (1972), New Directions: New York, USA

— *The Ascent to Truth* (1981), A Harvest Book, Harcourt, Brace & Company: New York, USA

— *Conjectures of a Guilty Bystander* (1994), Bantam Doubleday: New York, USA

— *Thoughts in Solitude* (2005), Rosetta Books LLC, eBook: New York, USA

John Jacob Raub:

— *Who told you that you were naked? Freedom from Judgement, Guilt and Fear of Punishment* (1992) The Crossroad Publishing Company, New York, USA

Israel Regardie:

— *Twelve Steps to Spiritual Enlightenment* (1969), Sangreal Foundation, Dallas, Texas, U.S.A (First edition – Christian perspective)

— *The Tree of Life: A Study in Magic* (1972) Samuel Weiser, Inc. York Beach, Maine, U.S.A

— *The One Year Manual* (1981), Samuel Weiser, Inc. (alternative Twelve Steps to Spiritual Enlightenment – Occult perspective), York Beach, Maine, U.S.A

— *A Garden of Pomegranates* (1987), Lewellyn Publications, St. Paul, Minnesota, U.S.A

Evelyn Underhill:

— *Mysticism: A Study in Nature and Development of Spiritual Consciousness,* 12th Revised Edition (1930), & *Practical Mysticism: A little book for normal people*: two books included within Kindle eBook (2011)

Online/Internet material

Mark Passio

Mark Passio is a researcher, activist, and public speaker on all things relating to the current state of human consciousness. Over his many years of study he has gathered a wealth of knowledge and made many videos on various topics such as 'Natural Law' and 'Street-Wise Spirituality', which can be found on his YouTube channel. https://www.youtube.com/user/WhatOnEarth93

Mark also has his own website, https://www.whatonearthishappening.com/ for those of you who may be interested.

Printed in Great Britain
by Amazon